DIANA:
PRINCESS
OF THE
AMAZONS

D0013206

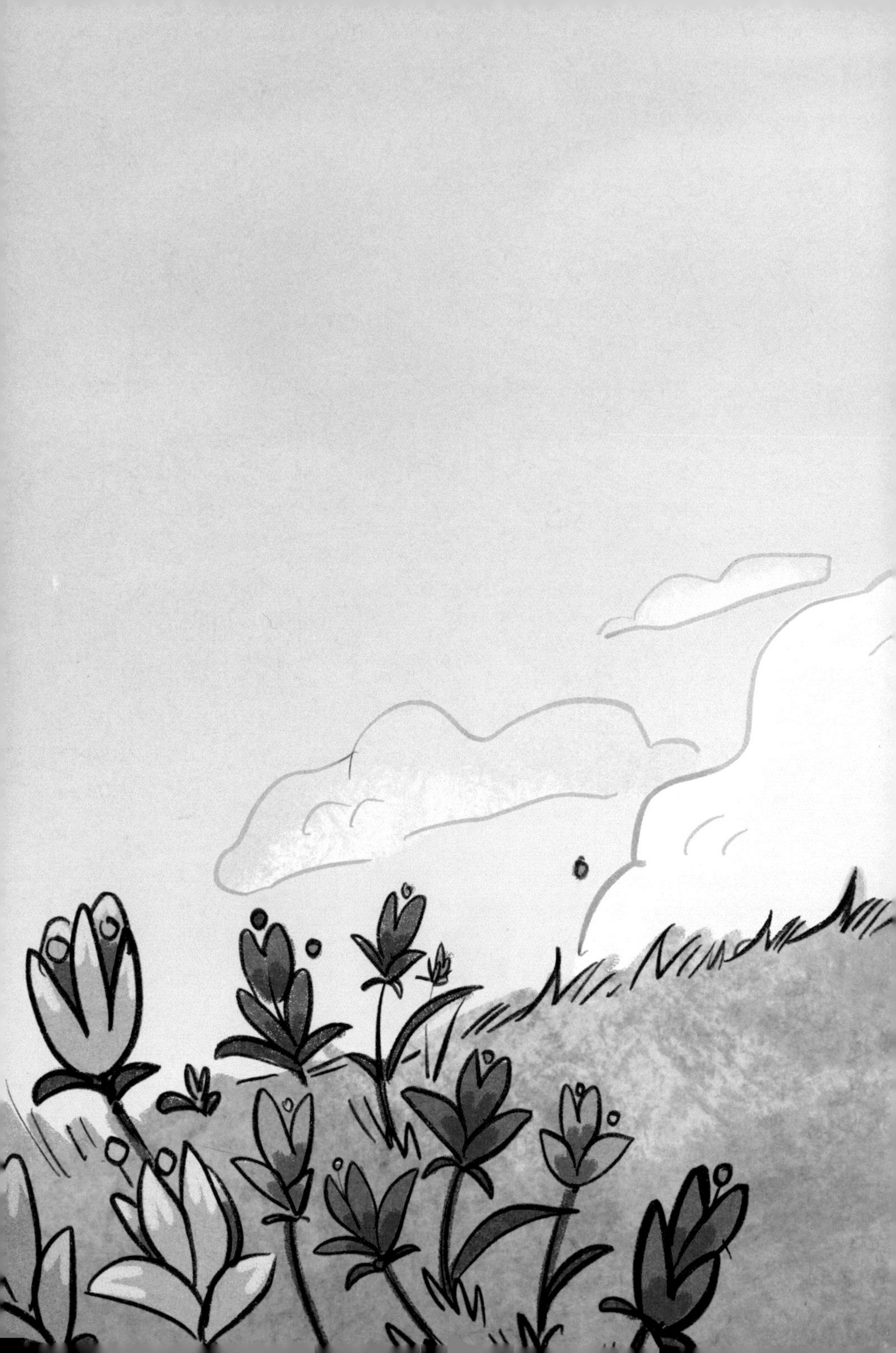

DIANA: PRINCESS OF THE AMAZONS

WRITTEN BY
**SHANNON HALE
& DEAN HALE**

ILLUSTRATED BY
VICTORIA YING

COLORS BY **LARK PIEN**
LETTERS BY **DAVE SHARPE**

WONDER WOMAN CREATED BY **WILLIAM MOULTON MARSTON**

LAUREN BISOM Editor
STEVE COOK Design Director – Books
AMIE BROCKWAY-METCALF Publication Design

BOB HARRAS Senior VP – Editor-in-Chief, DC Comics
MICHELE R. WELLS VP & Executive Editor, Young Reader

DAN DiDIO Publisher
JIM LEE Publisher & Chief Creative Officer
BOBBIE CHASE VP – New Publishing Initiatives
DON FALLETTI VP – Manufacturing Operations & Workflow Management
LAWRENCE GANEM VP – Talent Services
ALISON GILL Senior VP – Manufacturing & Operations
HANK KANALZ Senior VP – Publishing Strategy & Support Services
DAN MIRON VP – Publishing Operations
NICK J. NAPOLITANO VP – Manufacturing Administration & Design
JONAH WEILAND VP – Marketing & Creative Services
NANCY SPEARS VP – Sales

DIANA: PRINCESS OF THE AMAZONS

Published by DC Comics.
Copyright © 2020 DC Comics.
All Rights Reserved. All characters, their distinctive likenesses, and related elements featured in this publication are trademarks of DC Comics. The stories, characters, and incidents featured in this publication are entirely fictional. DC Comics does not read or accept unsolicited submissions of ideas, stories, or artwork. DC – a WarnerMedia Company.

DC Comics, 2900 West Alameda Ave., Burbank, CA 91505
Printed by LSC Communications, Crawfordsville, IN, USA.
3/13/20. Second Printing.
ISBN: 978-1-4012-9111-2
3/13/20. Third Printing.
School Market Edition ISBN: 978-1-77950-407-4

Library of Congress Cataloging-in-Publication Data

Names: Hale, Shannon, writer. | Hale, Dean, 1972- writer. | Ying, Victoria, illustrator. | Pien, Lark, colourist. | Sharpe, Dave (Letterer), letterer.
Title: Diana, Princess of the Amazons : a graphic novel / written by Shannon Hale & Dean Hale ; illustrated by Victoria Ying ; colors by Lark Pien ; letters by Dave Sharpe.
Description: Burbank, CA : DC Comics, [2020] | "Wonder Woman created by William Moulton Marston" | Audience: Ages 8-12 | Audience: Grades 4-6 | Summary: Eleven-year-old Diana, the gangly, sometimes clumsy, only child on the island of Themyscira, struggles to live up to the high Amazonian standards and longs for someone her own age whom she can talk to.
Identifiers: LCCN 2019040273 (print) | LCCN 2019040274 (ebook) | ISBN 9781401291112 (paperback) | ISBN 9781779500892 (ebook)
Subjects: LCSH: Graphic novels. | CYAC: Graphic novels. | Loneliness--Fiction. | Self-esteem--Fiction. | Amazons--Fiction.
Classification: LCC PZ7.7.H35 Di 2020 (print) | LCC PZ7.7.H35 (ebook) | DDC 741.5/973--dc23

PEFC Certified

This product is from sustainably managed forests and controlled sources

PEFC/29-31-337   www.pefc.org

TABLE OF CONTENTS

*For the kids who look up to Auntie Gal
and the former kids who spun
alongside Auntie Lynda.*

—Shannon and Dean Hale

For Lily.

—Victoria Ying

CHAPTER
ONE

Making a Friend

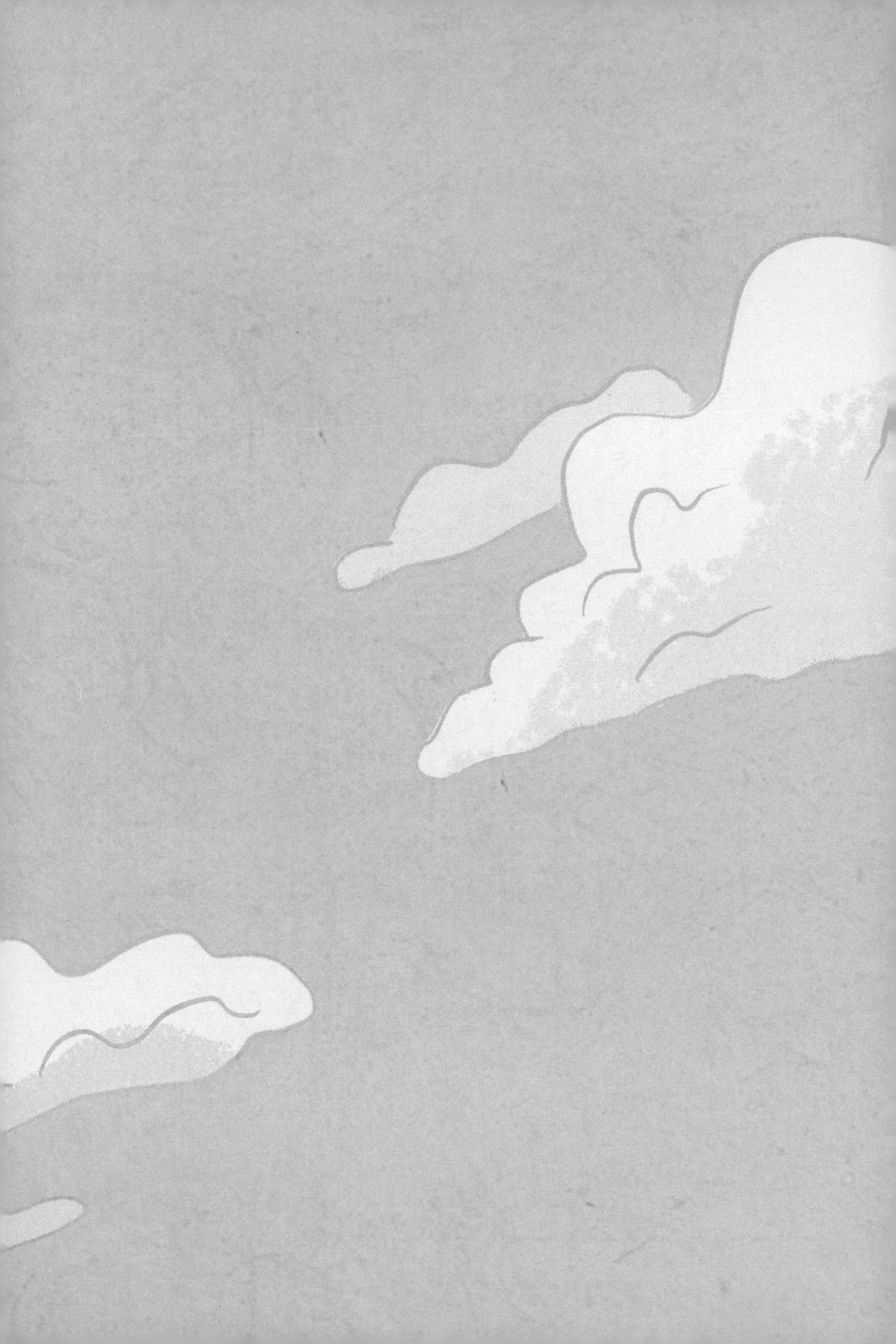

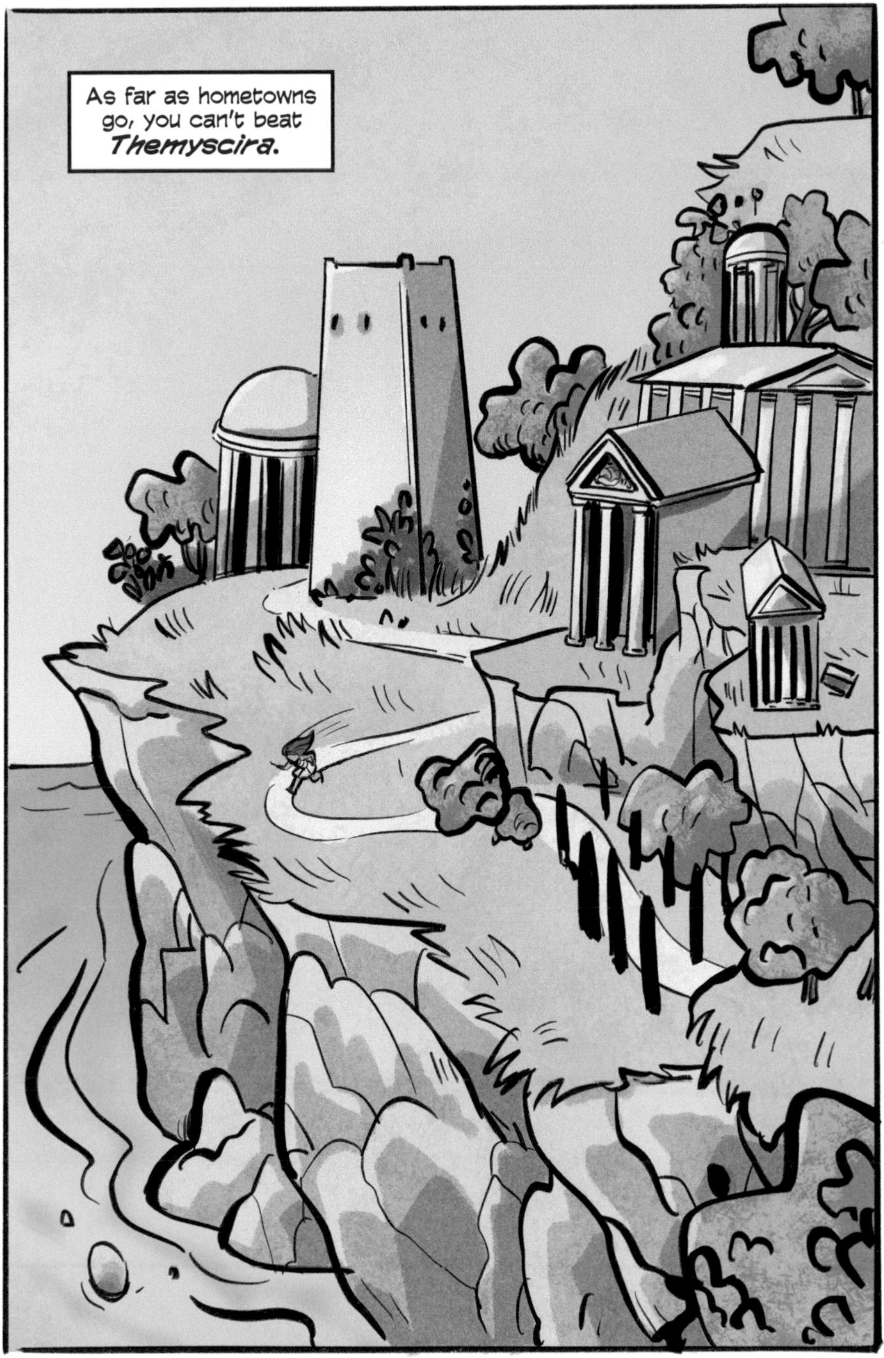
As far as hometowns go, you can't beat *Themyscira.*

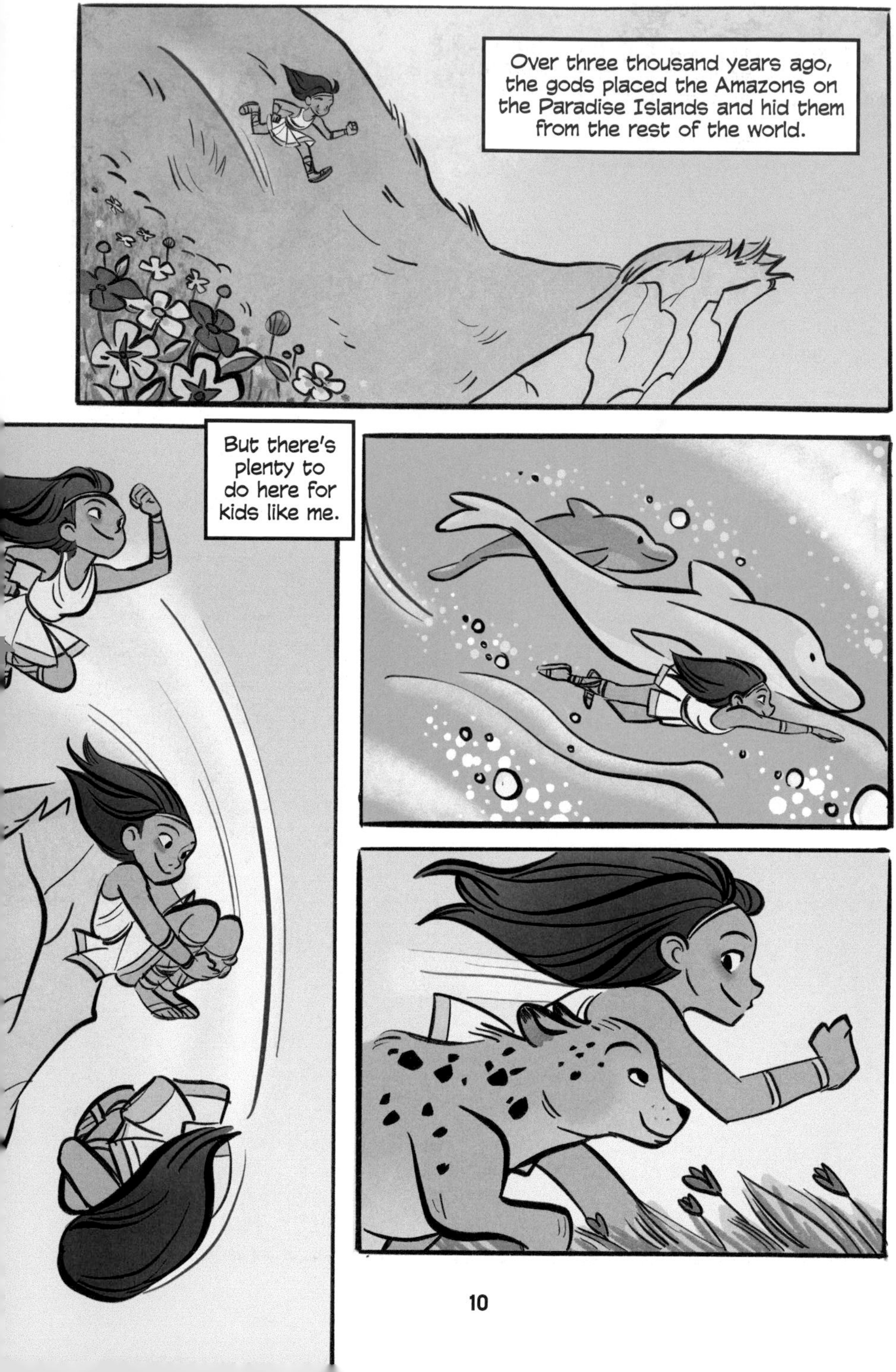
Over three thousand years ago, the gods placed the Amazons on the Paradise Islands and hid them from the rest of the world.
But there's plenty to do here for kids like me.

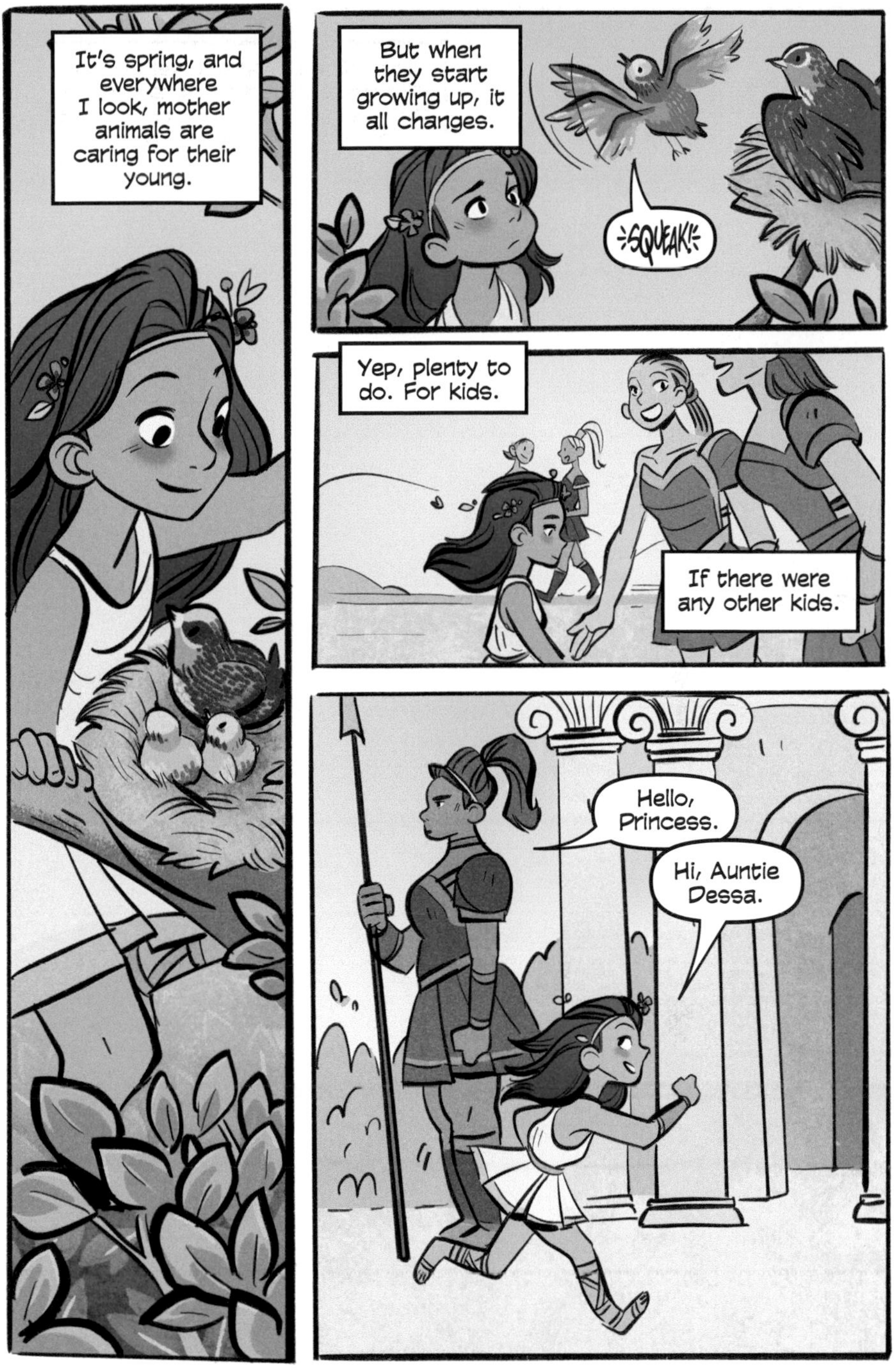

It's spring, and everywhere I look, mother animals are caring for their young.
But when they start growing up, it all changes.
SQUEAK!
Yep, plenty to do. For kids.
If there were any other kids.
Hello, Princess.
Hi, Auntie Dessa.

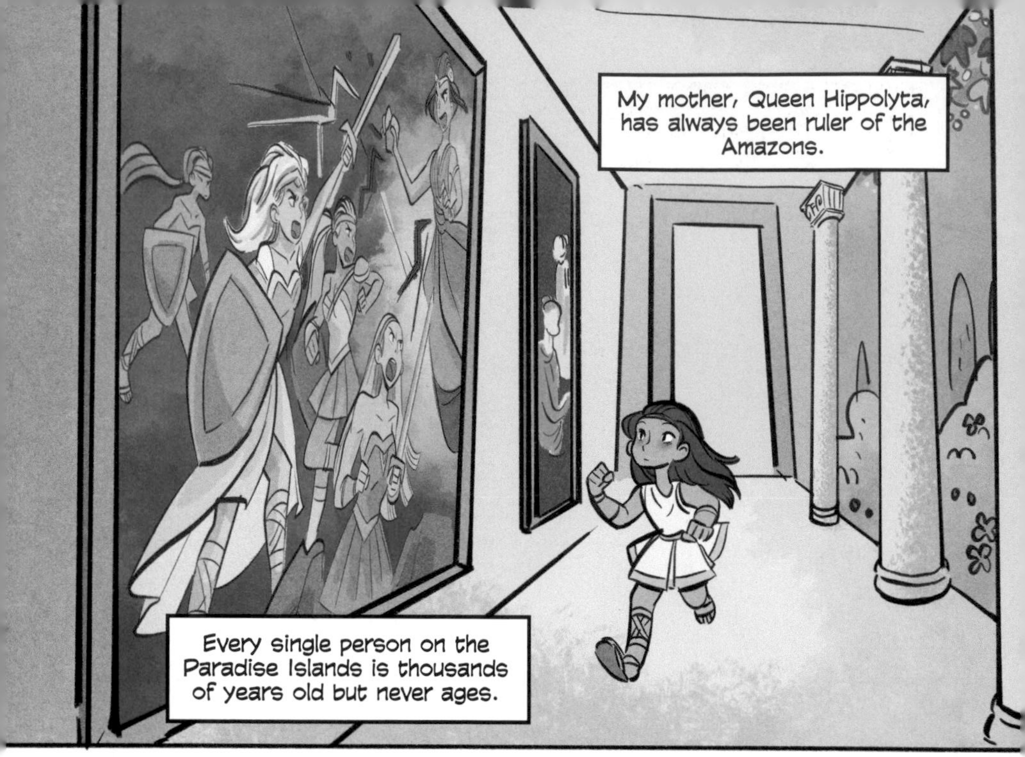
My mother, Queen Hippolyta, has always been ruler of the Amazons.
Every single person on the Paradise Islands is thousands of years old but never ages.

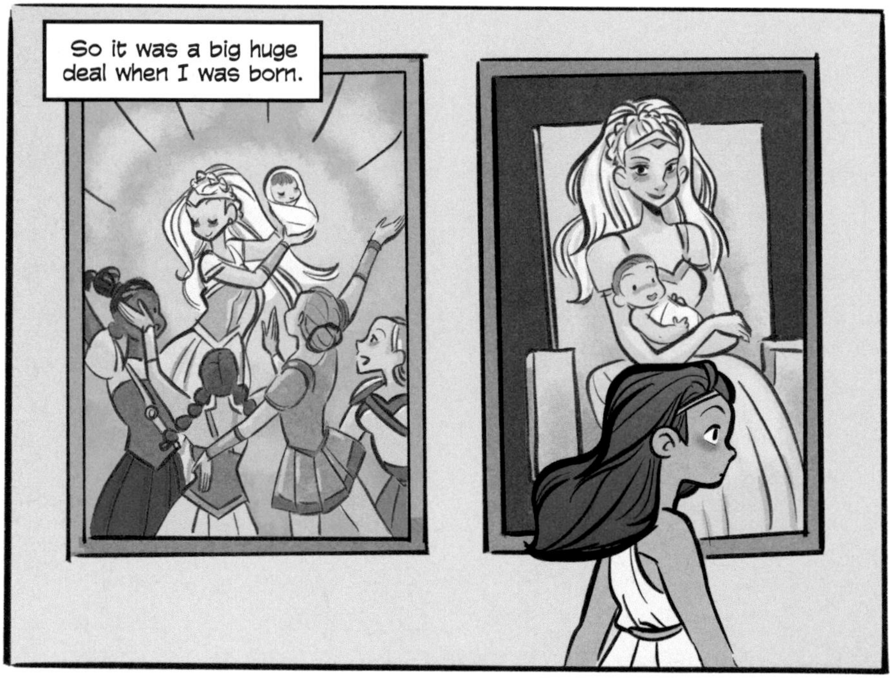
So it was a big huge deal when I was born.

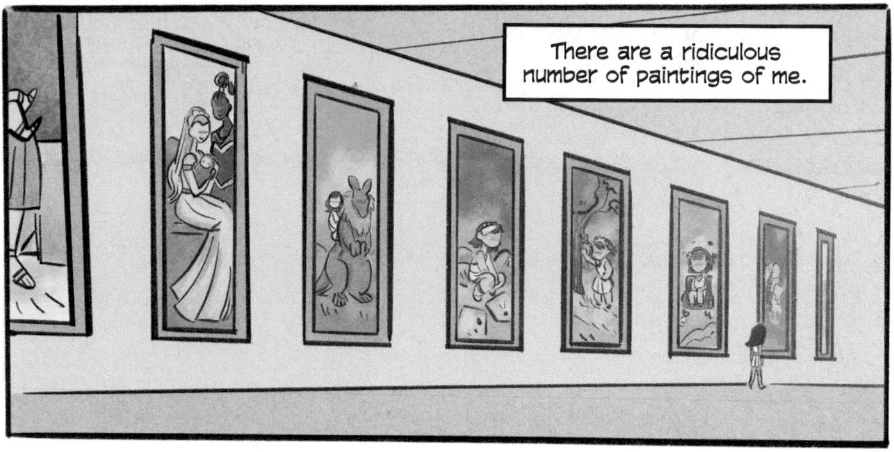
There are a ridiculous number of paintings of me.

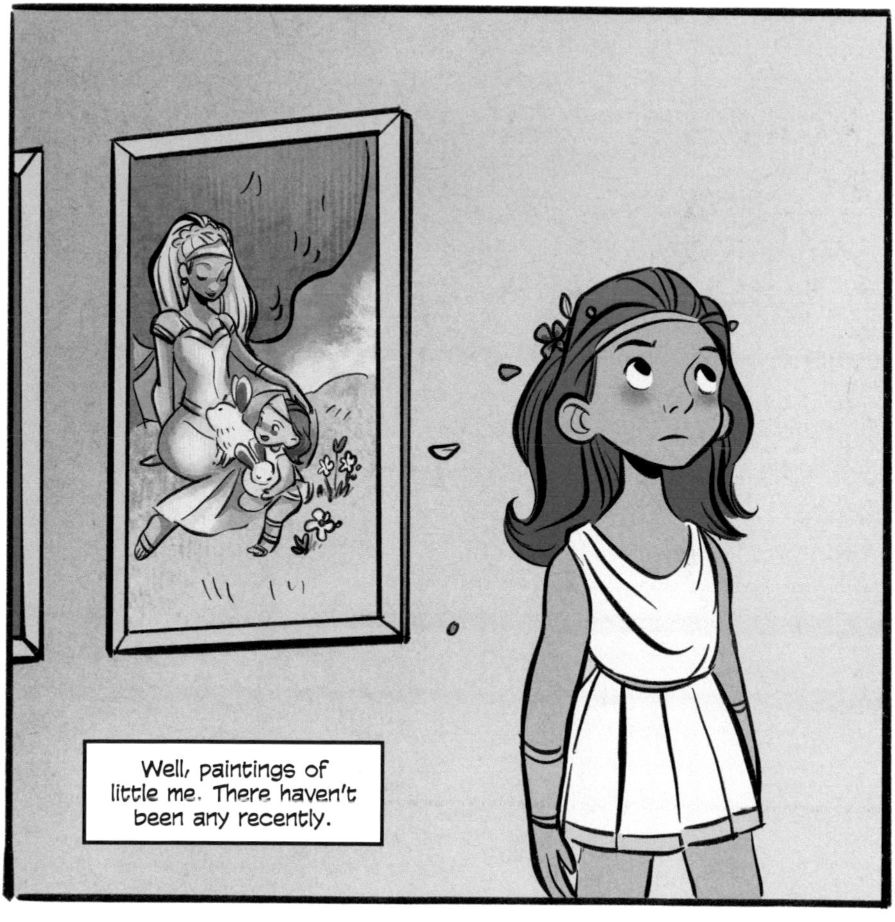
Well, paintings of little me. There haven't been any recently.

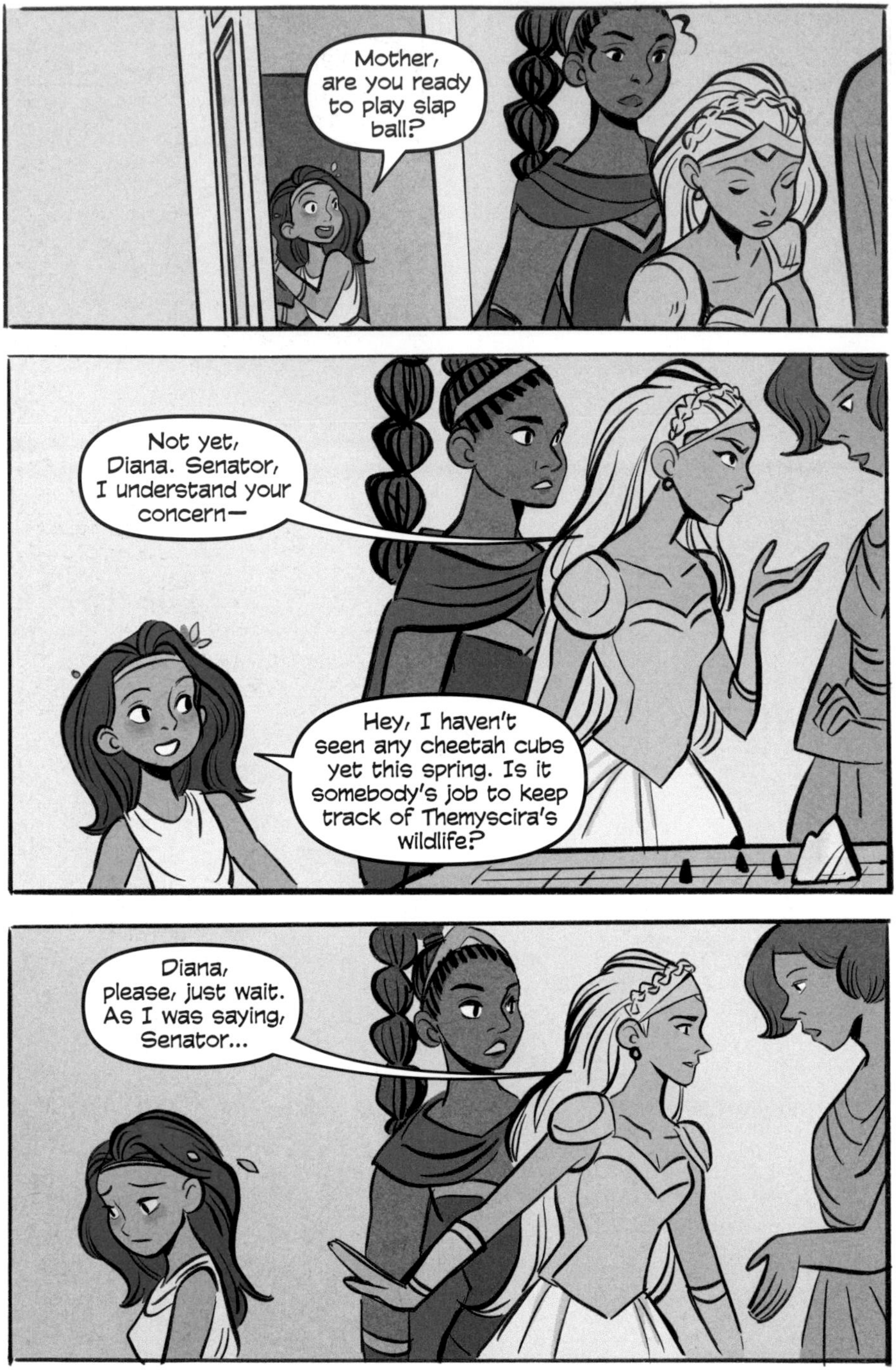
Mother, are you ready to play slap ball?
Not yet, Diana. Senator, I understand your concern—
Hey, I haven't seen any cheetah cubs yet this spring. Is it somebody's job to keep track of Themyscira's wildlife?
Diana, please, just wait. As I was saying, Senator...

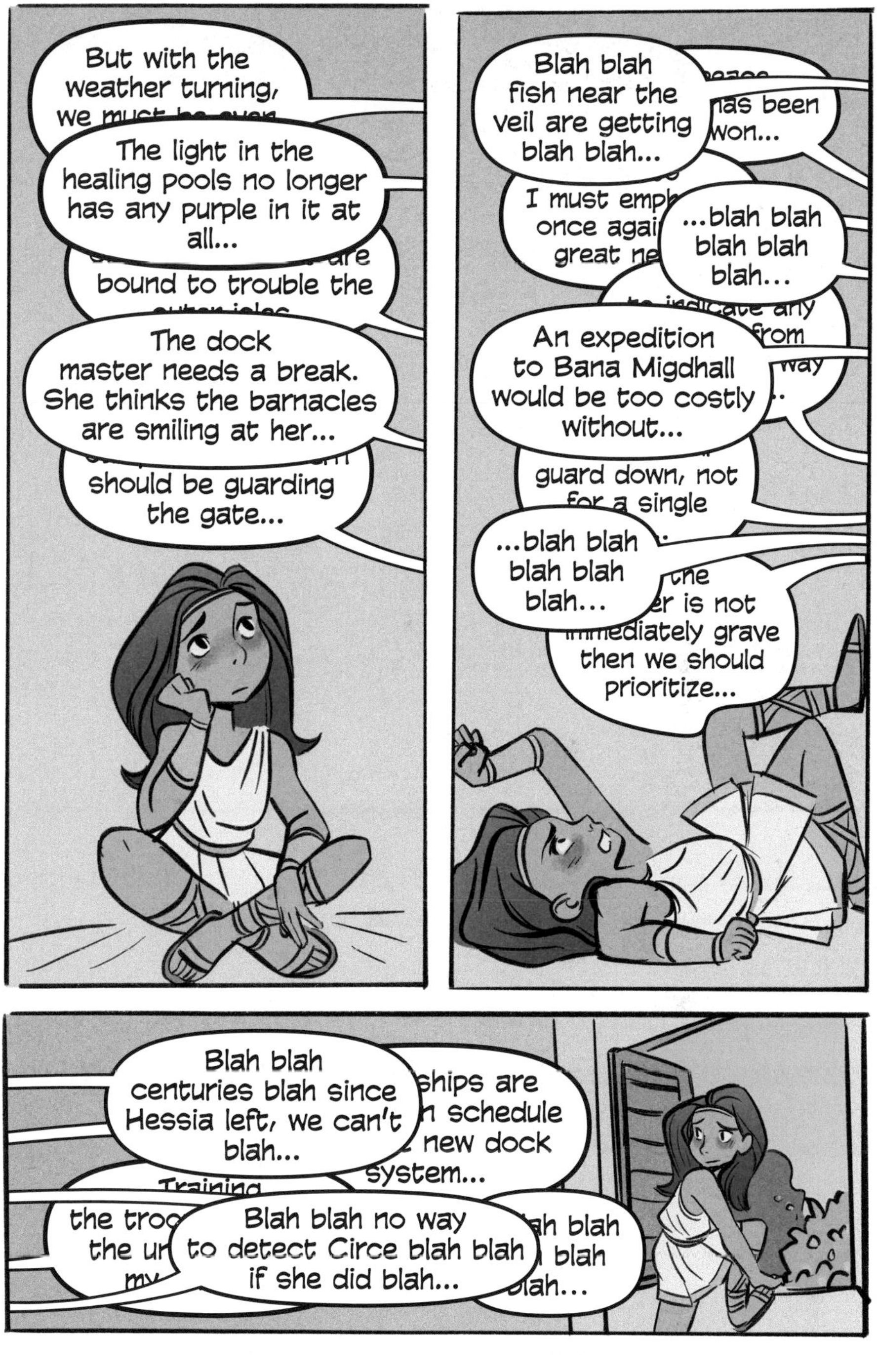
But with the weather turning,
The light in the healing pools no longer has any purple in it at all...
bound to trouble the
The dock master needs a break. She thinks the barnacles are smiling at her...
should be guarding the gate...
Blah blah fish near the veil are getting blah blah...
been won...
...blah blah blah blah blah...
An expedition to Bana Migdhall would be too costly without...
guard down, not for a single
...blah blah blah blah blah...
is not
then we should prioritize...
Blah blah centuries blah since Hessia left, we can't blah...
ships are
schedule
new dock
system...
Blah blah no way to detect Circe blah blah if she did blah...

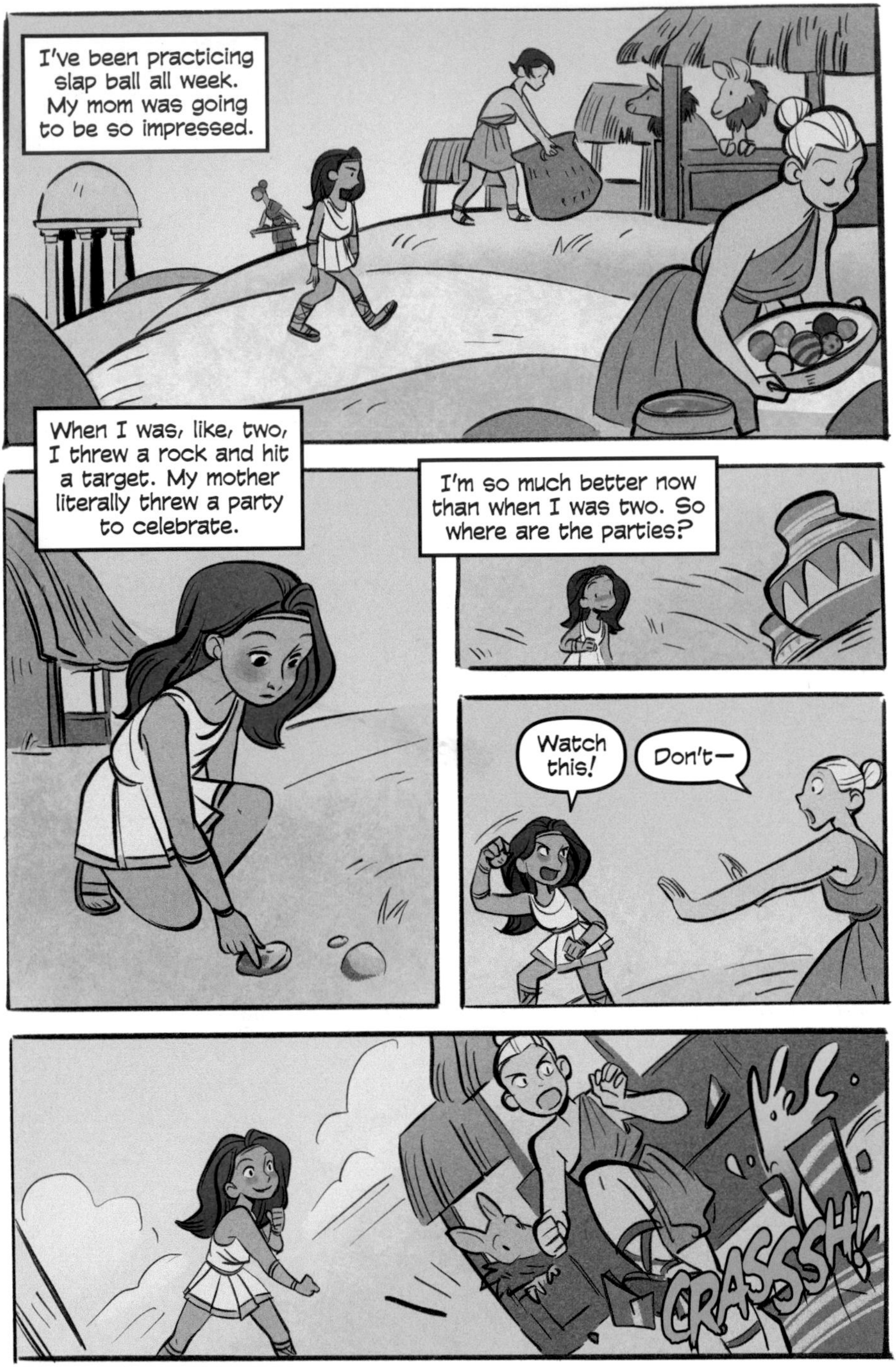
I've been practicing slap ball all week. My mom was going to be so impressed.
When I was, like, two, I threw a rock and hit a target. My mother literally threw a party to celebrate.
I'm so much better now than when I was two. So where are the parties?
Watch this!
Don't—
CRASSSH!

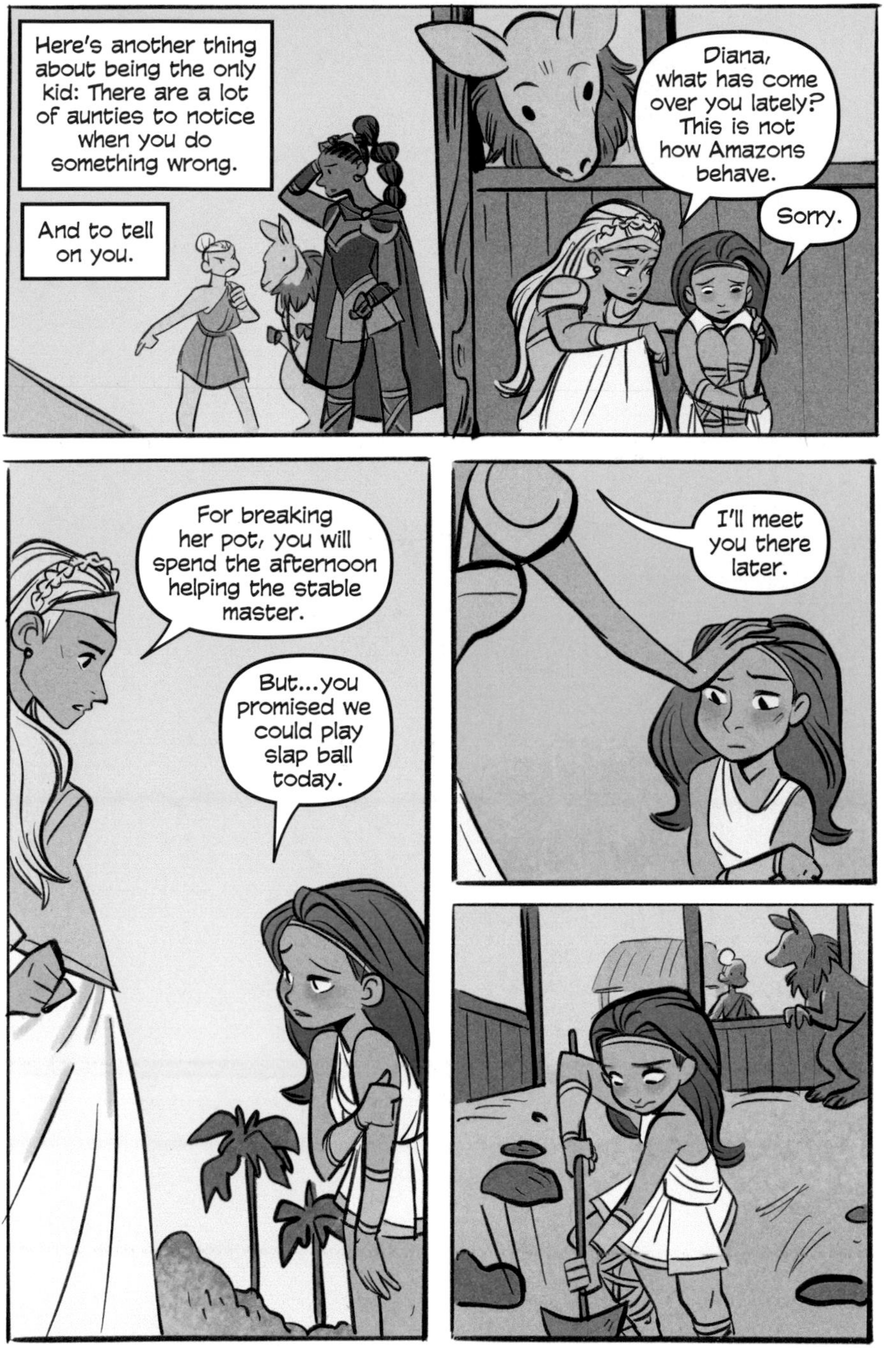
Here's another thing about being the only kid: There are a lot of aunties to notice when you do something wrong.
And to tell on you.
Diana, what has come over you lately? This is not how Amazons behave.
Sorry.
For breaking her pot, you will spend the afternoon helping the stable master.
But...you promised we could play slap ball today.
I'll meet you there later.

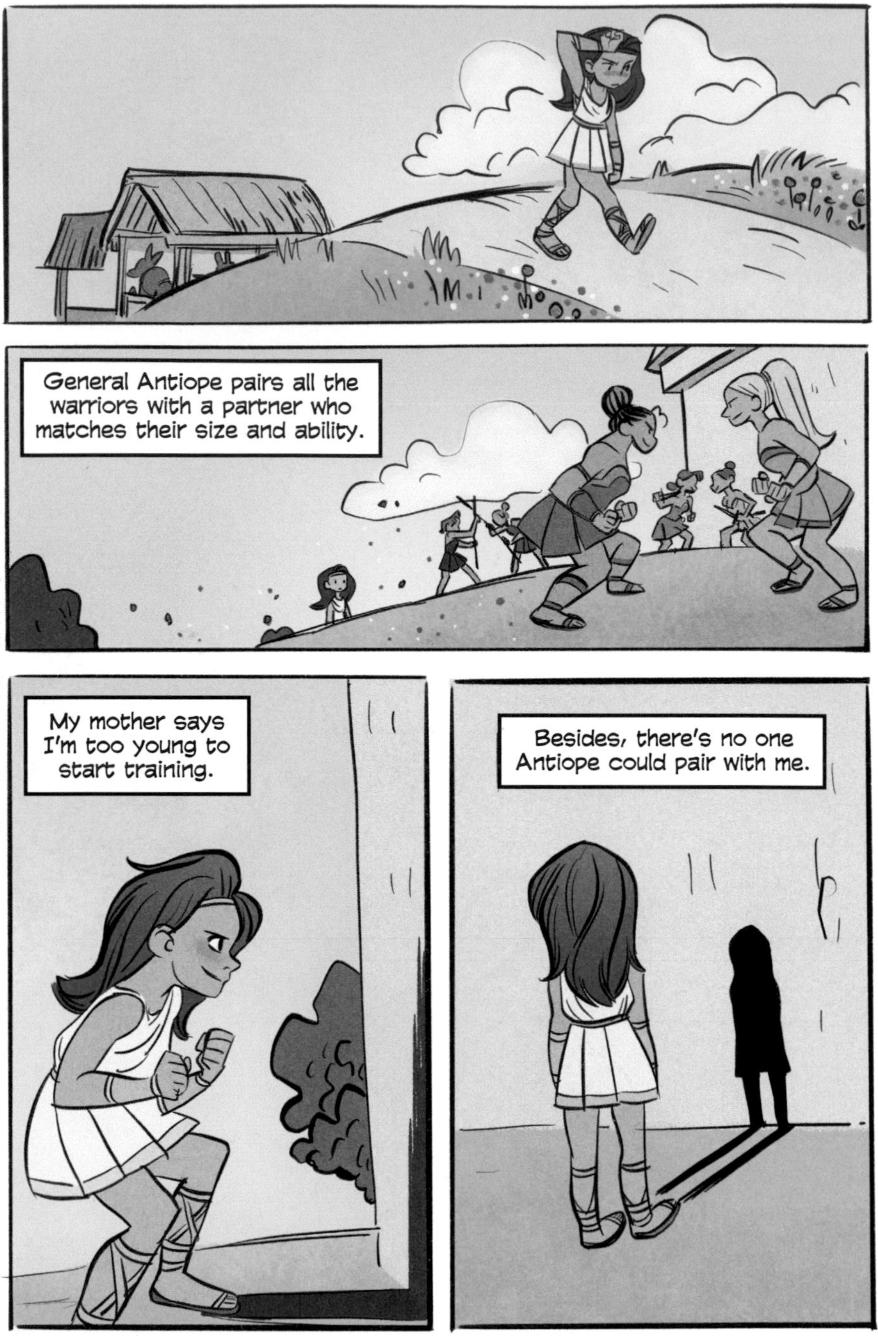
General Antiope pairs all the warriors with a partner who matches their size and ability.
My mother says I'm too young to start training.
Besides, there's no one Antiope could pair with me.

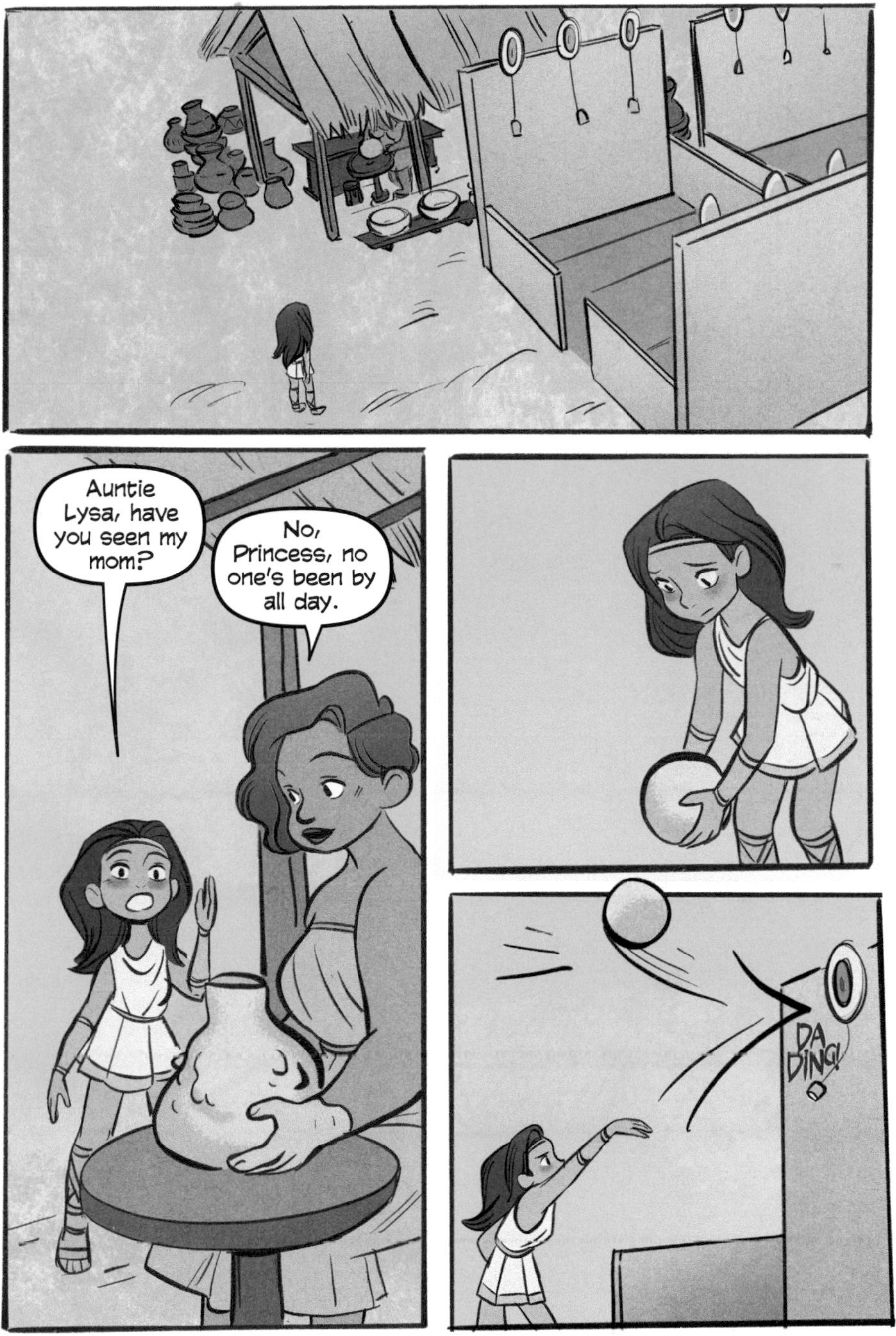
Auntie Lysa, have you seen my mom?
No, Princess, no one's been by all day.
DA DING!

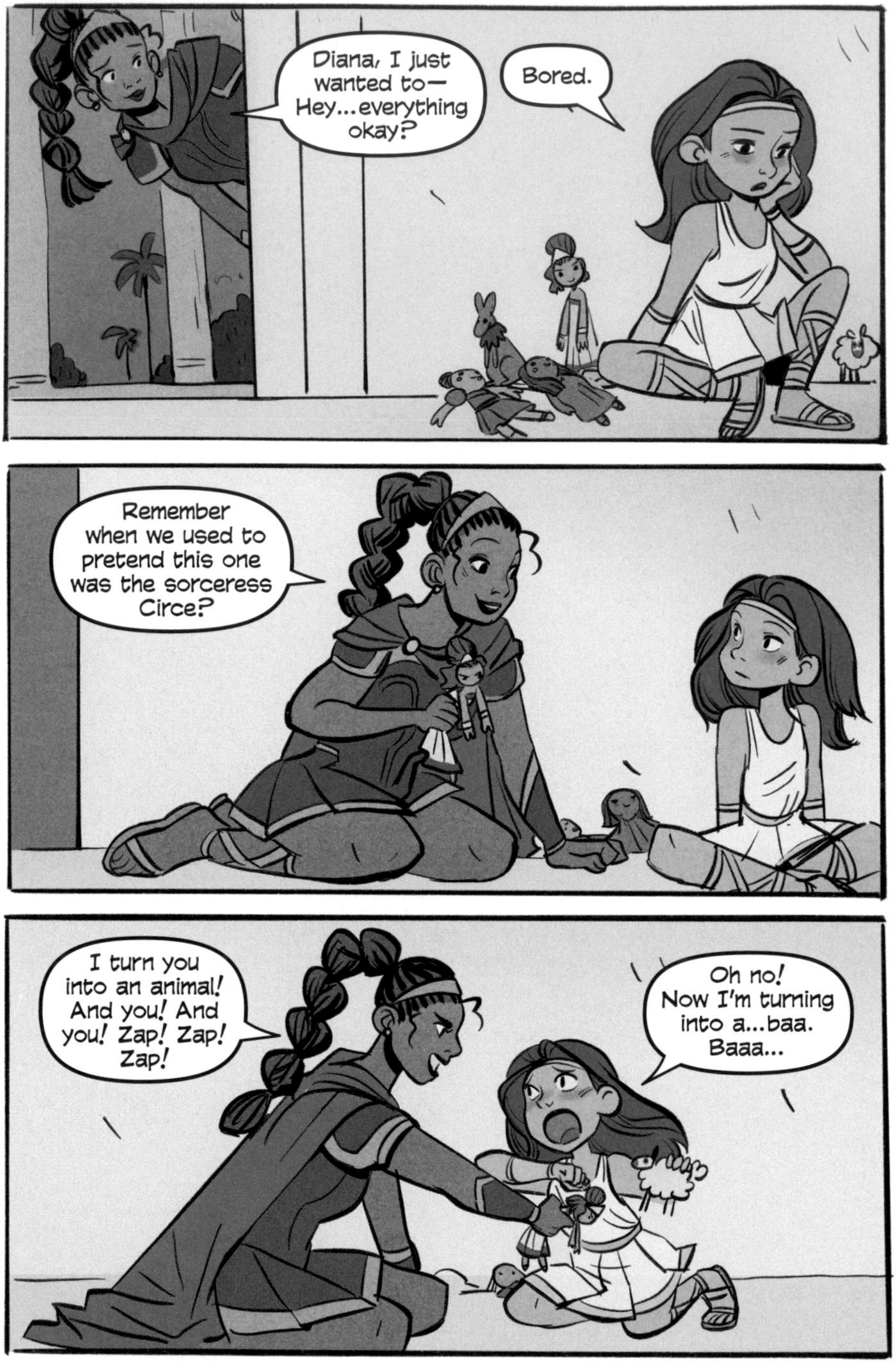
Diana, I just wanted to— Hey...everything okay?
Bored.
Remember when we used to pretend this one was the sorceress Circe?
I turn you into an animal! And you! And you! Zap! Zap! Zap!
Oh no! Now I'm turning into a...baa. Baaa...

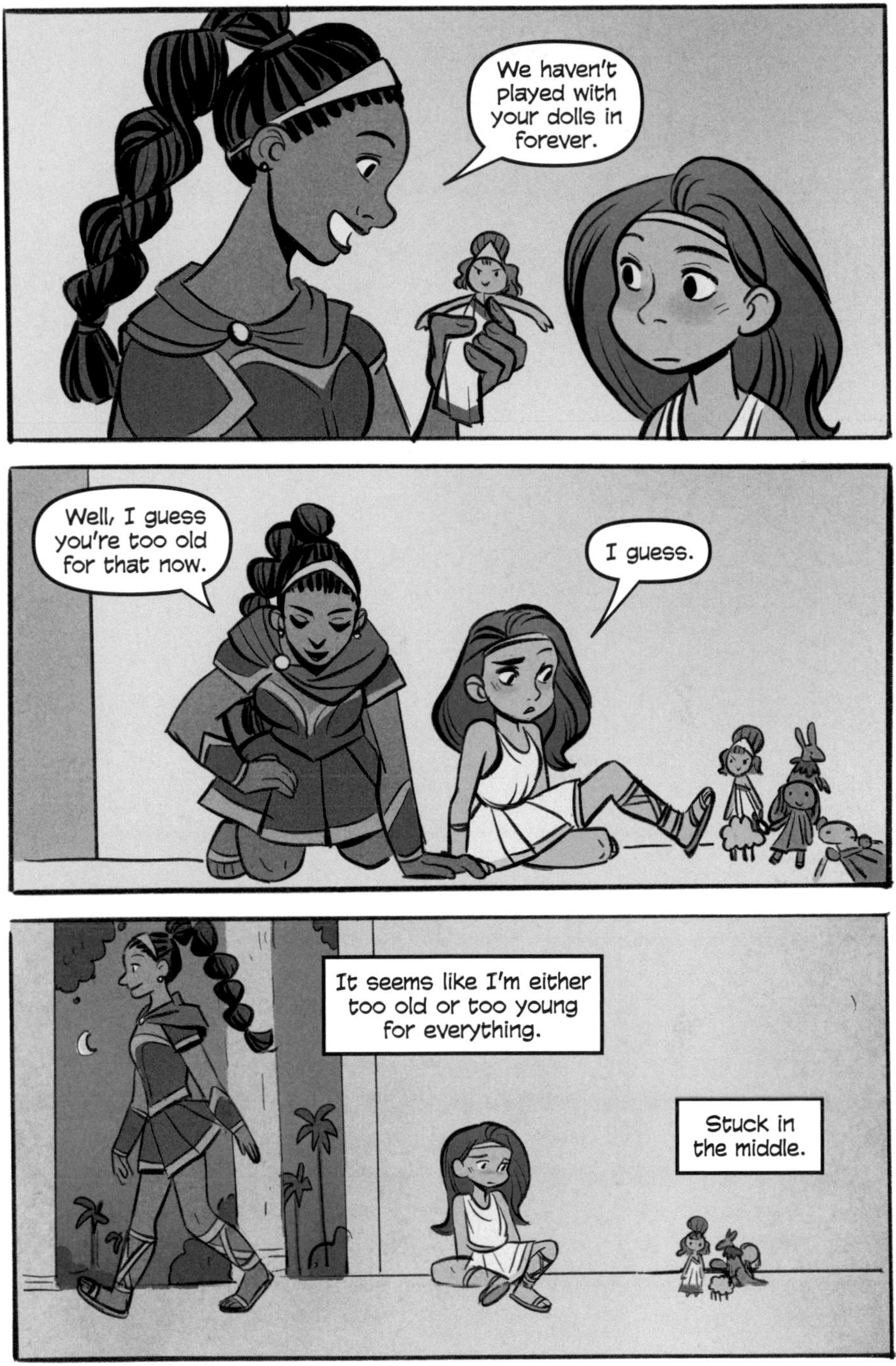
We haven't played with your dolls in forever.
Well, I guess you're too old for that now.
I guess.
It seems like I'm either too old or too young for everything.
Stuck in the middle.

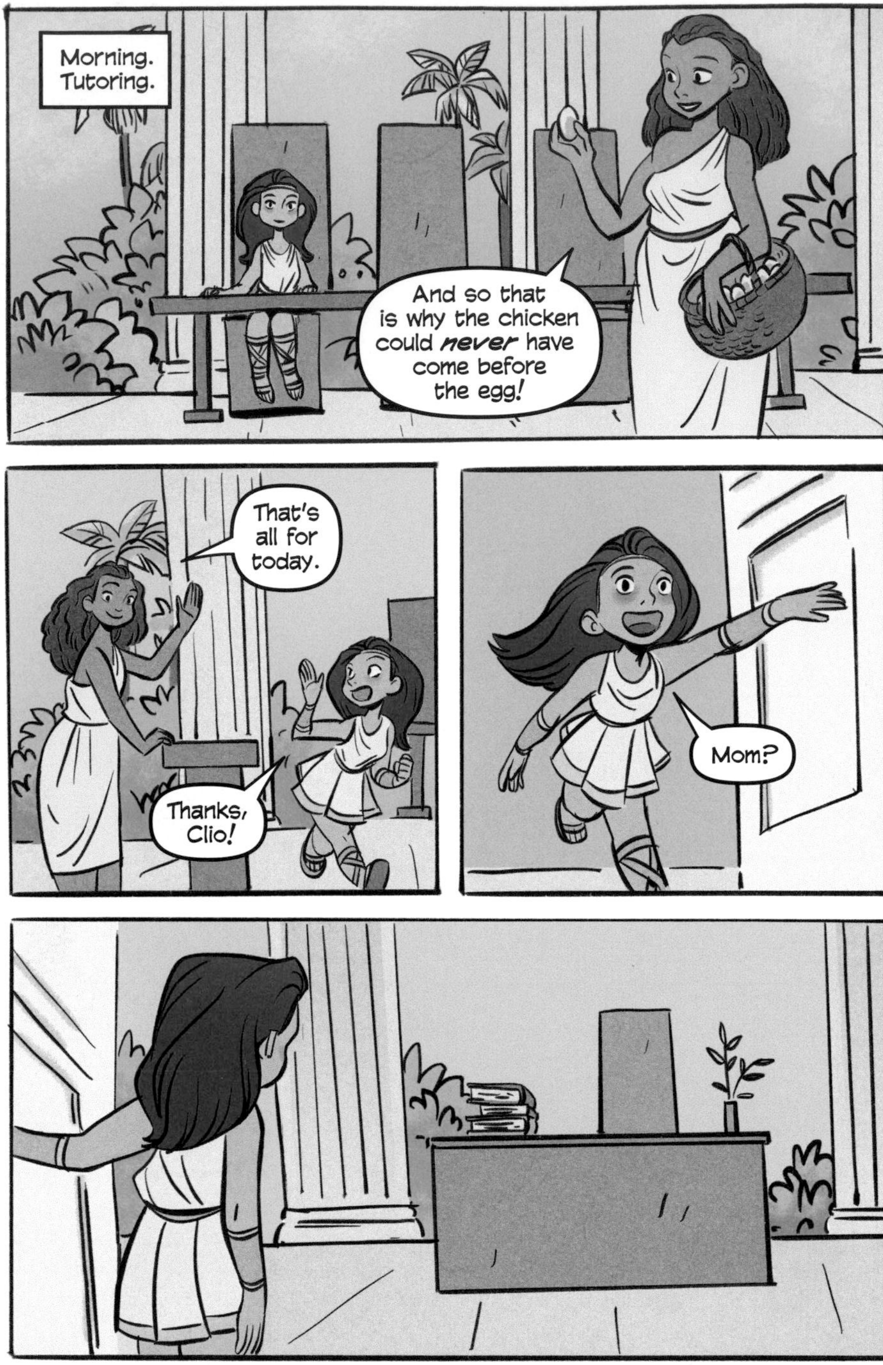
Morning.
Tutoring.
And so that is why the chicken could *never* have come before the egg!
That's all for today.
Thanks, Clio!
Mom?

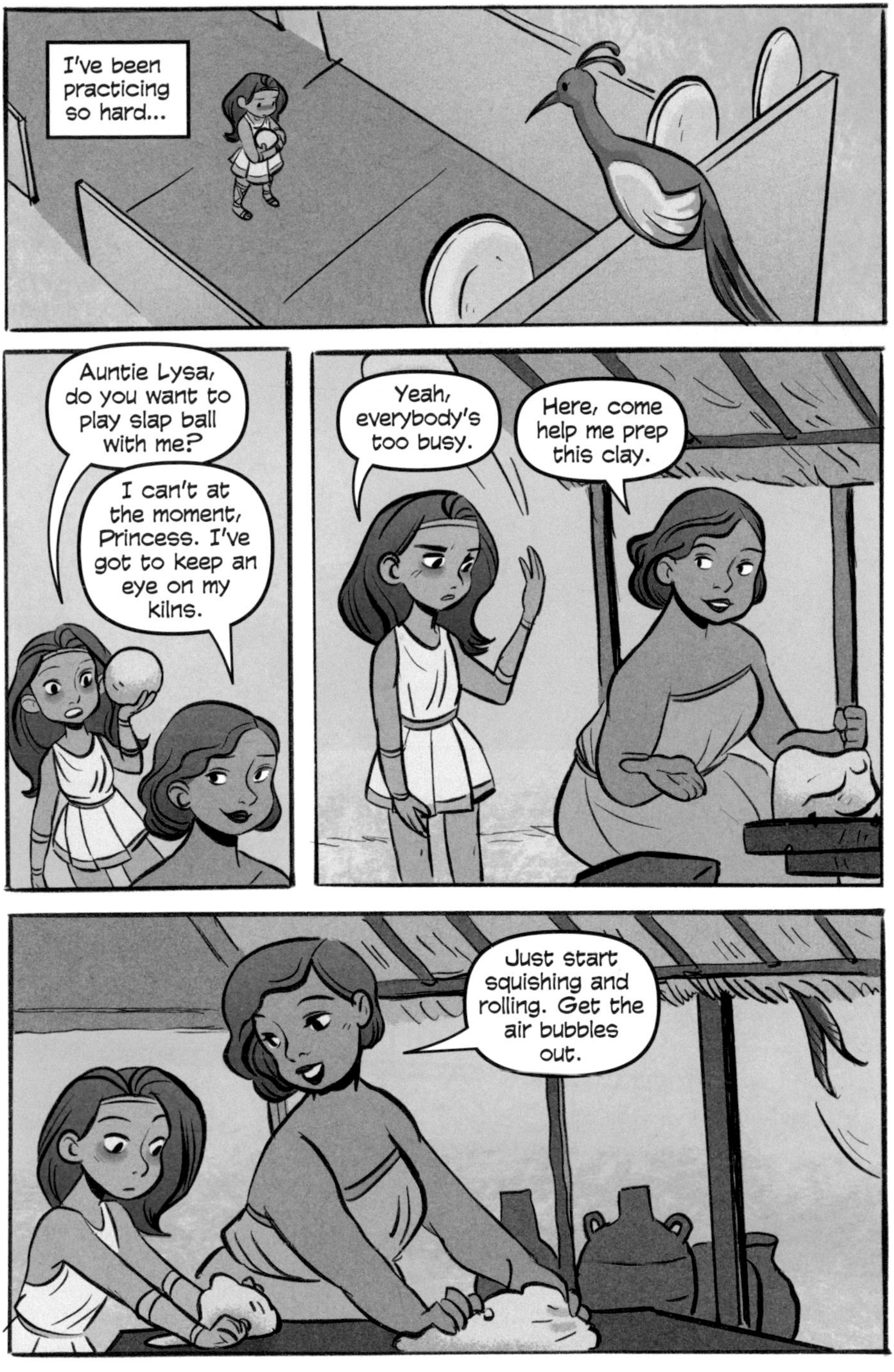
I've been practicing so hard...
Auntie Lysa, do you want to play slap ball with me?
I can't at the moment, Princess. I've got to keep an eye on my kilns.
Yeah, everybody's too busy.
Here, come help me prep this clay.
Just start squishing and rolling. Get the air bubbles out.

Once upon a time the queen of the Amazons wanted a daughter more than anything in the world...

Uh, I think I know this one.

My mother used to tell me the story of my birth all the time.

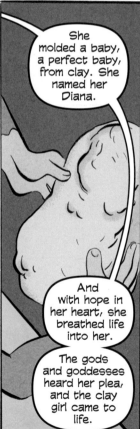

She molded a baby, a perfect baby, from clay. She named her Diana.

WHUFF

And with hope in her heart, she breathed life into her.

The gods and goddesses heard her plea, and the clay girl came to life.

Clearly, I am not queen of the Amazons!

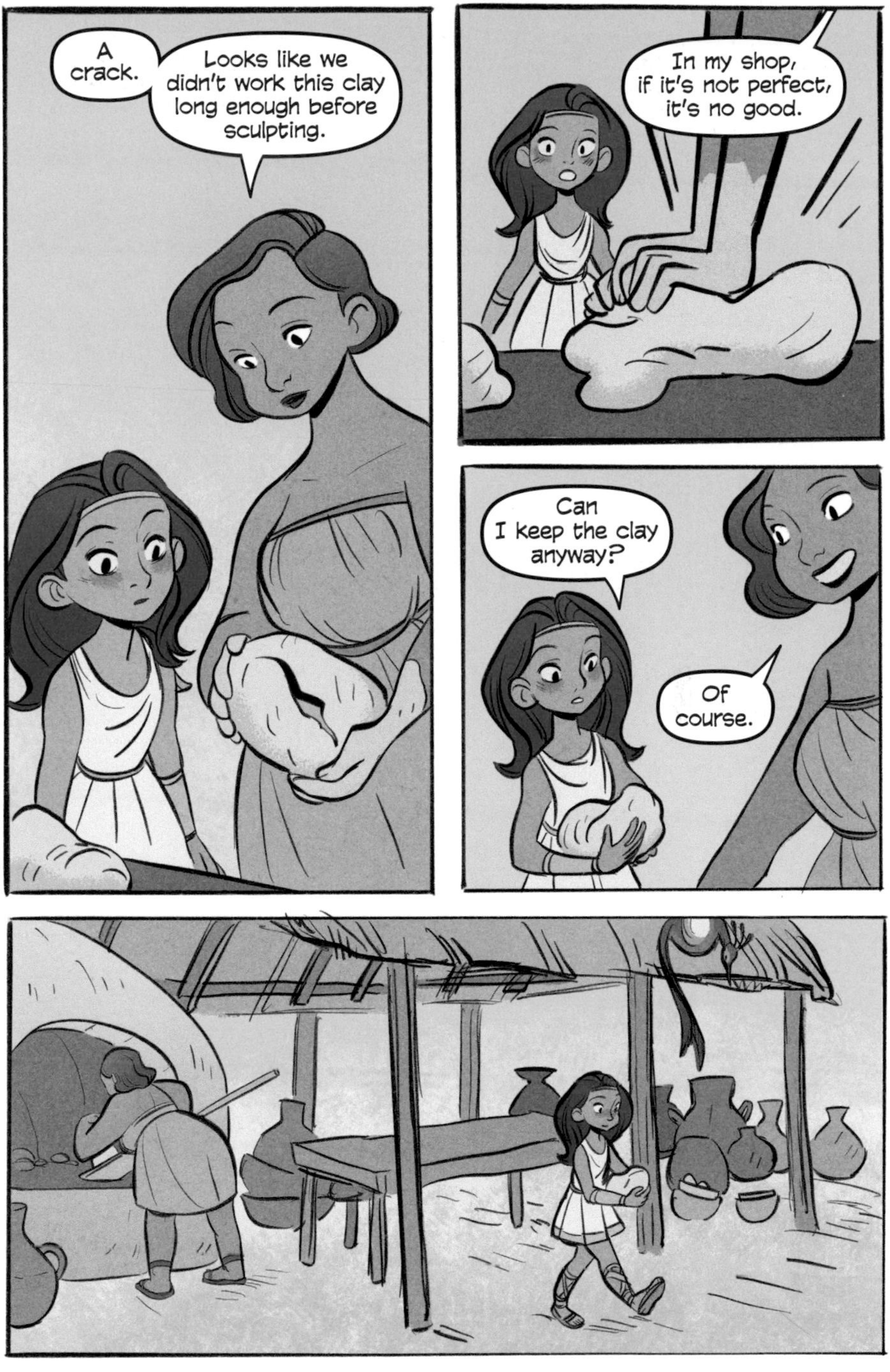
A crack.
Looks like we didn't work this clay long enough before sculpting.
In my shop, if it's not perfect, it's no good.
Can I keep the clay anyway?
Of course.

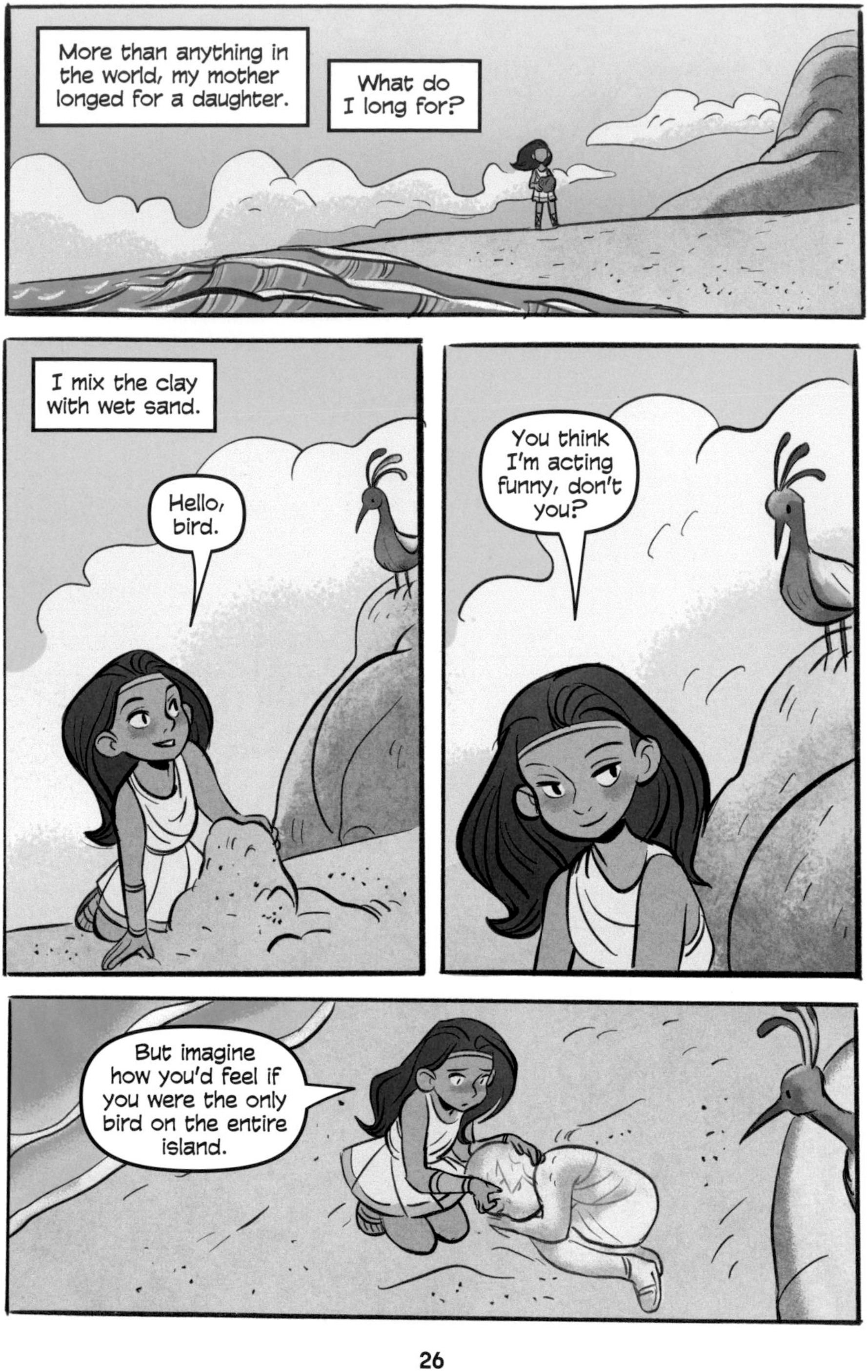
More than anything in the world, my mother longed for a daughter.
What do I long for?
I mix the clay with wet sand.
Hello, bird.
You think I'm acting funny, don't you?
But imagine how you'd feel if you were the only bird on the entire island.

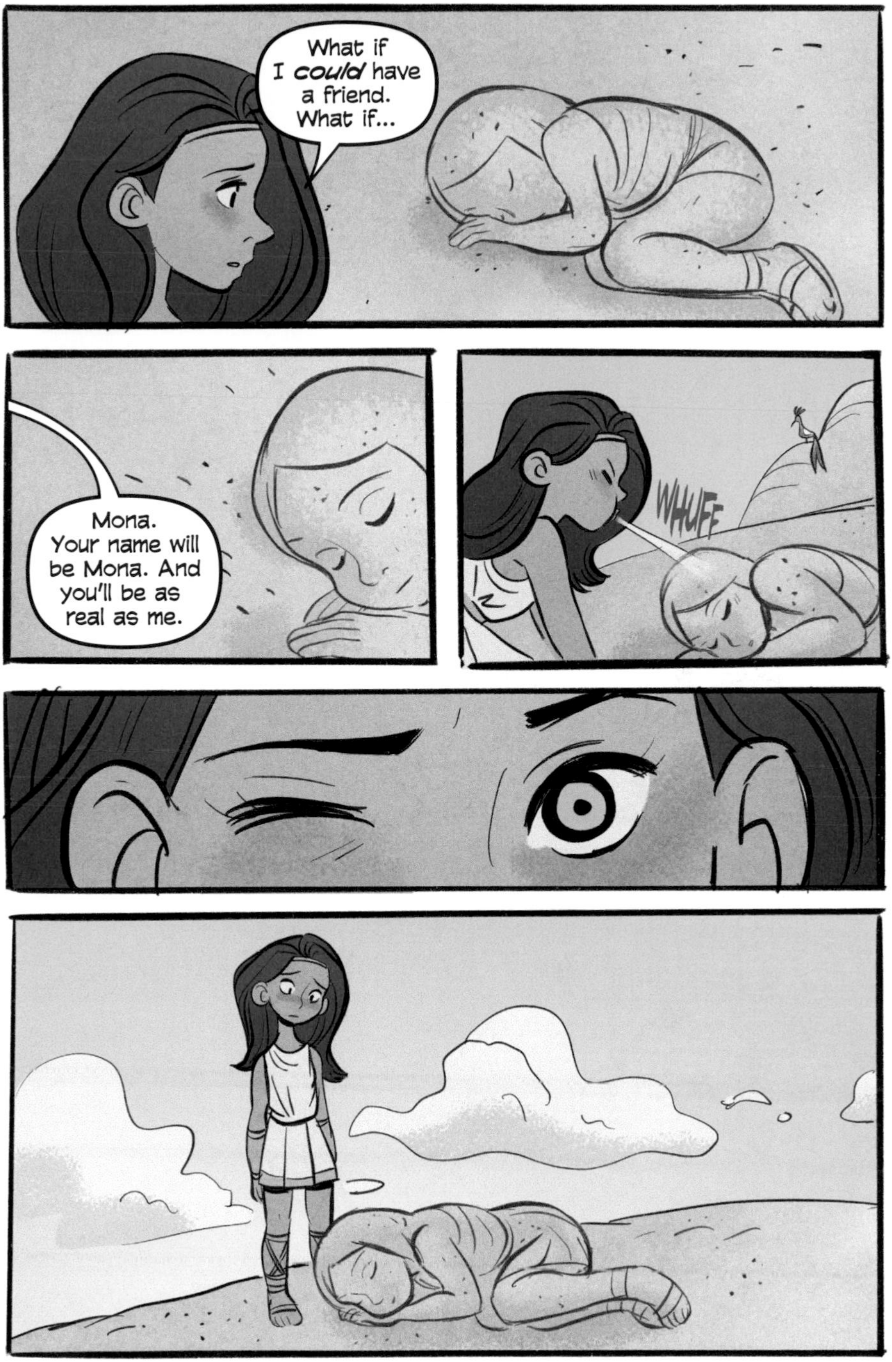
What if I *could* have a friend. What if...
Mona. Your name will be Mona. And you'll be as real as me.
WHUFF

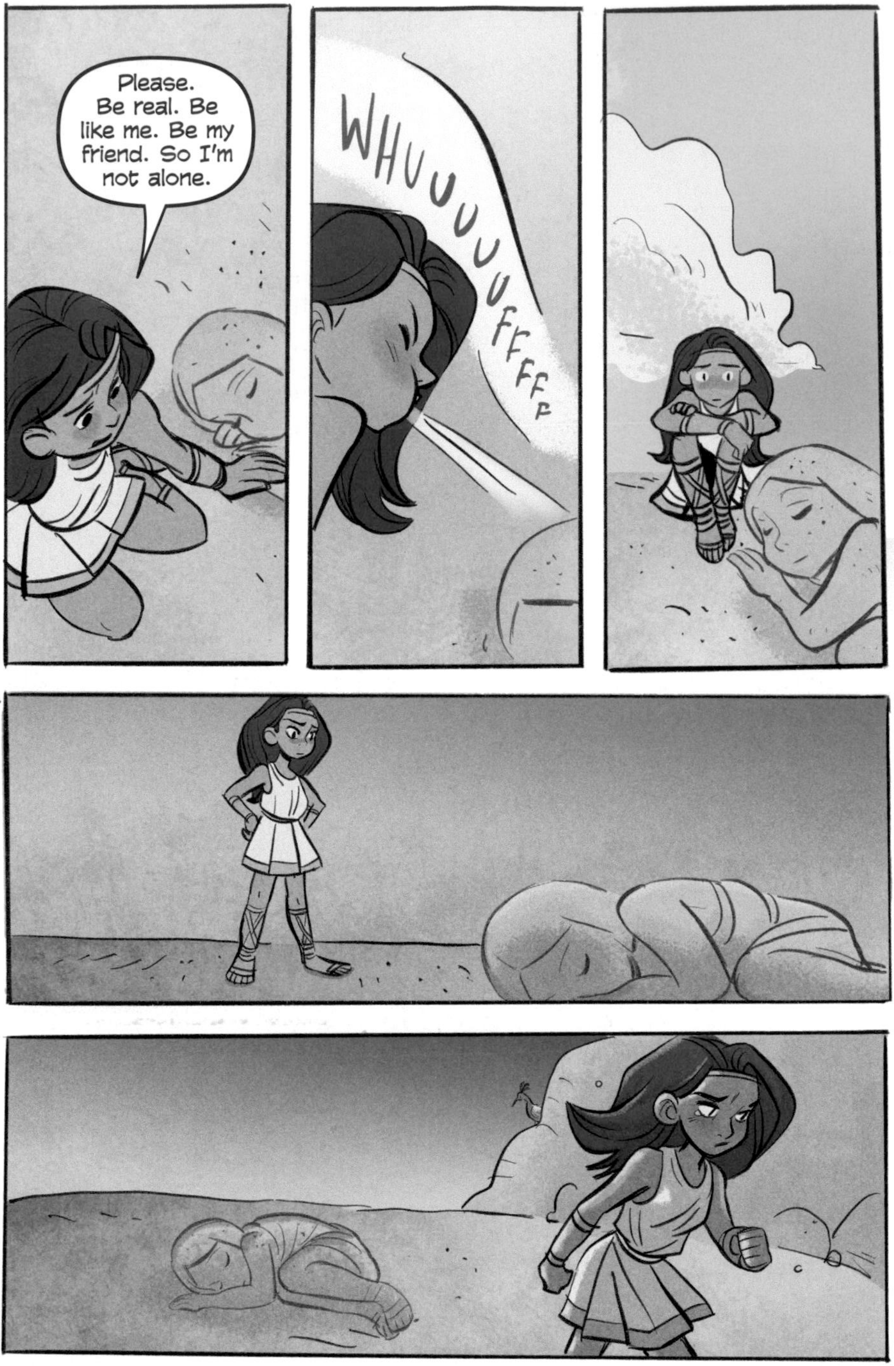
Please. Be real. Be like me. Be my friend. So I'm not alone.
WHUUUUUUFFFFF

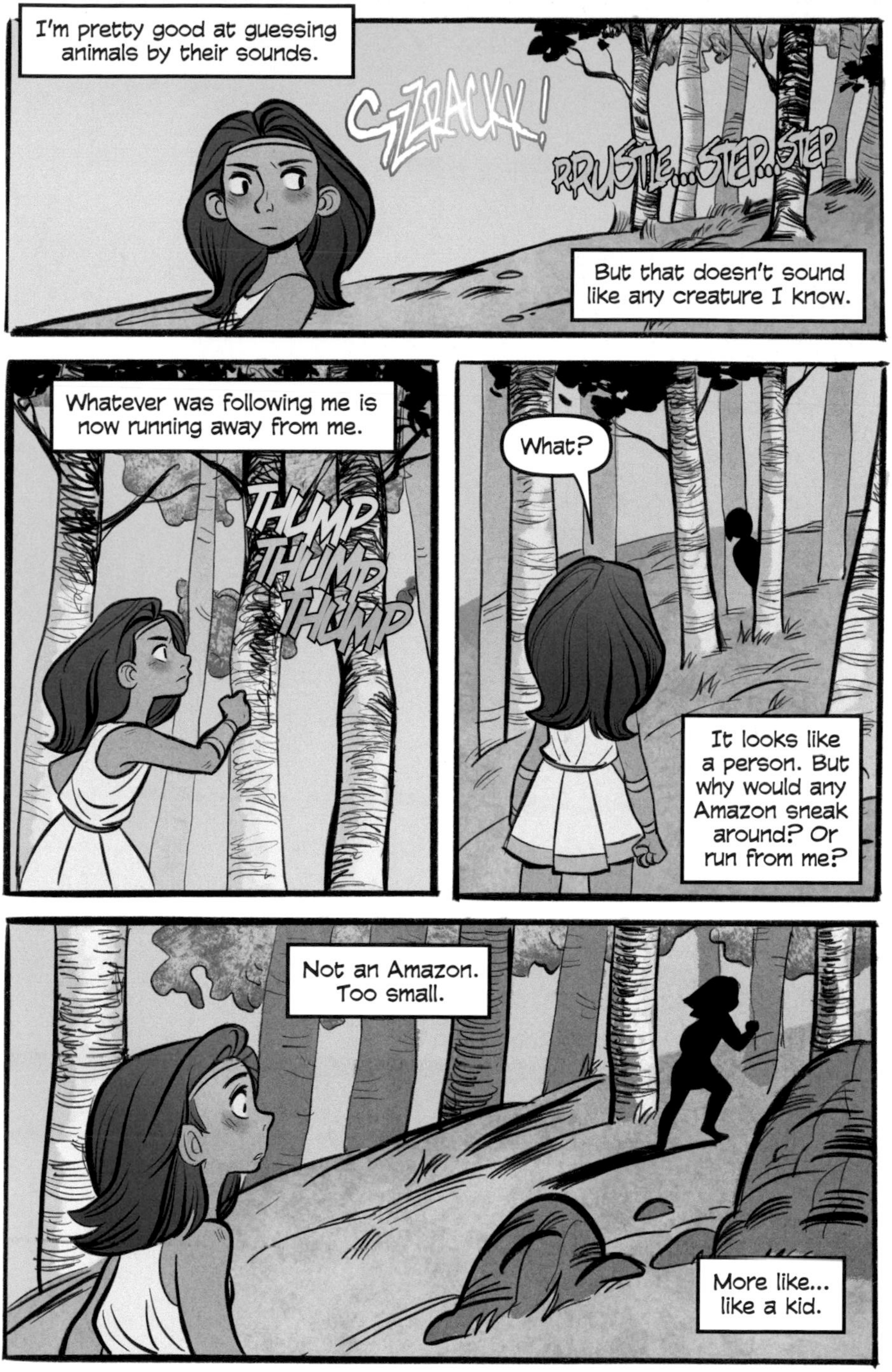

I'm pretty good at guessing animals by their sounds.
CZRACKK!
RRUSTLE...STEP...STEP
But that doesn't sound like any creature I know.
Whatever was following me is now running away from me.
THUMP THUMP THUMP
What?
It looks like a person. But why would any Amazon sneak around? Or run from me?
Not an Amazon. Too small.
More like... like a kid.

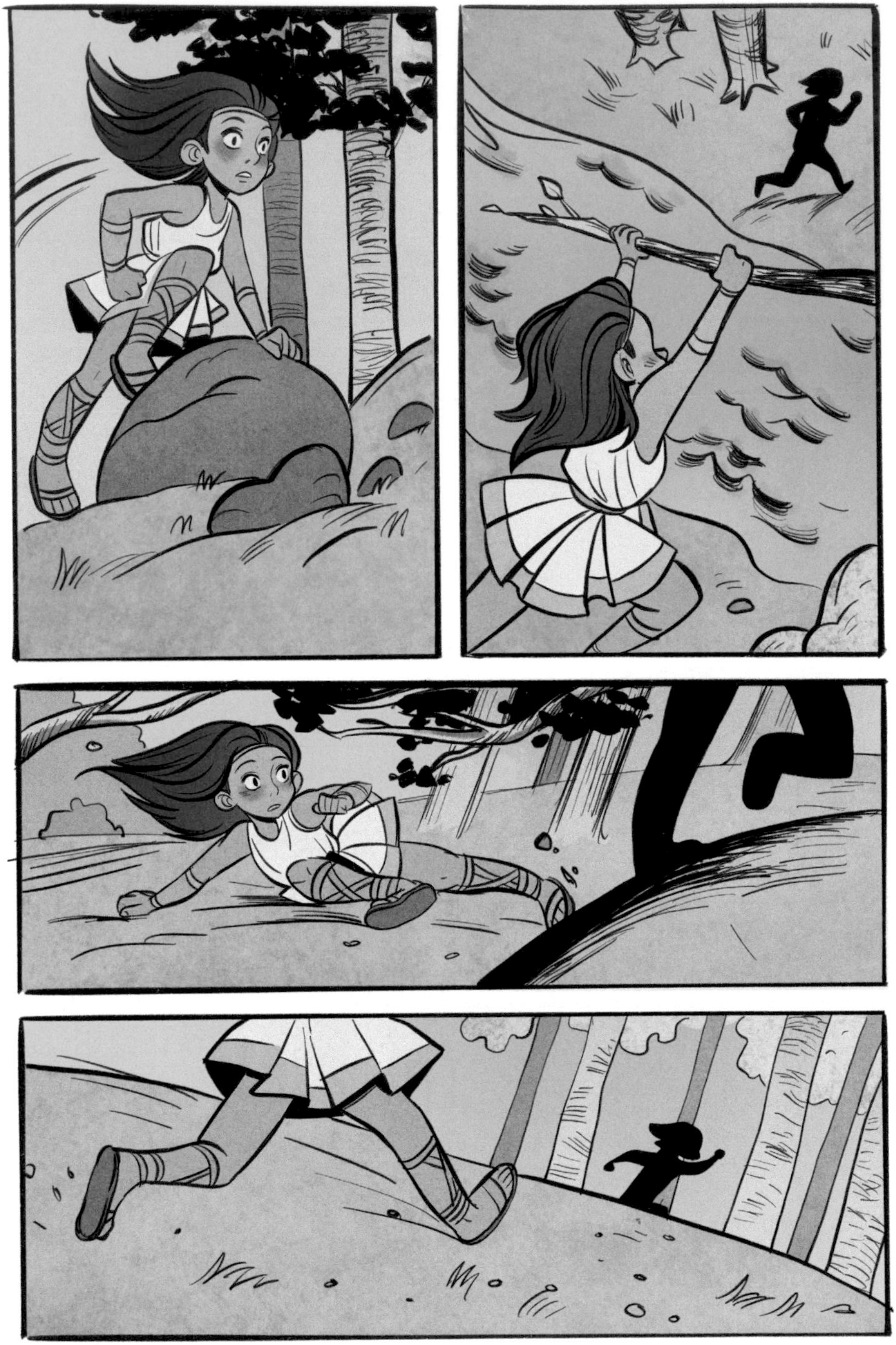

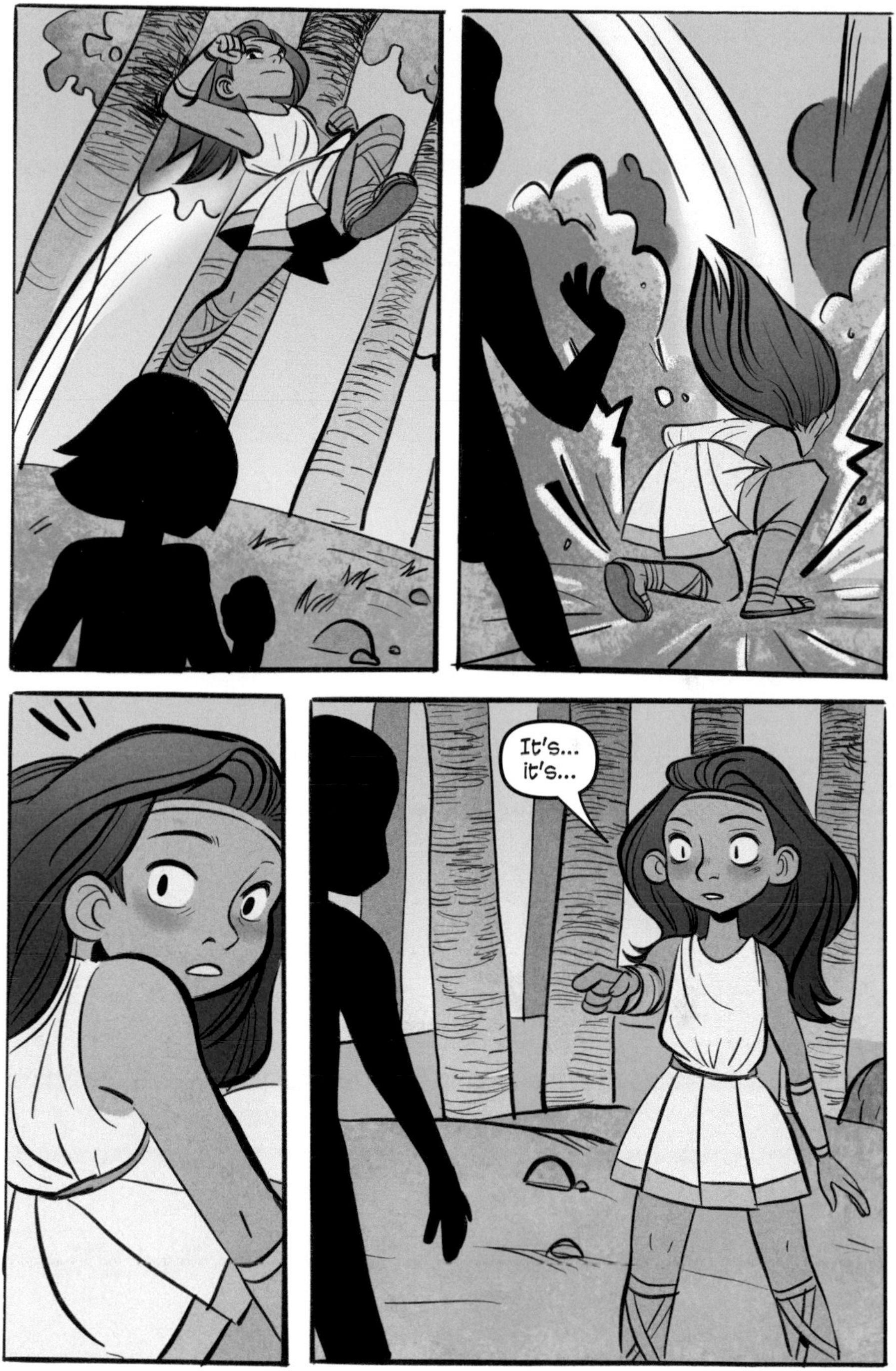
It's...
it's...

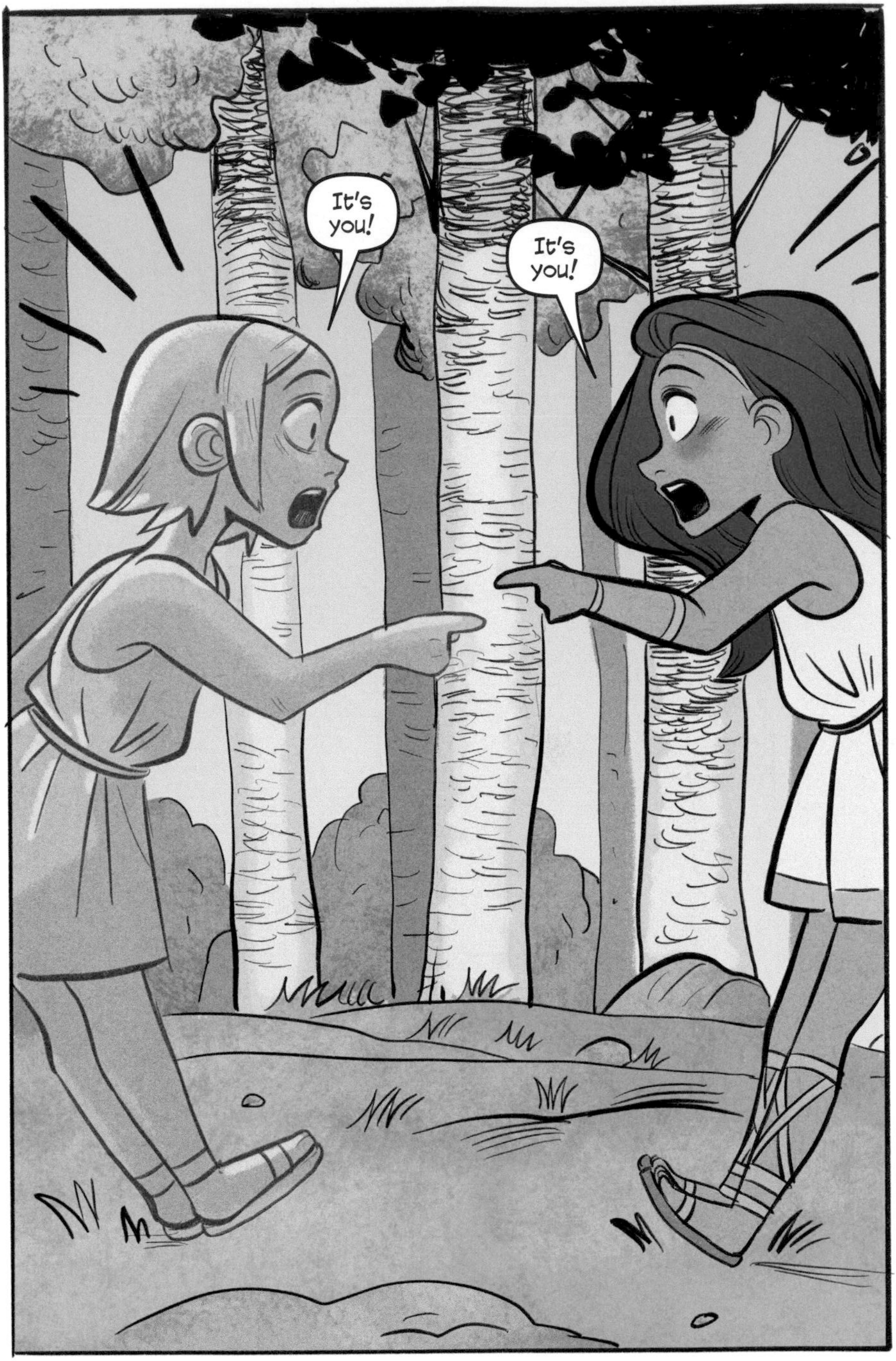
It's you!
It's you!

CHAPTER TWO

Cutting Class on Themyscira

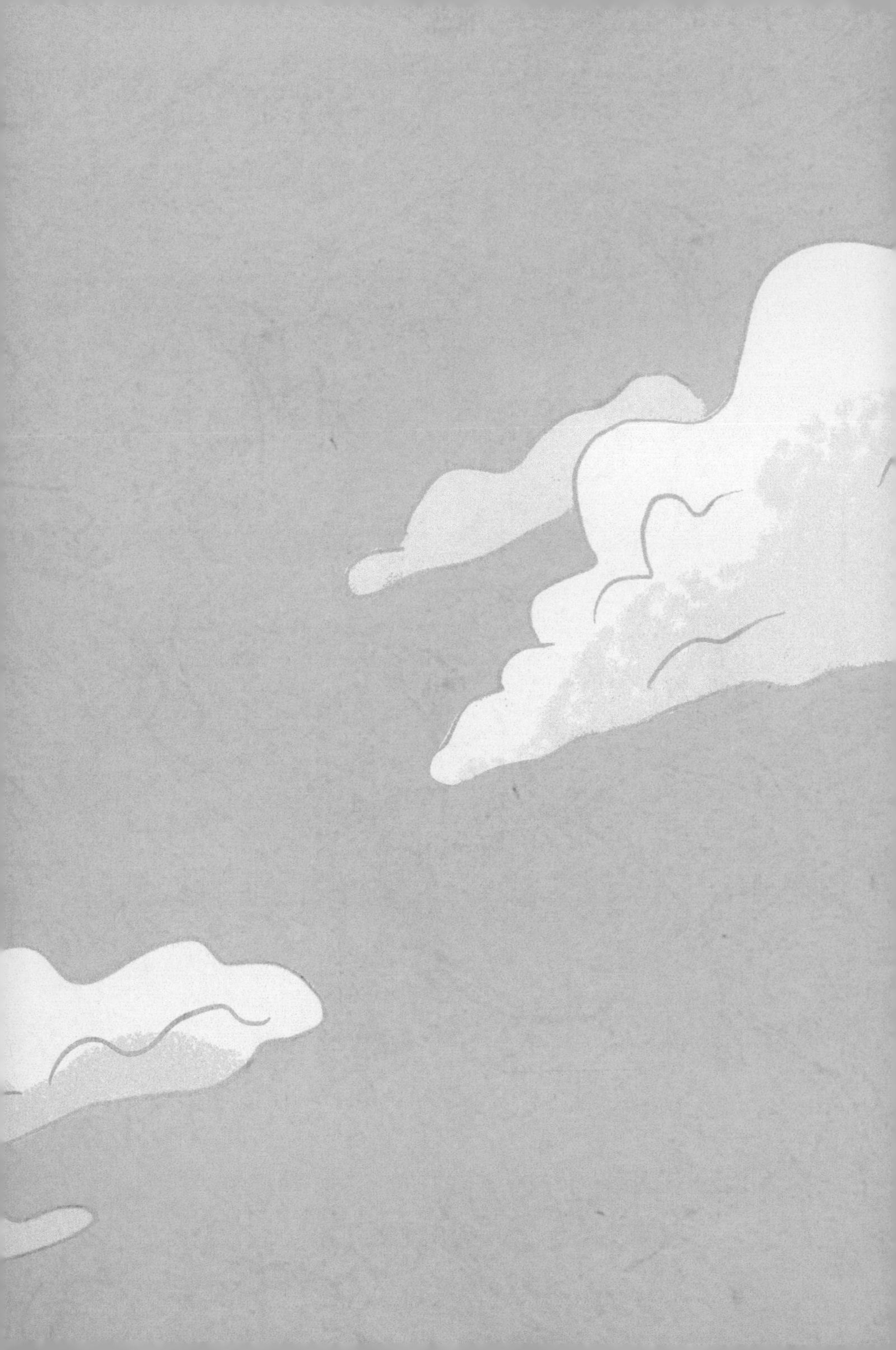

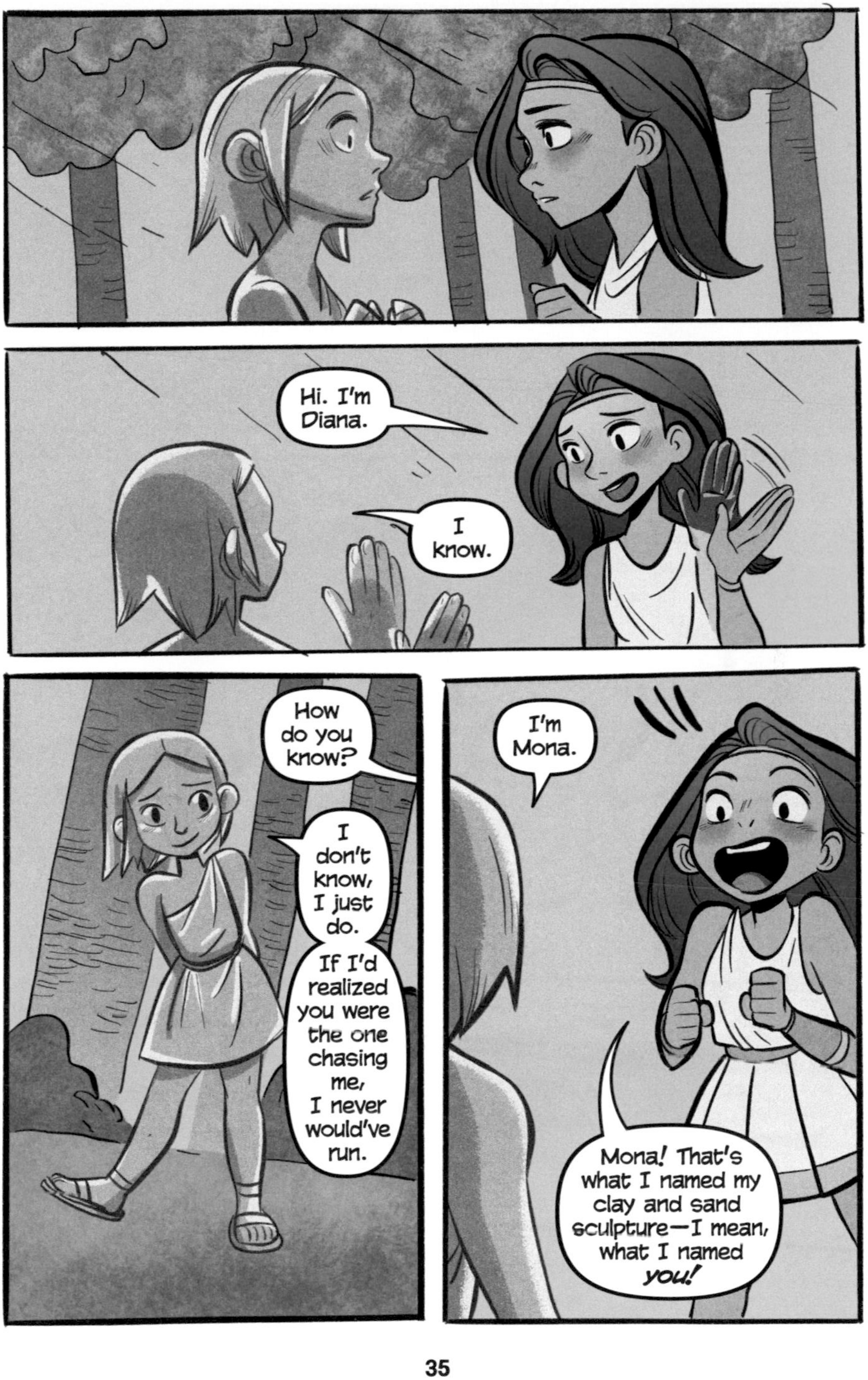
Hi. I'm Diana.
I know.
How do you know?
I don't know, I just do.
If I'd realized you were the one chasing me, I never would've run.
I'm Mona.
Mona! That's what I named my clay and sand sculpture—I mean, what I named *you!*

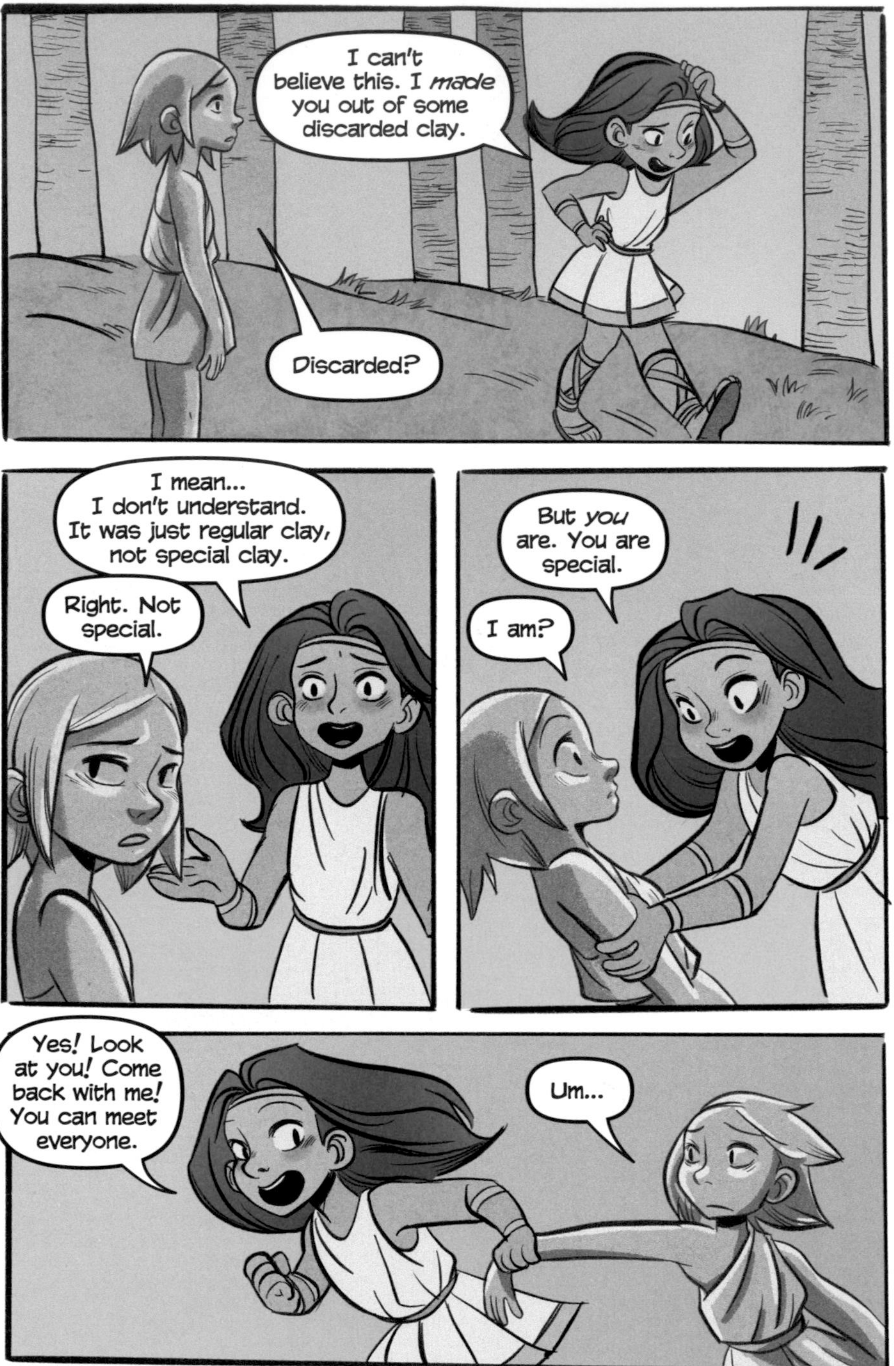
I can't believe this. I *made* you out of some discarded clay.
Discarded?
I mean... I don't understand. It was just regular clay, not special clay.
Right. Not special.
But *you* are. You are special.
I am?
Yes! Look at you! Come back with me! You can meet everyone.
Um...

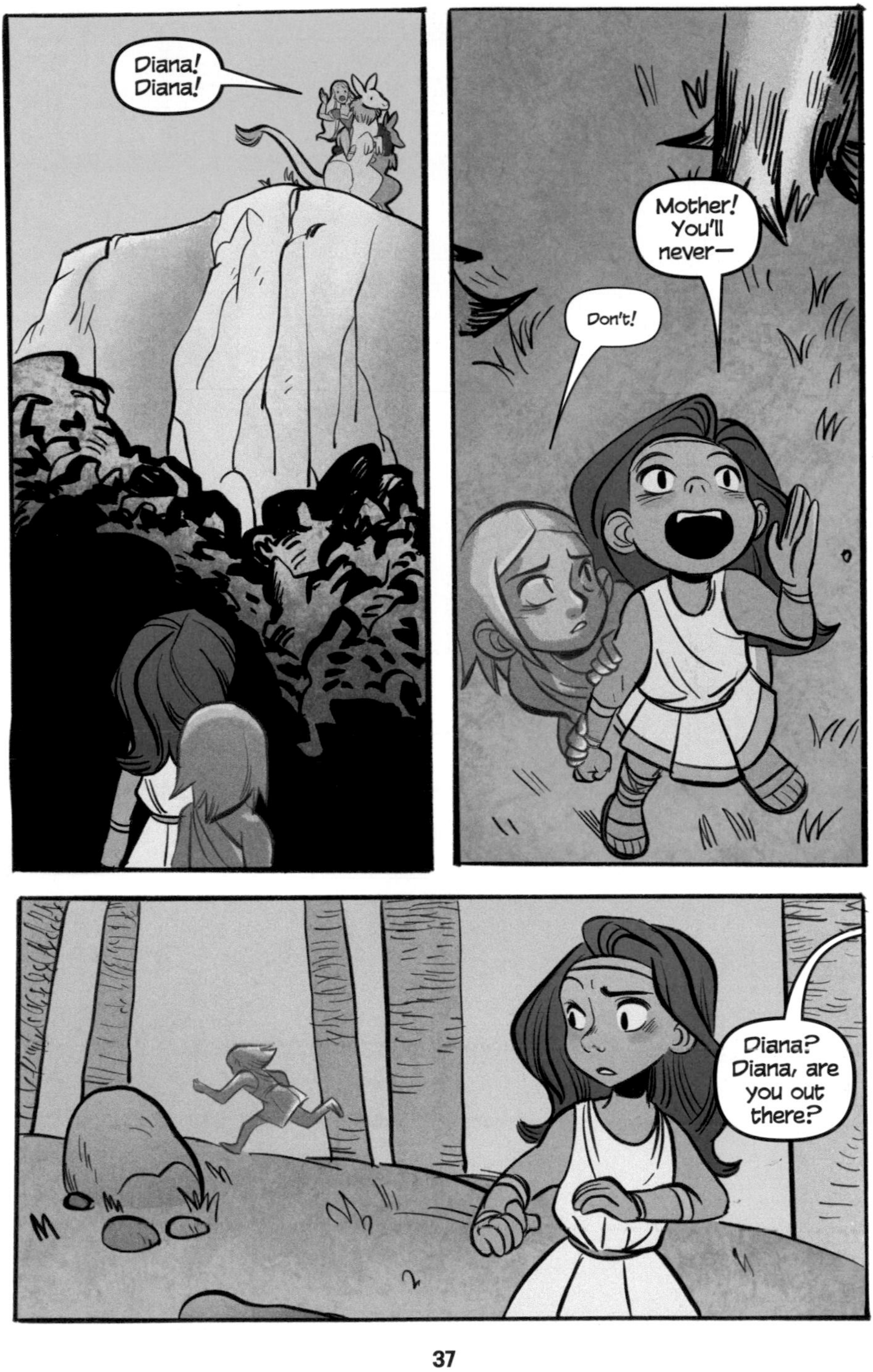
Diana!
Diana!
Mother!
You'll
never—
Don't!
Diana?
Diana, are
you out
there?

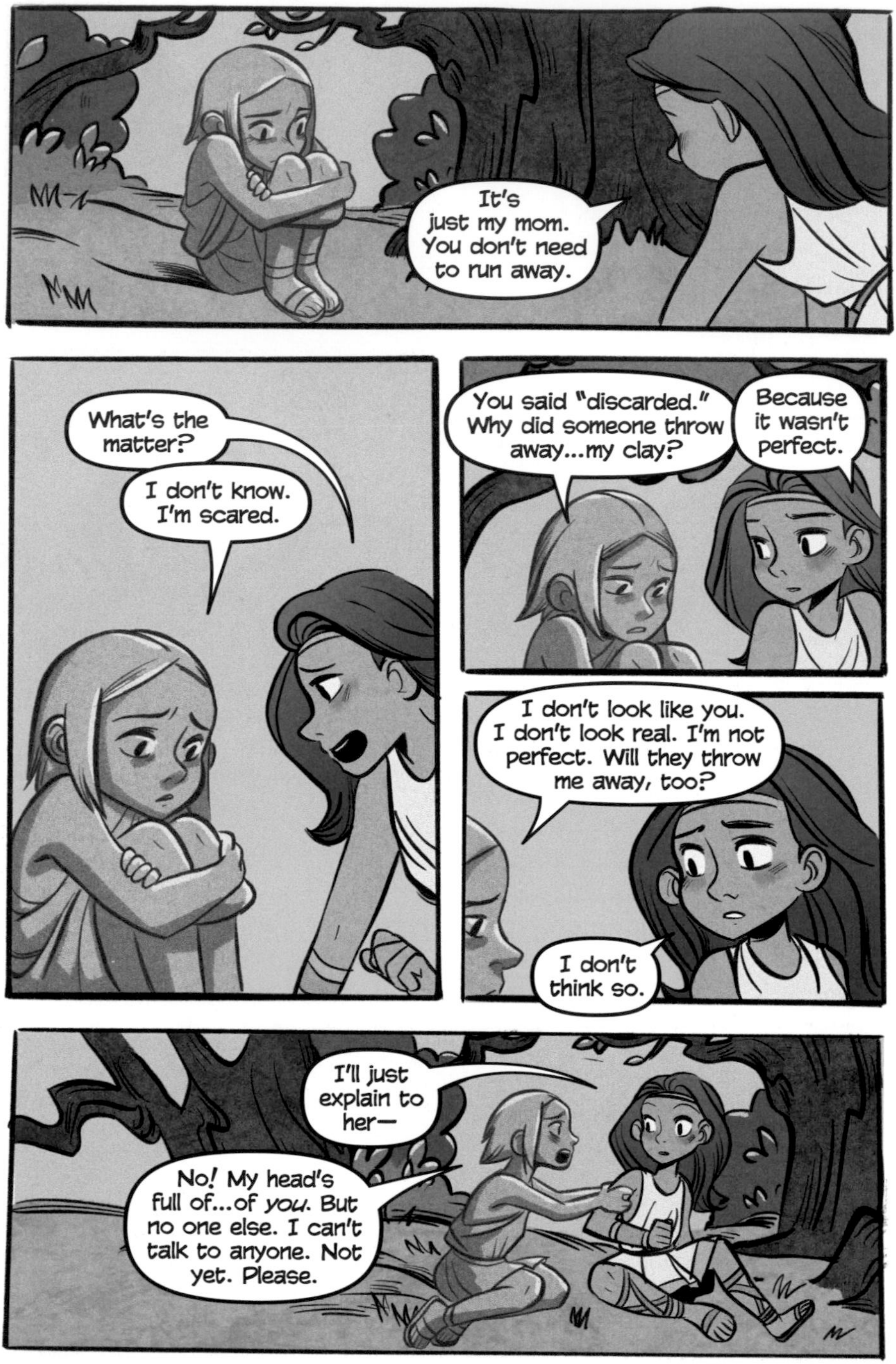
It's just my mom. You don't need to run away.
What's the matter?
I don't know. I'm scared.
You said "discarded." Why did someone throw away...my clay?
Because it wasn't perfect.
I don't look like you. I don't look real. I'm not perfect. Will they throw me away, too?
I don't think so.
I'll just explain to her—
No! My head's full of...of *you*. But no one else. I can't talk to anyone. Not yet. Please.

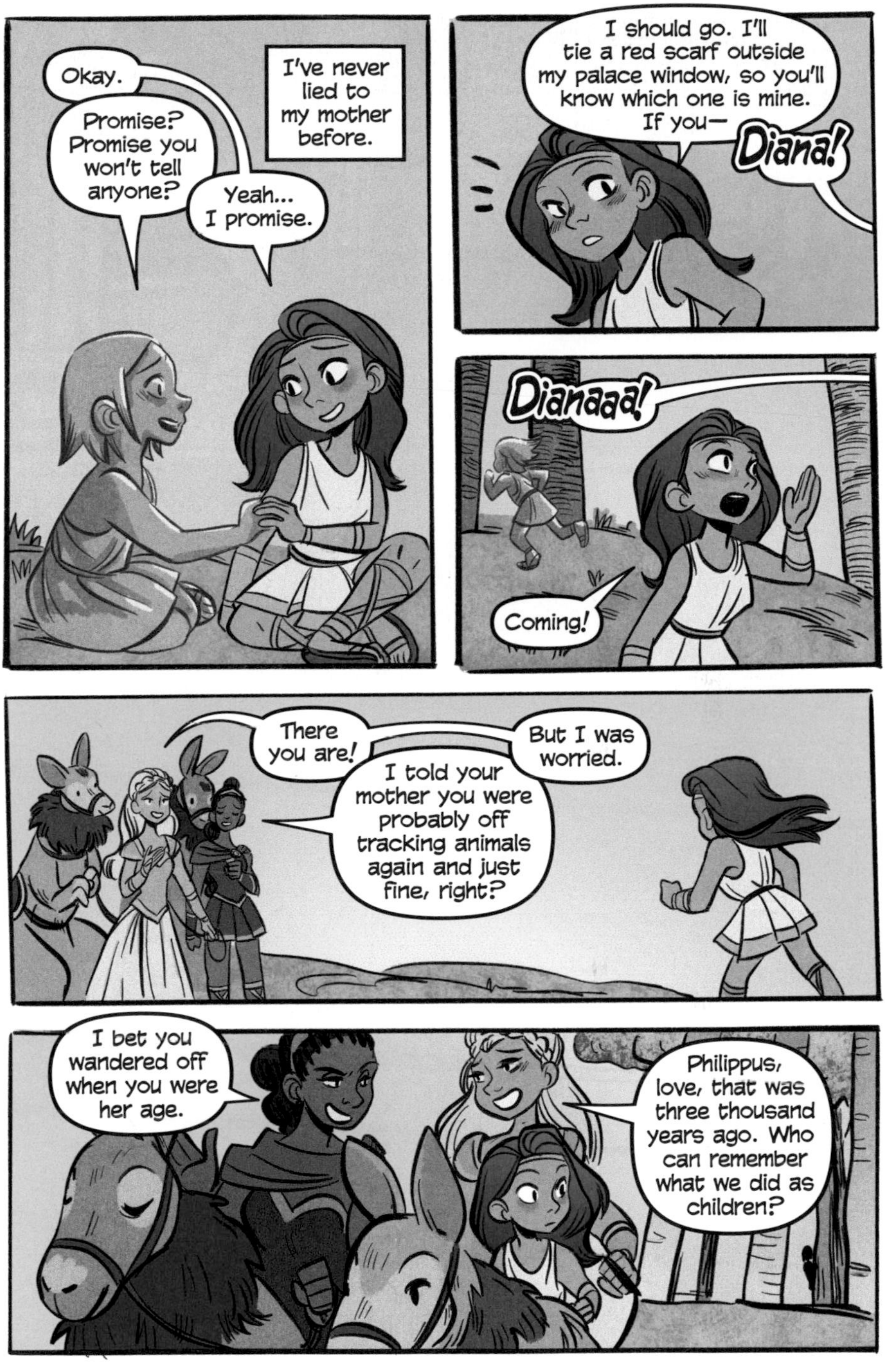
Okay.
I've never lied to my mother before.
Promise? Promise you won't tell anyone?
Yeah... I promise.
I should go. I'll tie a red scarf outside my palace window, so you'll know which one is mine. If you—
Diana!
Dianaaa!
Coming!
There you are!
But I was worried.
I told your mother you were probably off tracking animals again and just fine, right?
I bet you wandered off when you were her age.
Philippus, love, that was three thousand years ago. Who can remember what we did as children?

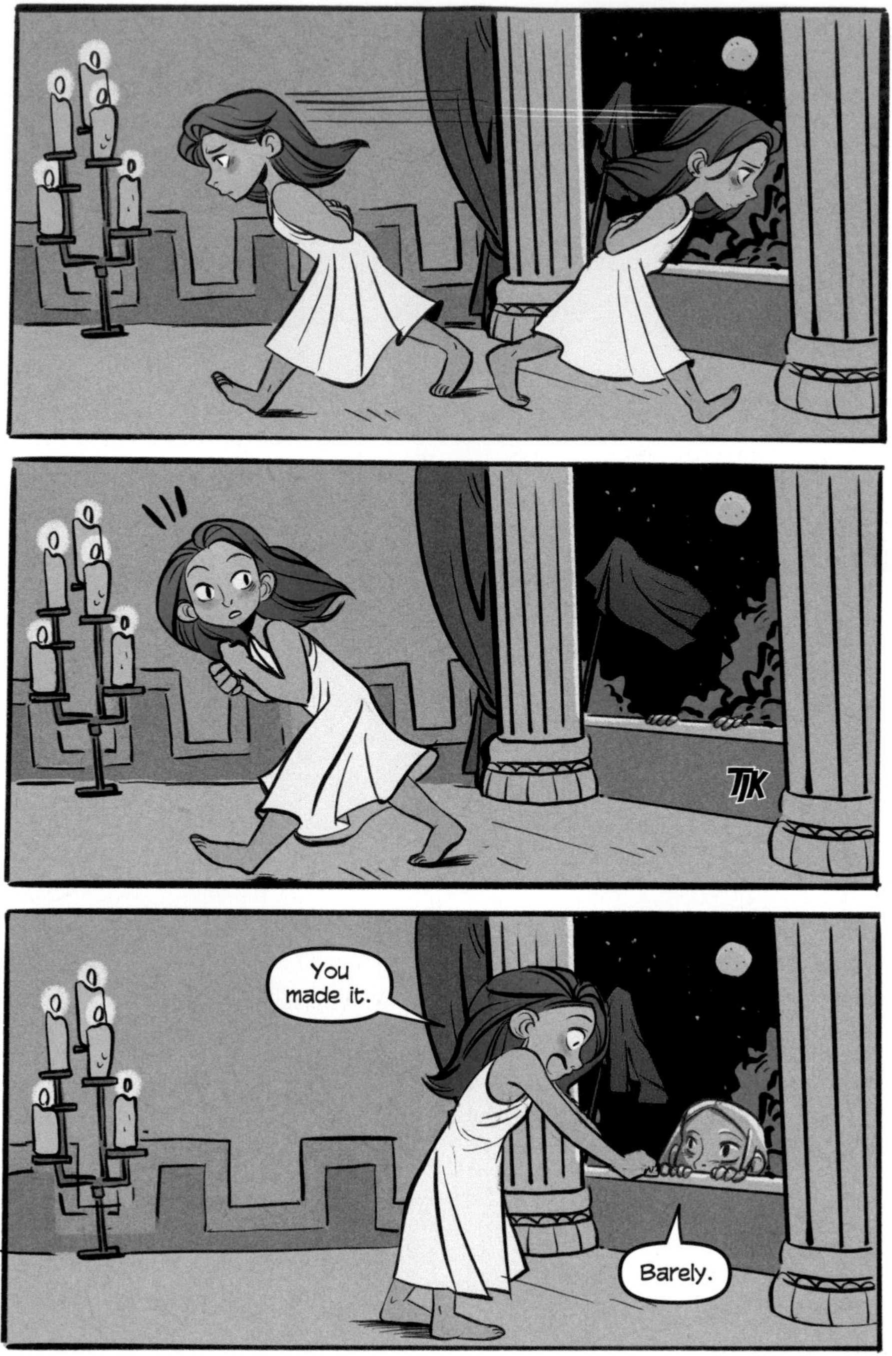
TJK
You made it.
Barely.

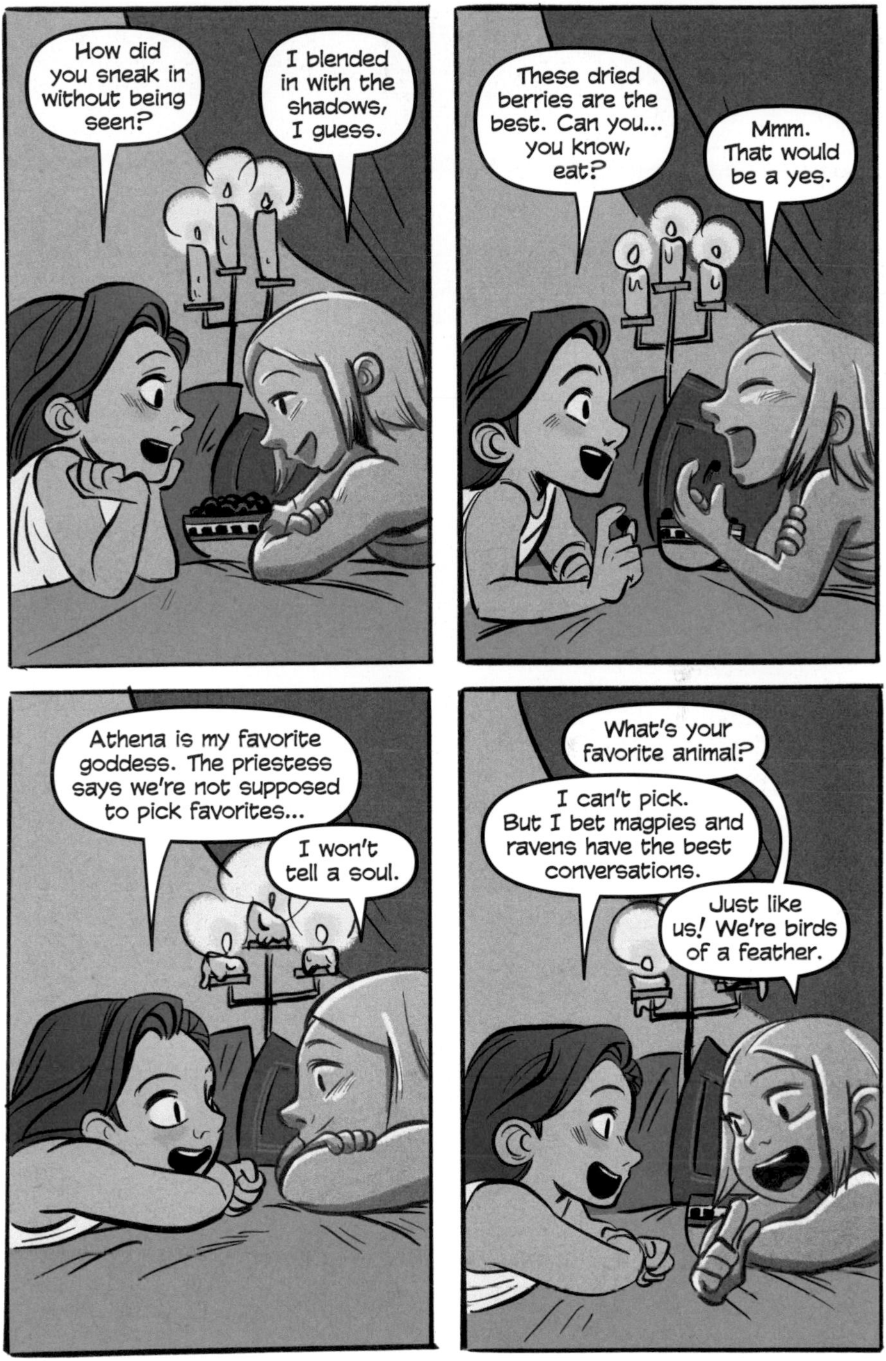
How did you sneak in without being seen?
I blended in with the shadows, I guess.
These dried berries are the best. Can you... you know, eat?
Mmm. That would be a yes.
Athena is my favorite goddess. The priestess says we're not supposed to pick favorites...
I won't tell a soul.
What's your favorite animal?
I can't pick. But I bet magpies and ravens have the best conversations.
Just like us! We're birds of a feather.

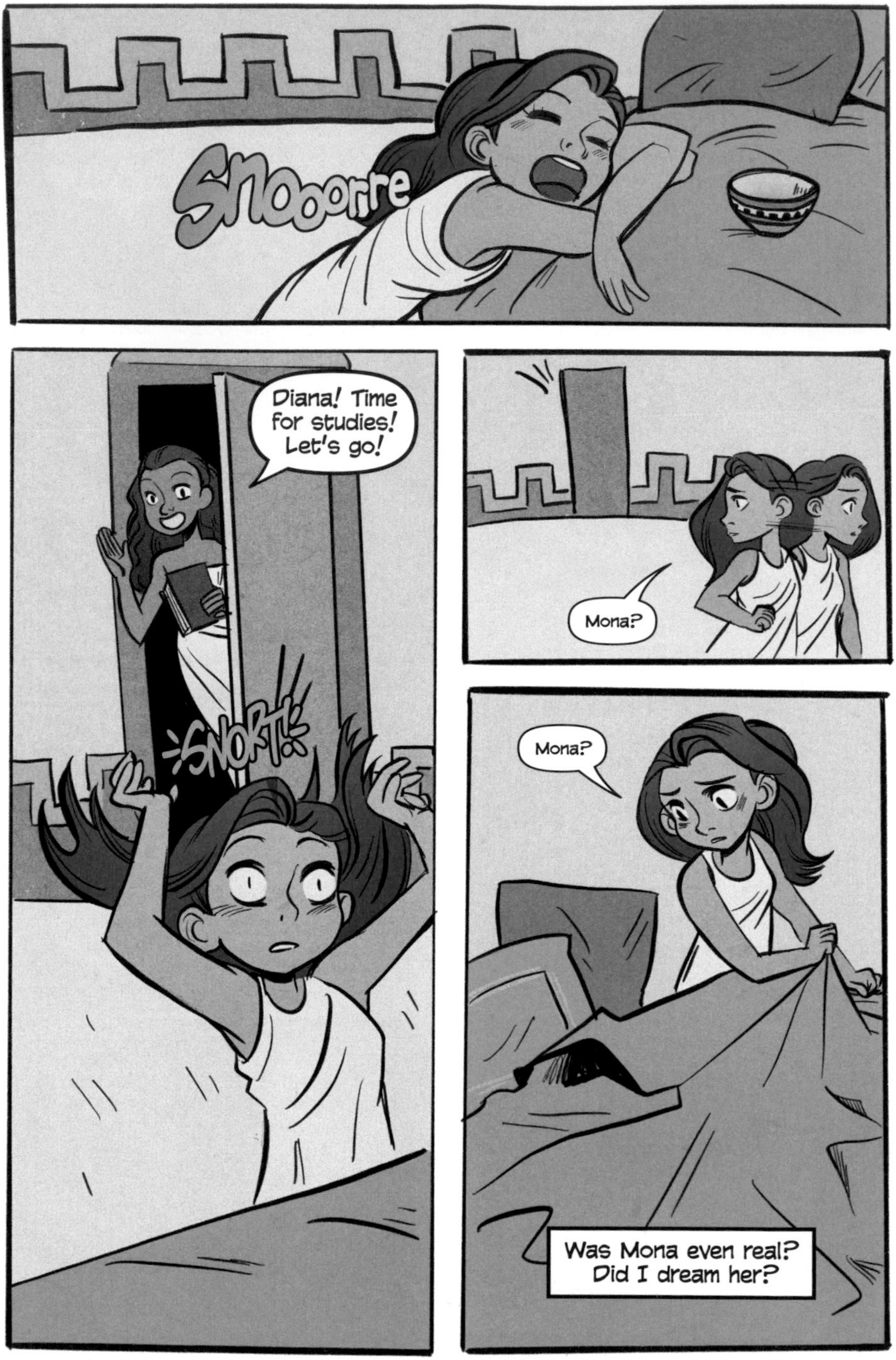
SNOOORRE
Diana! Time for studies! Let's go!
SNORT!
Mona?
Mona?
Was Mona even real? Did I dream her?

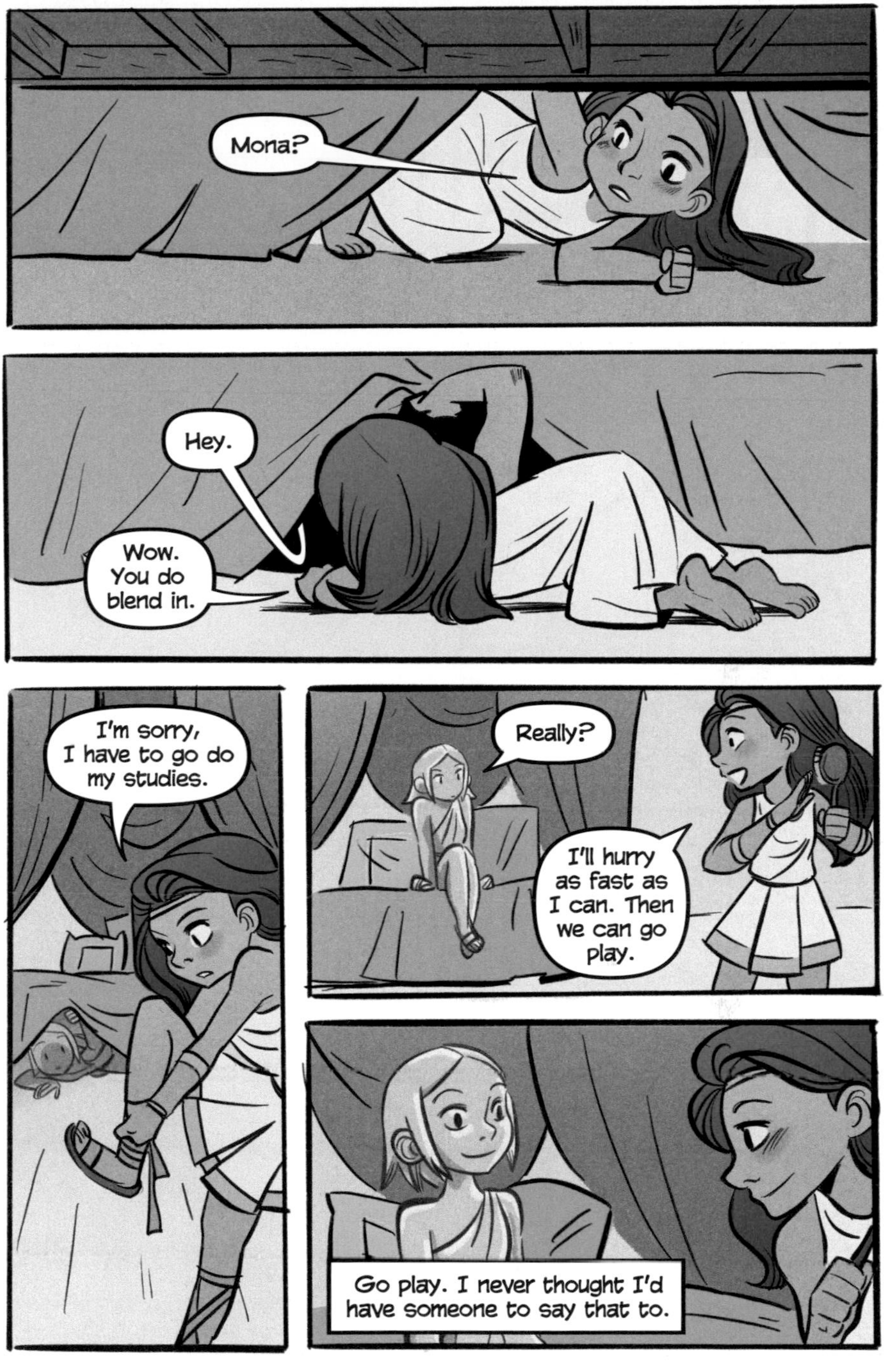
Mona?
Hey.
Wow. You do blend in.
I'm sorry, I have to go do my studies.
Really?
I'll hurry as fast as I can. Then we can go play.
Go play. I never thought I'd have someone to say that to.

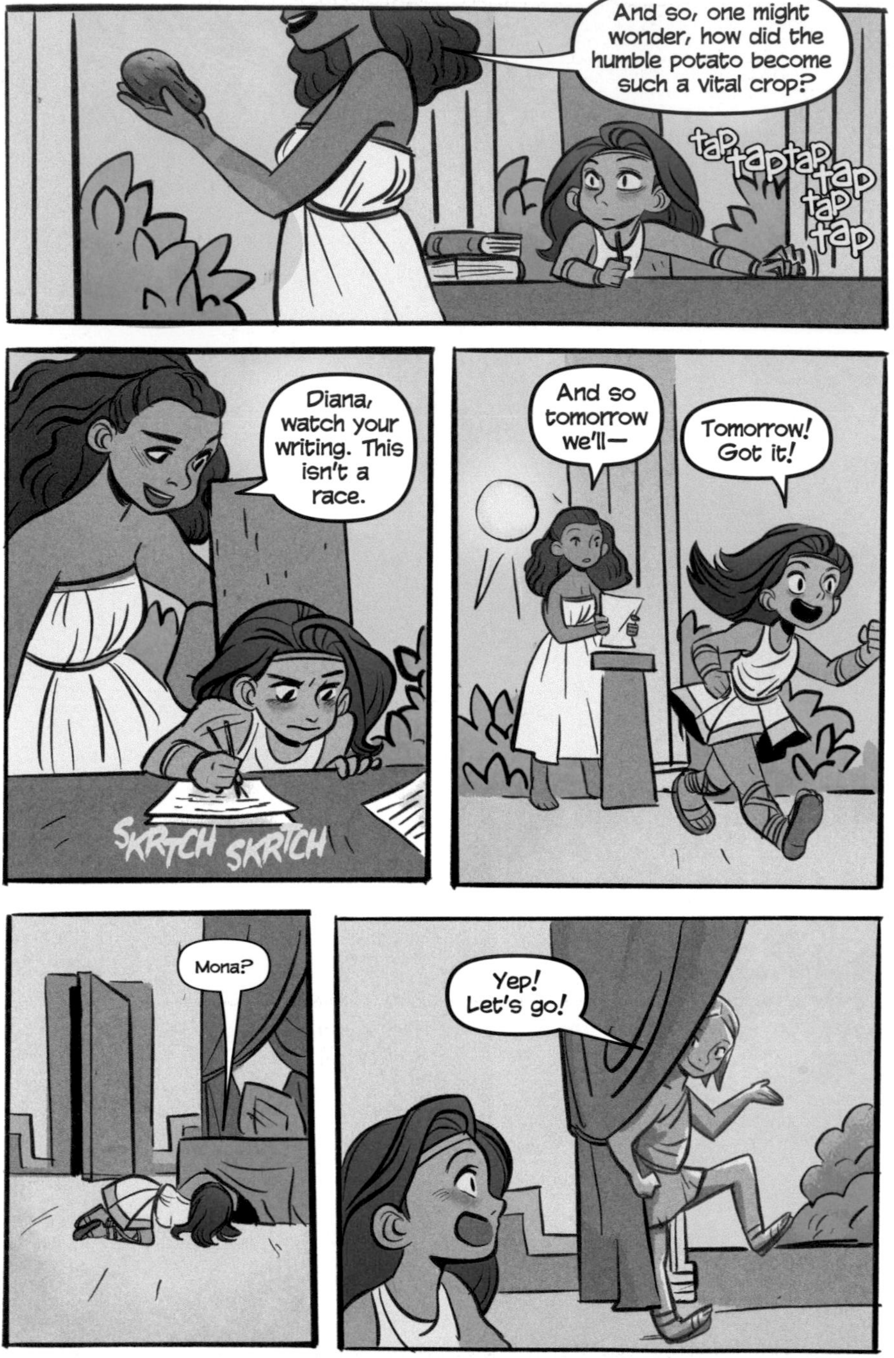
And so, one might wonder, how did the humble potato become such a vital crop?
tap taptaptap tap tap tap
Diana, watch your writing. This isn't a race.
SKRTCH SKRTCH
And so tomorrow we'll—
Tomorrow! Got it!
Mona?
Yep! Let's go!

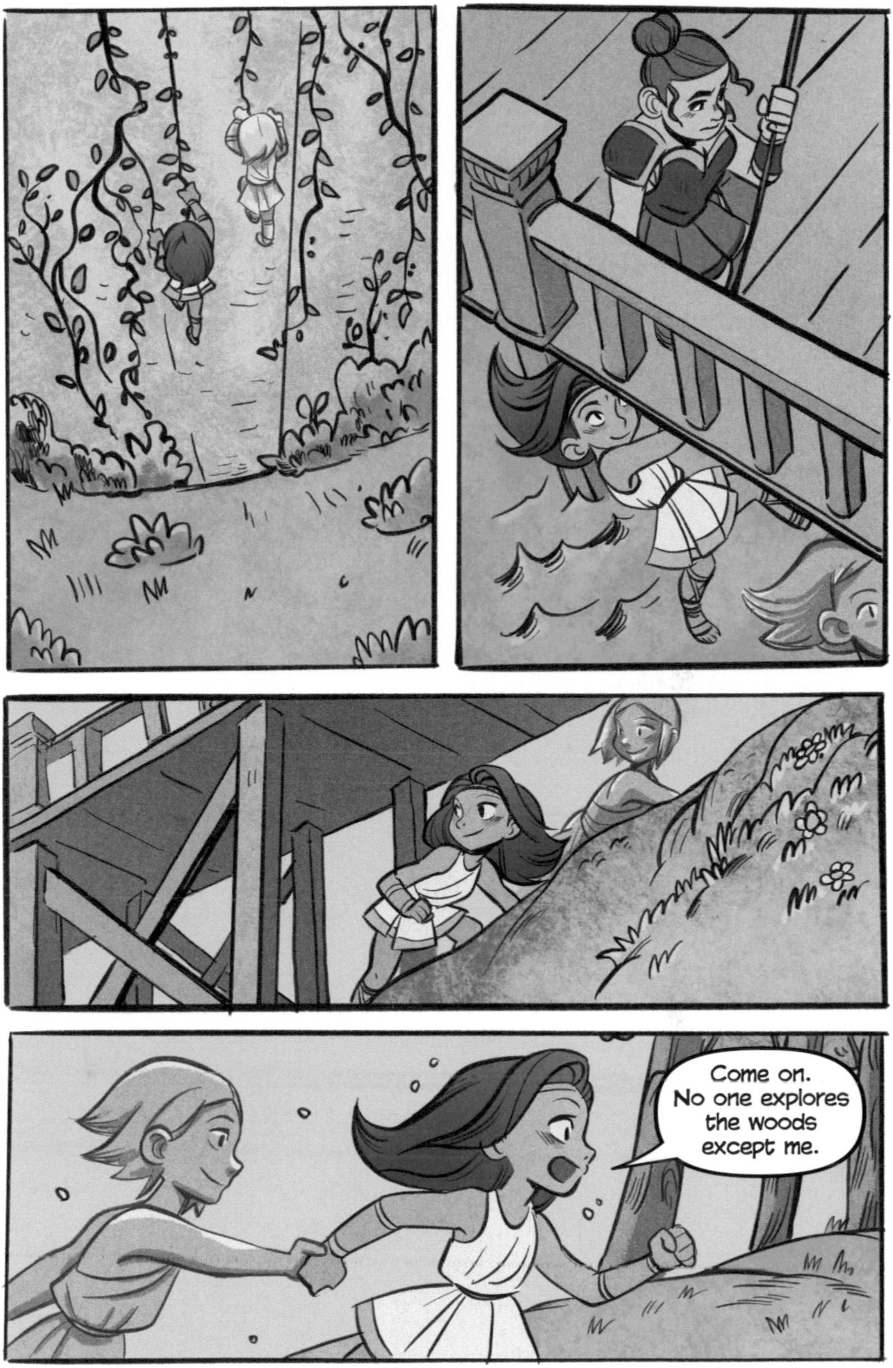
Come on.
No one explores
the woods
except me.

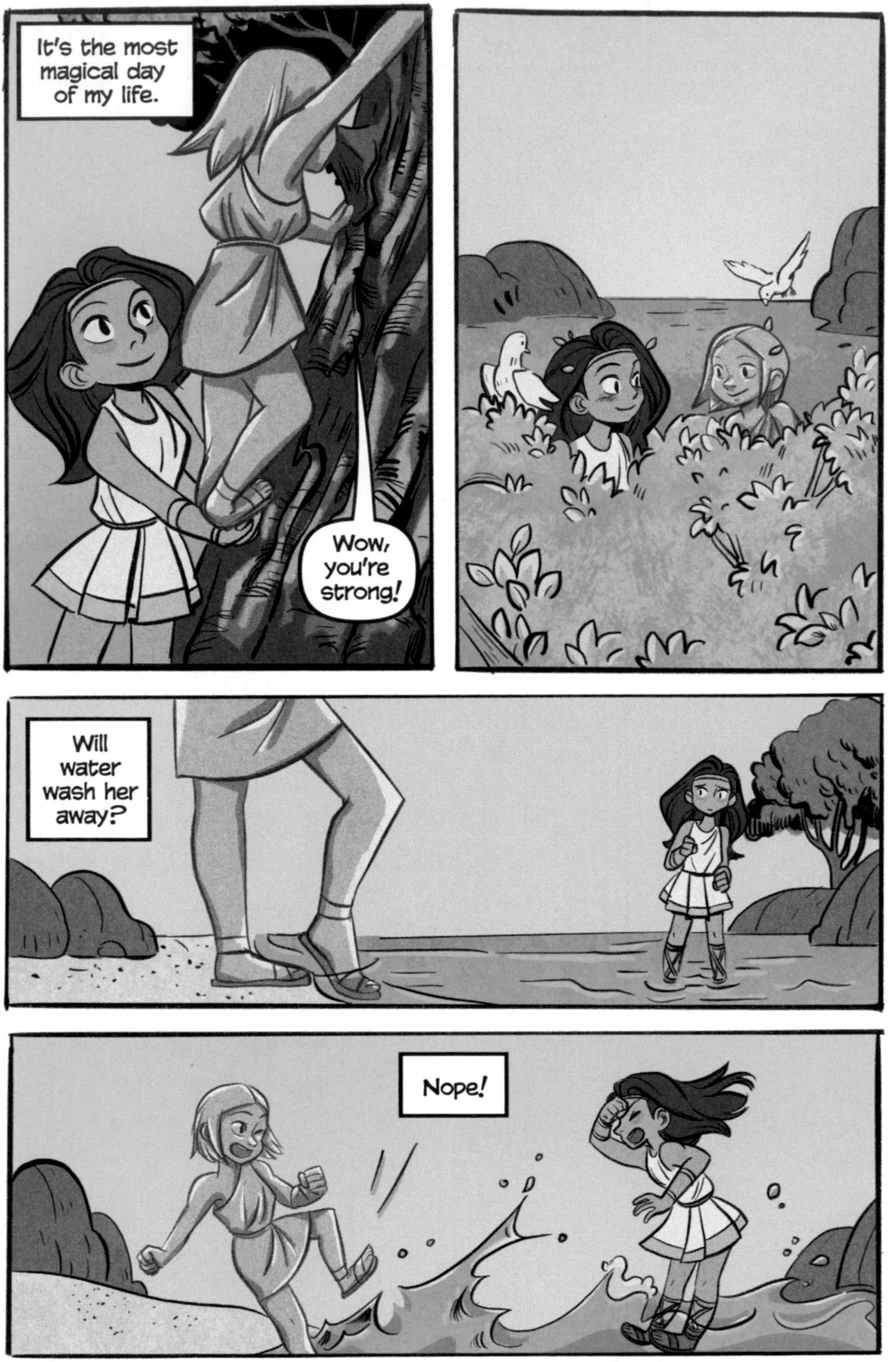
It's the most magical day of my life.
Wow, you're strong!
Will water wash her away?
Nope!

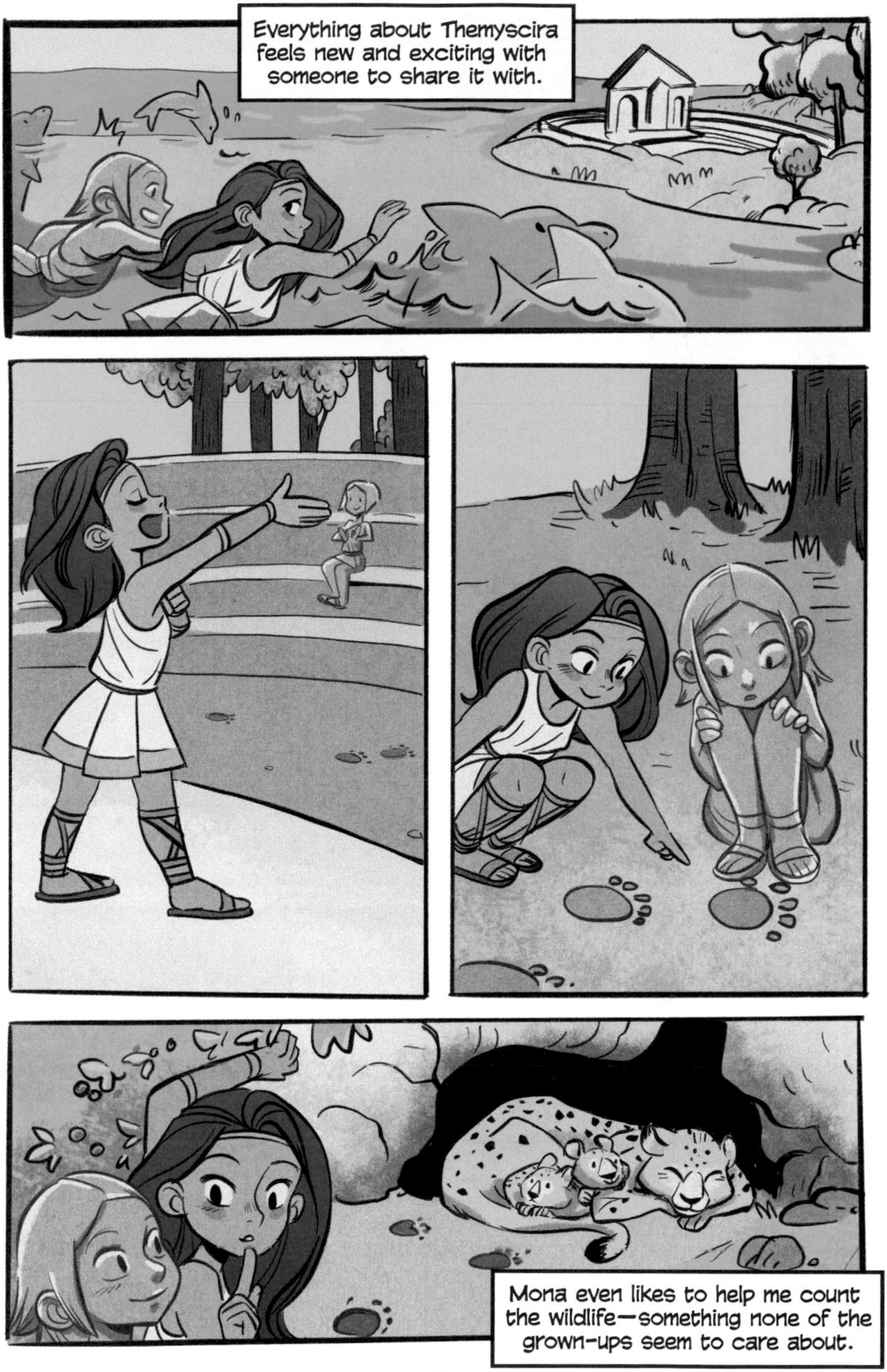
Everything about Themyscira feels new and exciting with someone to share it with.
Mona even likes to help me count the wildlife—something none of the grown-ups seem to care about.

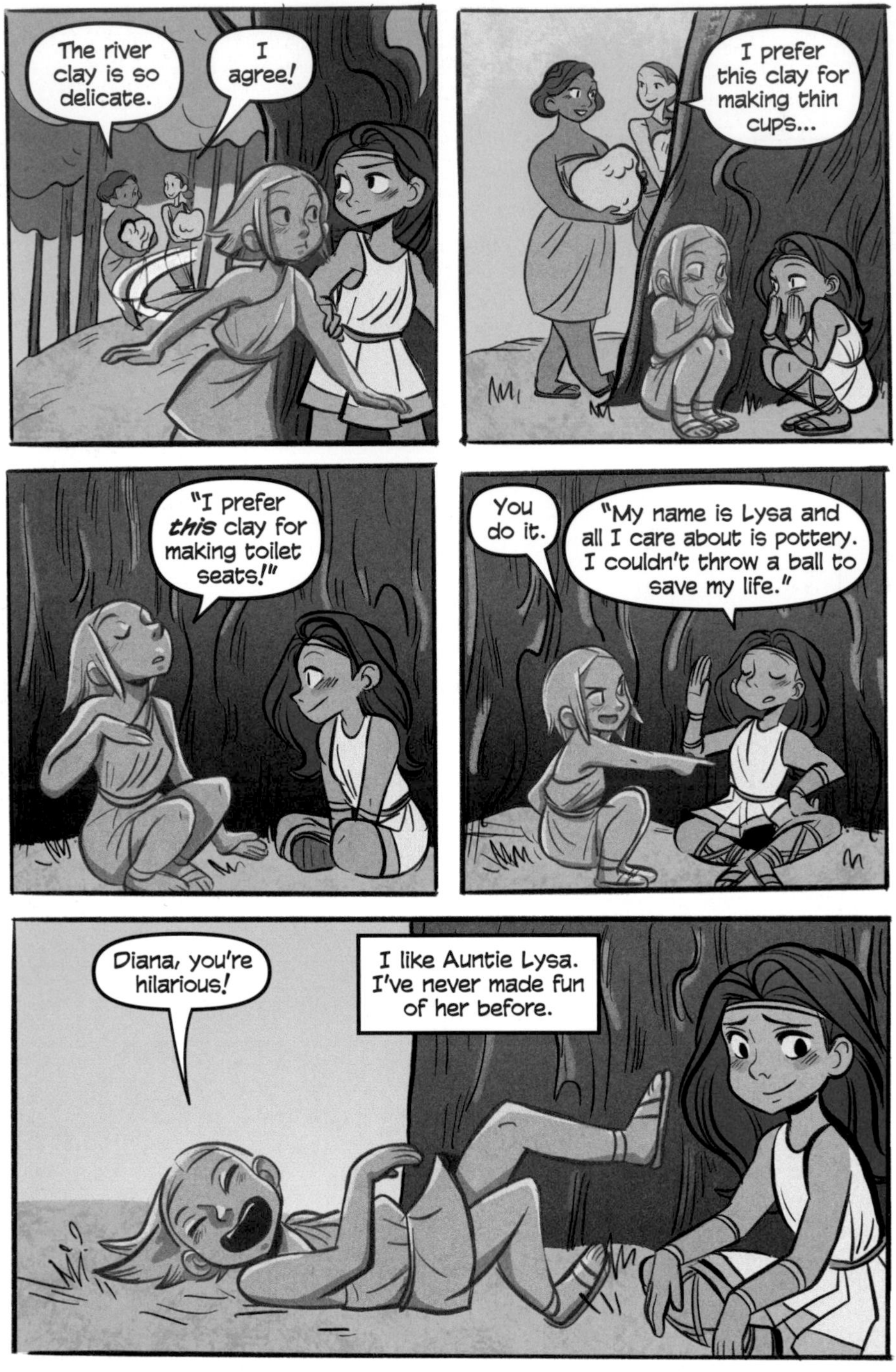
The river clay is so delicate.
I agree!
I prefer this clay for making thin cups...
"I prefer *this* clay for making toilet seats!"
You do it.
"My name is Lysa and all I care about is pottery. I couldn't throw a ball to save my life."
Diana, you're hilarious!
I like Auntie Lysa. I've never made fun of her before.

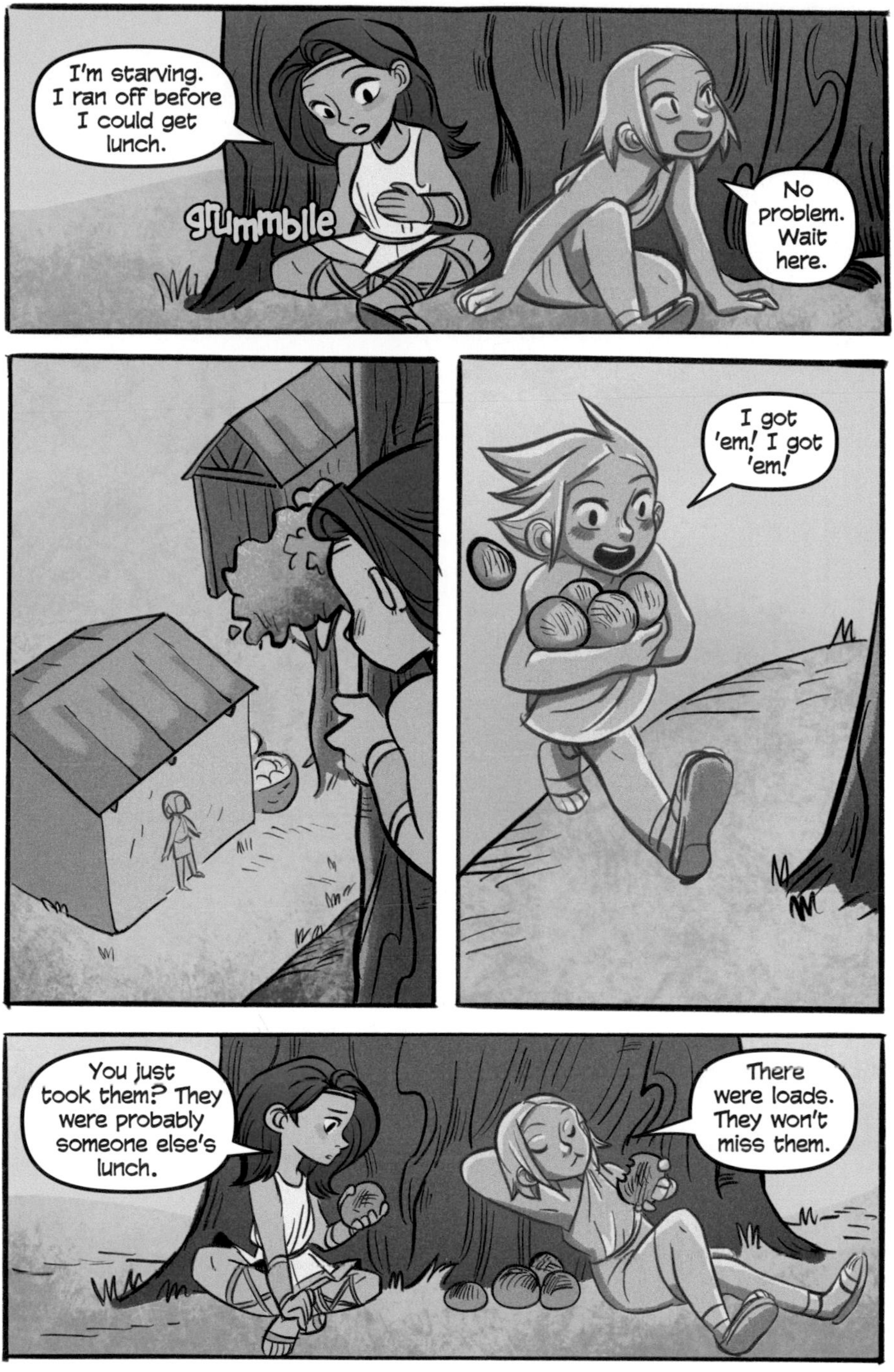
I'm starving. I ran off before I could get lunch.
grummblle
No problem. Wait here.
I got 'em! I got 'em!
You just took them? They were probably someone else's lunch.
There were loads. They won't miss them.

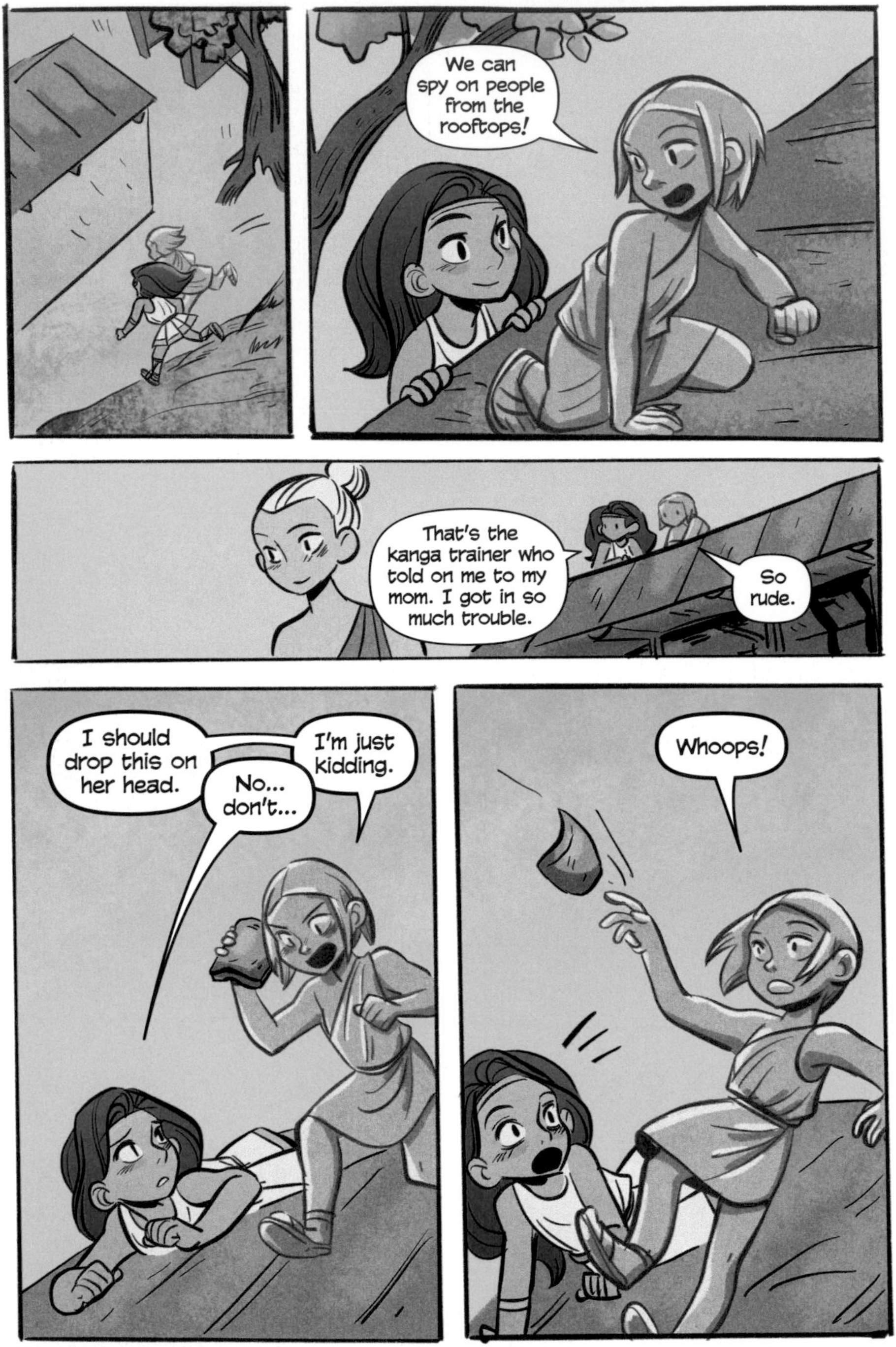
We can spy on people from the rooftops!
That's the kanga trainer who told on me to my mom. I got in so much trouble.
So rude.
I should drop this on her head.
No... don't...
I'm just kidding.
Whoops!

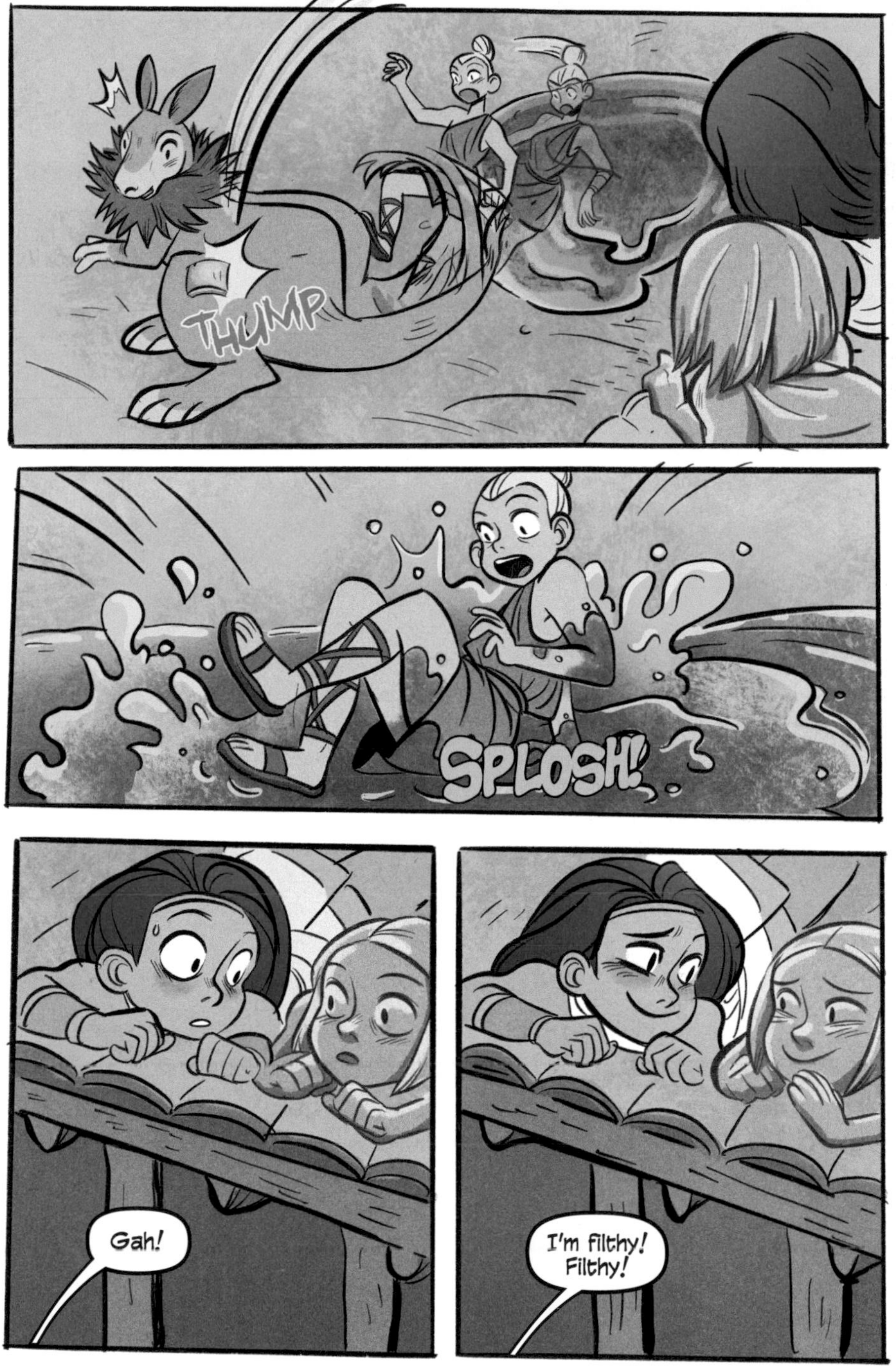
THUMP
SPLOSH!
Gah!
I'm filthy! Filthy!

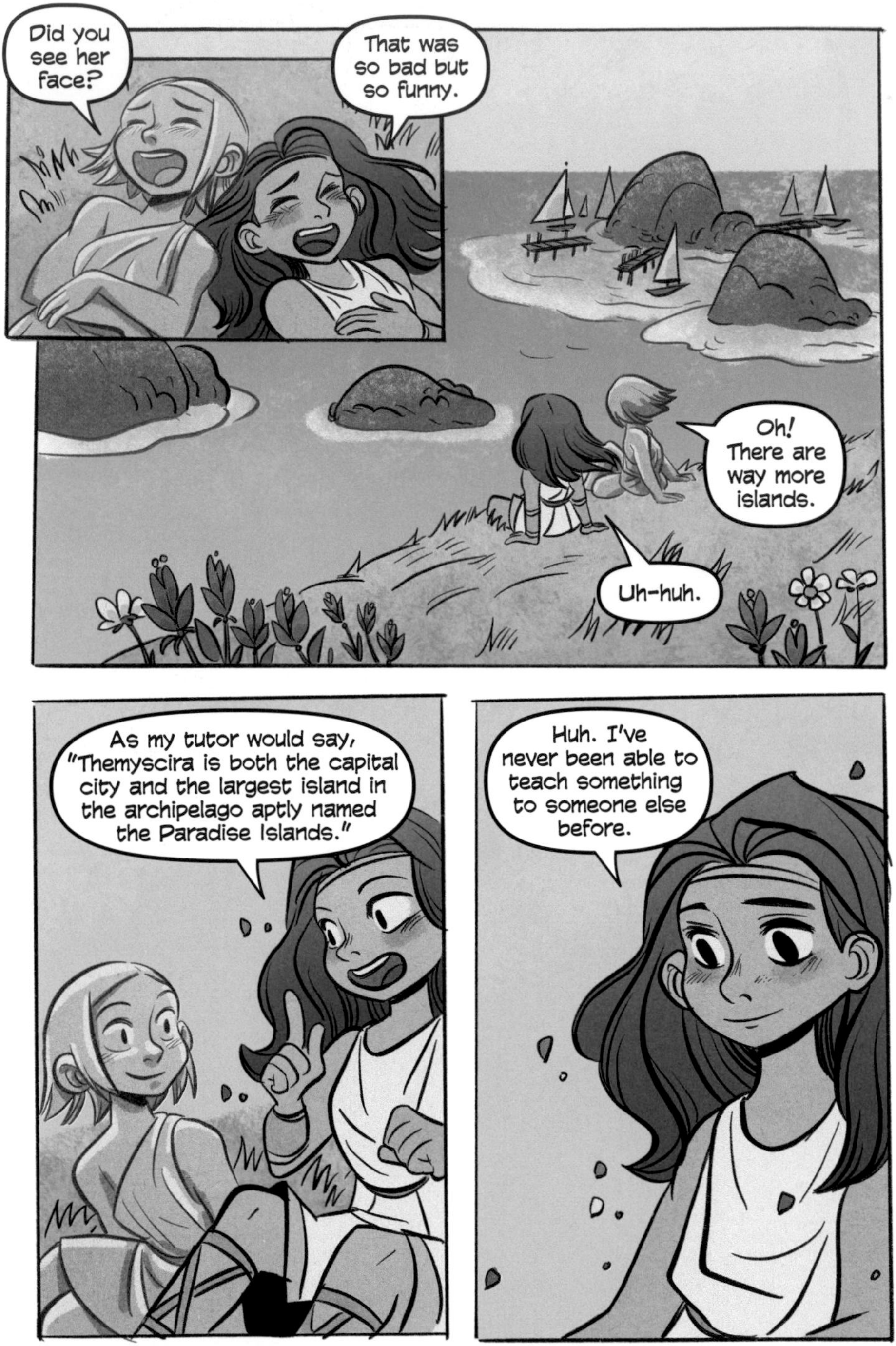
Did you see her face?
That was so bad but so funny.
Oh! There are way more islands.
Uh-huh.
As my tutor would say, "Themyscira is both the capital city and the largest island in the archipelago aptly named the Paradise Islands."
Huh. I've never been able to teach something to someone else before.

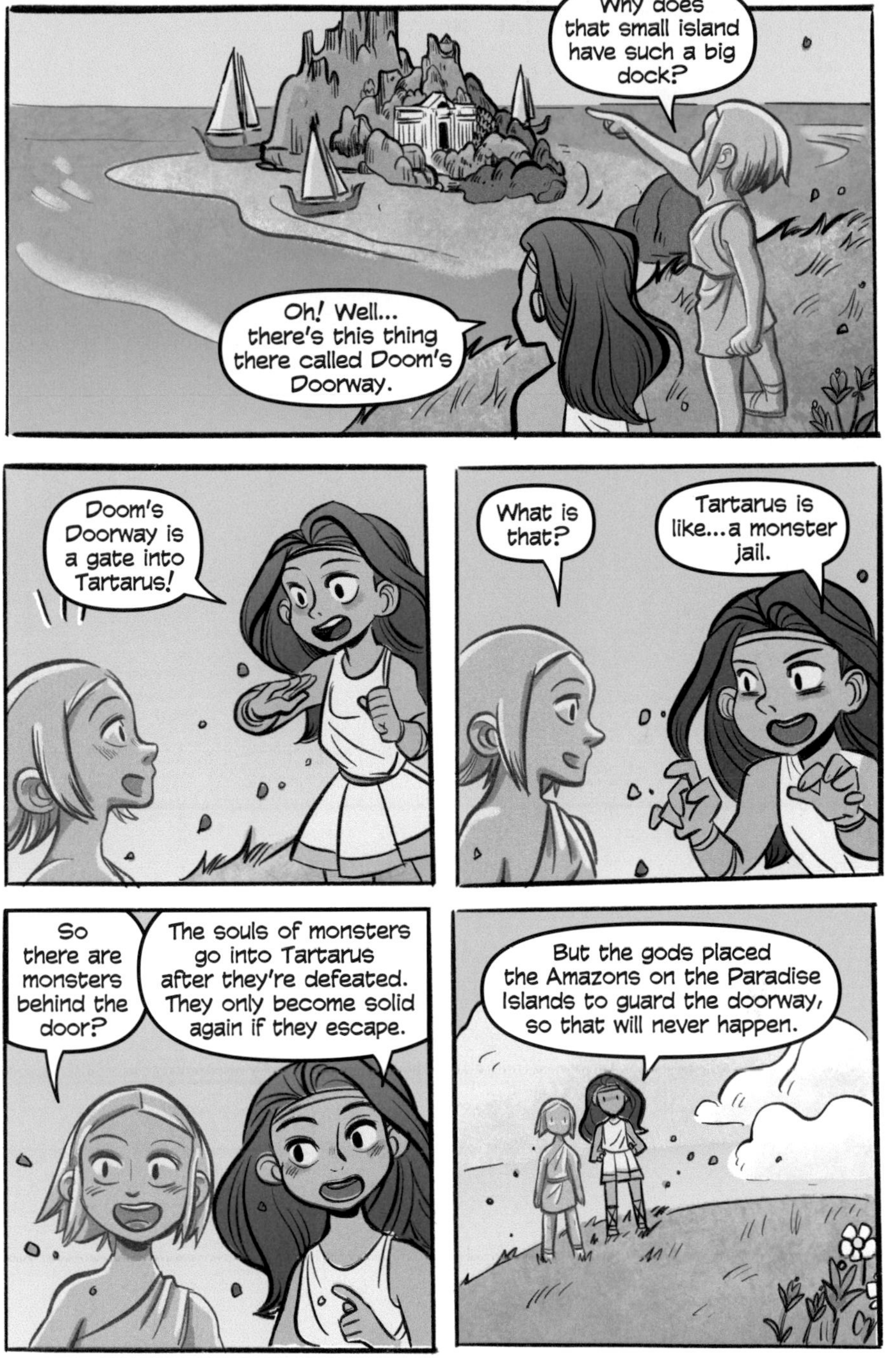

Why does that small island have such a big dock?
Oh! Well... there's this thing there called Doom's Doorway.
Doom's Doorway is a gate into Tartarus!
What is that?
Tartarus is like...a monster jail.
So there are monsters behind the door?
The souls of monsters go into Tartarus after they're defeated. They only become solid again if they escape.
But the gods placed the Amazons on the Paradise Islands to guard the doorway, so that will never happen.

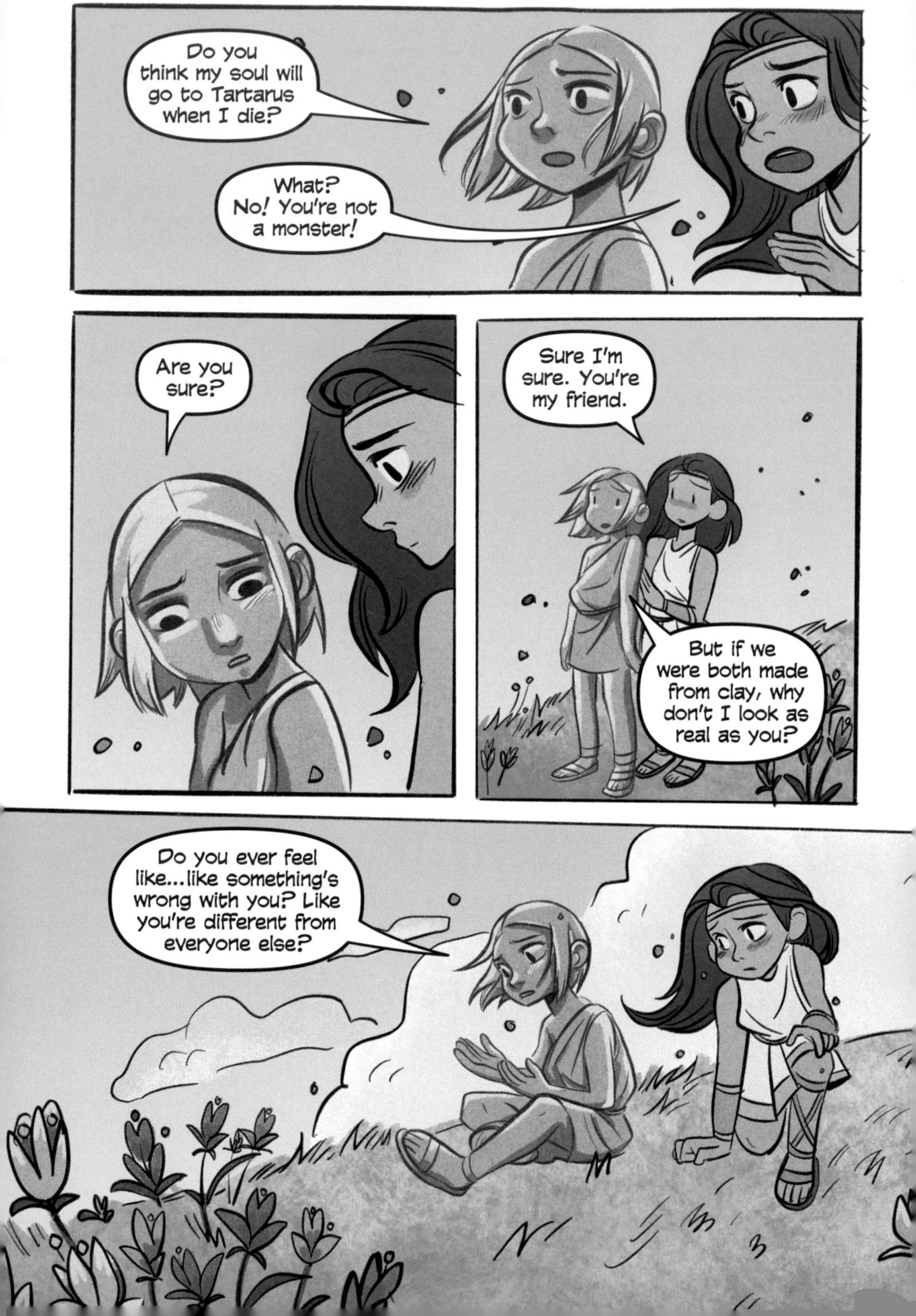

Do you think my soul will go to Tartarus when I die?
What? No! You're not a monster!
Are you sure?
Sure I'm sure. You're my friend.
But if we were both made from clay, why don't I look as real as you?
Do you ever feel like...like something's wrong with you? Like you're different from everyone else?

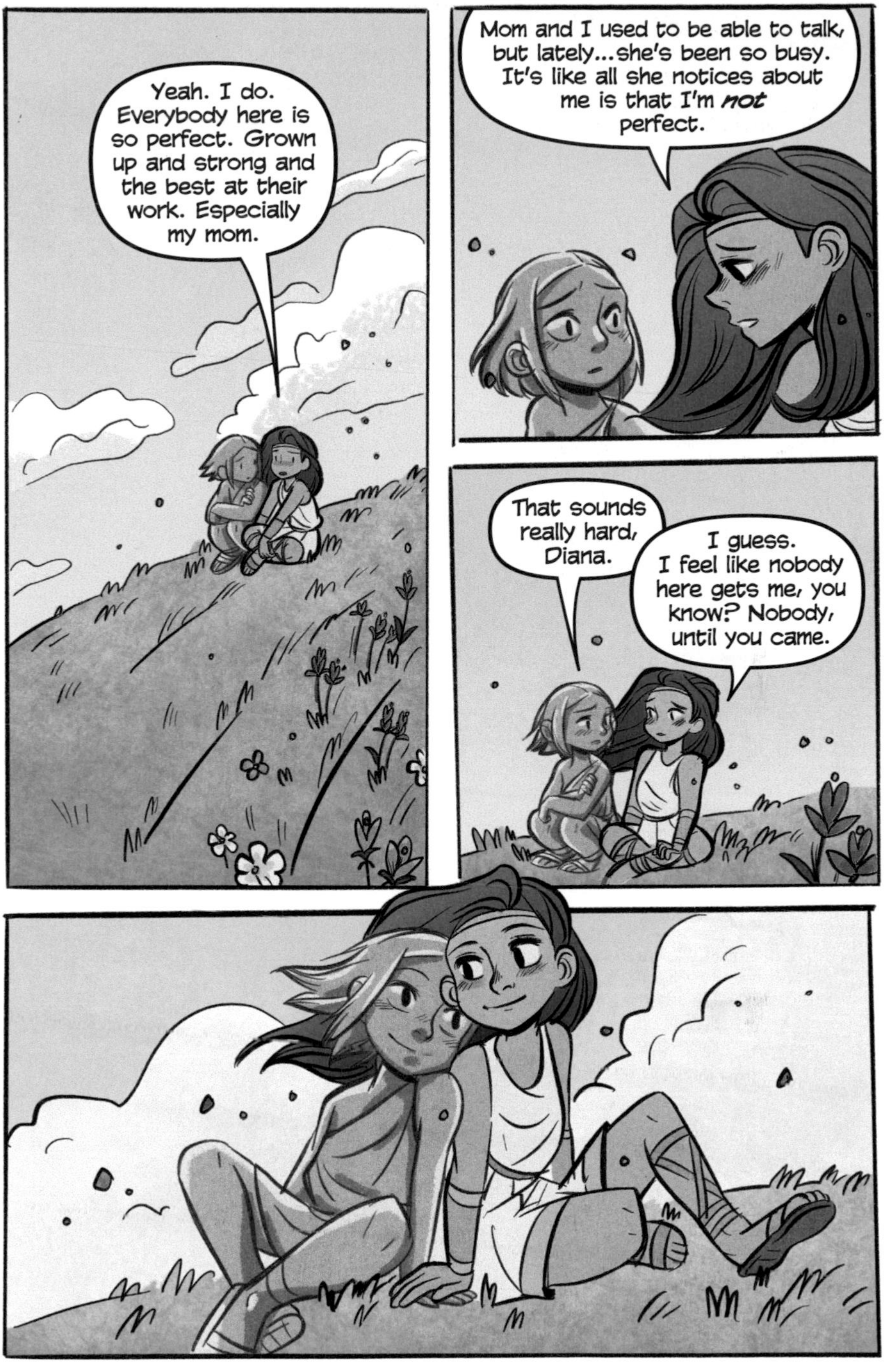
Yeah. I do. Everybody here is so perfect. Grown up and strong and the best at their work. Especially my mom.
Mom and I used to be able to talk, but lately...she's been so busy. It's like all she notices about me is that I'm *not* perfect.
That sounds really hard, Diana.
I guess. I feel like nobody here gets me, you know? Nobody, until you came.

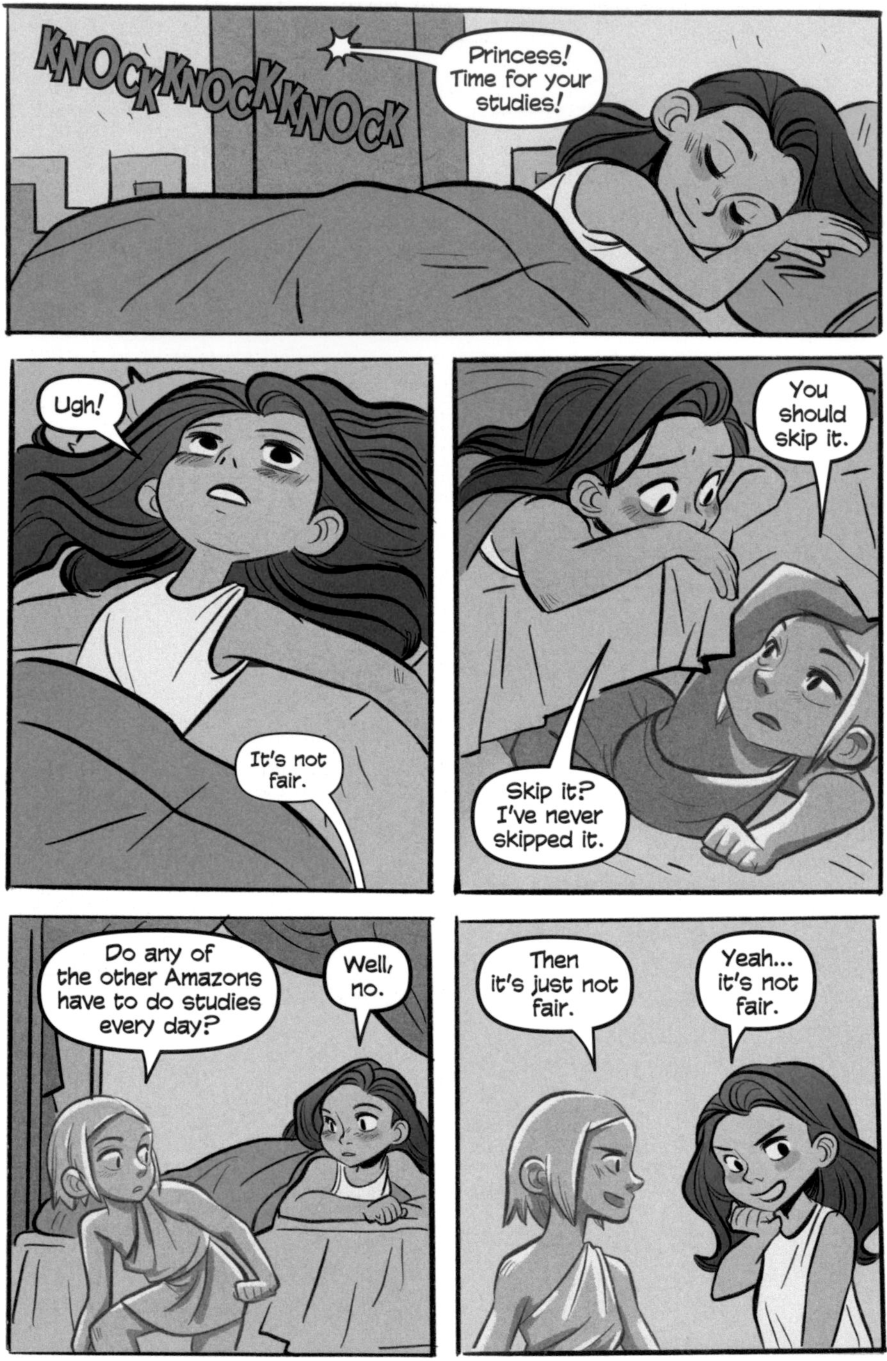
KNOCK KNOCK KNOCK
Princess! Time for your studies!
Ugh!
It's not fair.
You should skip it.
Skip it? I've never skipped it.
Do any of the other Amazons have to do studies every day?
Well, no.
Then it's just not fair.
Yeah... it's not fair.

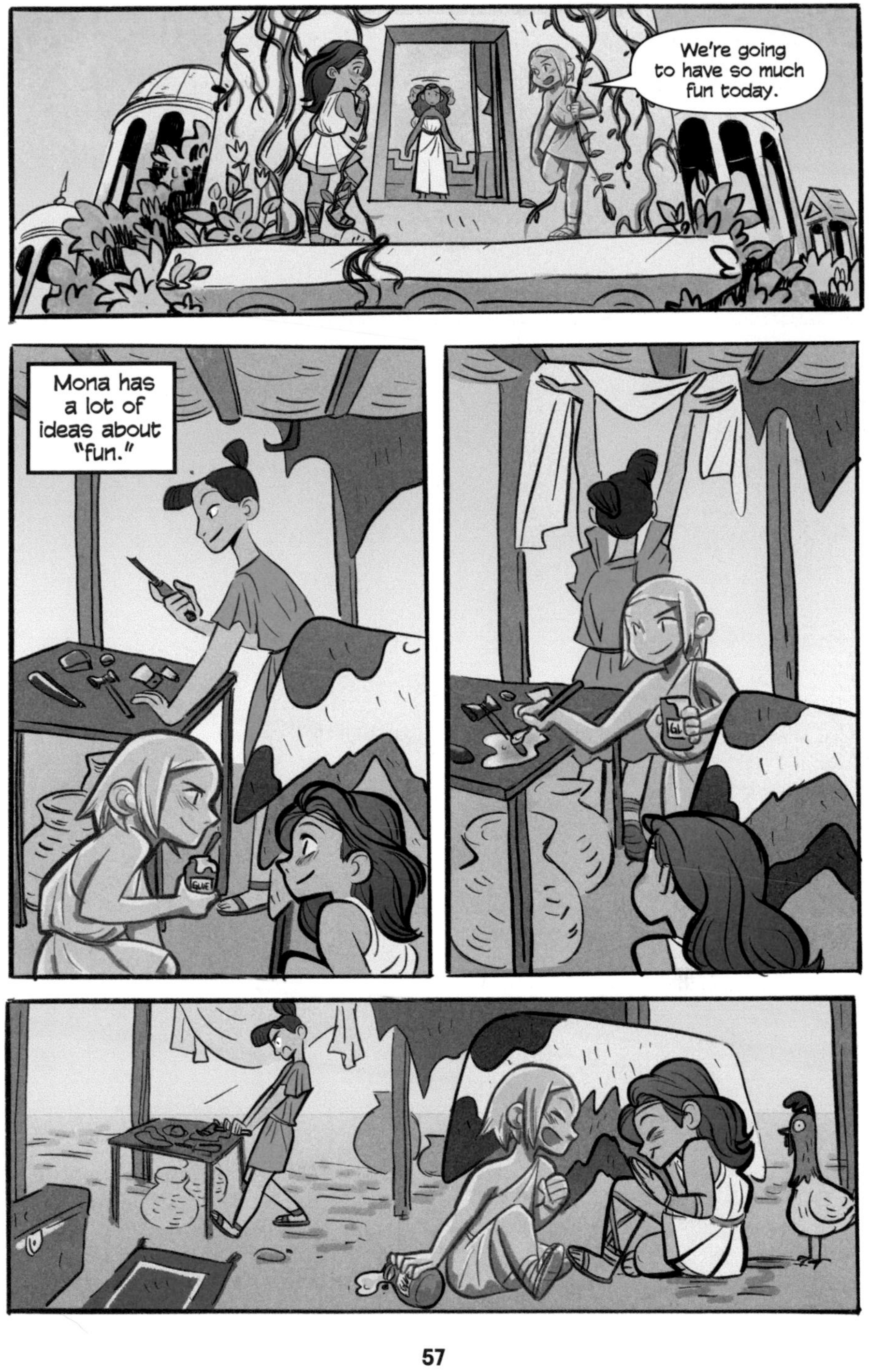
We're going to have so much fun today.
Mona has a lot of ideas about "fun."
GLUE

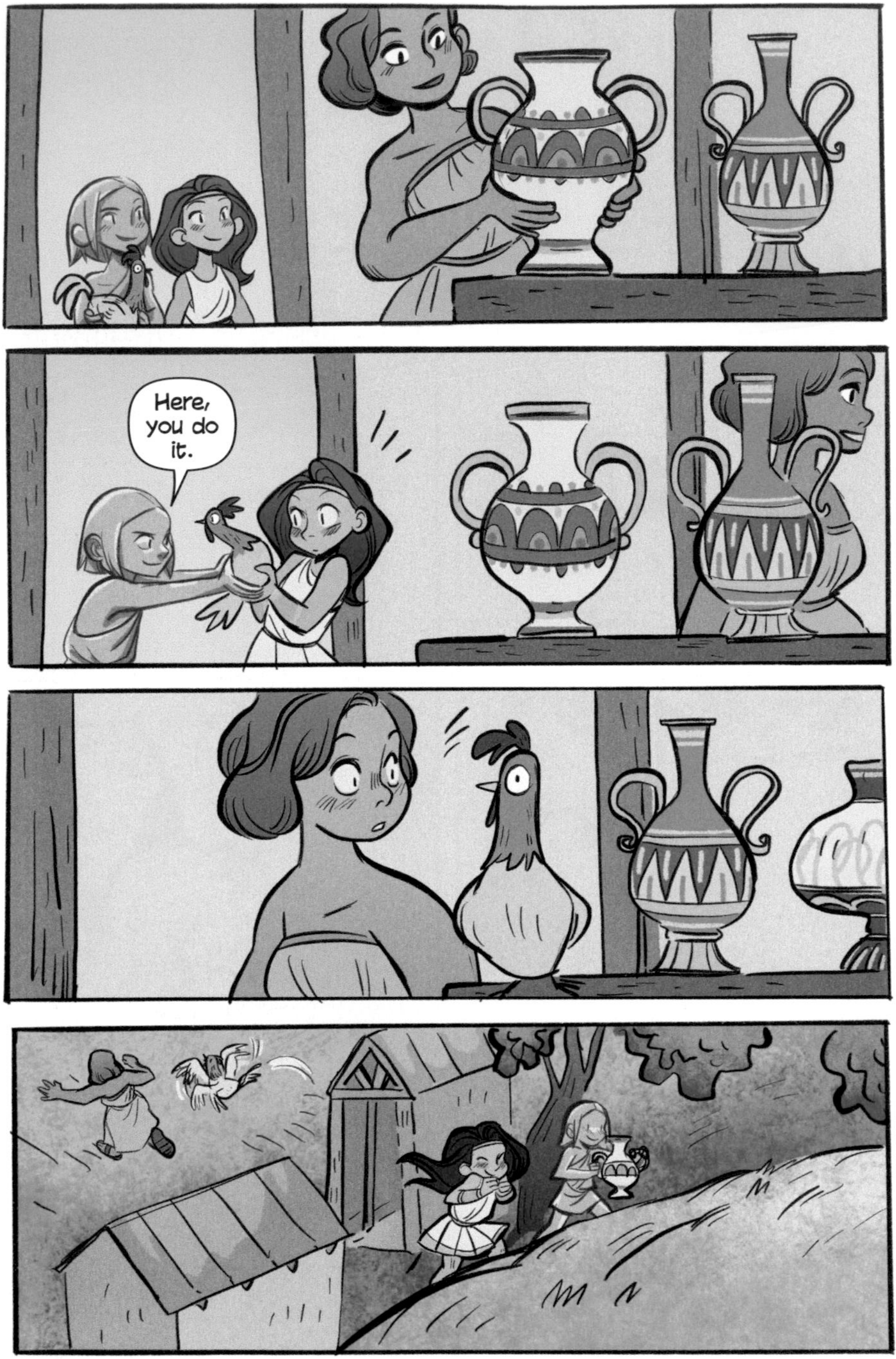
Here, you do it.

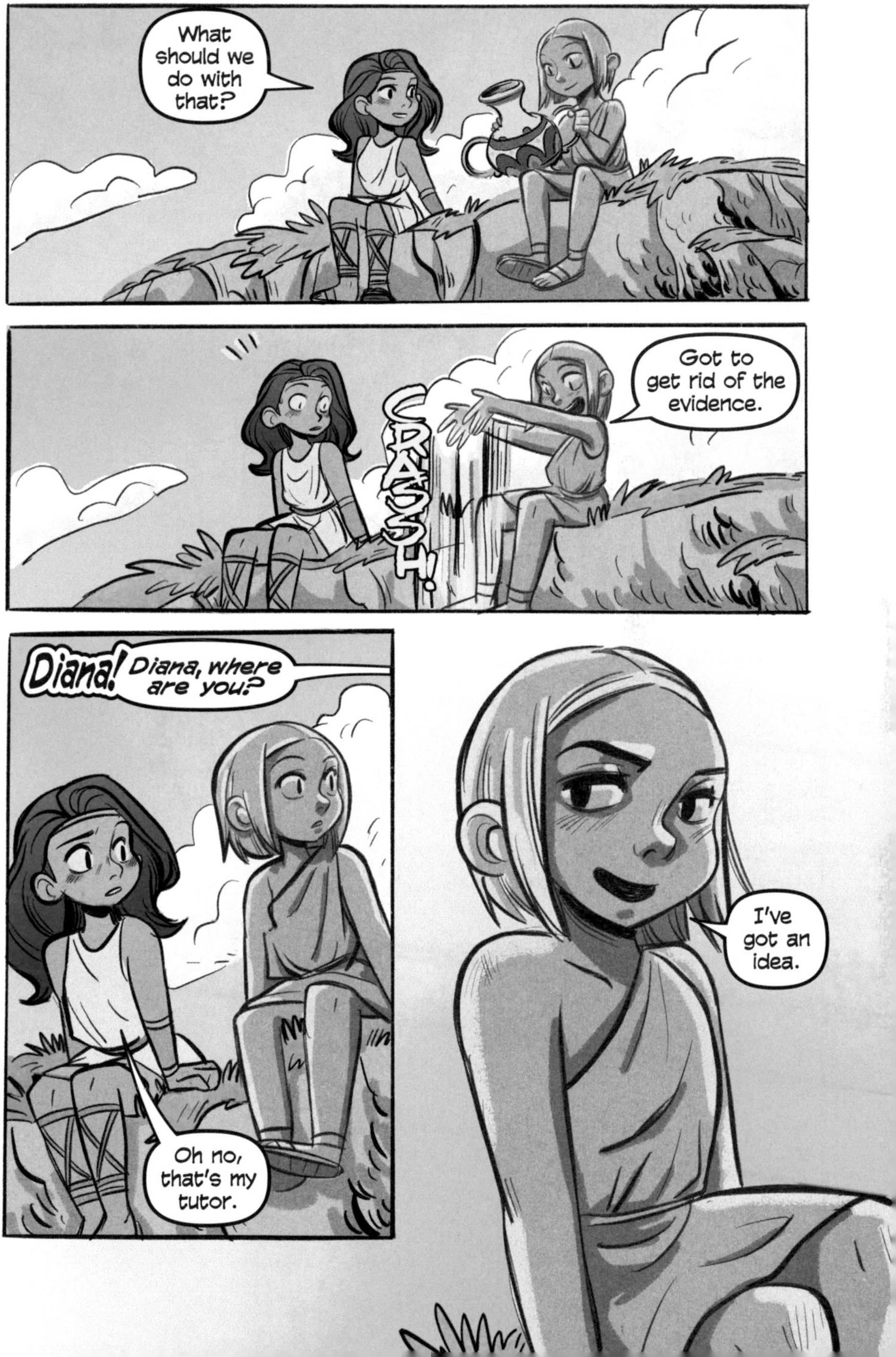
What should we do with that?
Got to get rid of the evidence.
CRASSH!
Diana!
Diana, where are you?
Oh no, that's my tutor.
I've got an idea.

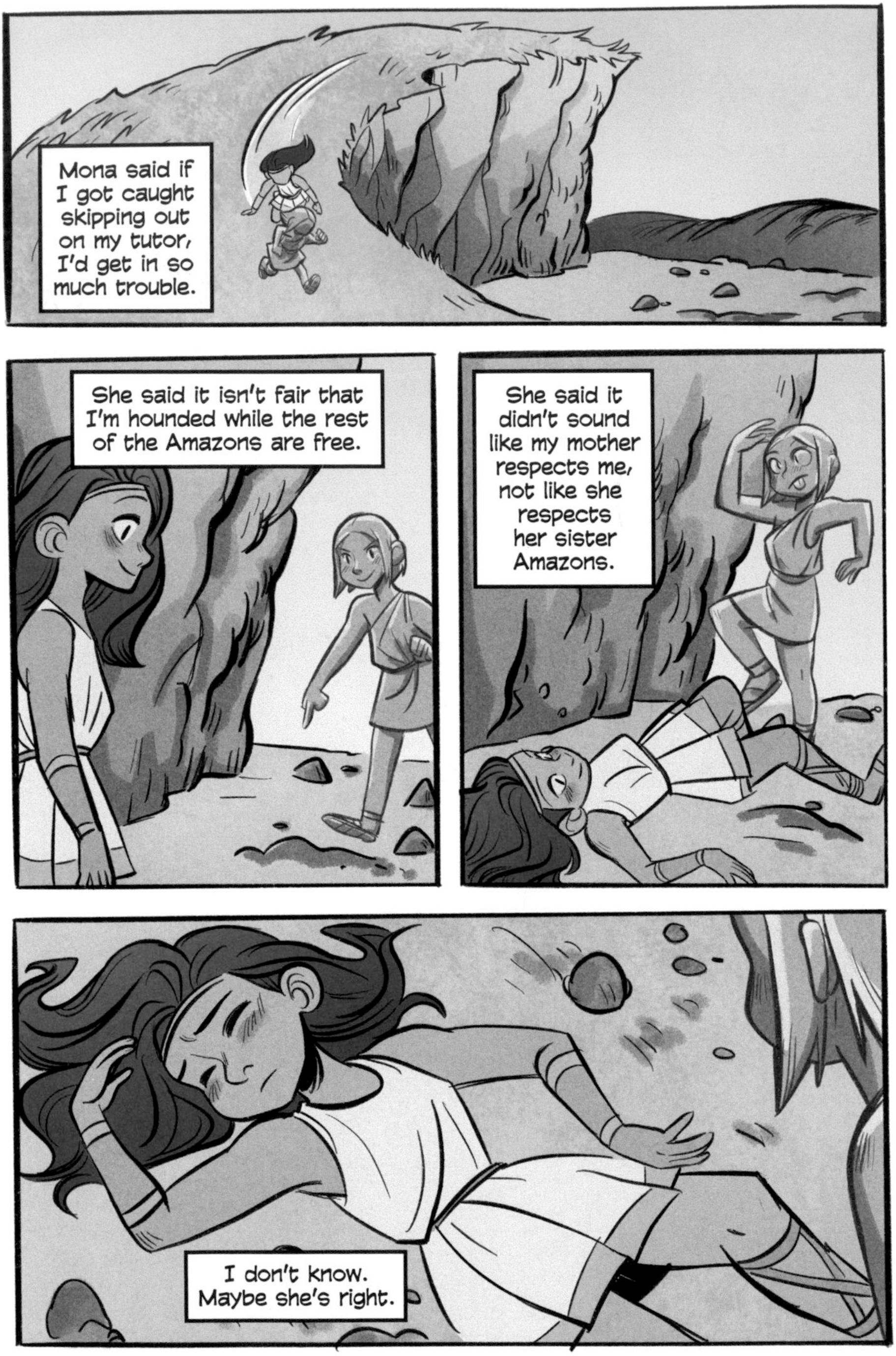
Mona said if I got caught skipping out on my tutor, I'd get in so much trouble.
She said it isn't fair that I'm hounded while the rest of the Amazons are free.
She said it didn't sound like my mother respects me, not like she respects her sister Amazons.
I don't know. Maybe she's right.

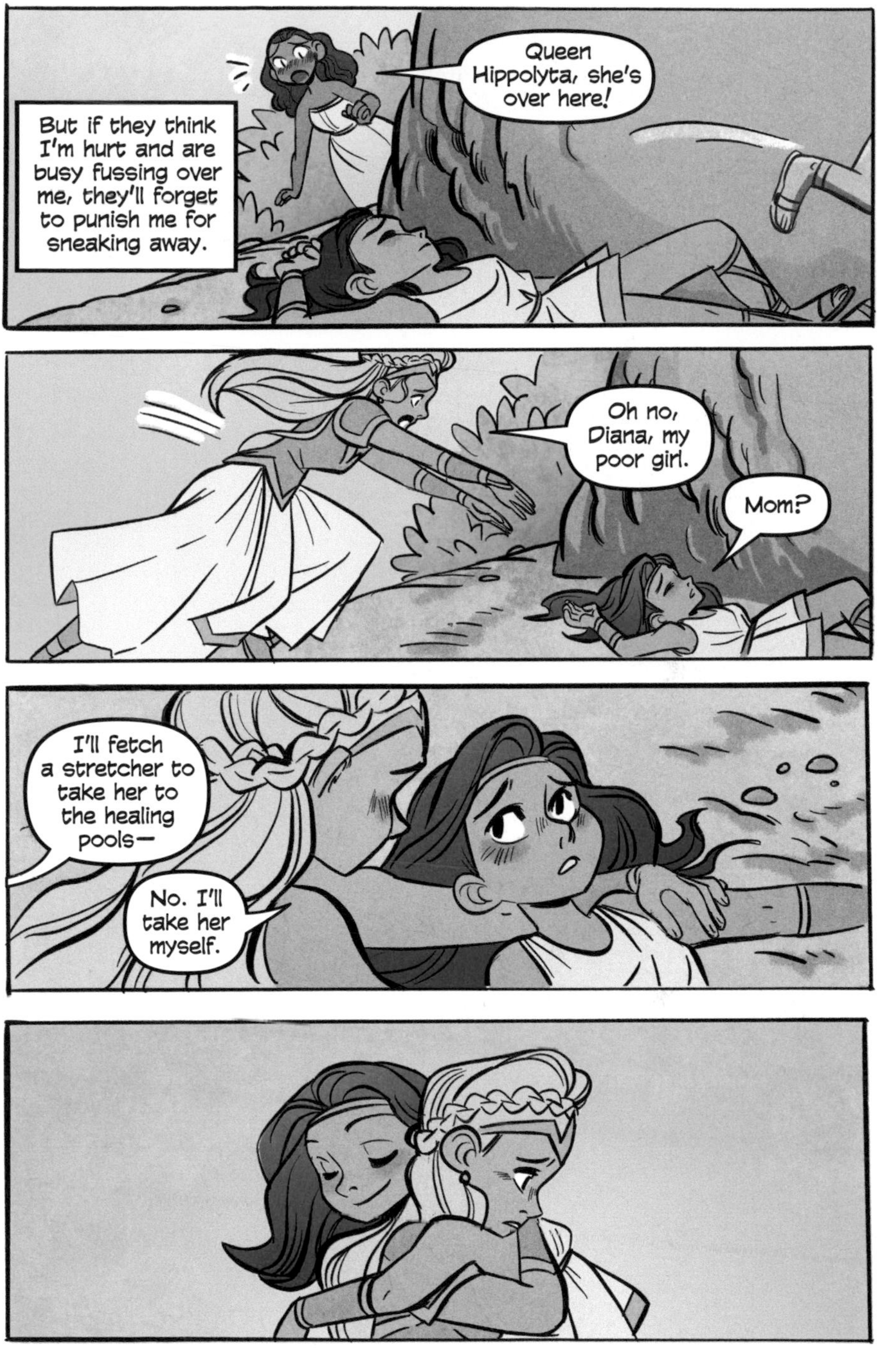
But if they think I'm hurt and are busy fussing over me, they'll forget to punish me for sneaking away.
Queen Hippolyta, she's over here!
Oh no, Diana, my poor girl.
Mom?
I'll fetch a stretcher to take her to the healing pools—
No. I'll take her myself.

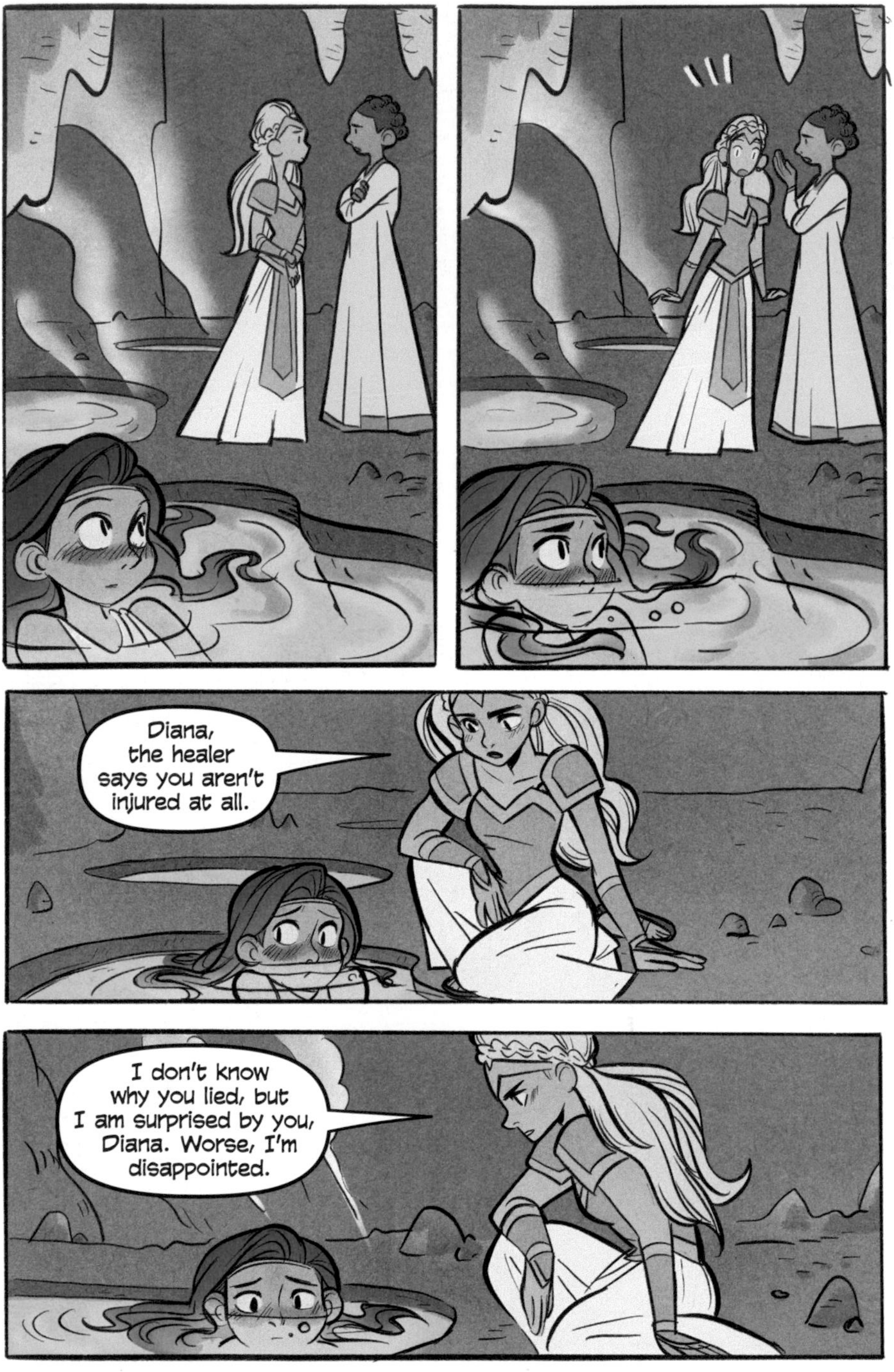

Diana, the healer says you aren't injured at all.
I don't know why you lied, but I am surprised by you, Diana. Worse, I'm disappointed.

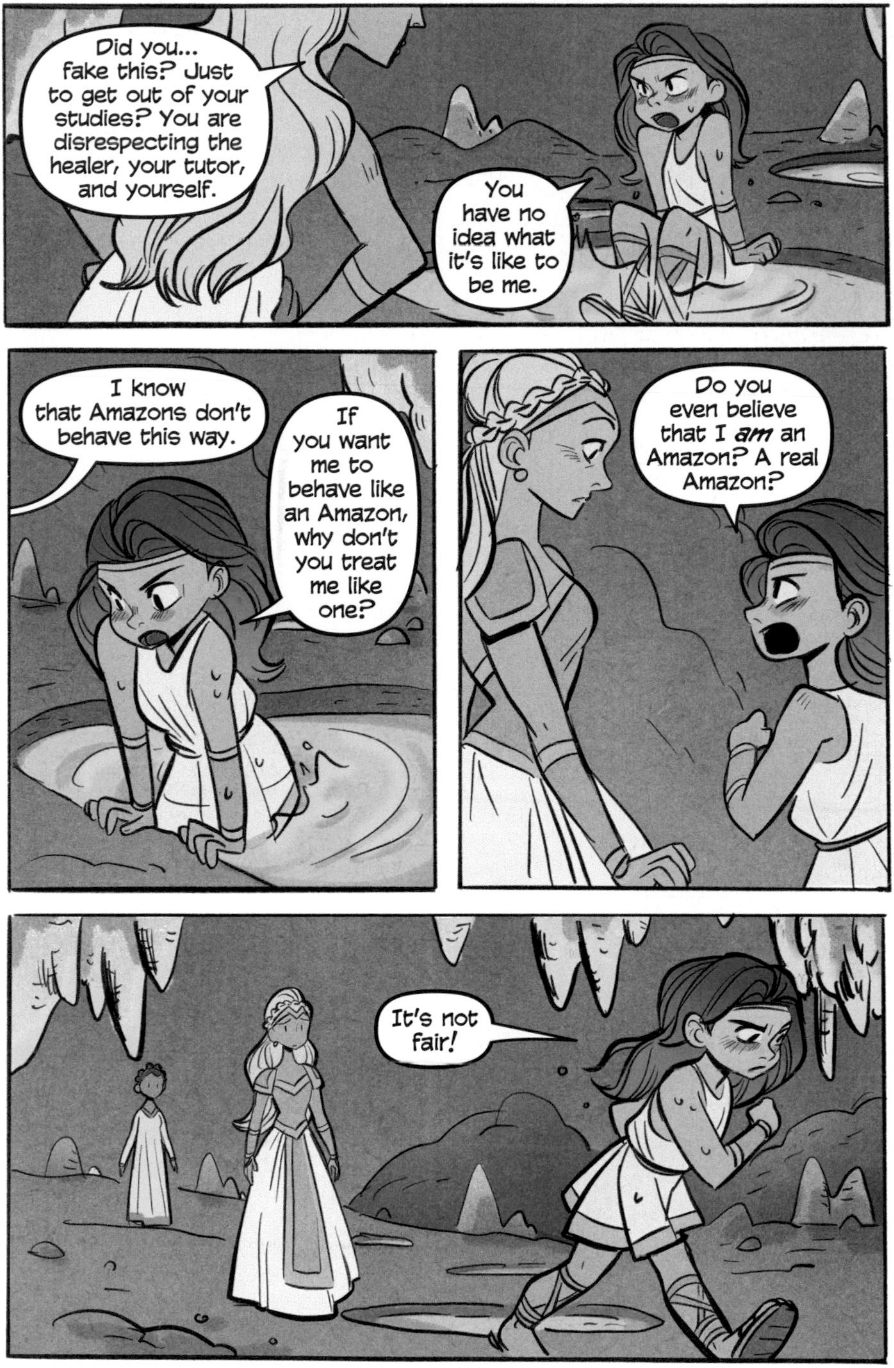
Did you... fake this? Just to get out of your studies? You are disrespecting the healer, your tutor, and yourself.
You have no idea what it's like to be me.
I know that Amazons don't behave this way.
If you want me to behave like an Amazon, why don't you treat me like one?
Do you even believe that I *am* an Amazon? A real Amazon?
It's not fair!

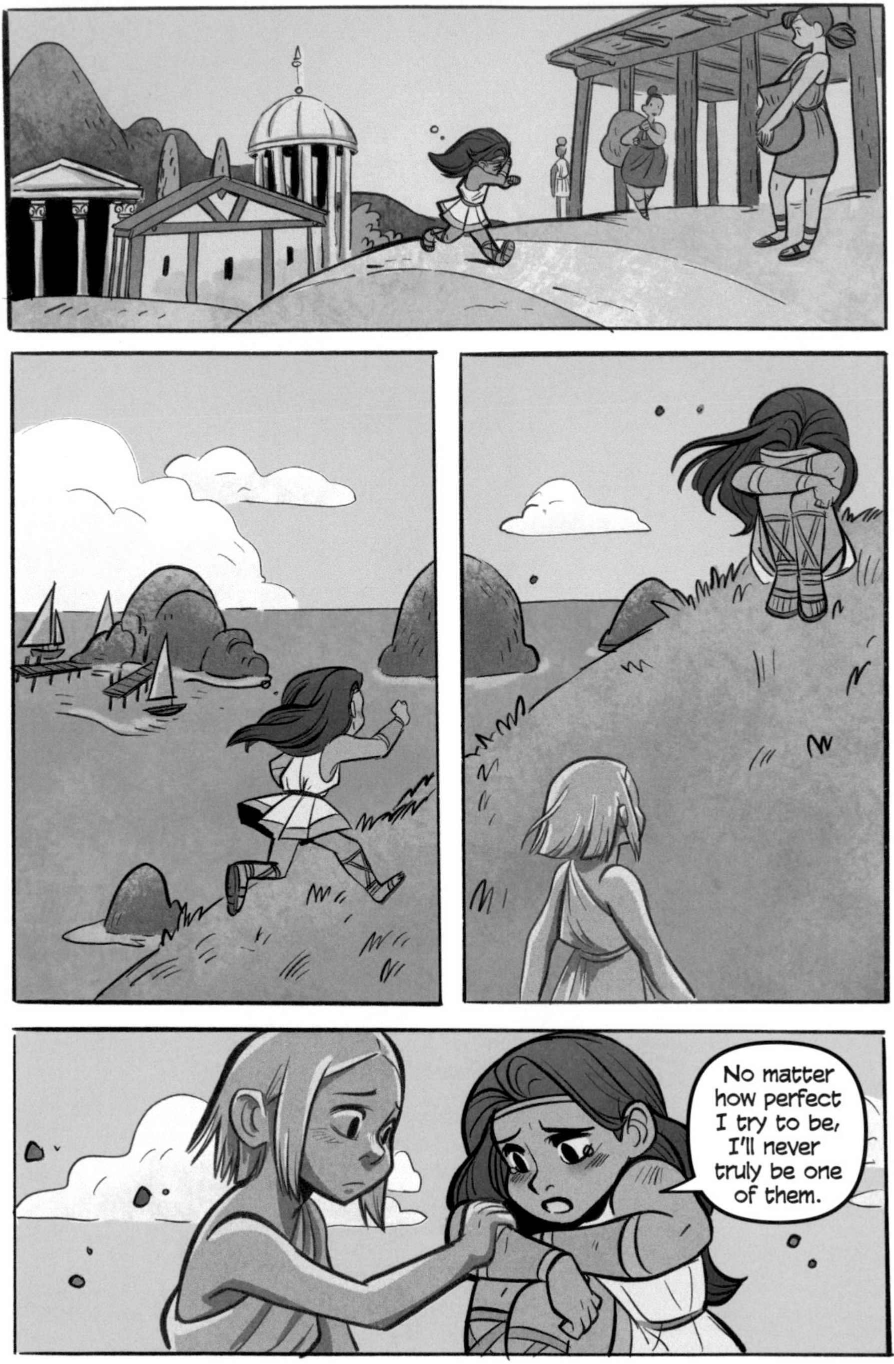
No matter how perfect I try to be, I'll never truly be one of them.

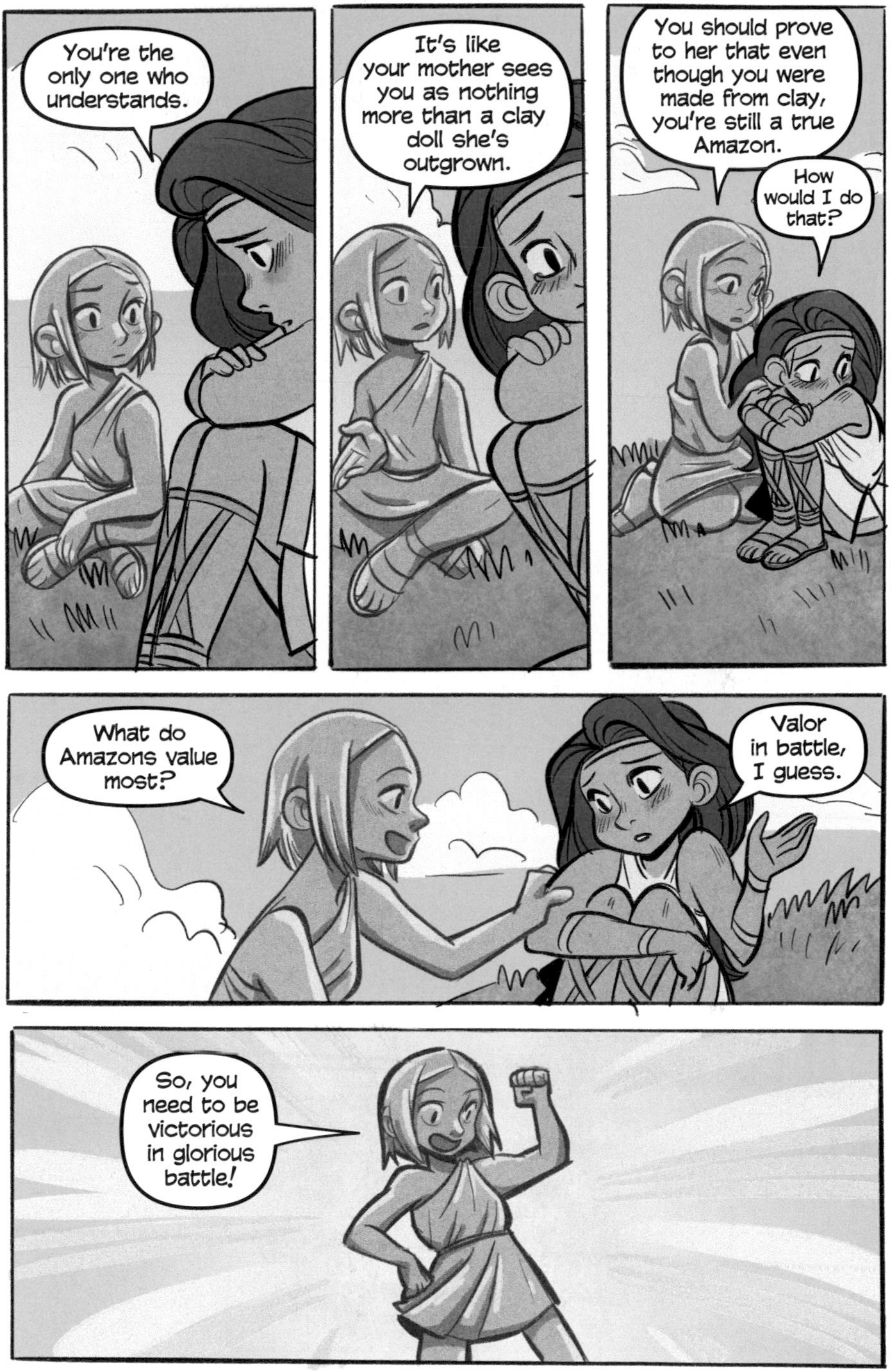
You're the only one who understands.
It's like your mother sees you as nothing more than a clay doll she's outgrown.
You should prove to her that even though you were made from clay, you're still a true Amazon.
How would I do that?
What do Amazons value most?
Valor in battle, I guess.
So, you need to be victorious in glorious battle!

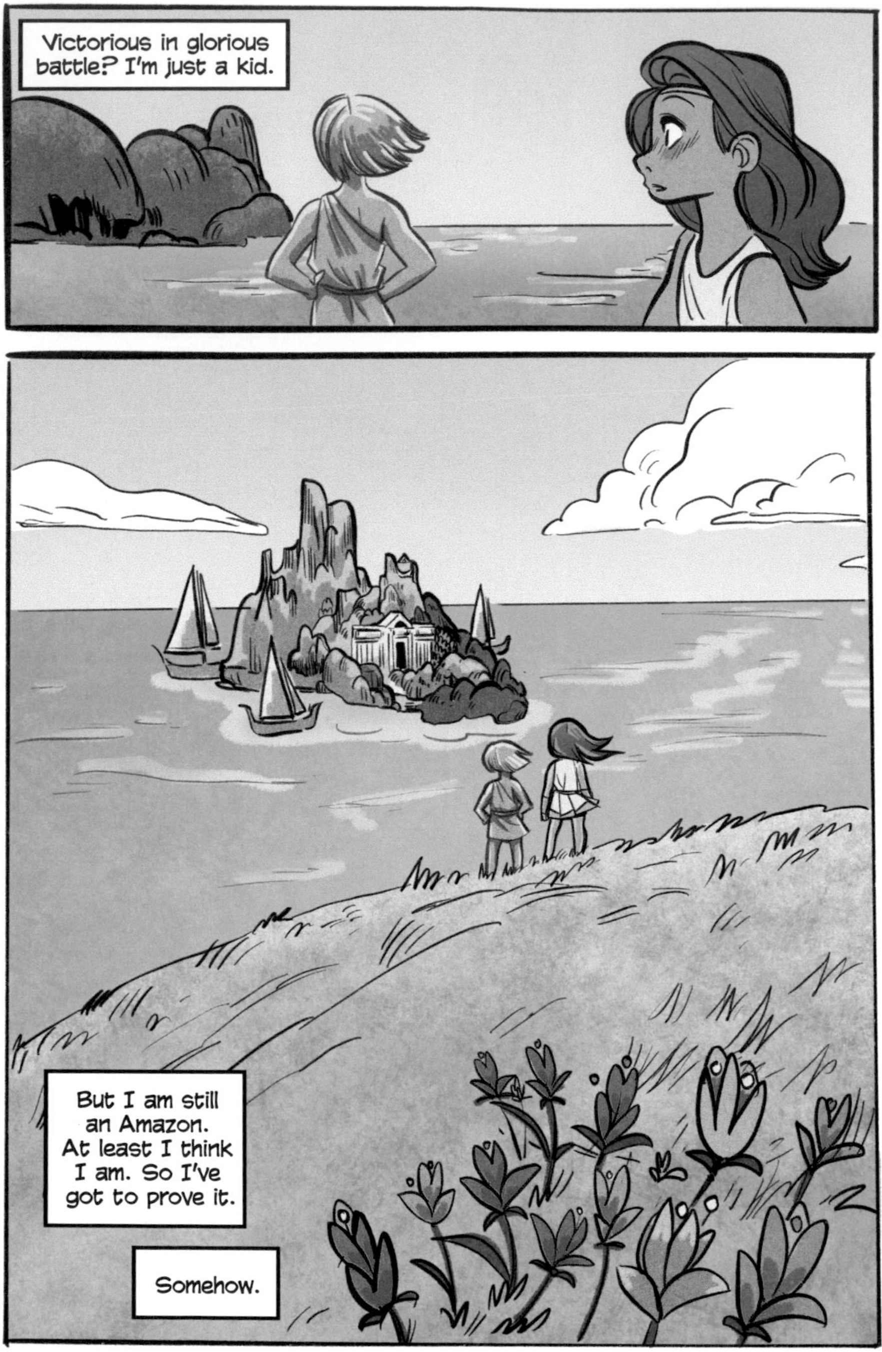
Victorious in glorious battle? I'm just a kid.
But I am still an Amazon. At least I think I am. So I've got to prove it.
Somehow.

CHAPTER THREE

Only an Amazon

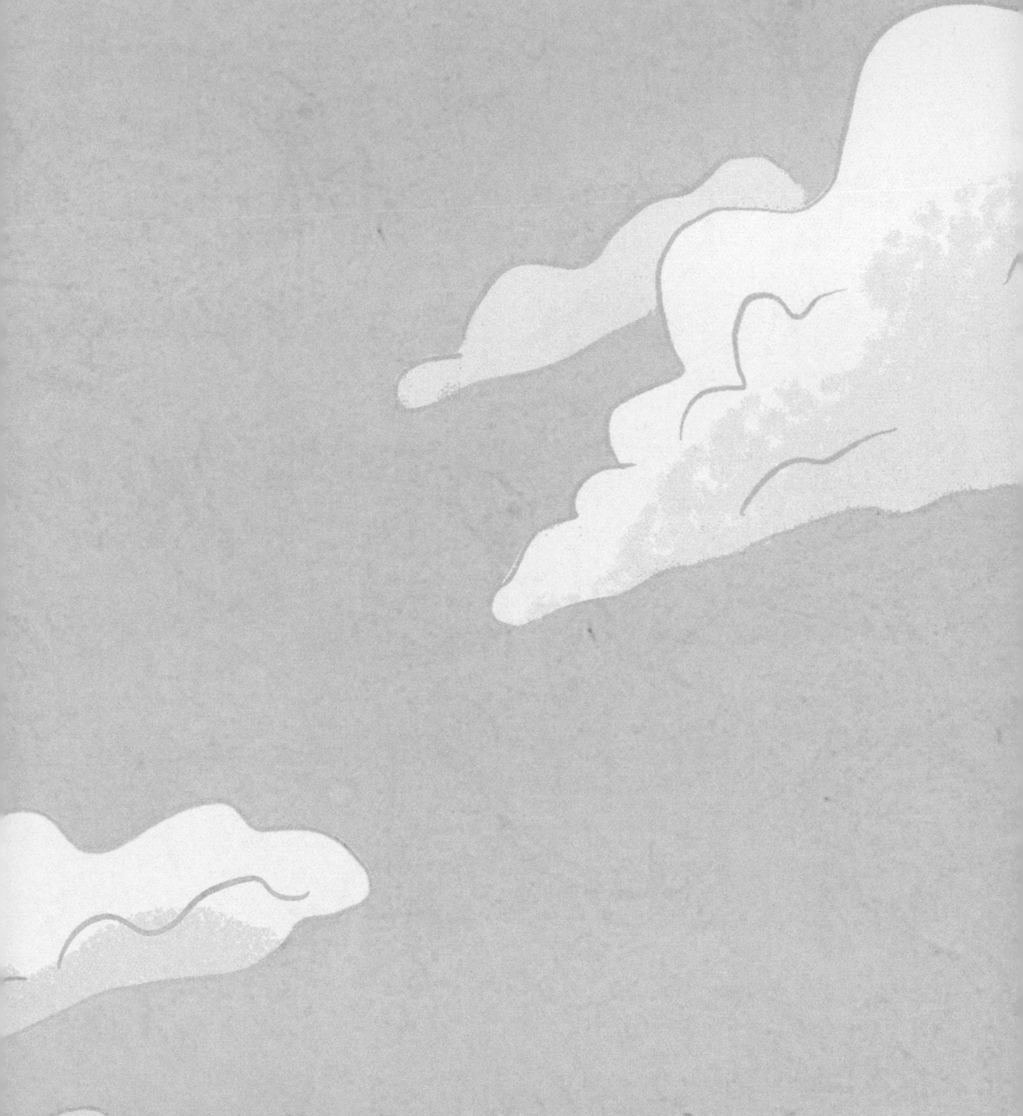

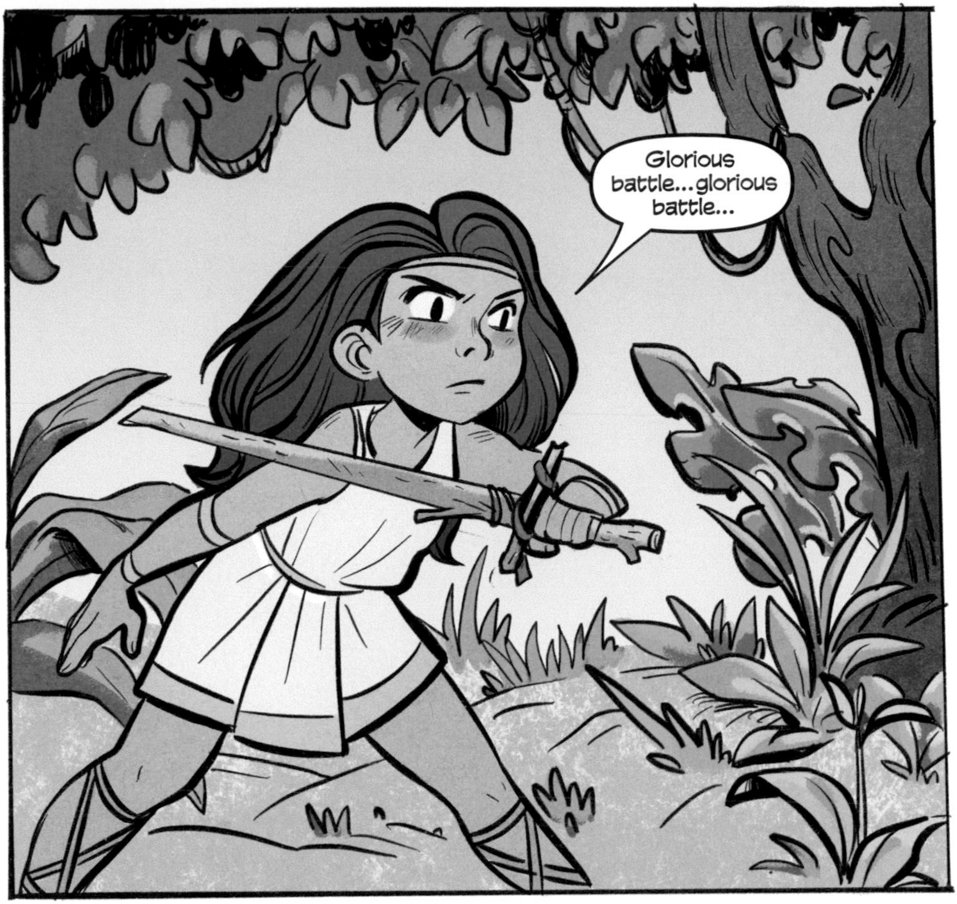
Glorious battle...glorious battle...

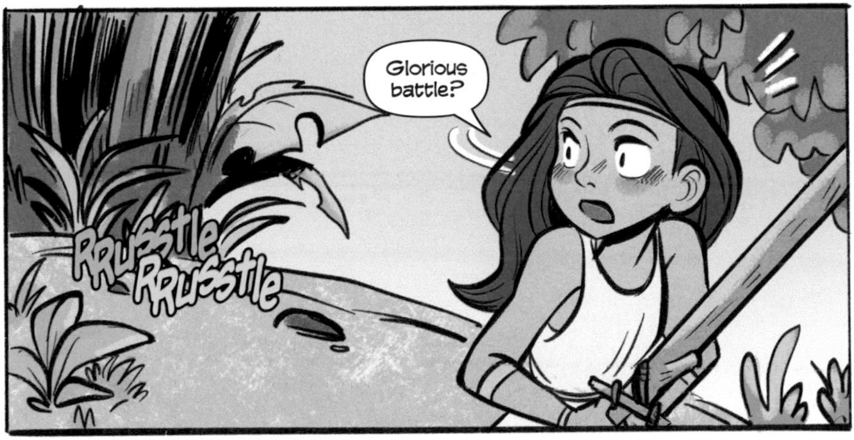
Glorious battle?
RRUSSTLE RRUSSTLE

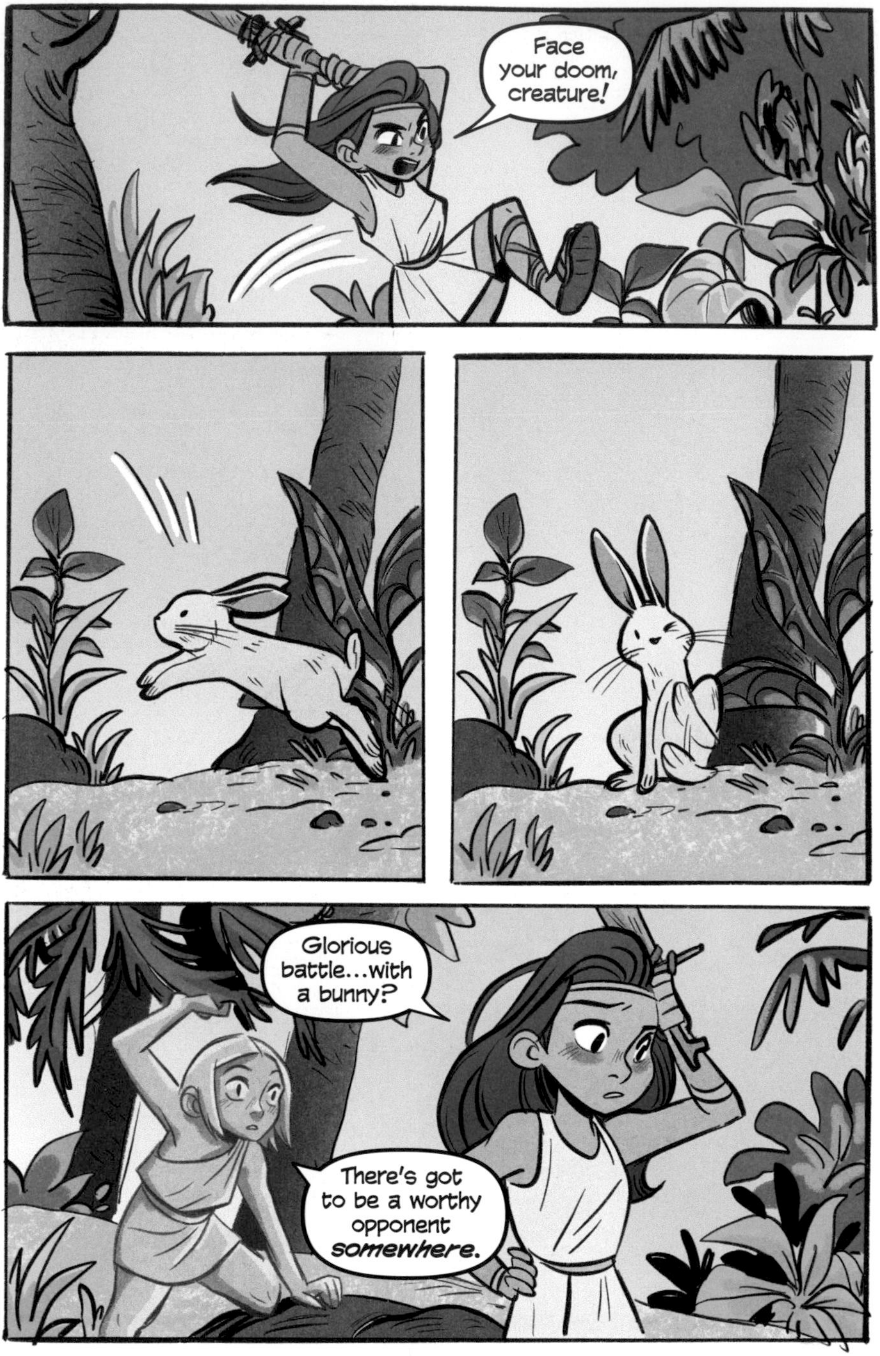
Face your doom, creature!
Glorious battle...with a bunny?
There's got to be a worthy opponent *somewhere*.

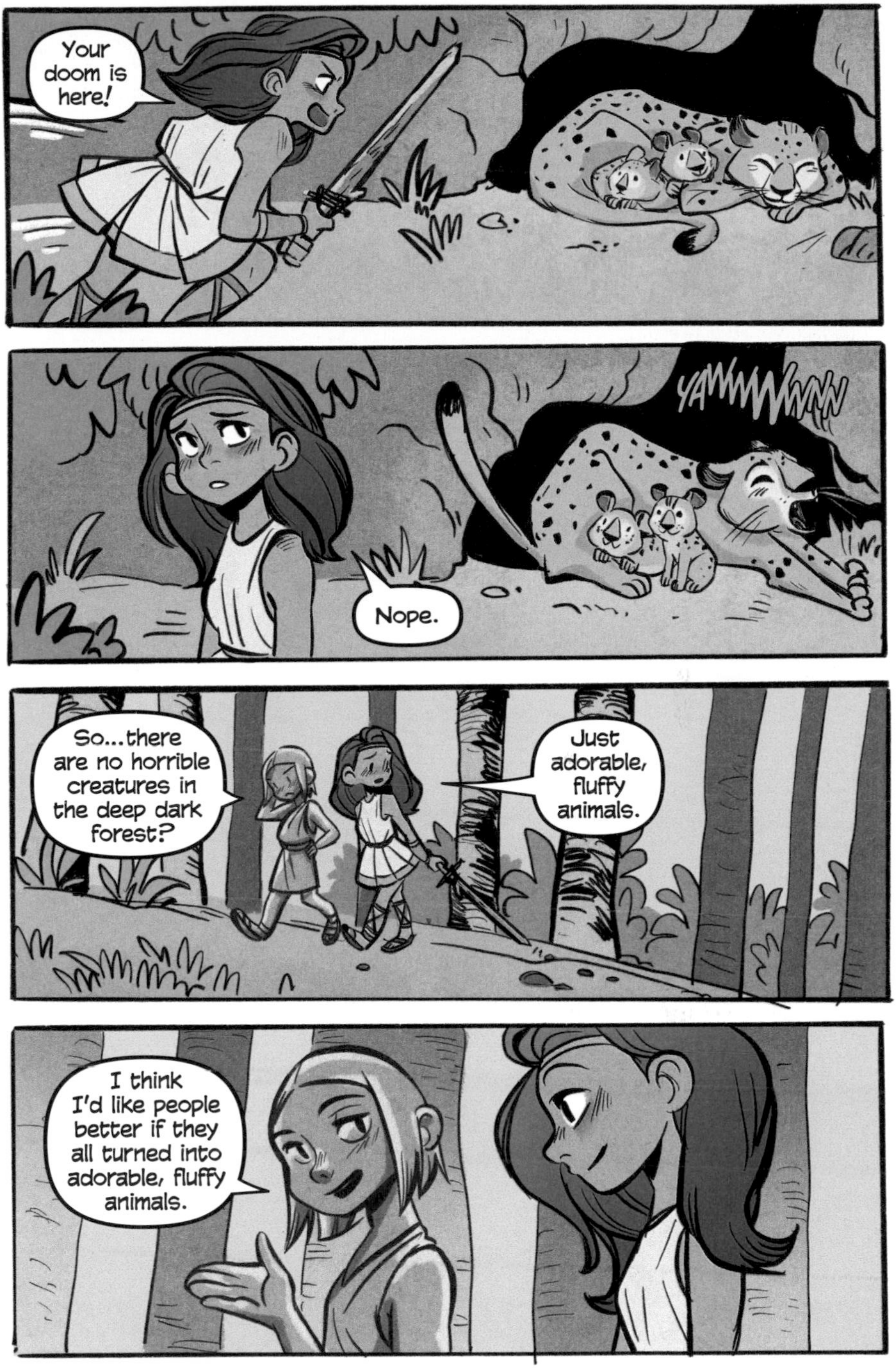
Your doom is here!
YAWWWWNN
Nope.
So...there are no horrible creatures in the deep dark forest?
Just adorable, fluffy animals.
I think I'd like people better if they all turned into adorable, fluffy animals.

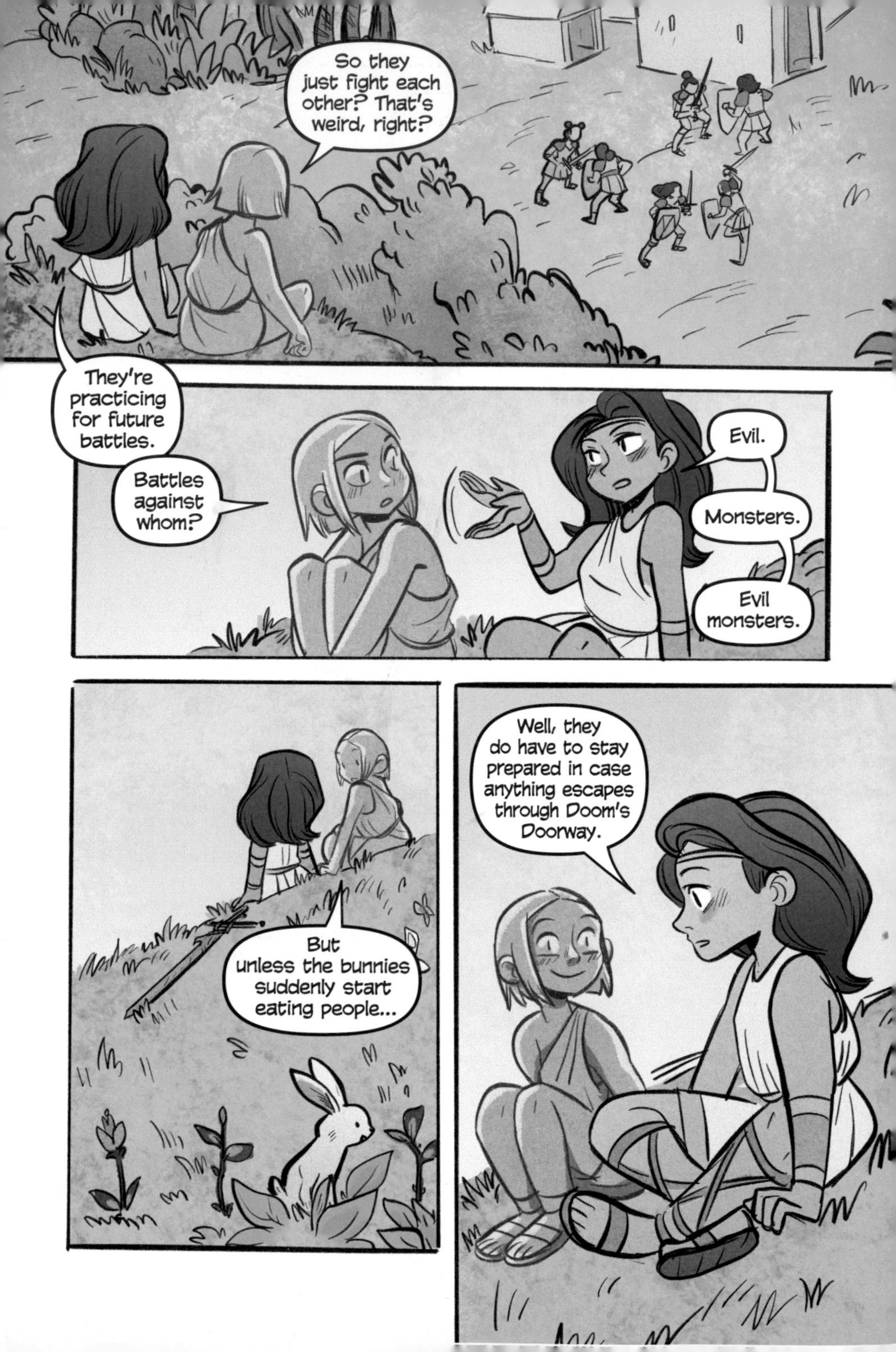
So they just fight each other? That's weird, right?
They're practicing for future battles.
Battles against whom?
Evil.
Monsters.
Evil monsters.
But unless the bunnies suddenly start eating people...
Well, they do have to stay prepared in case anything escapes through Doom's Doorway.

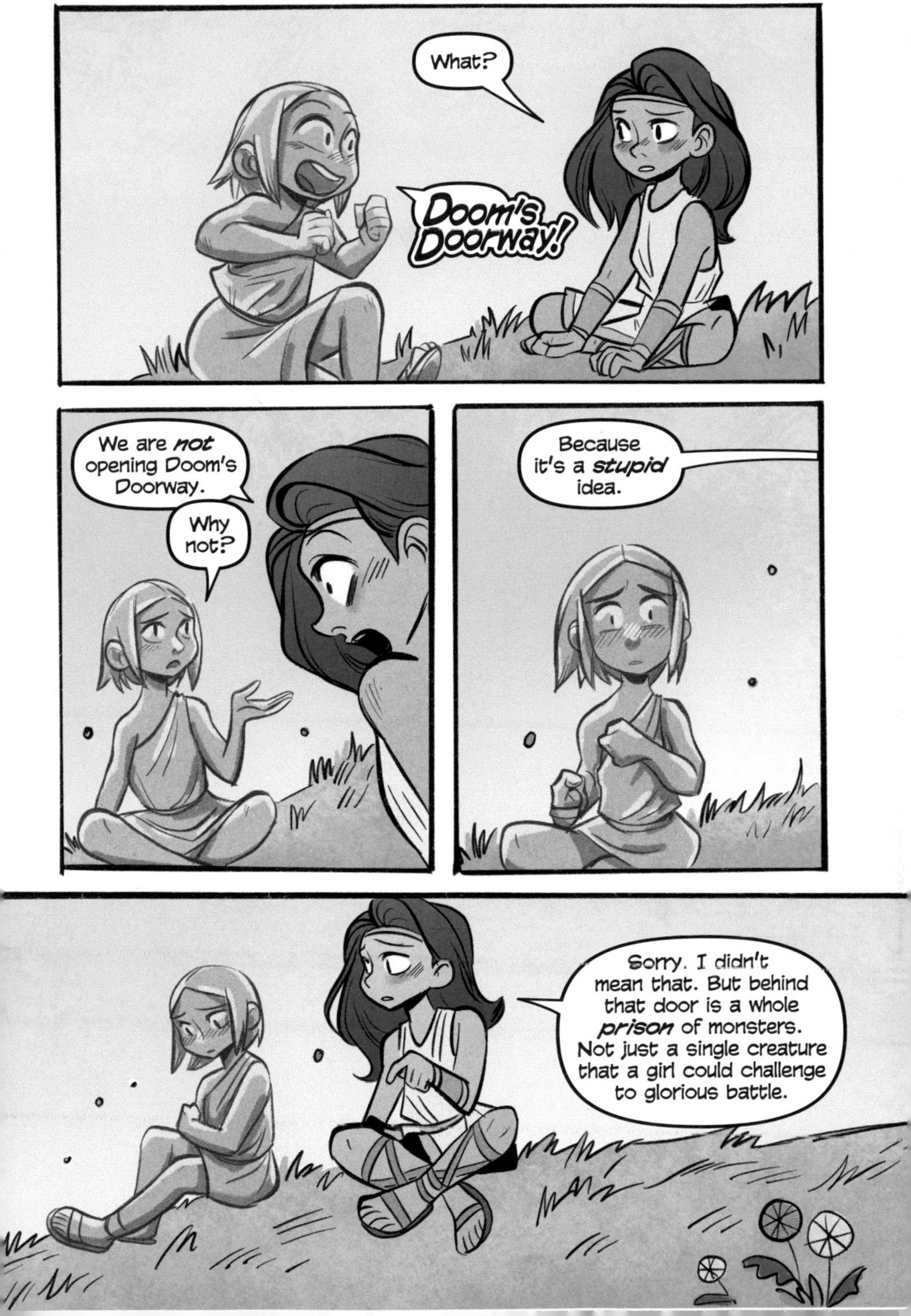
What?
Doom's Doorway!
We are *not* opening Doom's Doorway.
Why not?
Because it's a *stupid* idea.
Sorry. I didn't mean that. But behind that door is a whole *prison* of monsters. Not just a single creature that a girl could challenge to glorious battle.

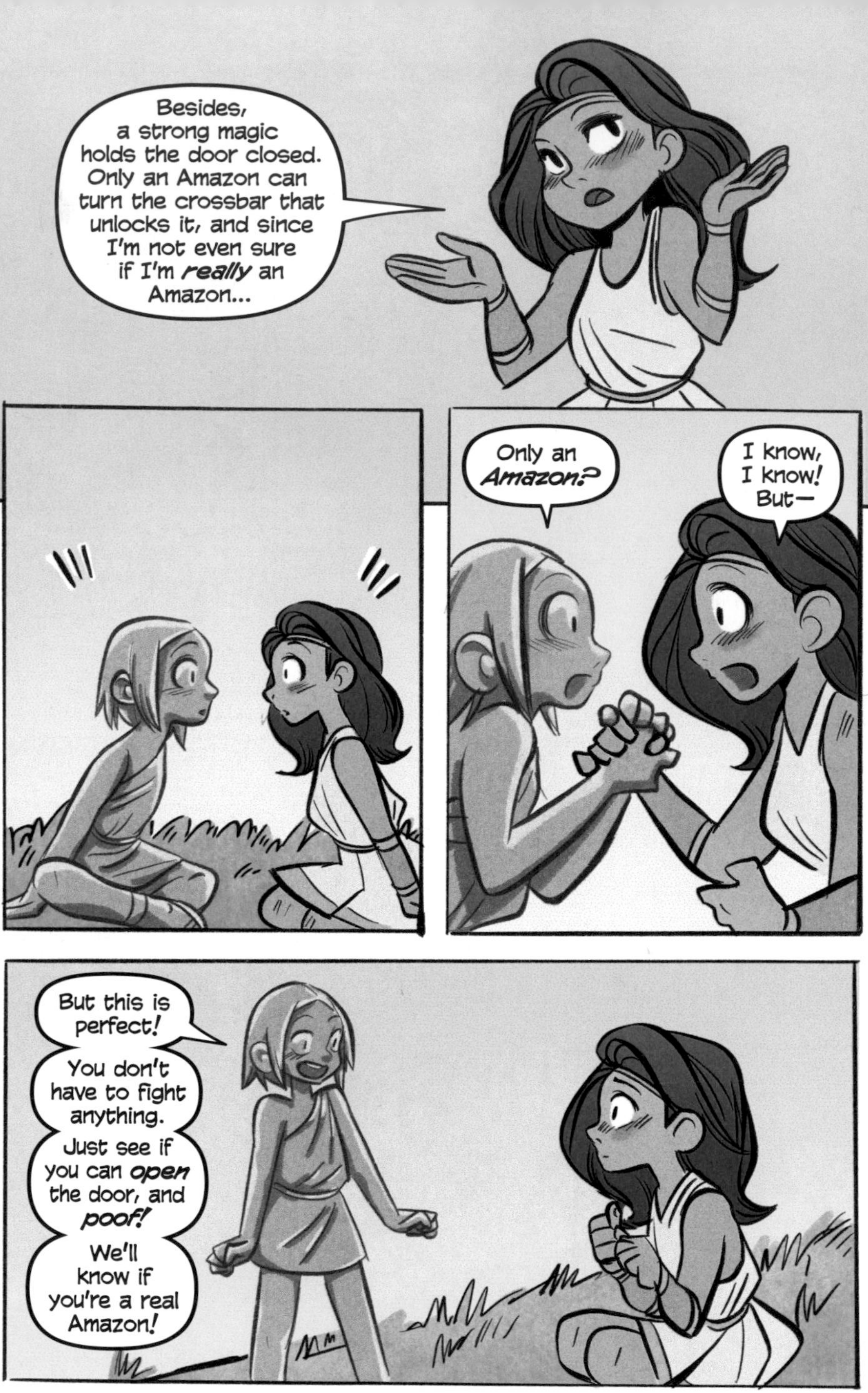
Besides, a strong magic holds the door closed. Only an Amazon can turn the crossbar that unlocks it, and since I'm not even sure if I'm *really* an Amazon...
Only an *Amazon?*
I know, I know! But—
But this is perfect!
You don't have to fight anything.
Just see if you can *open* the door, and *poof!*
We'll know if you're a real Amazon!

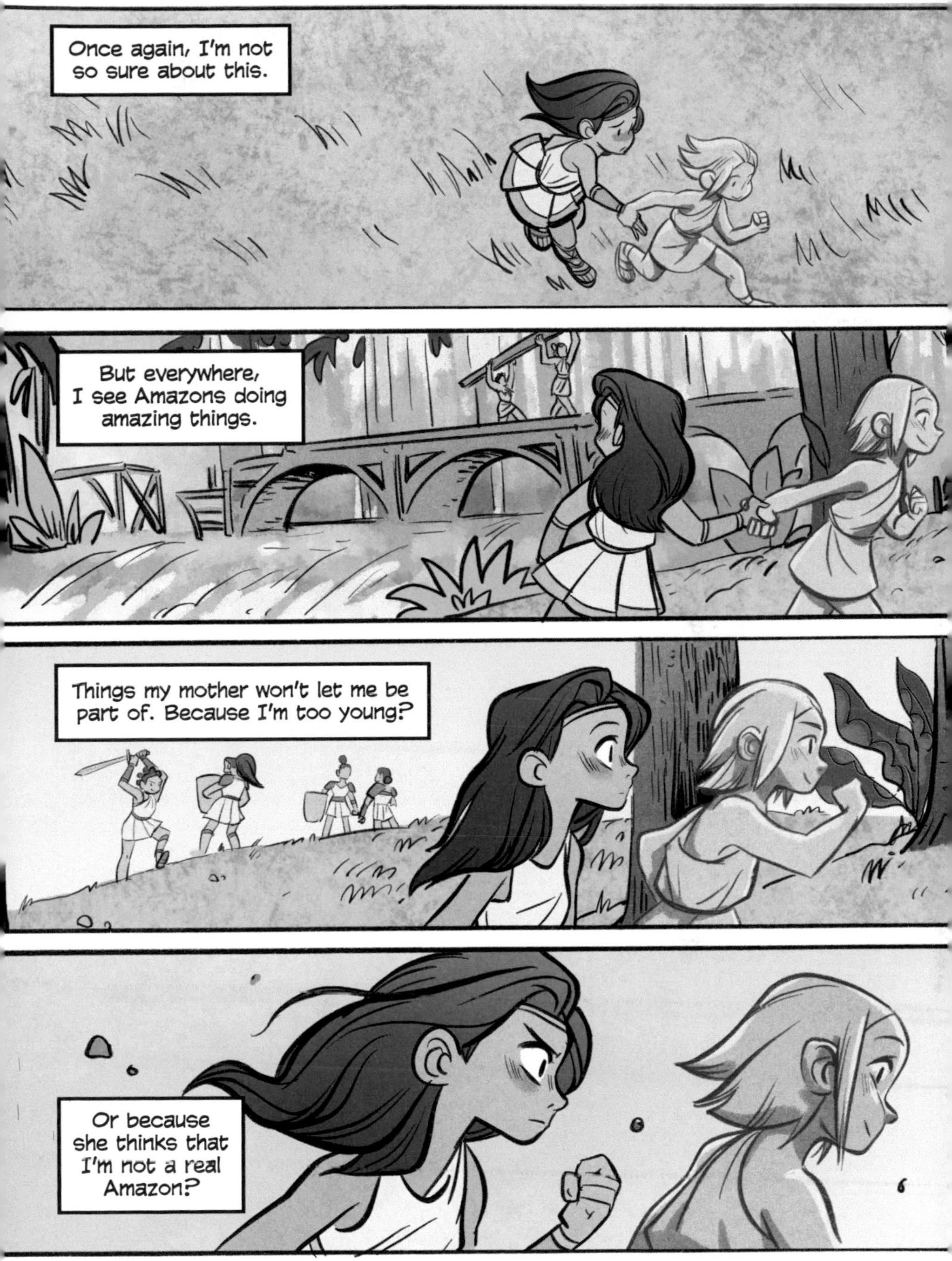
Once again, I'm not so sure about this.
But everywhere, I see Amazons doing amazing things.
Things my mother won't let me be part of. Because I'm too young?
Or because she thinks that I'm not a real Amazon?

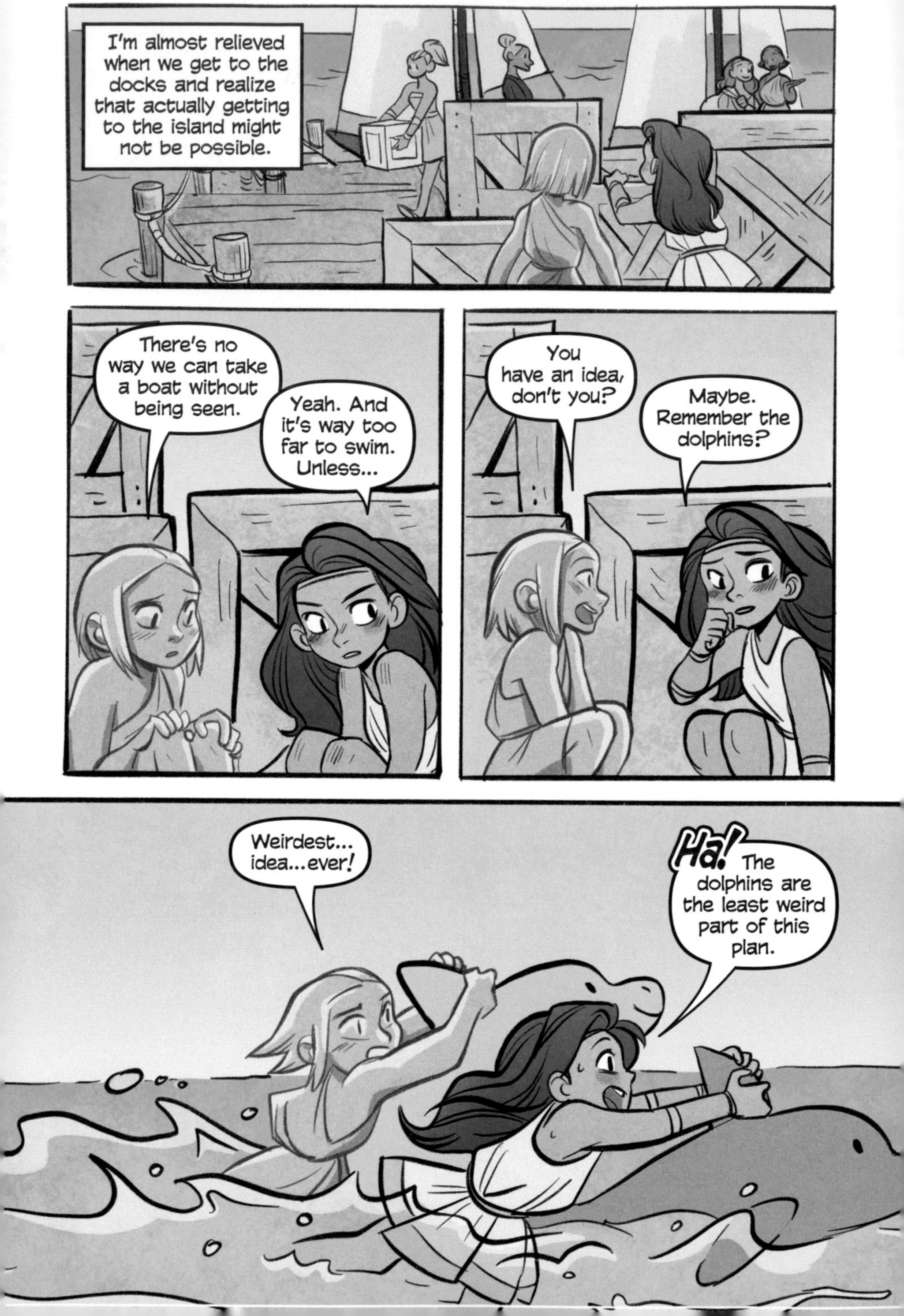
I'm almost relieved when we get to the docks and realize that actually getting to the island might not be possible.
There's no way we can take a boat without being seen.
Yeah. And it's way too far to swim. Unless...
You have an idea, don't you?
Maybe. Remember the dolphins?
Weirdest... idea...ever!
Ha! The dolphins are the least weird part of this plan.

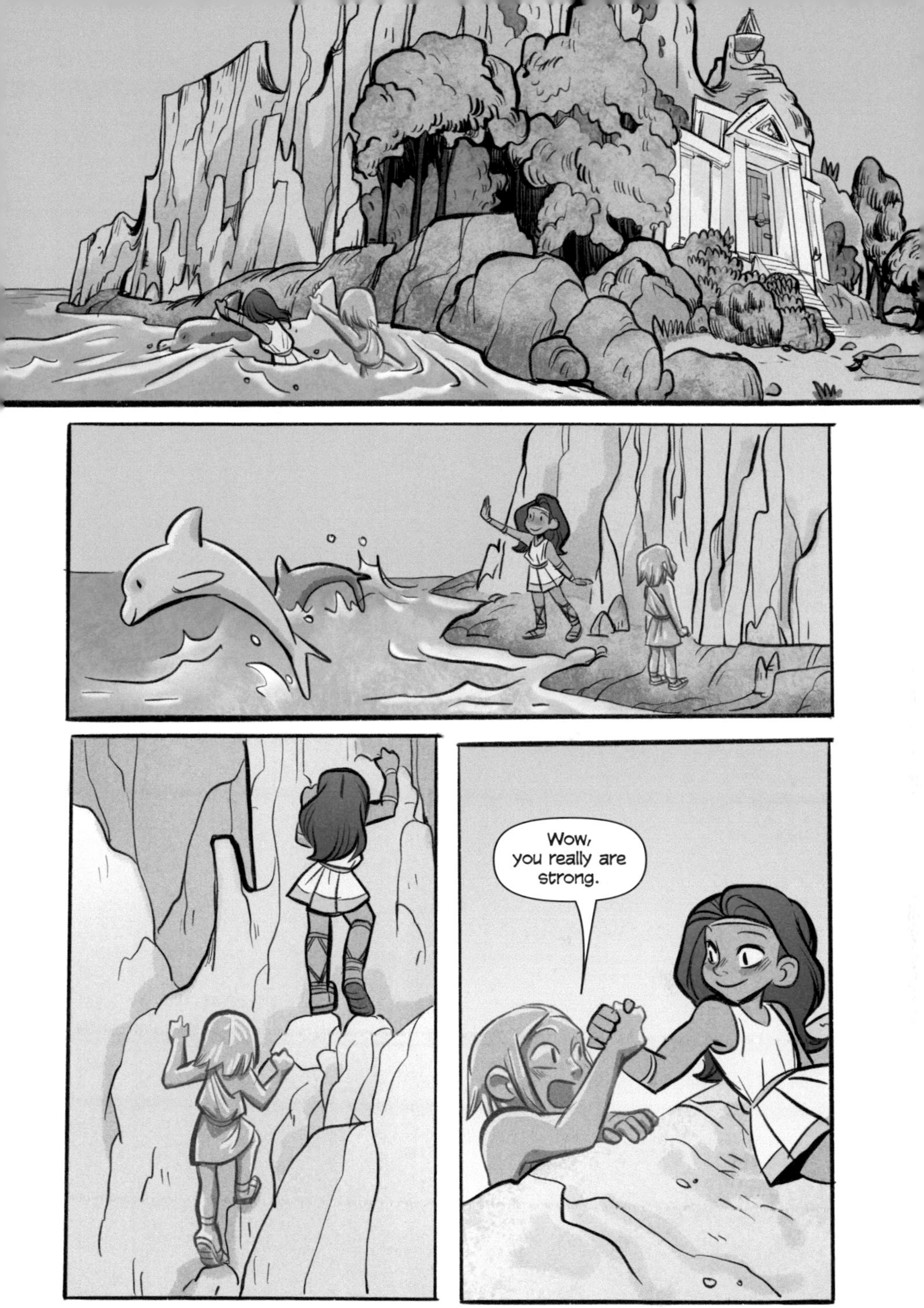
Wow, you really are strong.

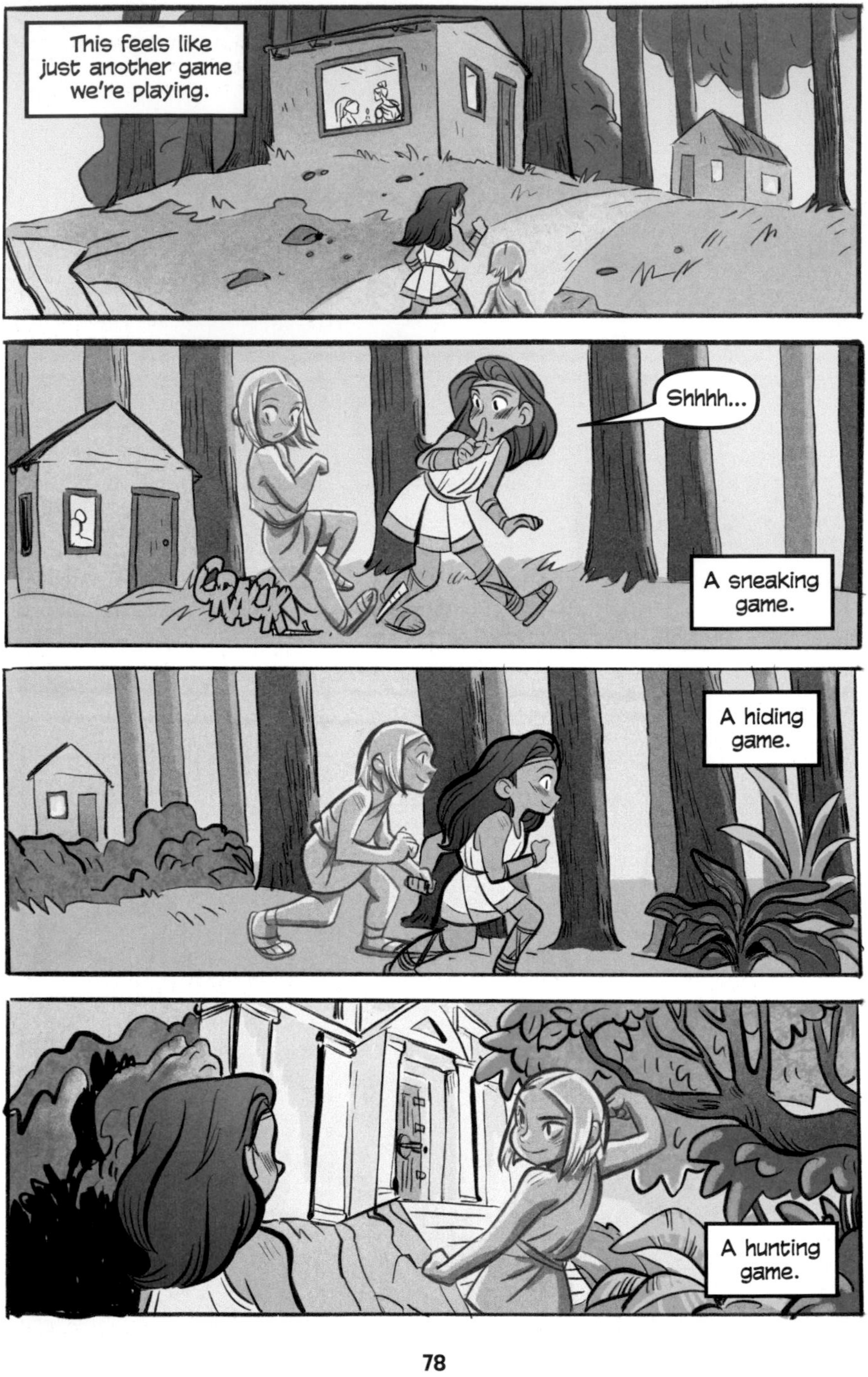
This feels like just another game we're playing.
Shhhh...
CRACK
A sneaking game.
A hiding game.
A hunting game.

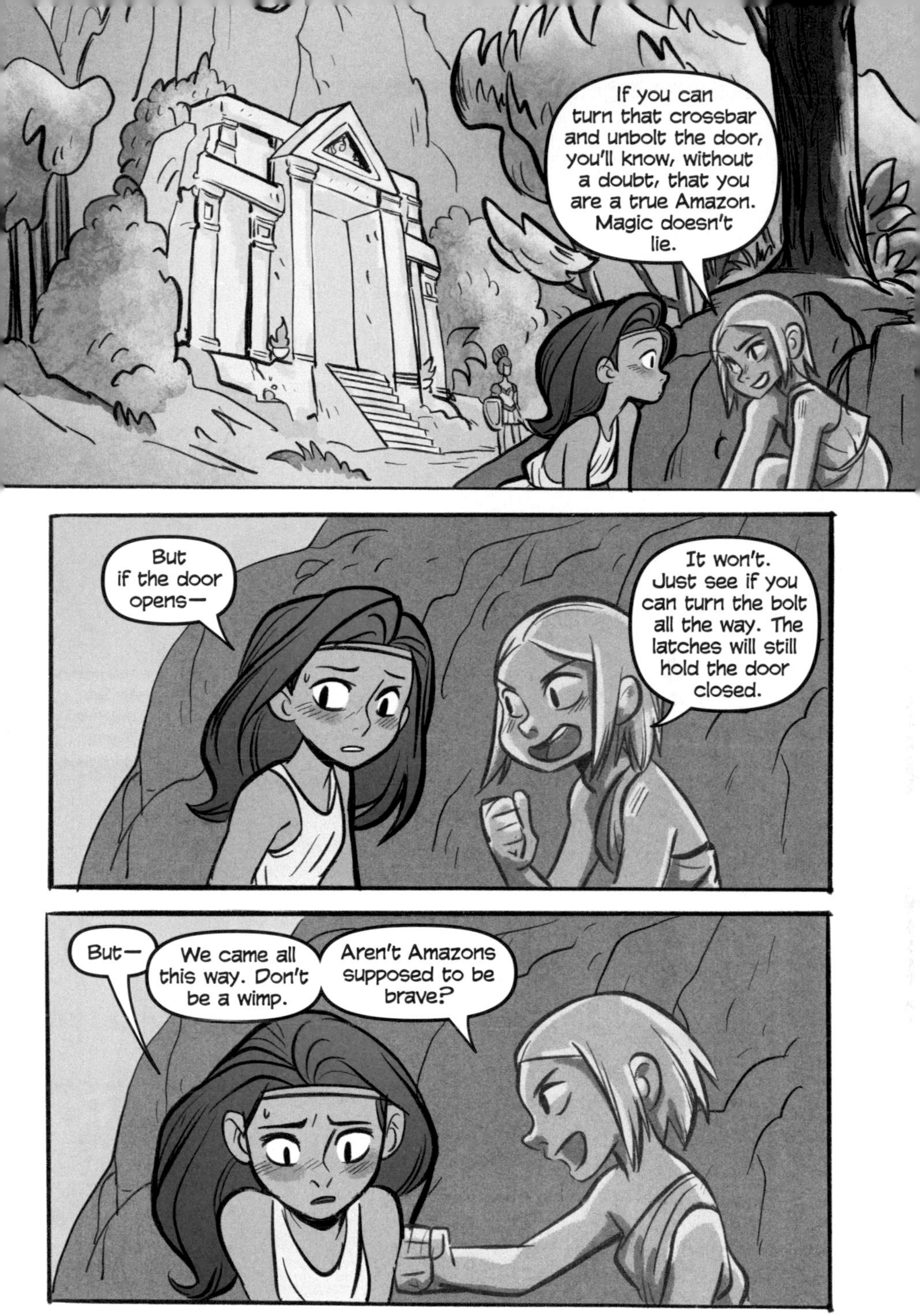
If you can turn that crossbar and unbolt the door, you'll know, without a doubt, that you are a true Amazon. Magic doesn't lie.
But if the door opens—
It won't. Just see if you can turn the bolt all the way. The latches will still hold the door closed.
But—
We came all this way. Don't be a wimp.
Aren't Amazons supposed to be brave?

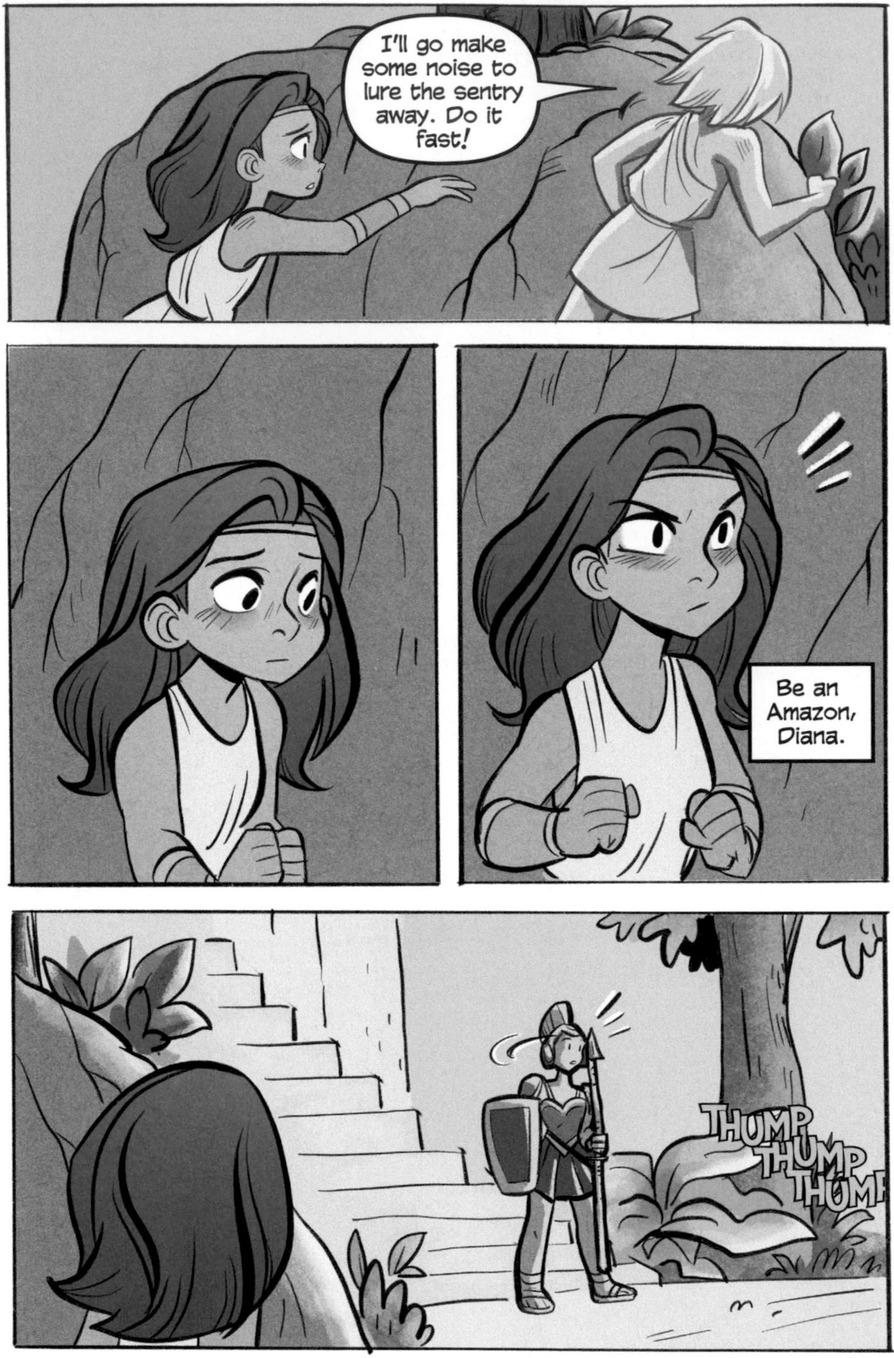

I'll go make some noise to lure the sentry away. Do it fast!
Be an Amazon, Diana.
THUMP THUMP THUMP

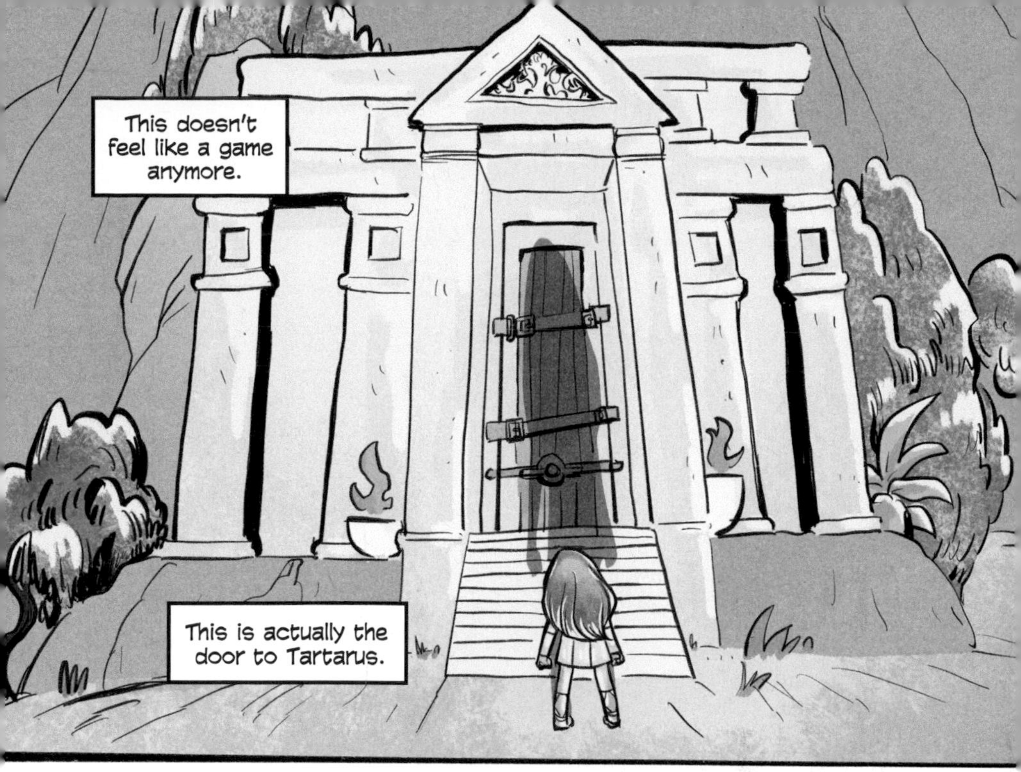
This doesn't feel like a game anymore.
This is actually the door to Tartarus.

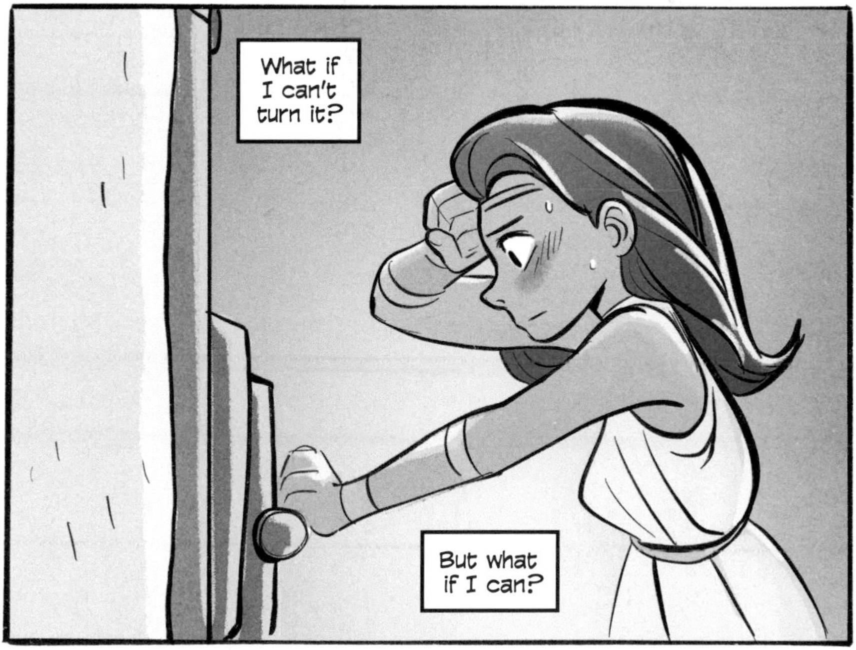
What if I can't turn it?
But what if I can?

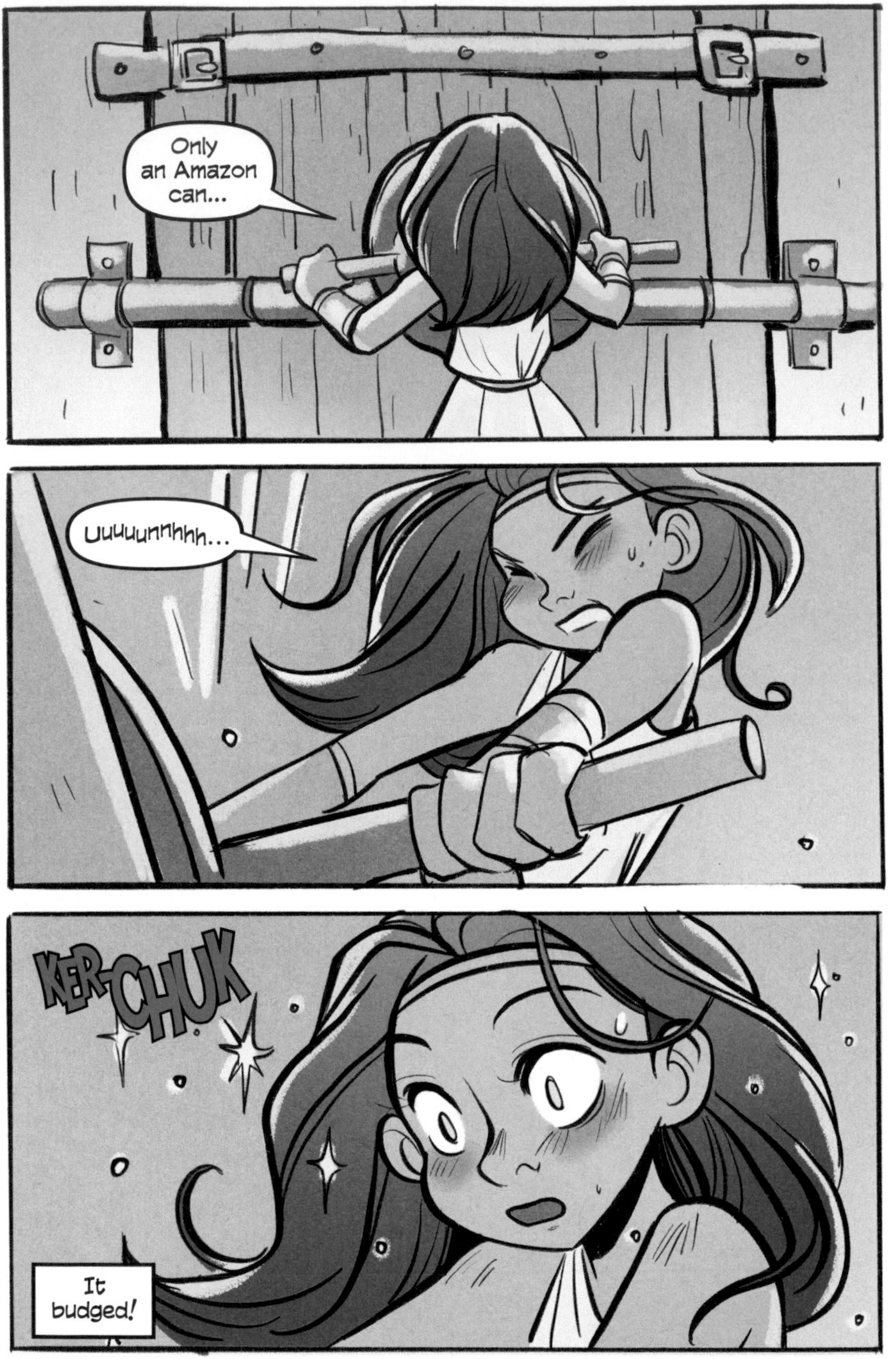
Only an Amazon can...
Uuuuunnhhh...
KER-CHUK
It budged!

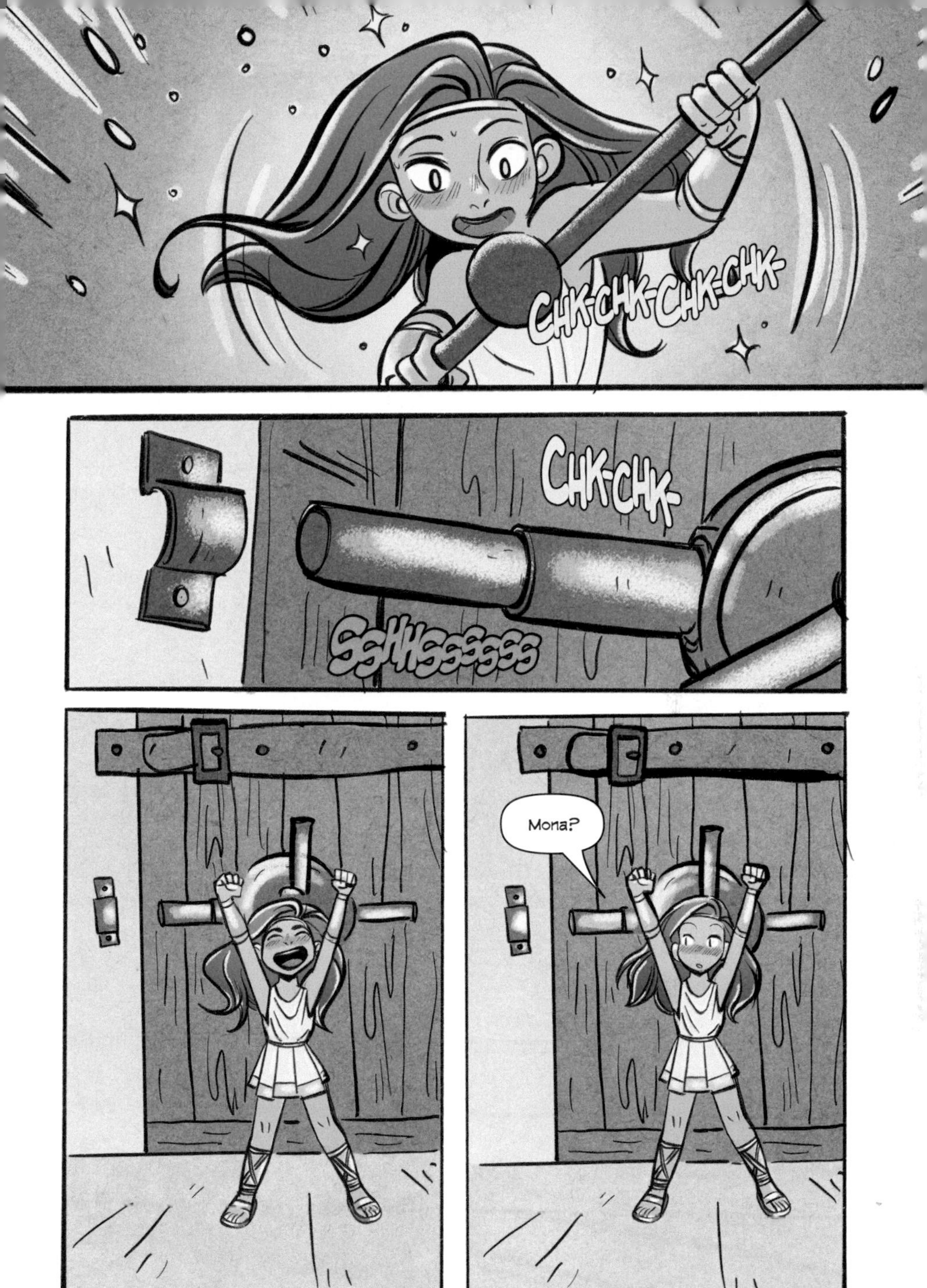
CHK-CHK-CHK-CHK
CHK-CHK
SSHHSSSSSS
Mona?

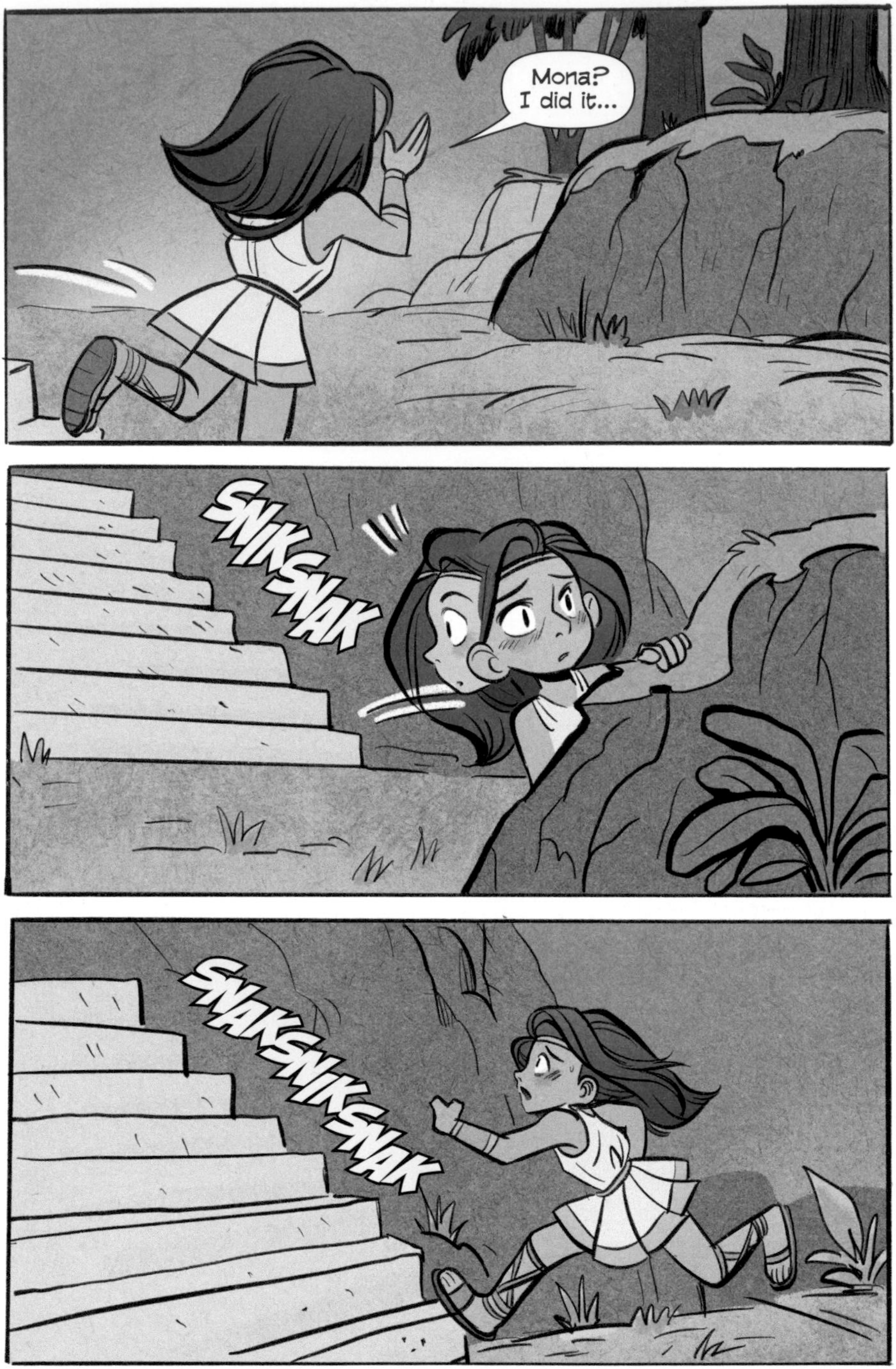
Mona?
I did it...
SNIKSNAK
SNAKSNIKSNAK

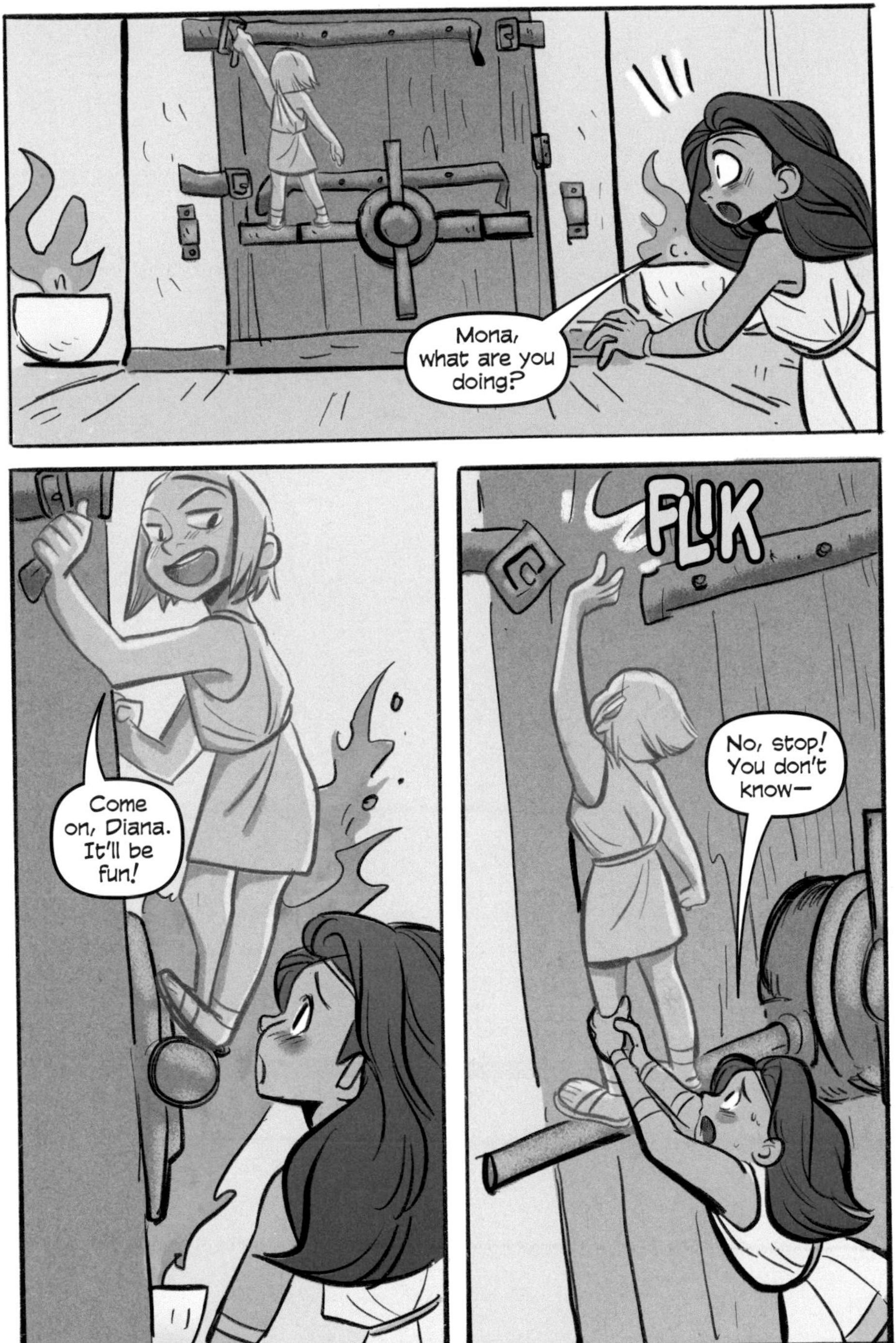
Mona, what are you doing?
Come on, Diana. It'll be fun!
FLIK
No, stop! You don't know—

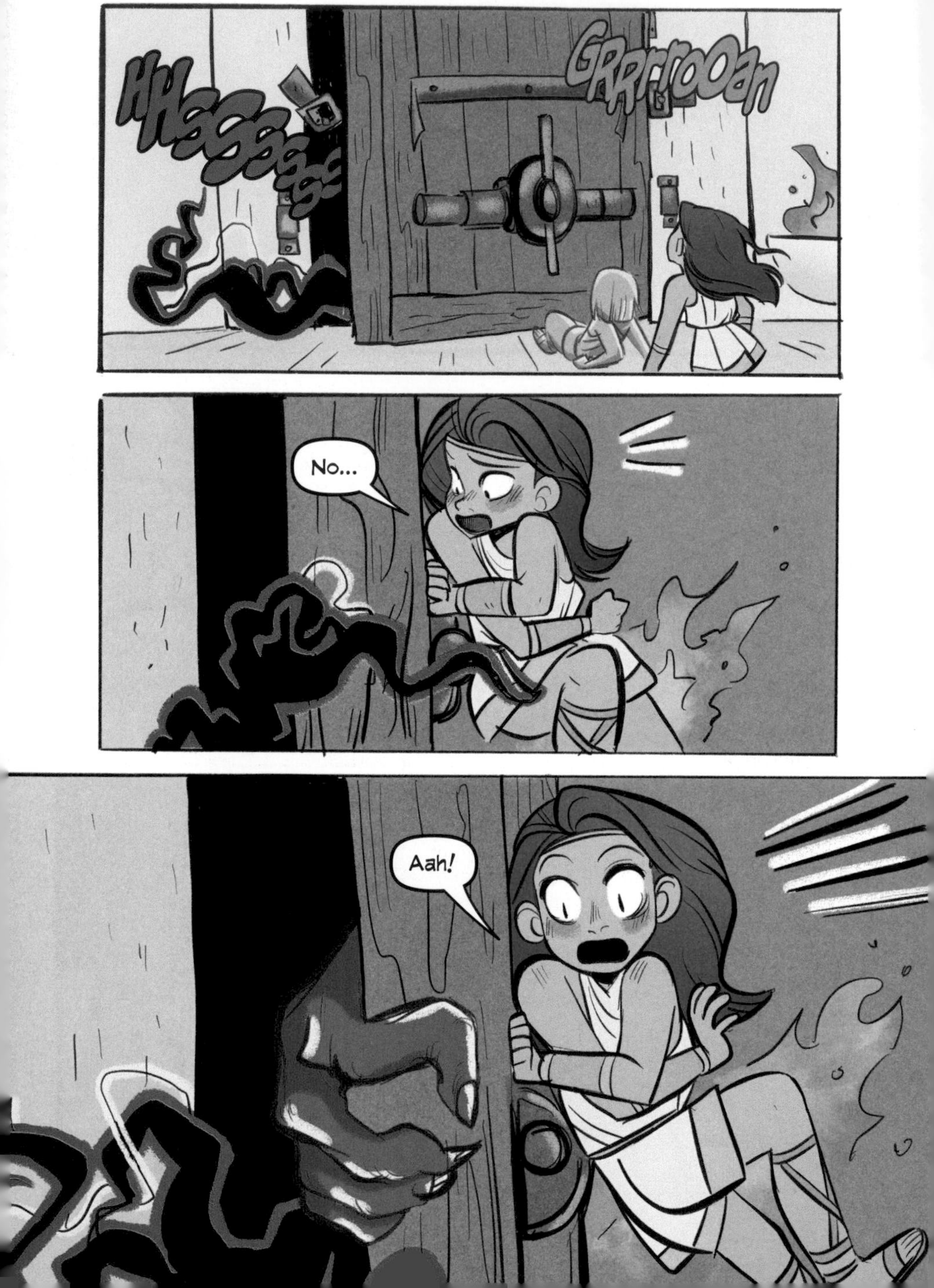
HHSSSSsss
GRRrrooOan
No...
Aah!

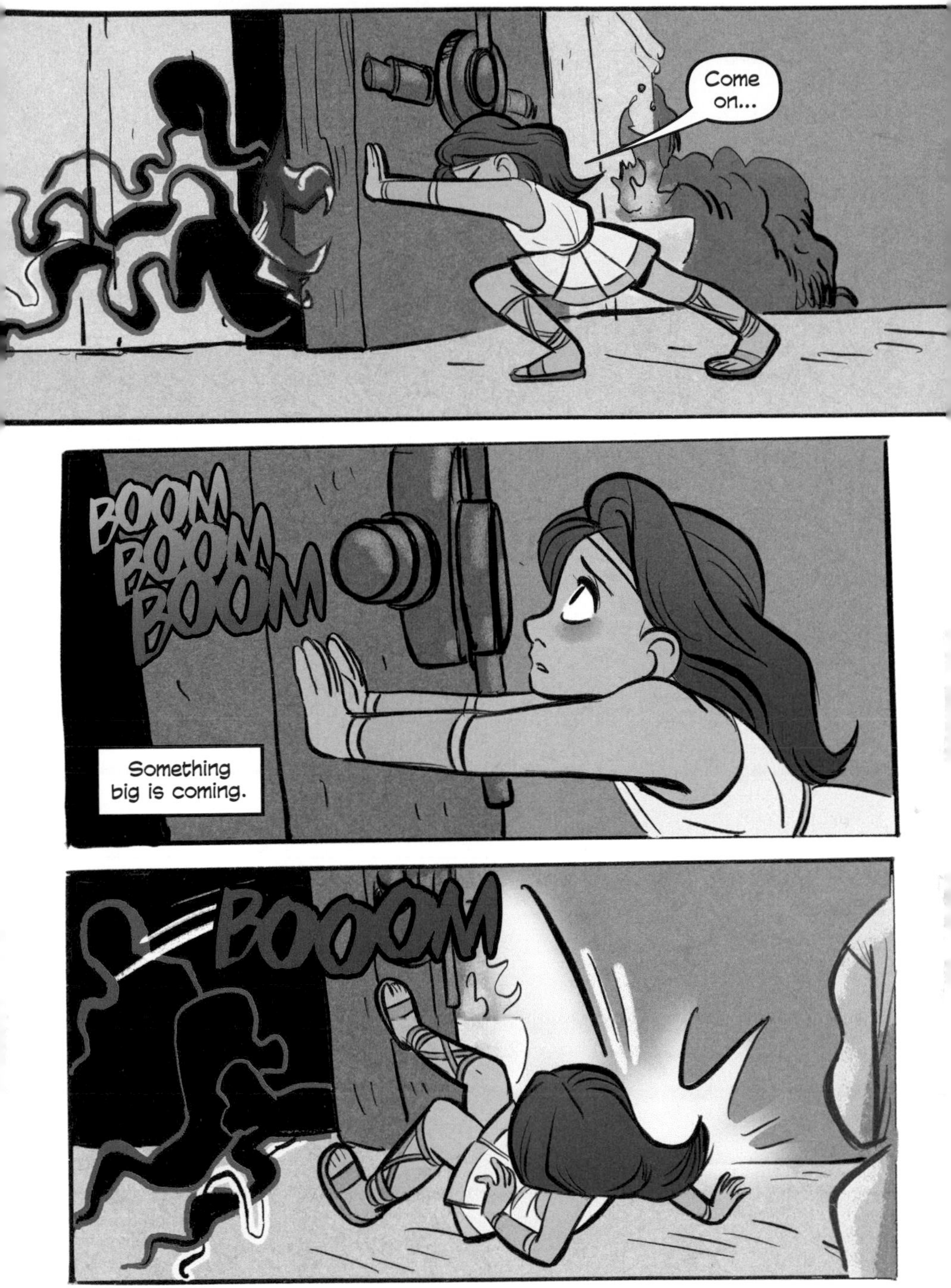
Come on...
BOOM
BOOM
BOOM
Something big is coming.
BOOOM

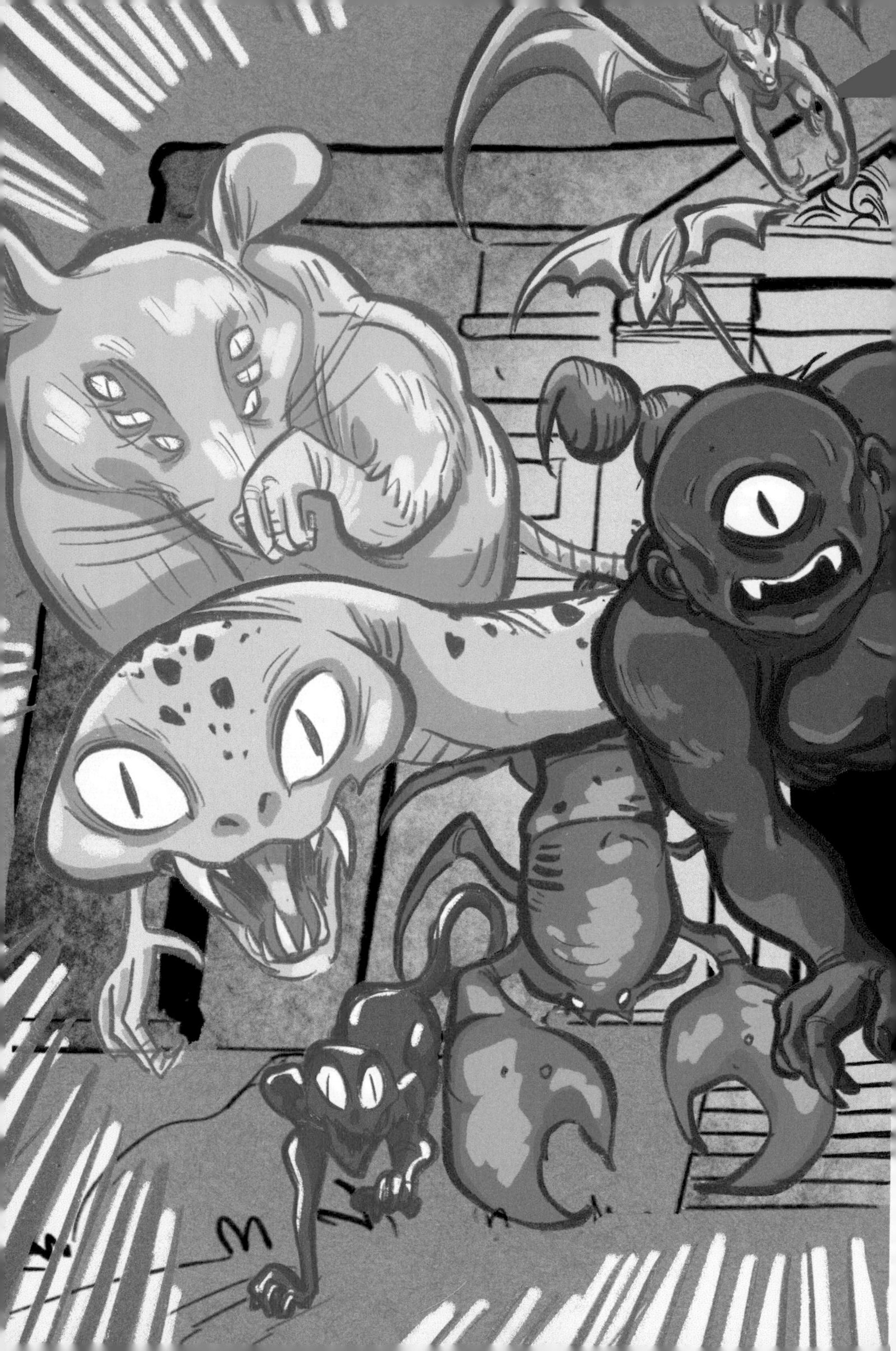

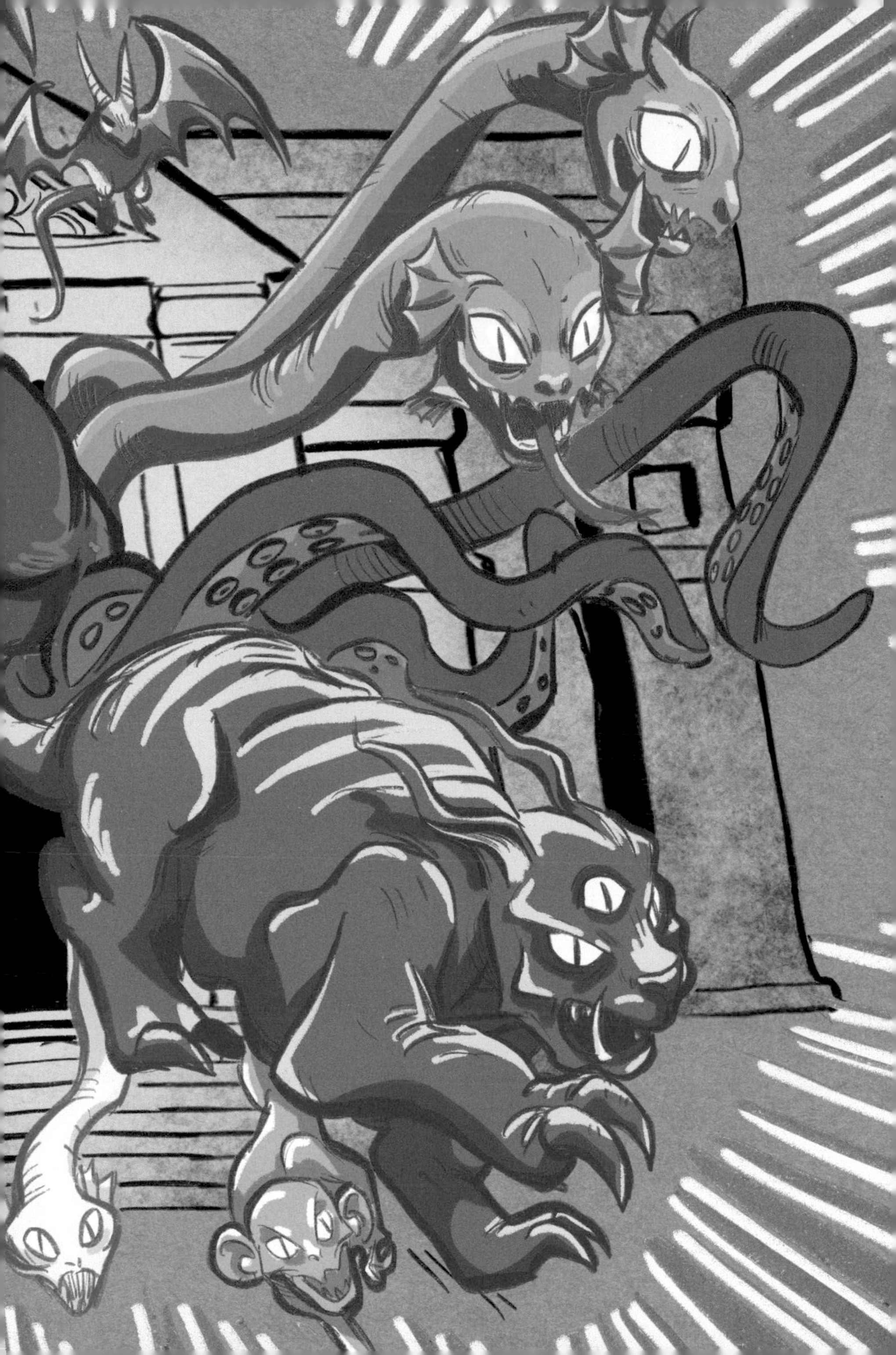

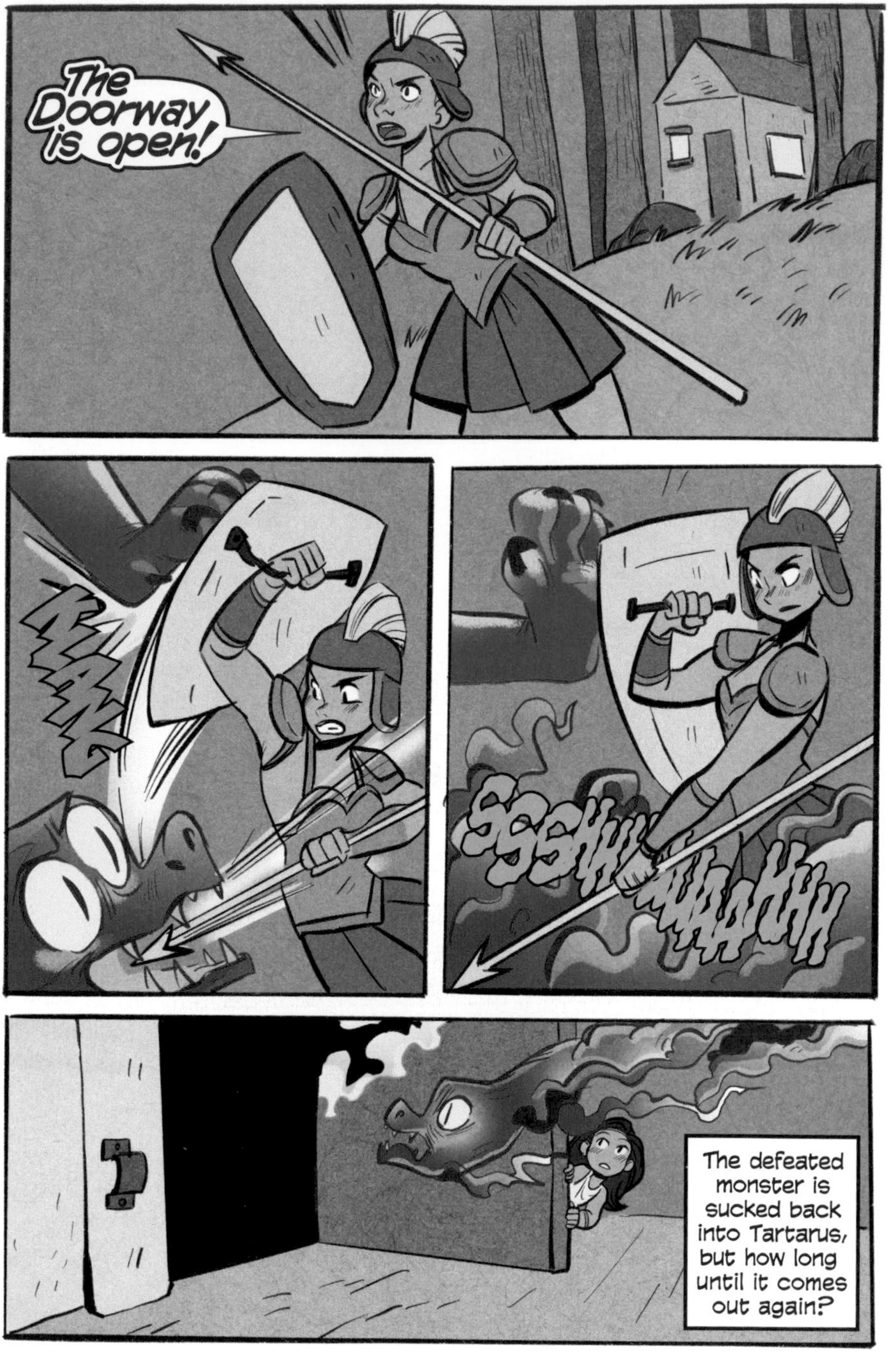
The Doorway is open!
KLANK
SSSHHWAAAHHH
The defeated monster is sucked back into Tartarus, but how long until it comes out again?

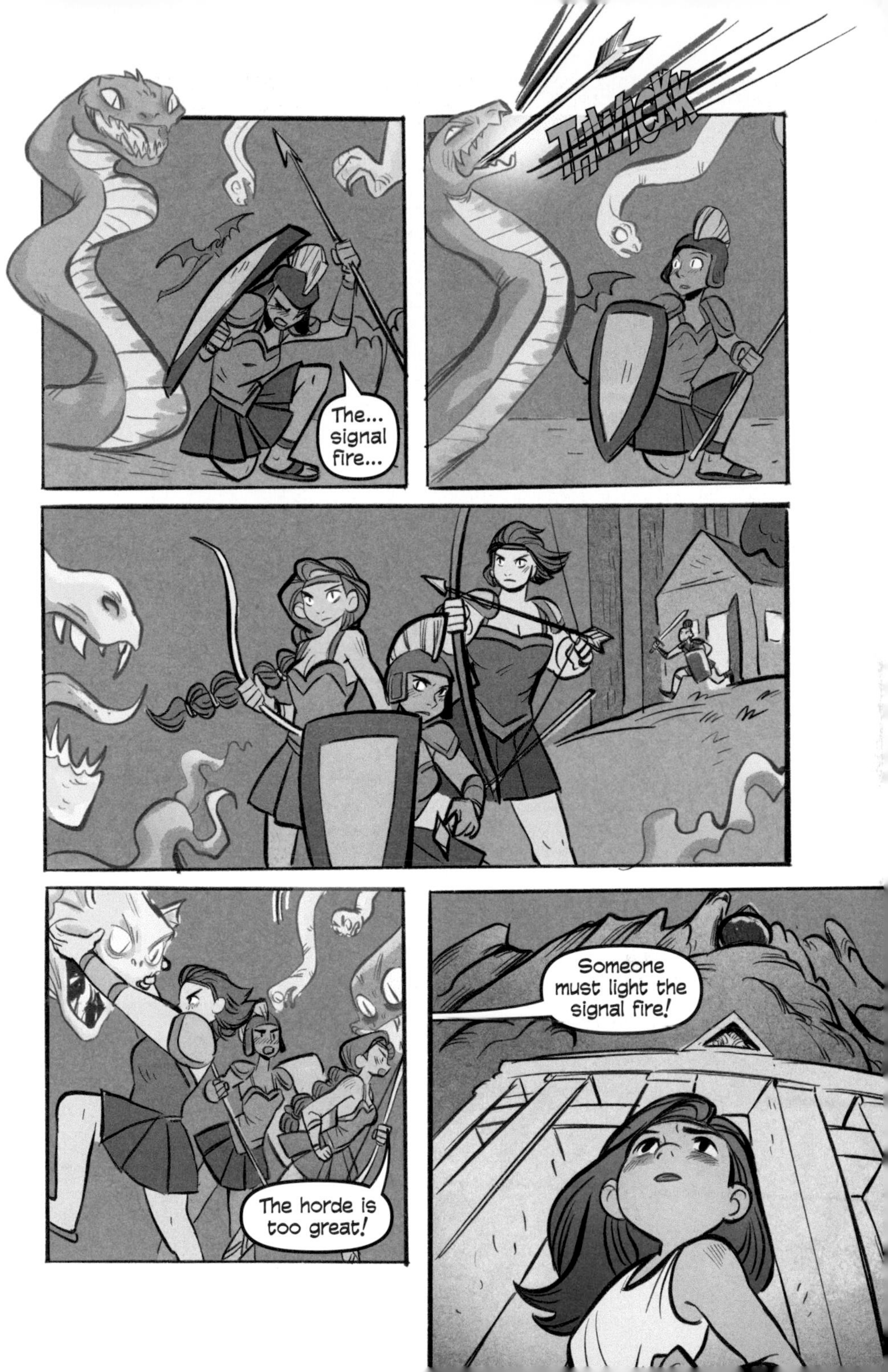
The... signal fire...
THWICK
Someone must light the signal fire!
The horde is too great!

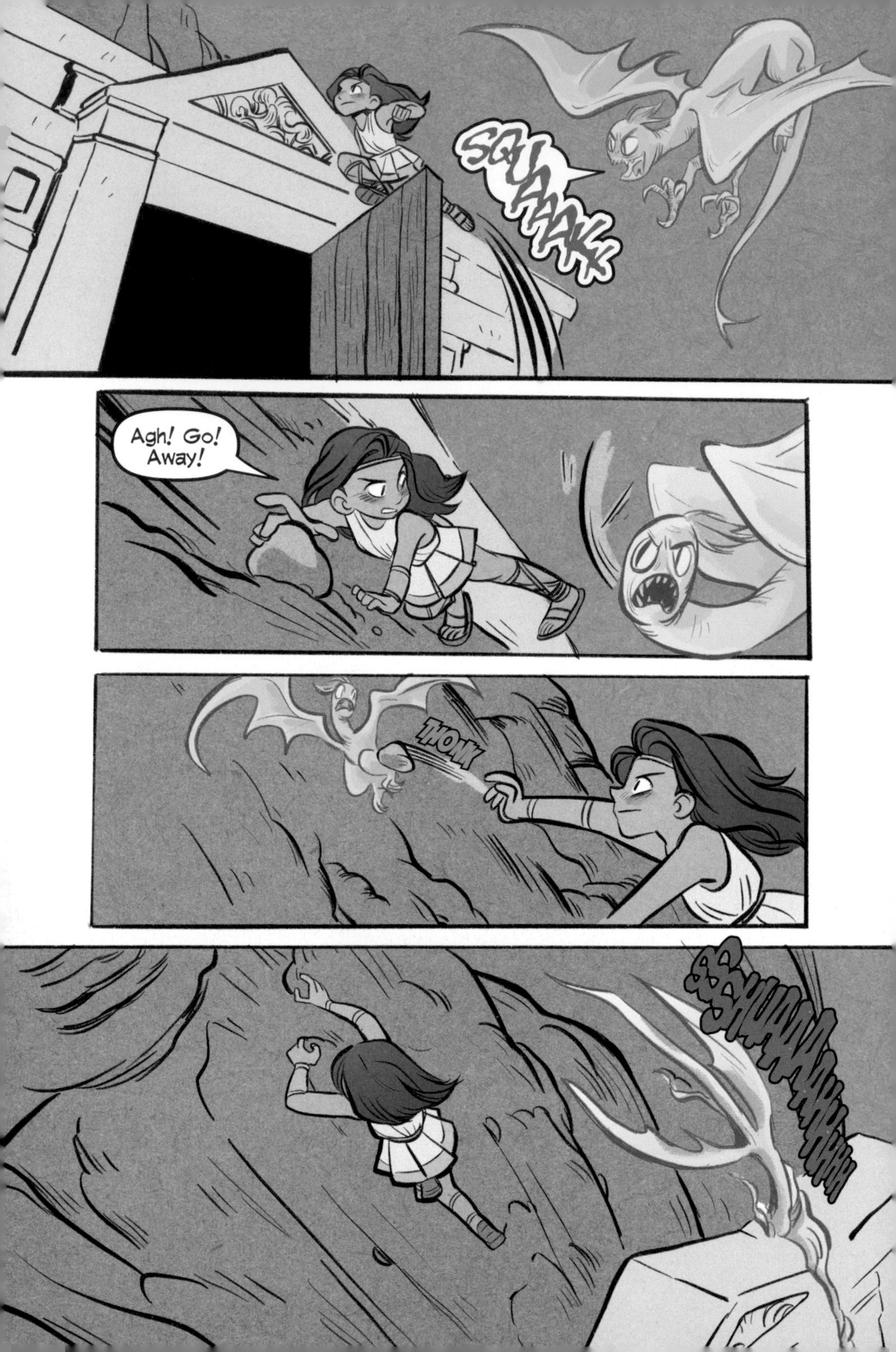
SQUAAAK!
Agh! Go! Away!
THONK
SSSHUHAAAHHHHH

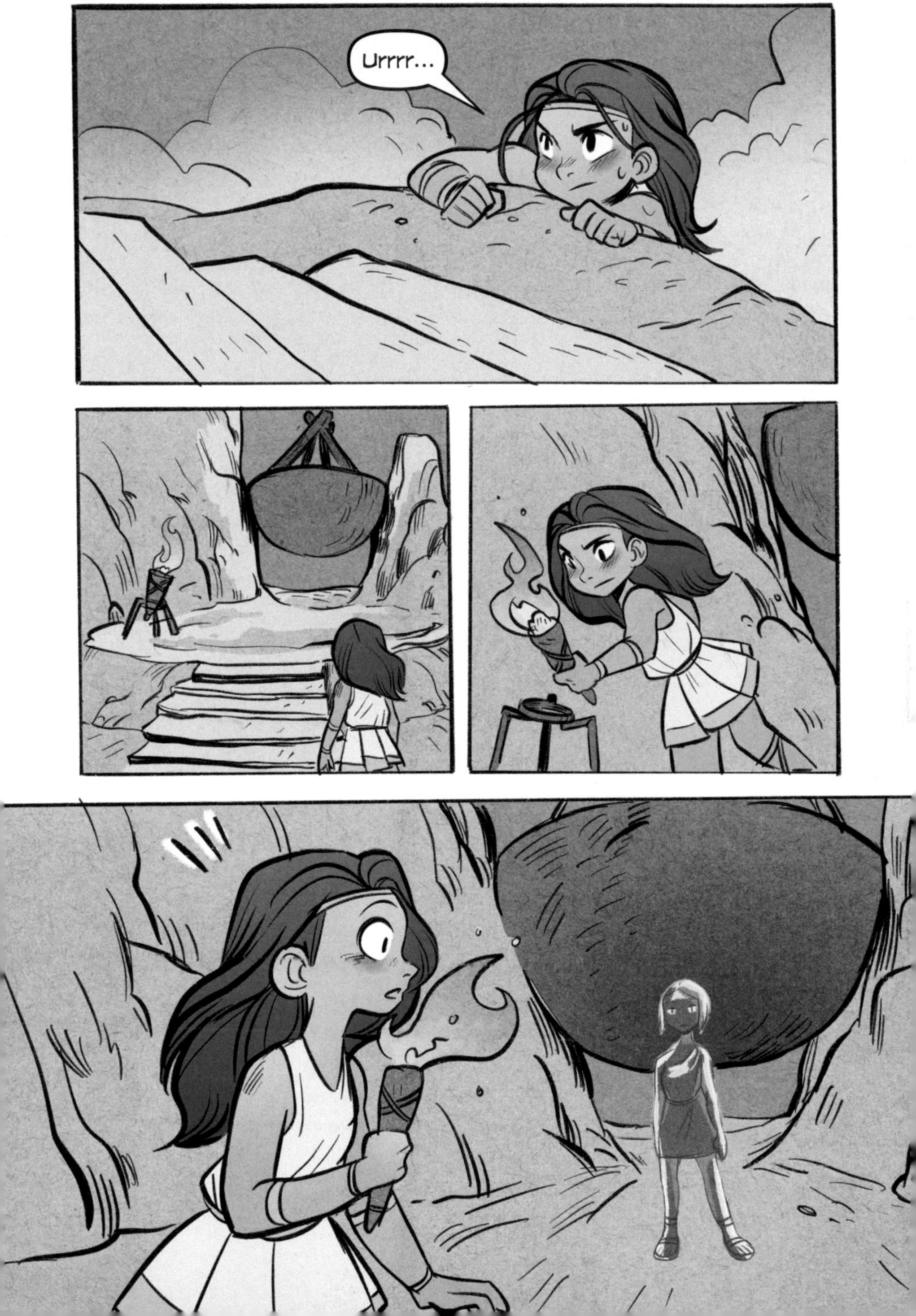
Urrrr...

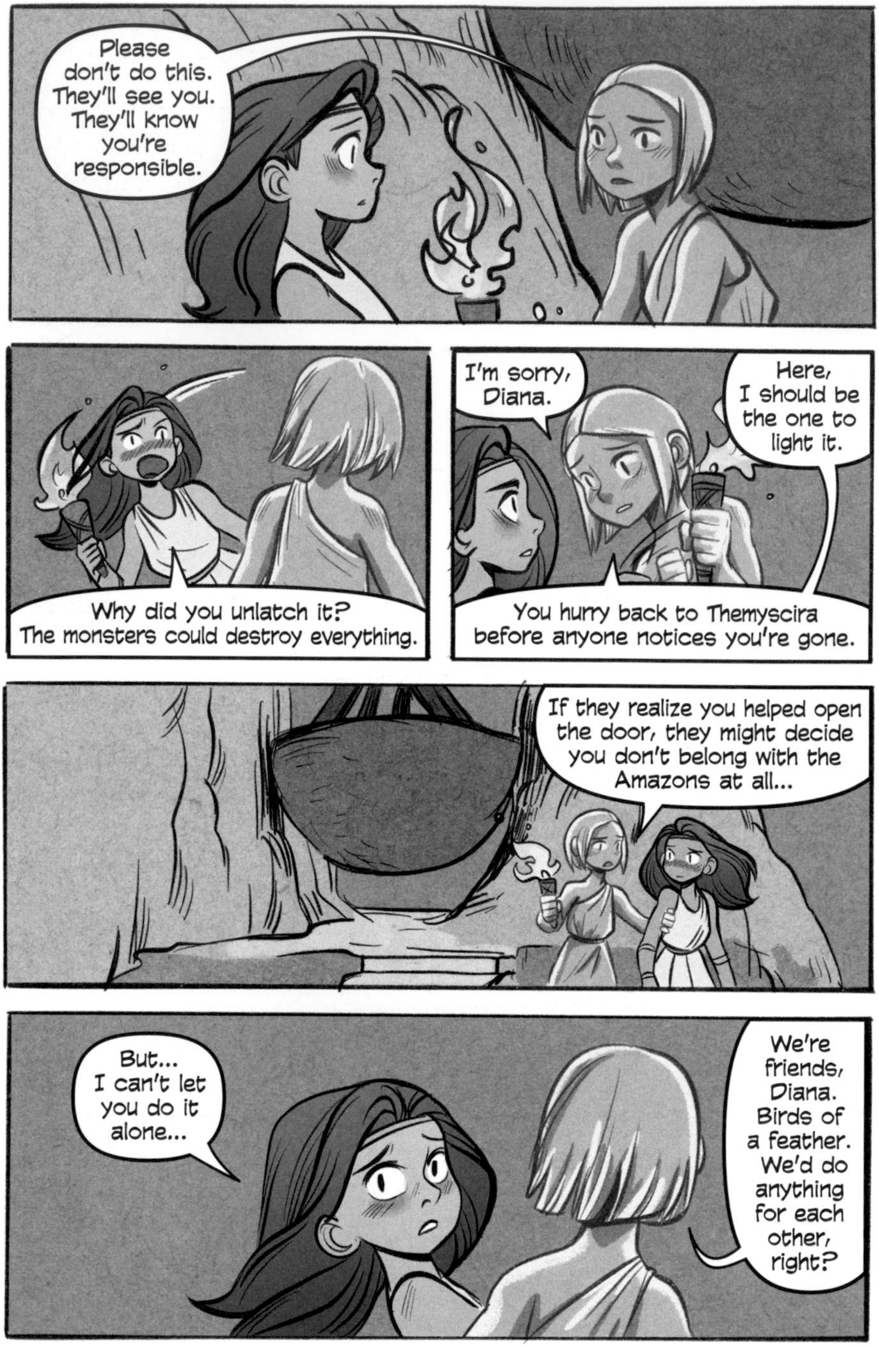
Please don't do this. They'll see you. They'll know you're responsible.
Why did you unlatch it? The monsters could destroy everything.
I'm sorry, Diana.
Here, I should be the one to light it.
You hurry back to Themyscira before anyone notices you're gone.
If they realize you helped open the door, they might decide you don't belong with the Amazons at all...
But... I can't let you do it alone...
We're friends, Diana. Birds of a feather. We'd do anything for each other, right?

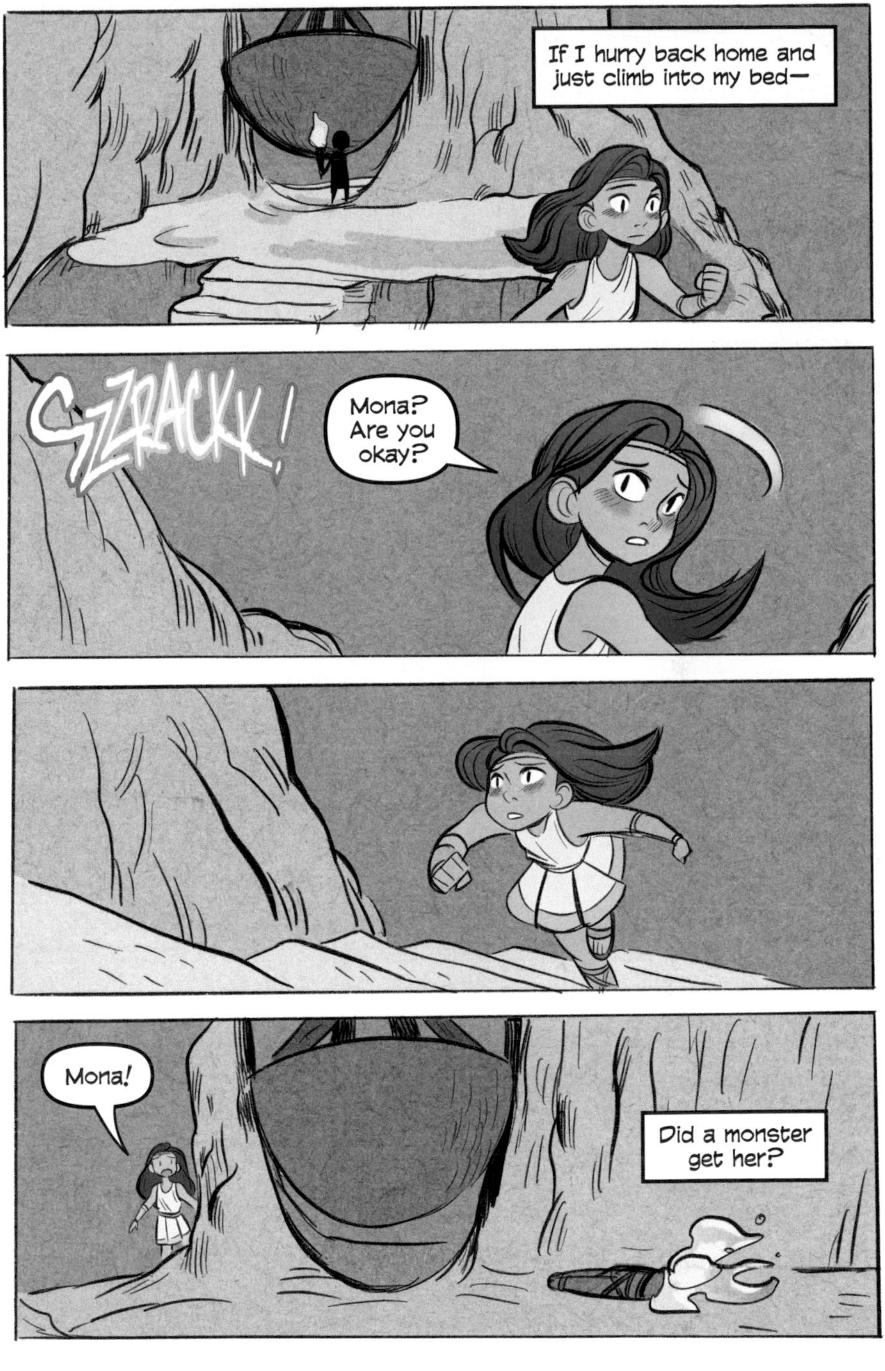
If I hurry back home and just climb into my bed—
SZZRACKK!
Mona? Are you okay?
Mona!
Did a monster get her?

Mona! Where are you?

Mona!

I never should have left her to do it alone.

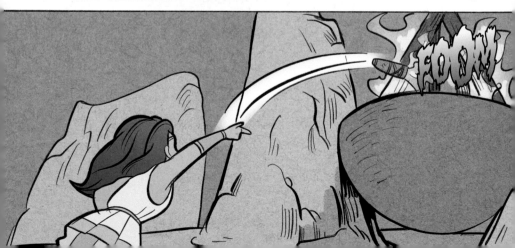

FOOM

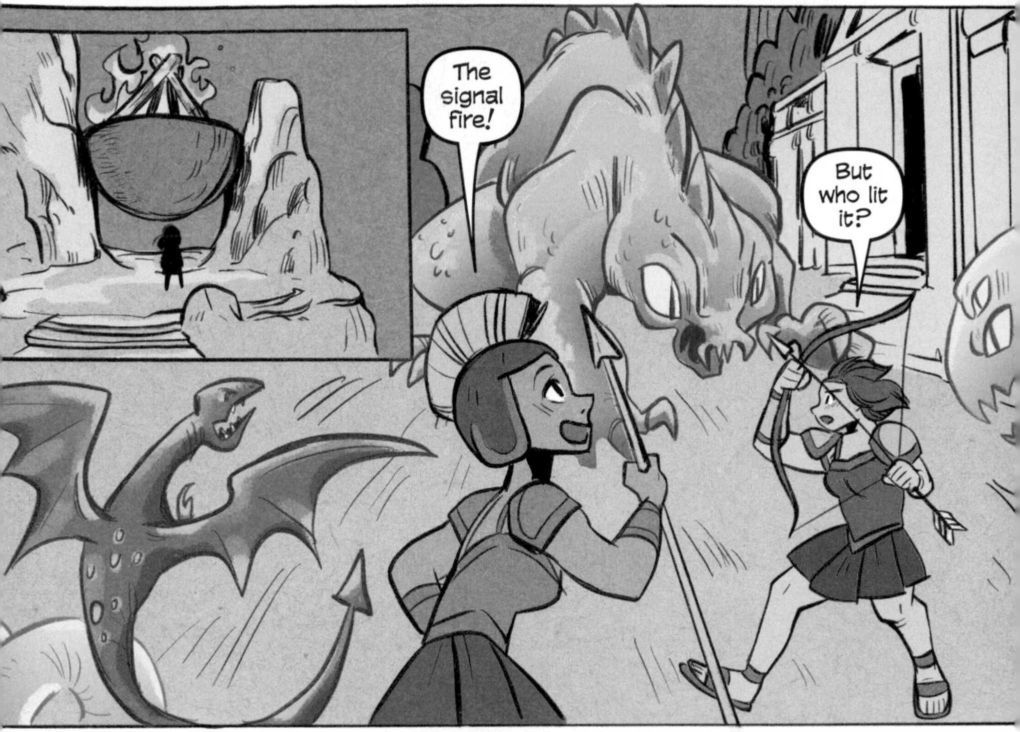
The signal fire!
But who lit it?

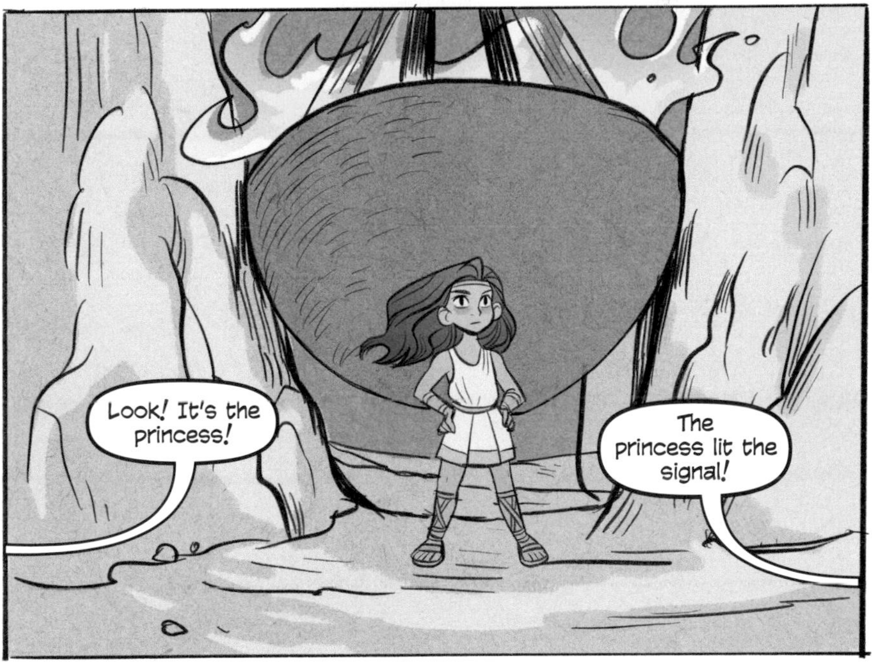
Look! It's the princess!
The princess lit the signal!

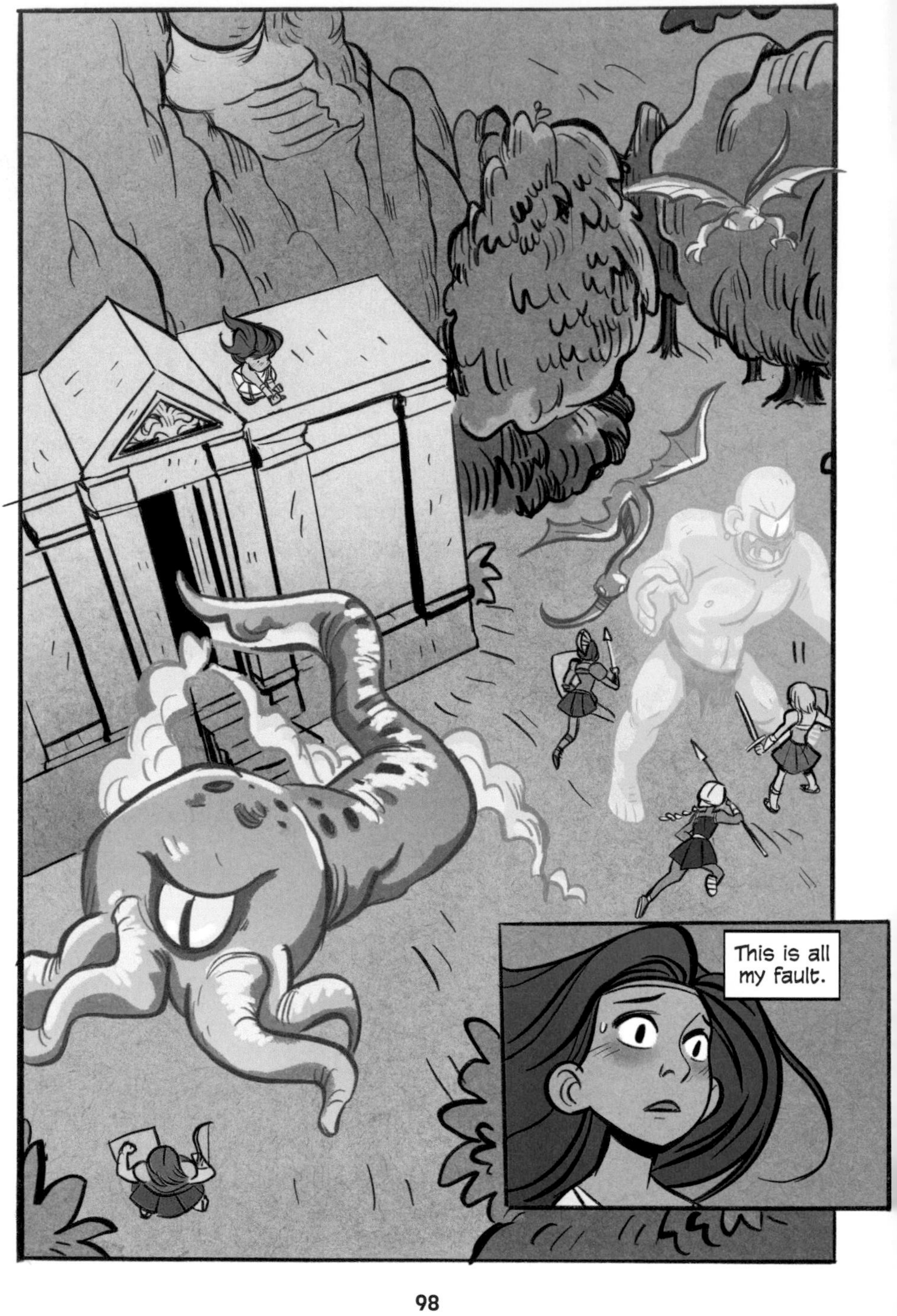
This is all my fault.

CHAPTER
FOUR

The Best of Us

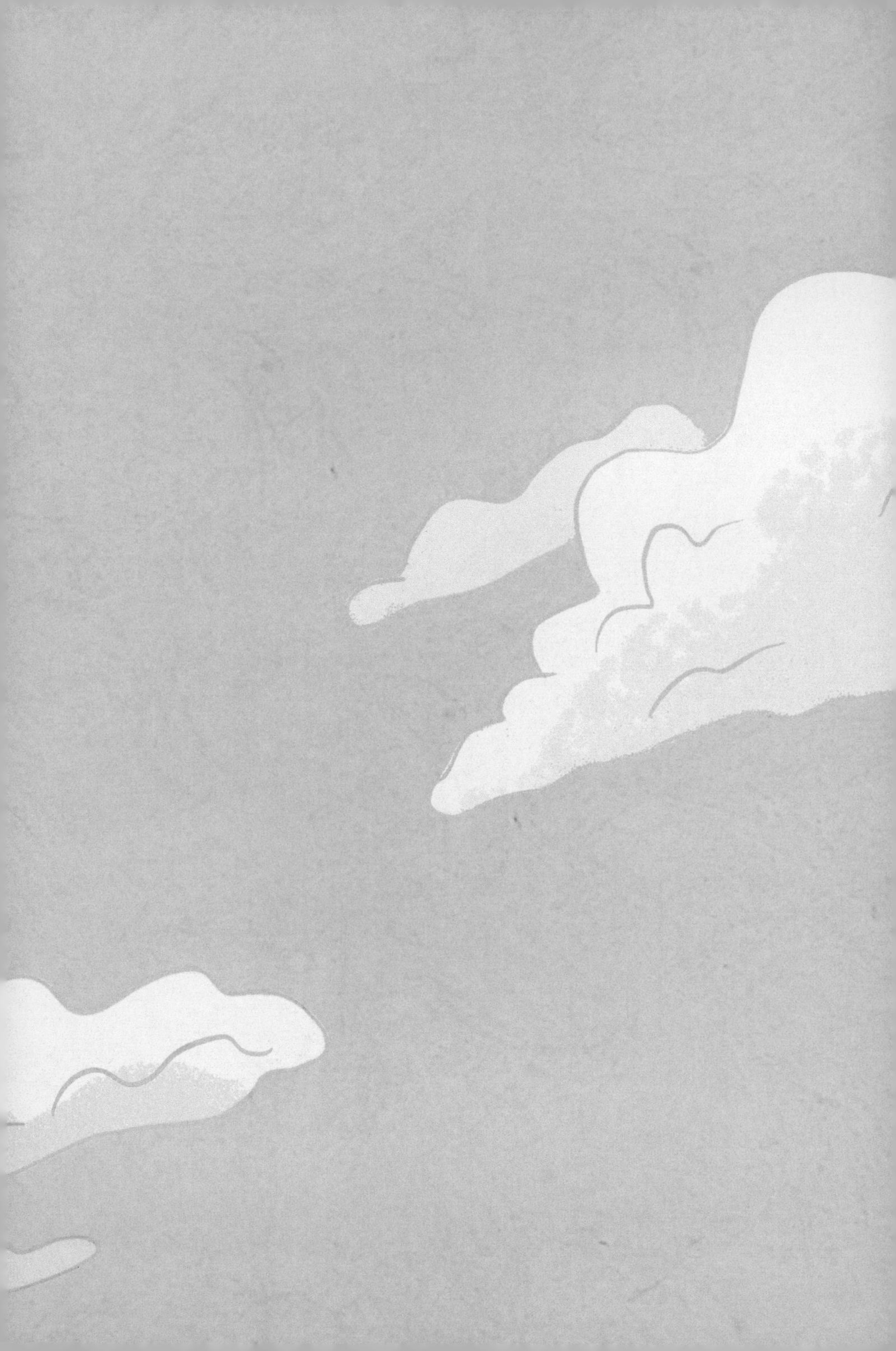

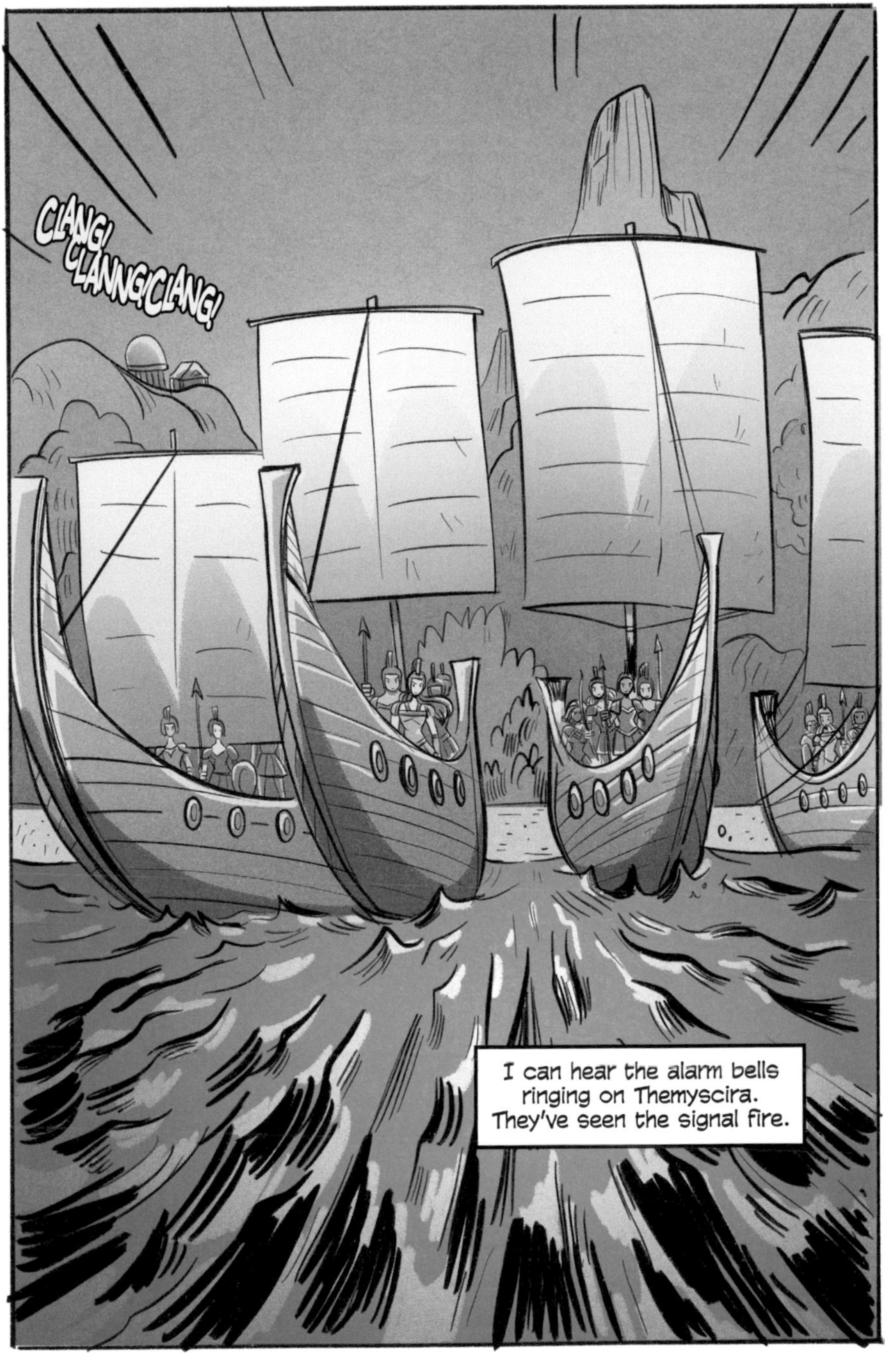
CLANG! CLANNG! CLANG!
I can hear the alarm bells ringing on Themyscira. They've seen the signal fire.

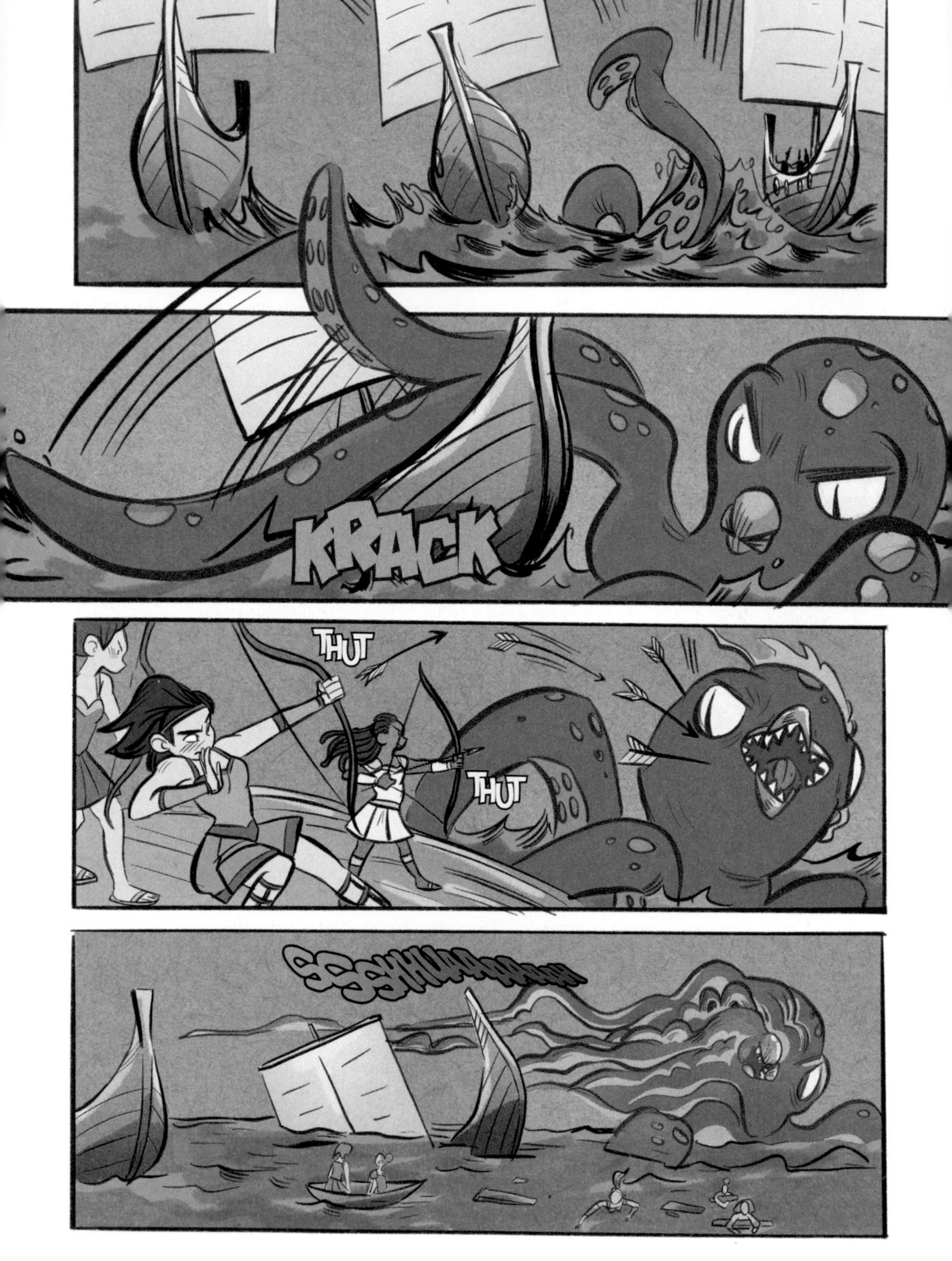
KRACK
THUT
THUT

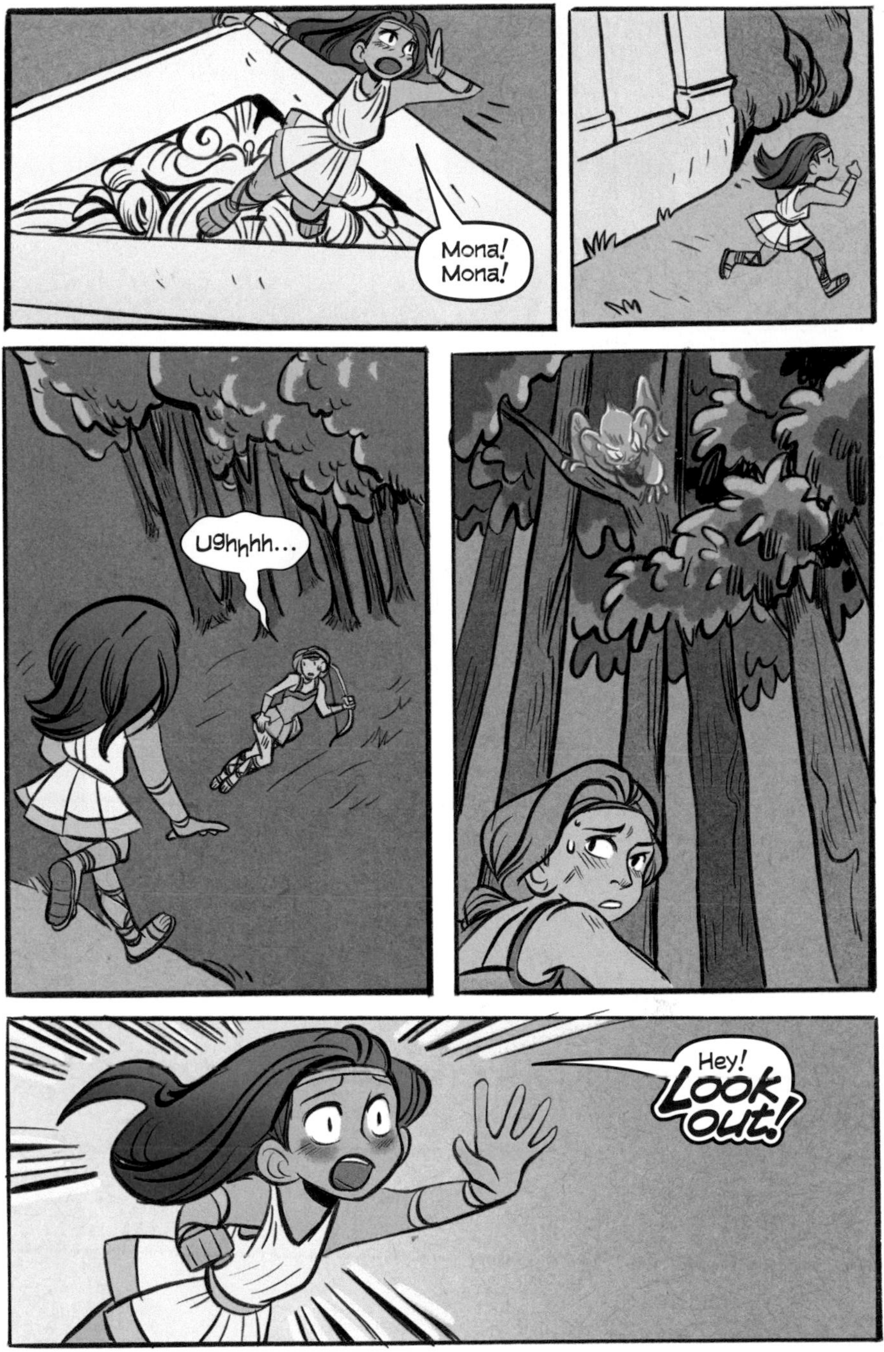
Mona! Mona!
Ughhhh...
Hey! Look out!

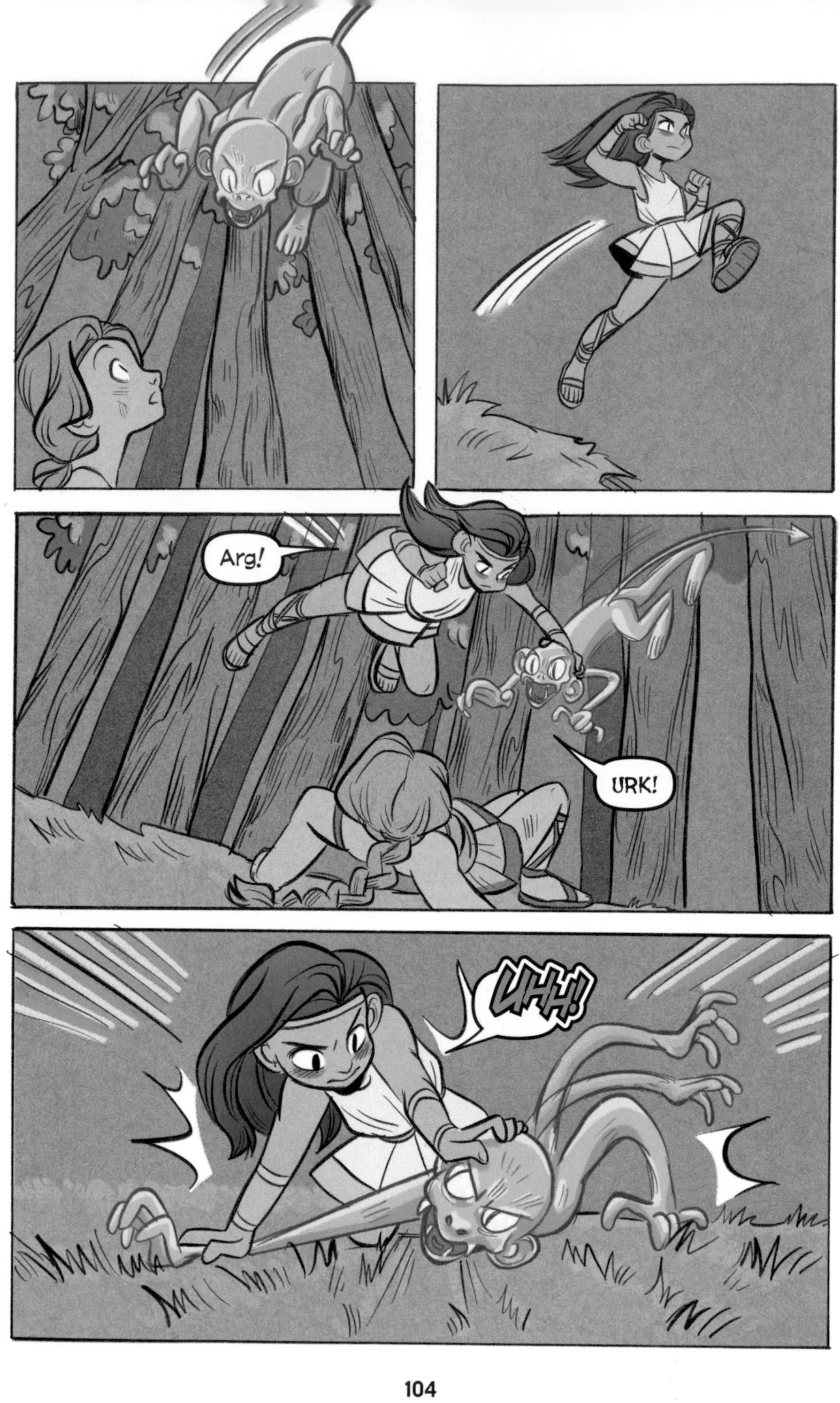
Arg!
URK!
UHH!

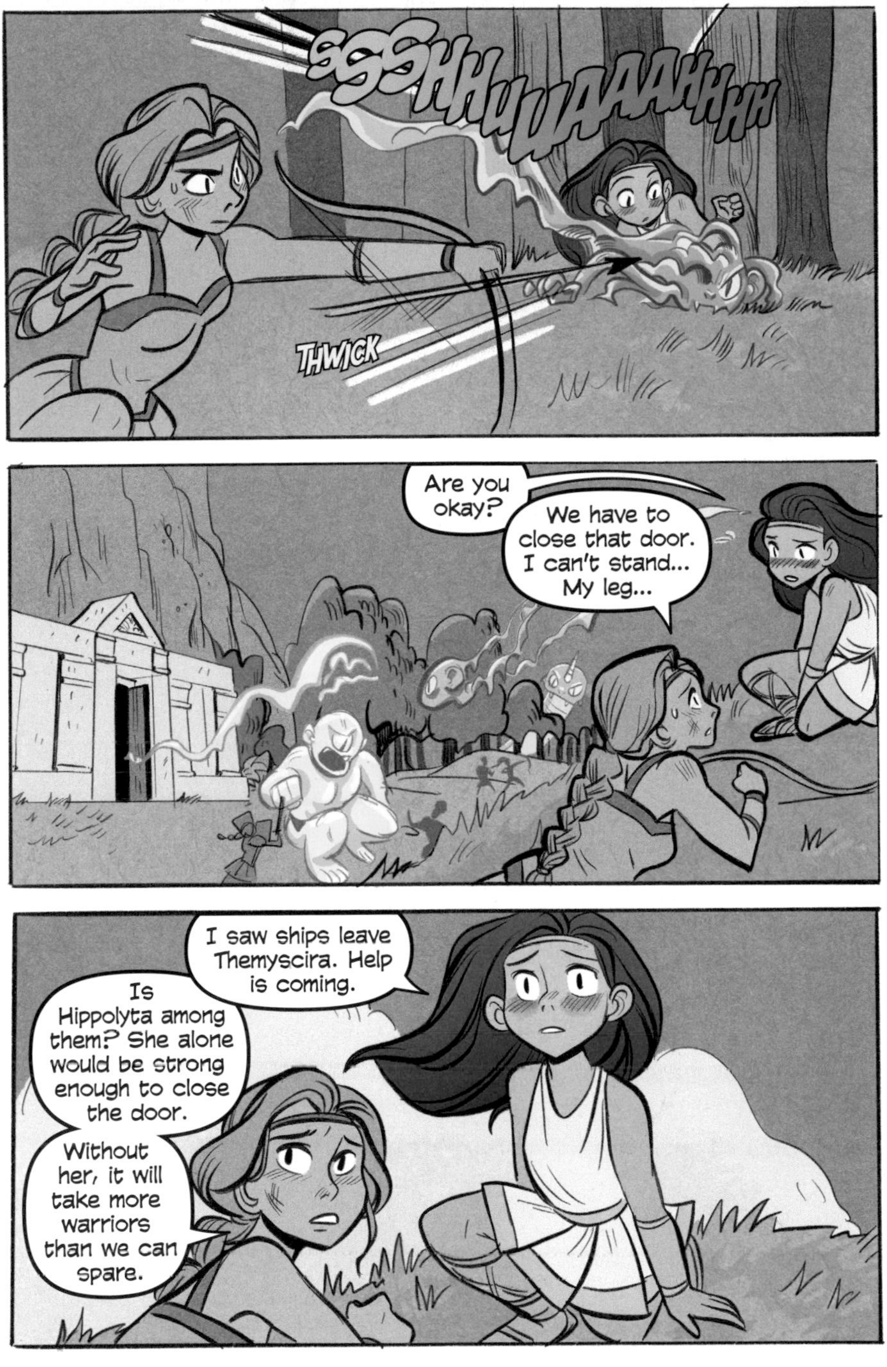

SSSHHUUAAAAHHHH
THWICK
Are you okay?
We have to close that door. I can't stand... My leg...
I saw ships leave Themyscira. Help is coming.
Is Hippolyta among them? She alone would be strong enough to close the door.
Without her, it will take more warriors than we can spare.

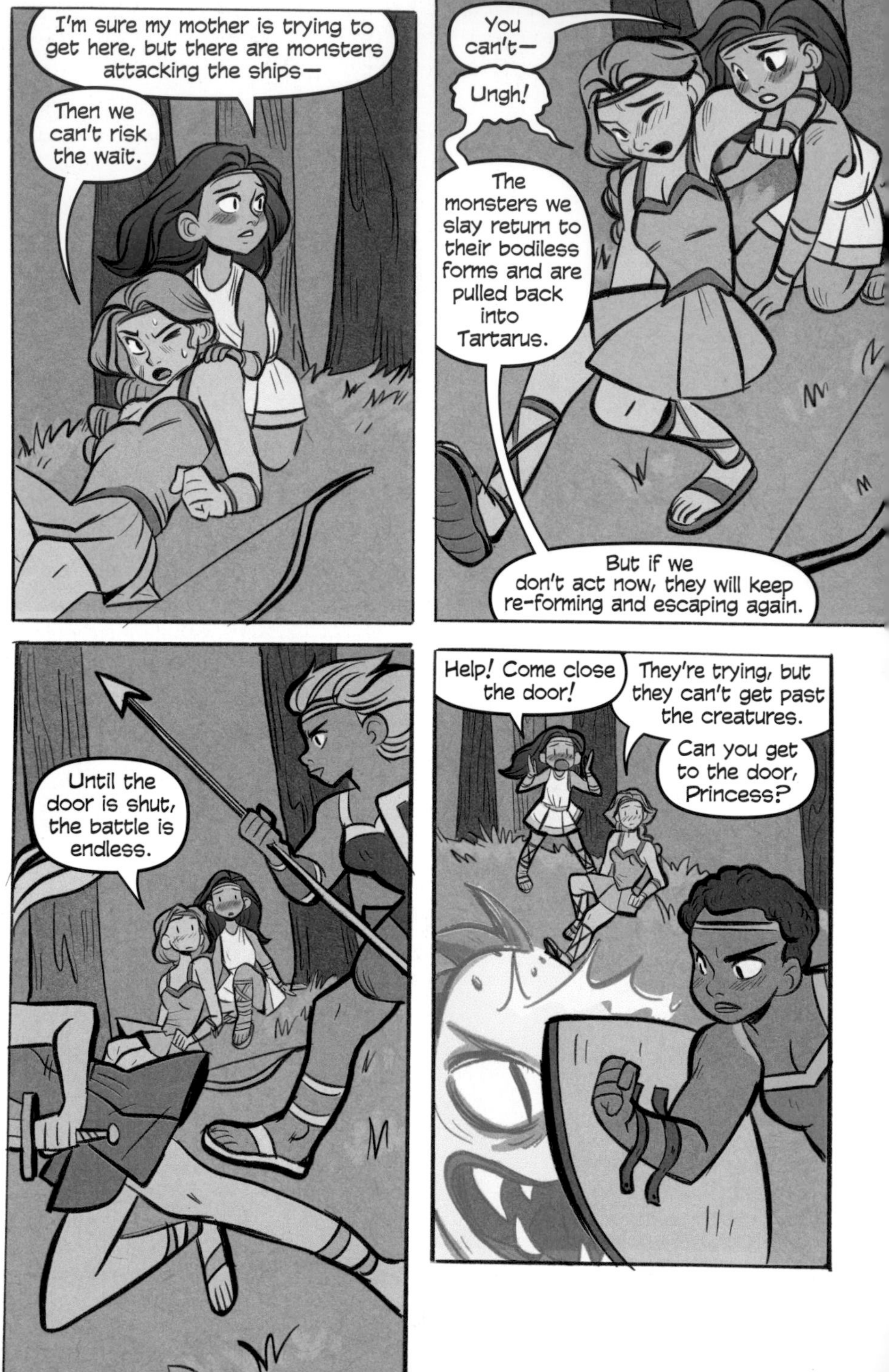
I'm sure my mother is trying to get here, but there are monsters attacking the ships—
Then we can't risk the wait.
You can't—
Ungh!
The monsters we slay return to their bodiless forms and are pulled back into Tartarus.
But if we don't act now, they will keep re-forming and escaping again.
Until the door is shut, the battle is endless.
Help! Come close the door!
They're trying, but they can't get past the creatures.
Can you get to the door, Princess?

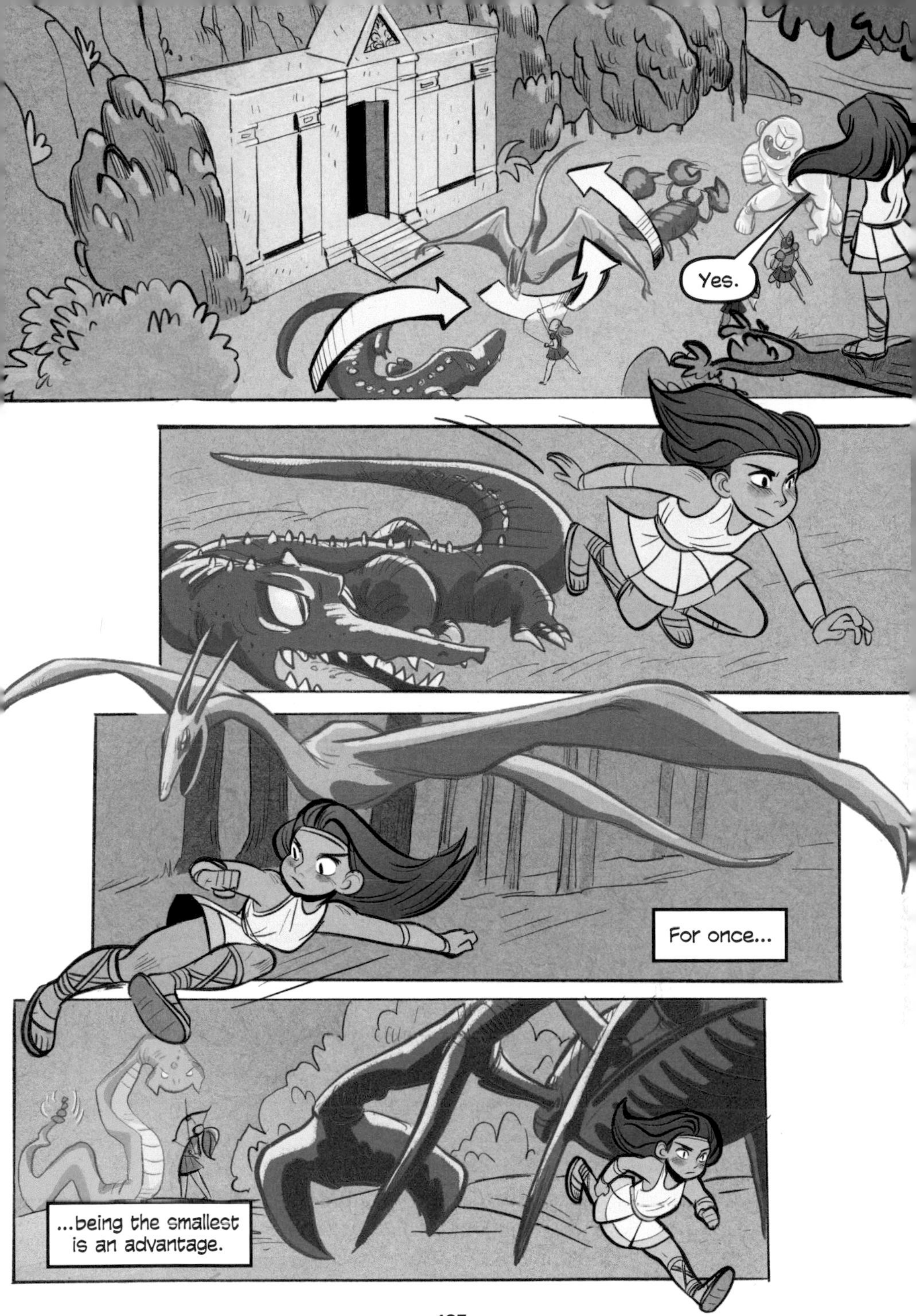
Yes.
For once...
...being the smallest
is an advantage.

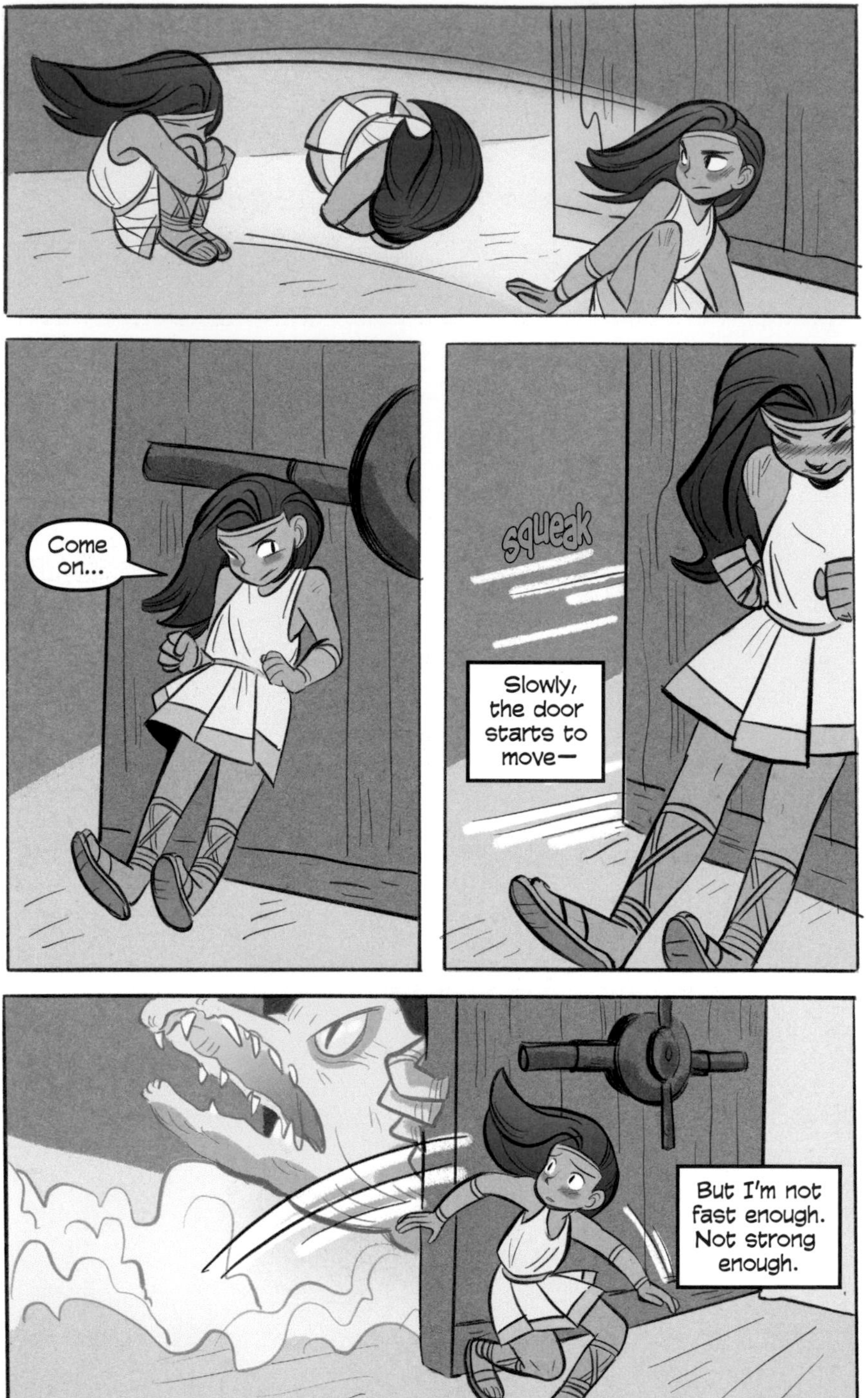
Come on...
squeak
Slowly, the door starts to move—
But I'm not fast enough. Not strong enough.

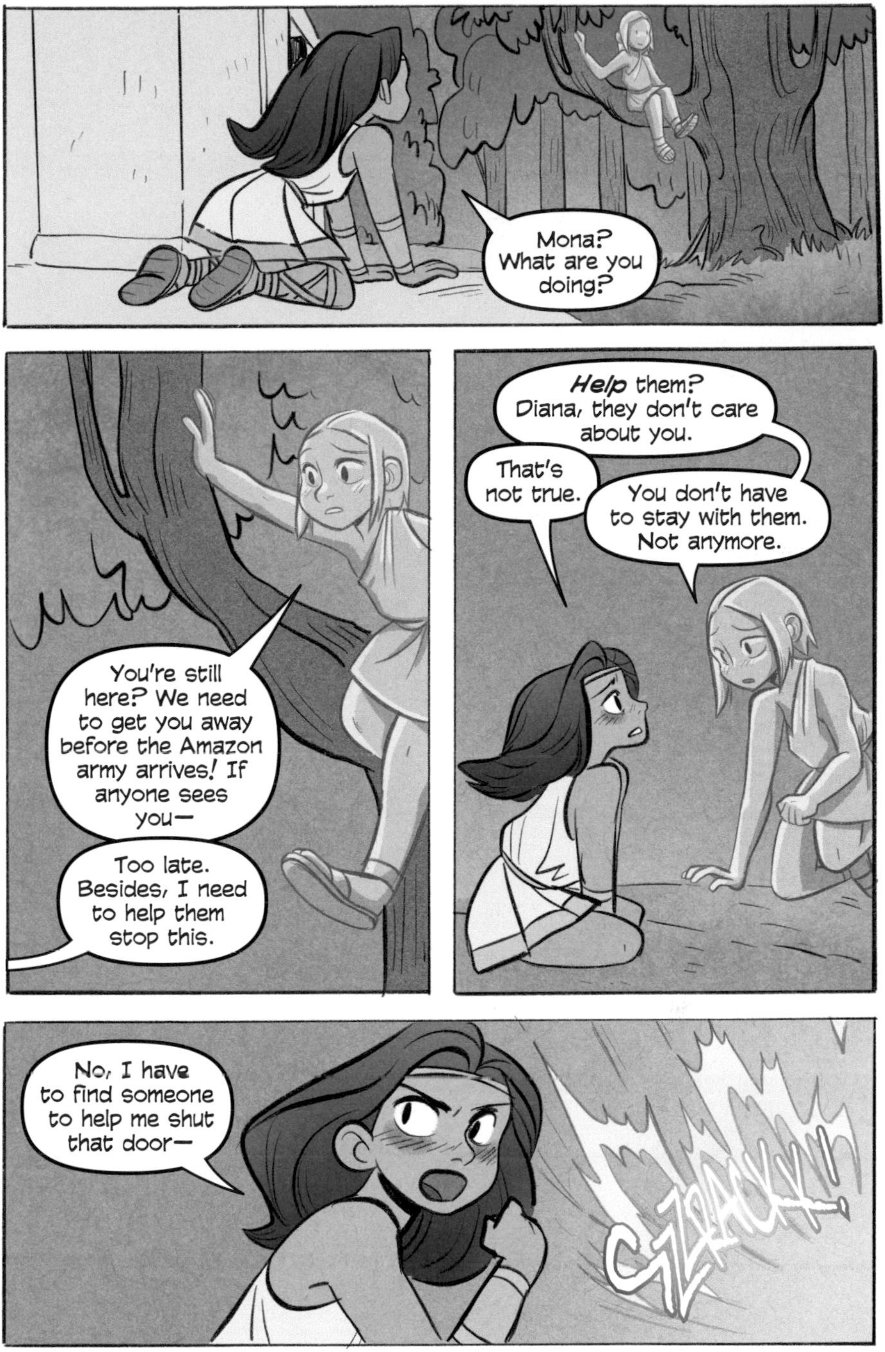
Mona? What are you doing?
You're still here? We need to get you away before the Amazon army arrives! If anyone sees you—
Too late. Besides, I need to help them stop this.
Help them? Diana, they don't care about you.
That's not true.
You don't have to stay with them. Not anymore.
No, I have to find someone to help me shut that door—
CZZACK!

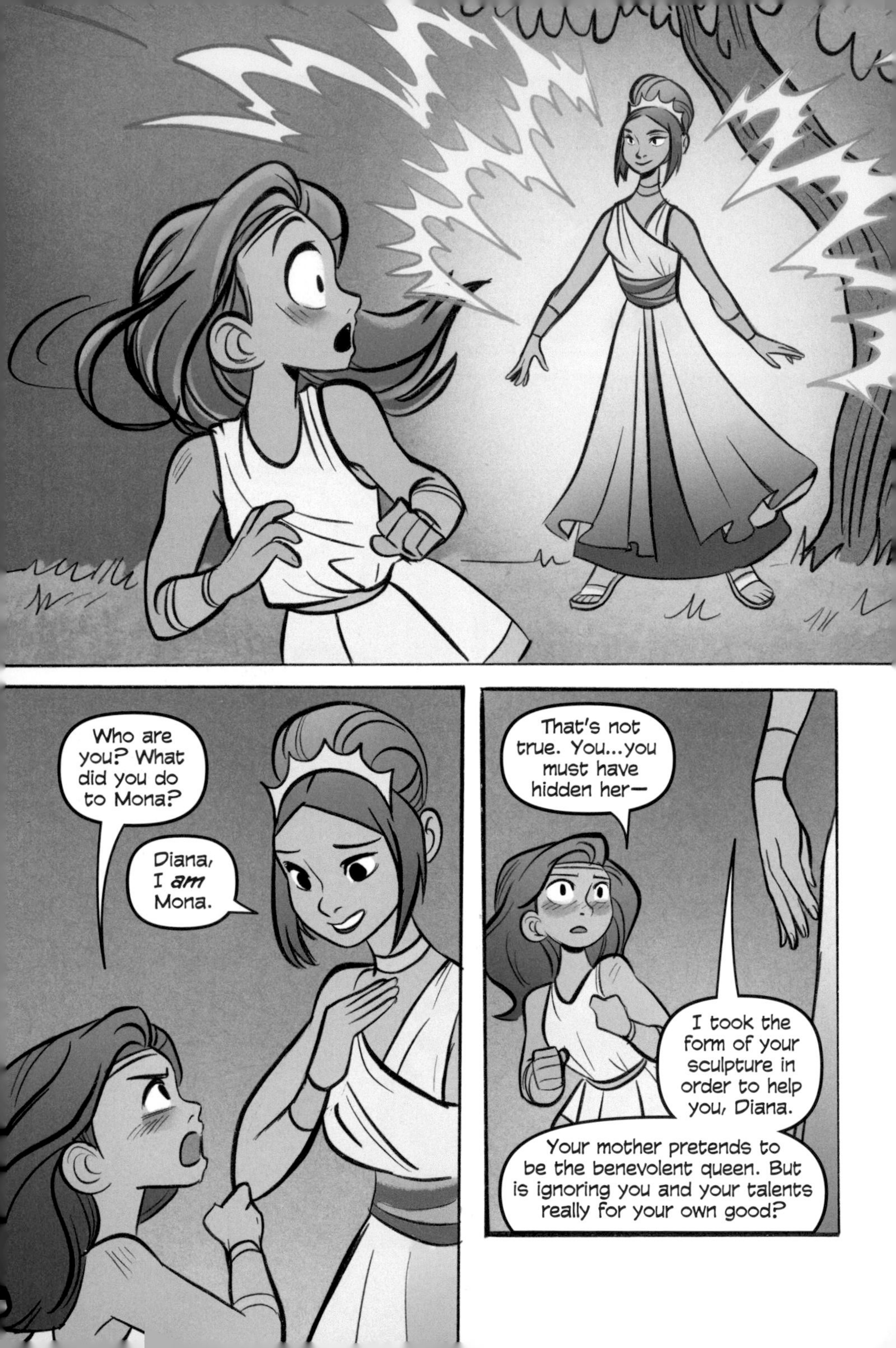
Who are you? What did you do to Mona?
Diana, I *am* Mona.
That's not true. You...you must have hidden her—
I took the form of your sculpture in order to help you, Diana.
Your mother pretends to be the benevolent queen. But is ignoring you and your talents really for your own good?

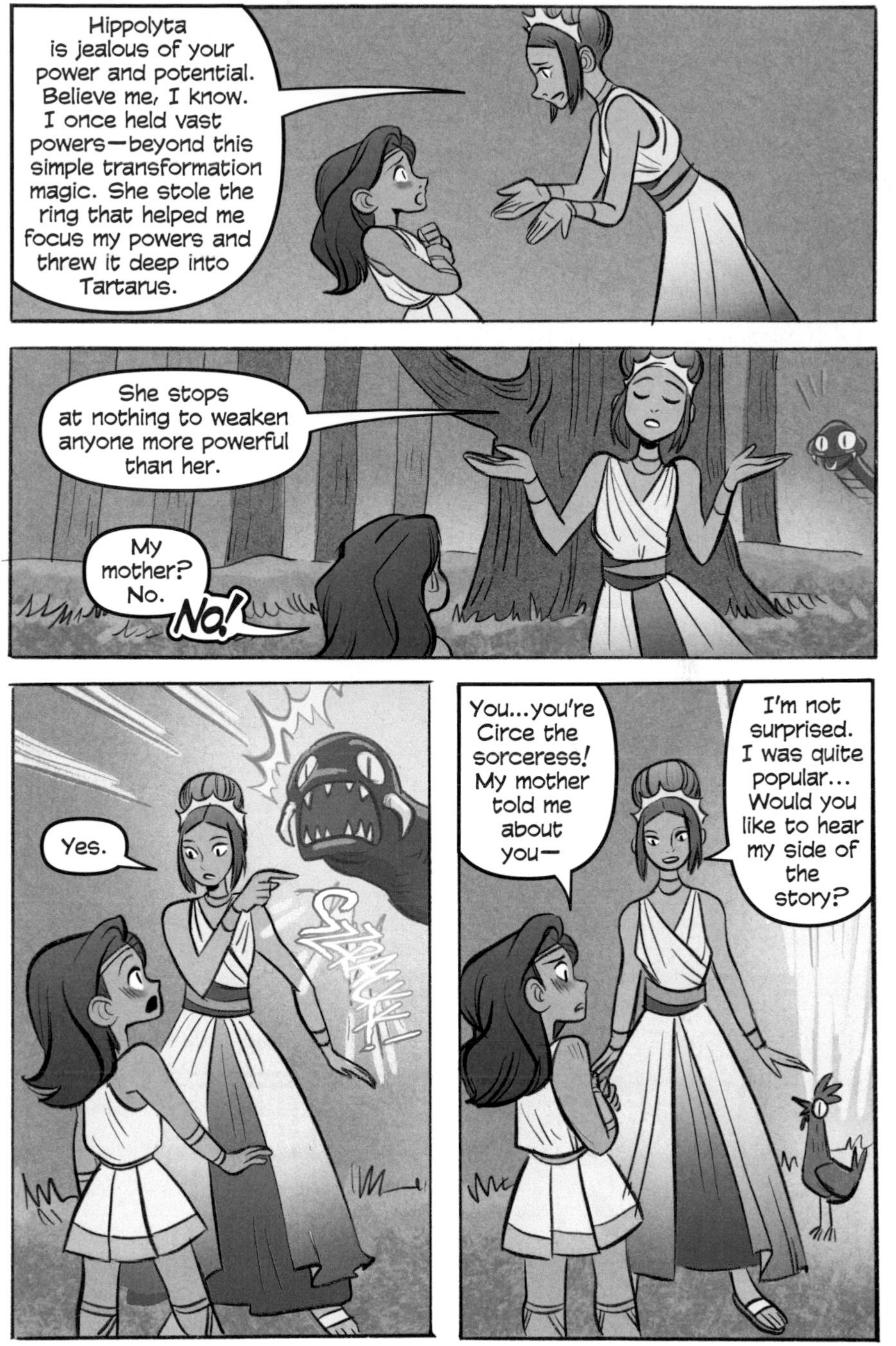
Hippolyta is jealous of your power and potential. Believe me, I know. I once held vast powers—beyond this simple transformation magic. She stole the ring that helped me focus my powers and threw it deep into Tartarus.
She stops at nothing to weaken anyone more powerful than her.
My mother? No.
No!
Yes.
You...you're Circe the sorceress! My mother told me about you—
I'm not surprised. I was quite popular... Would you like to hear my side of the story?

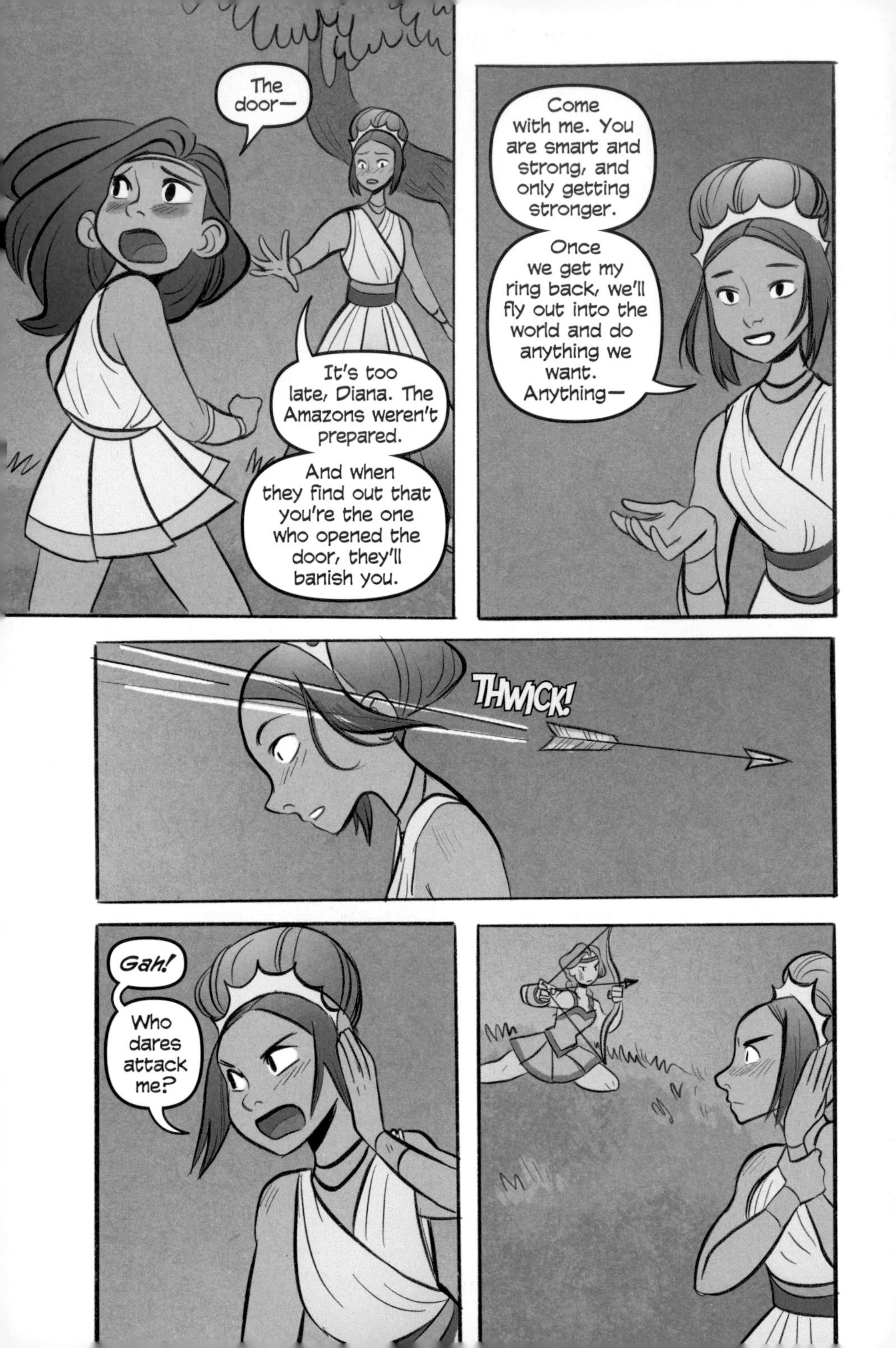
The door—
It's too late, Diana. The Amazons weren't prepared.
And when they find out that you're the one who opened the door, they'll banish you.
Come with me. You are smart and strong, and only getting stronger.
Once we get my ring back, we'll fly out into the world and do anything we want. Anything—
THWICK!
Gah!
Who dares attack me?

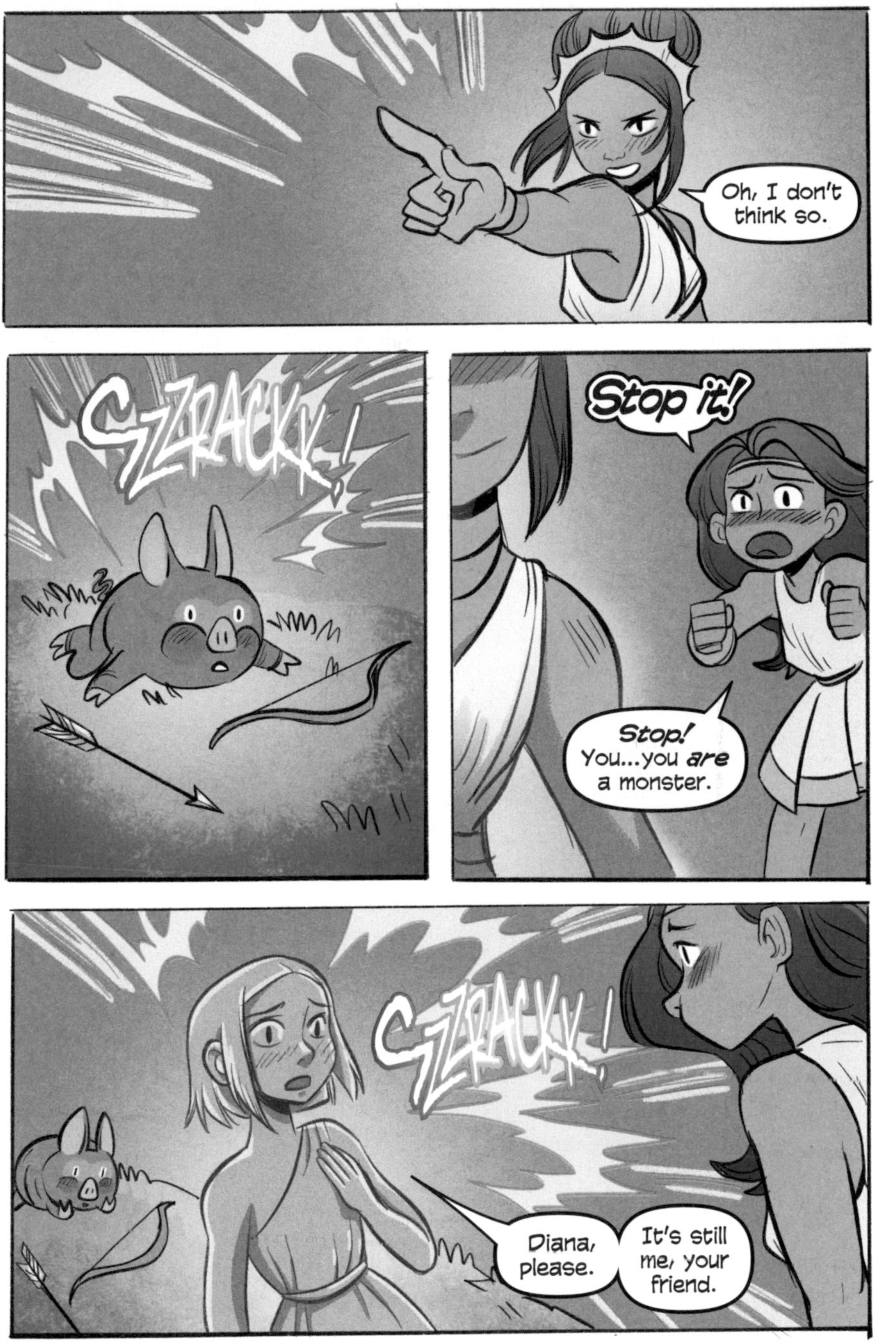
Oh, I don't think so.
SZZRACKK!
Stop it!
Stop! You...you *are* a monster.
SZZRACKK!
Diana, please.
It's still me, your friend.

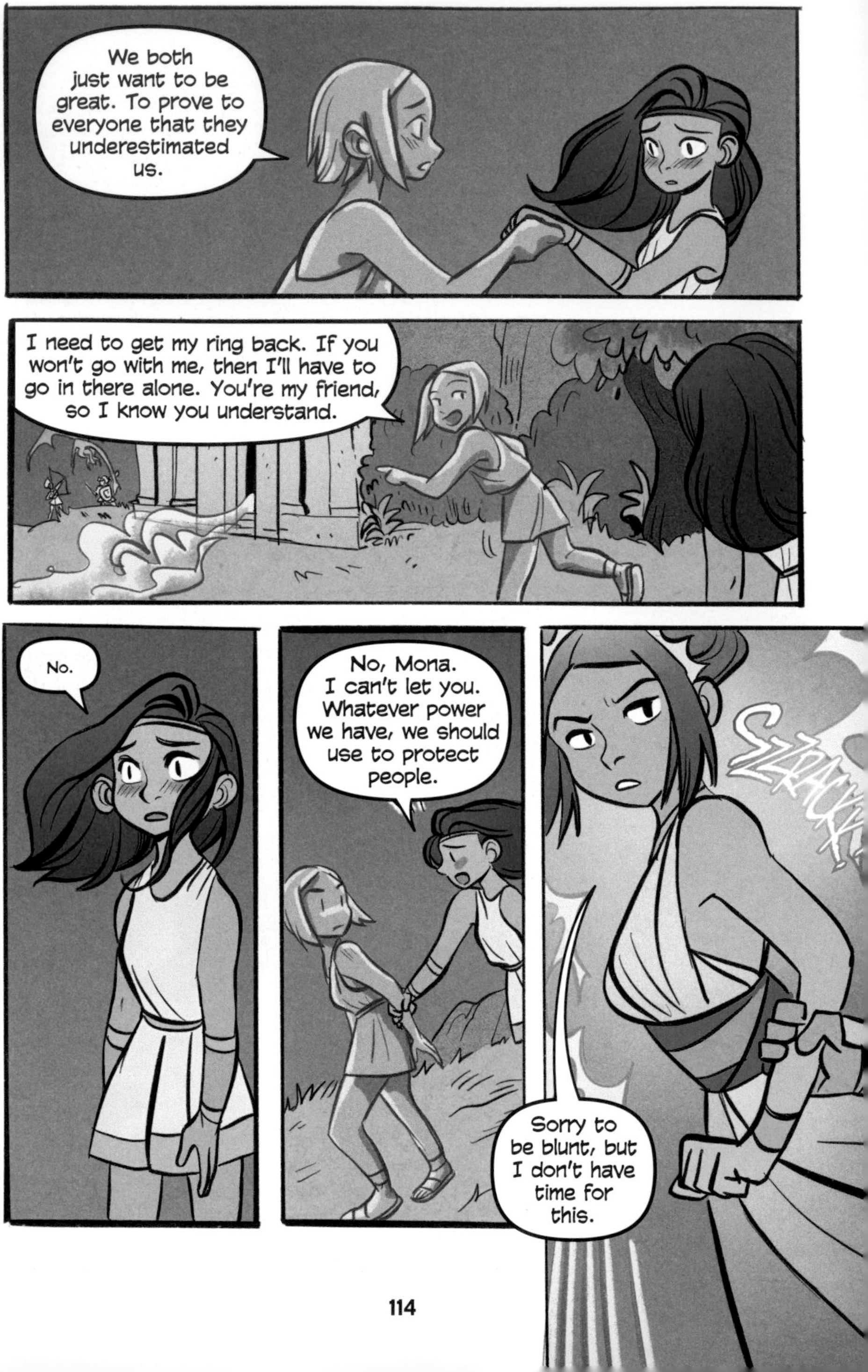
We both just want to be great. To prove to everyone that they underestimated us.
I need to get my ring back. If you won't go with me, then I'll have to go in there alone. You're my friend, so I know you understand.
No.
No, Mona. I can't let you. Whatever power we have, we should use to protect people.
SZZRACKK!
Sorry to be blunt, but I don't have time for this.

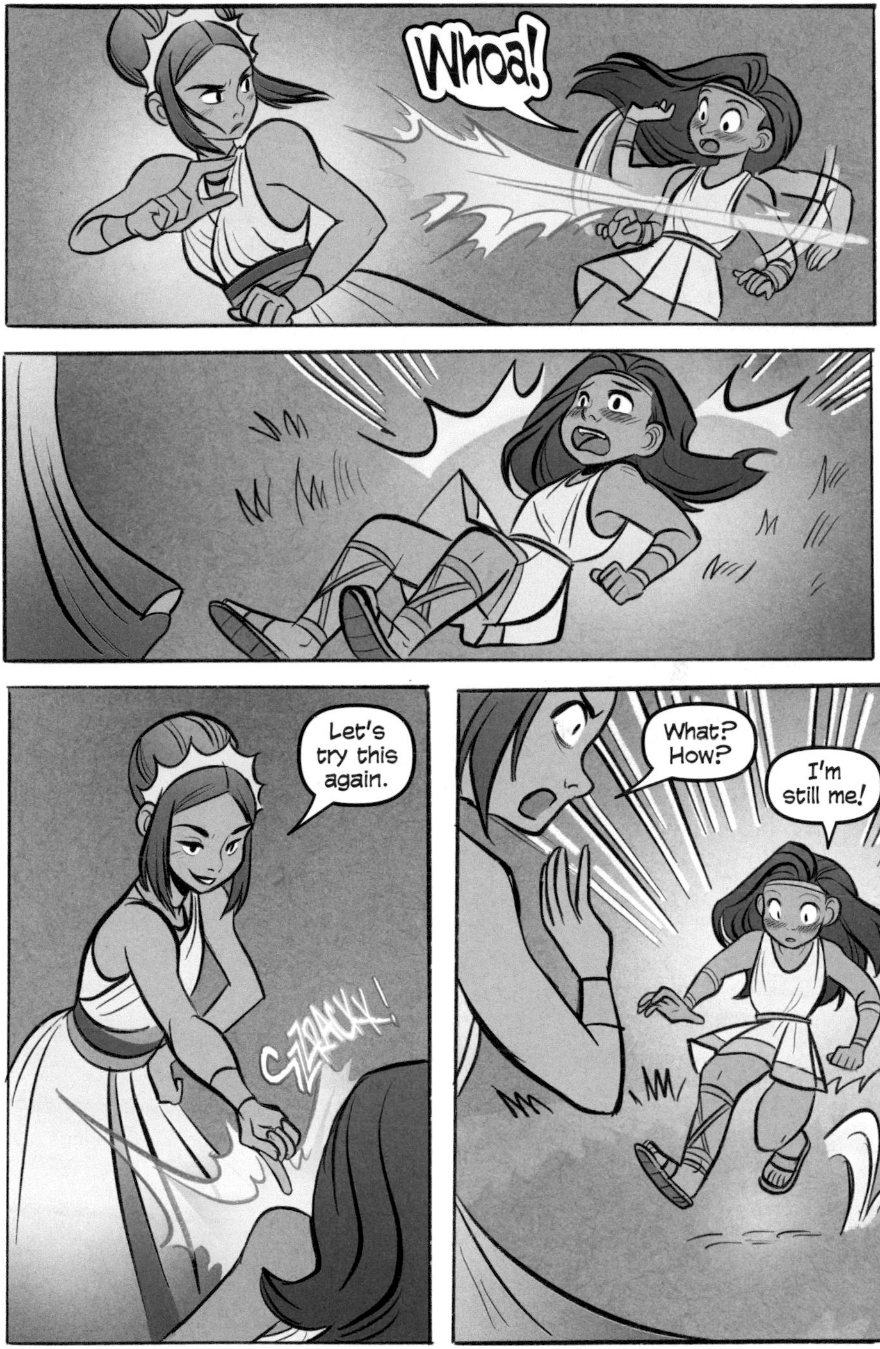
Whoa!
Let's try this again.
What? How?
I'm still me!

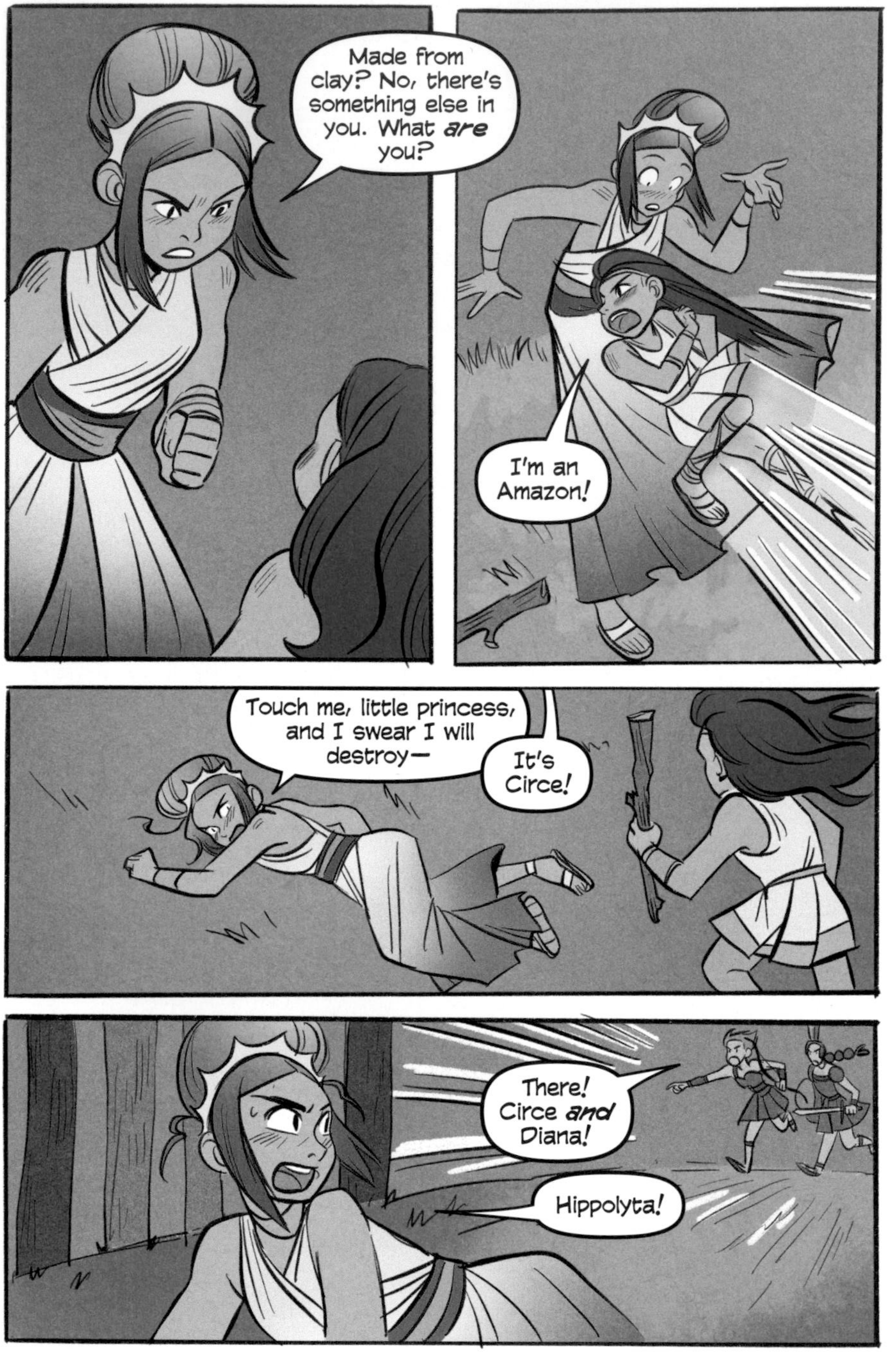

Made from clay? No, there's something else in you. What *are* you?
I'm an Amazon!
Touch me, little princess, and I swear I will destroy—
It's Circe!
There! Circe *and* Diana!
Hippolyta!

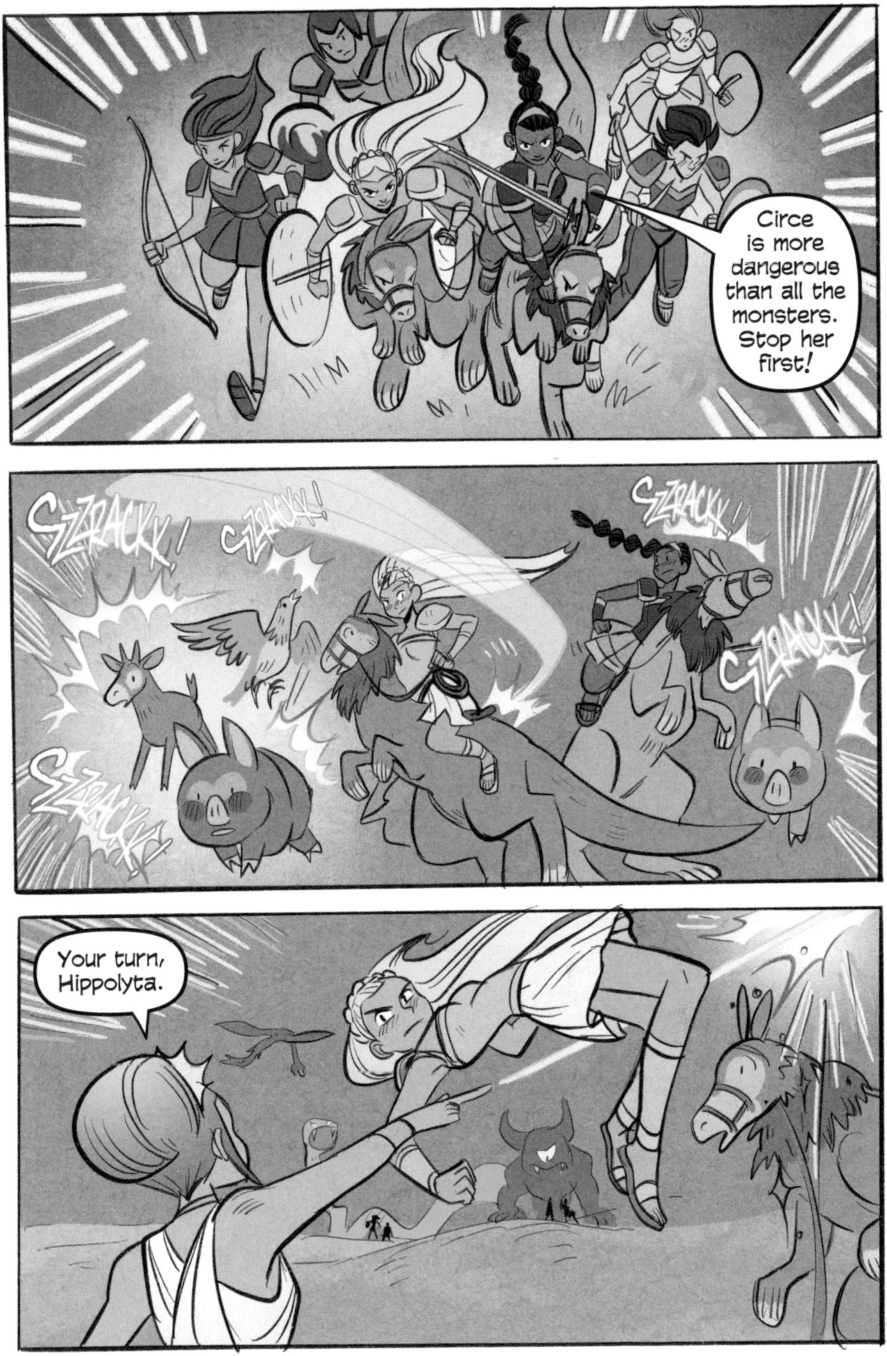
Circe is more dangerous than all the monsters. Stop her first!
SZZRACKK!
SZZRACKK!
SZZRACKK!
SZZRACKK!
SZZRACKK!
Your turn, Hippolyta.

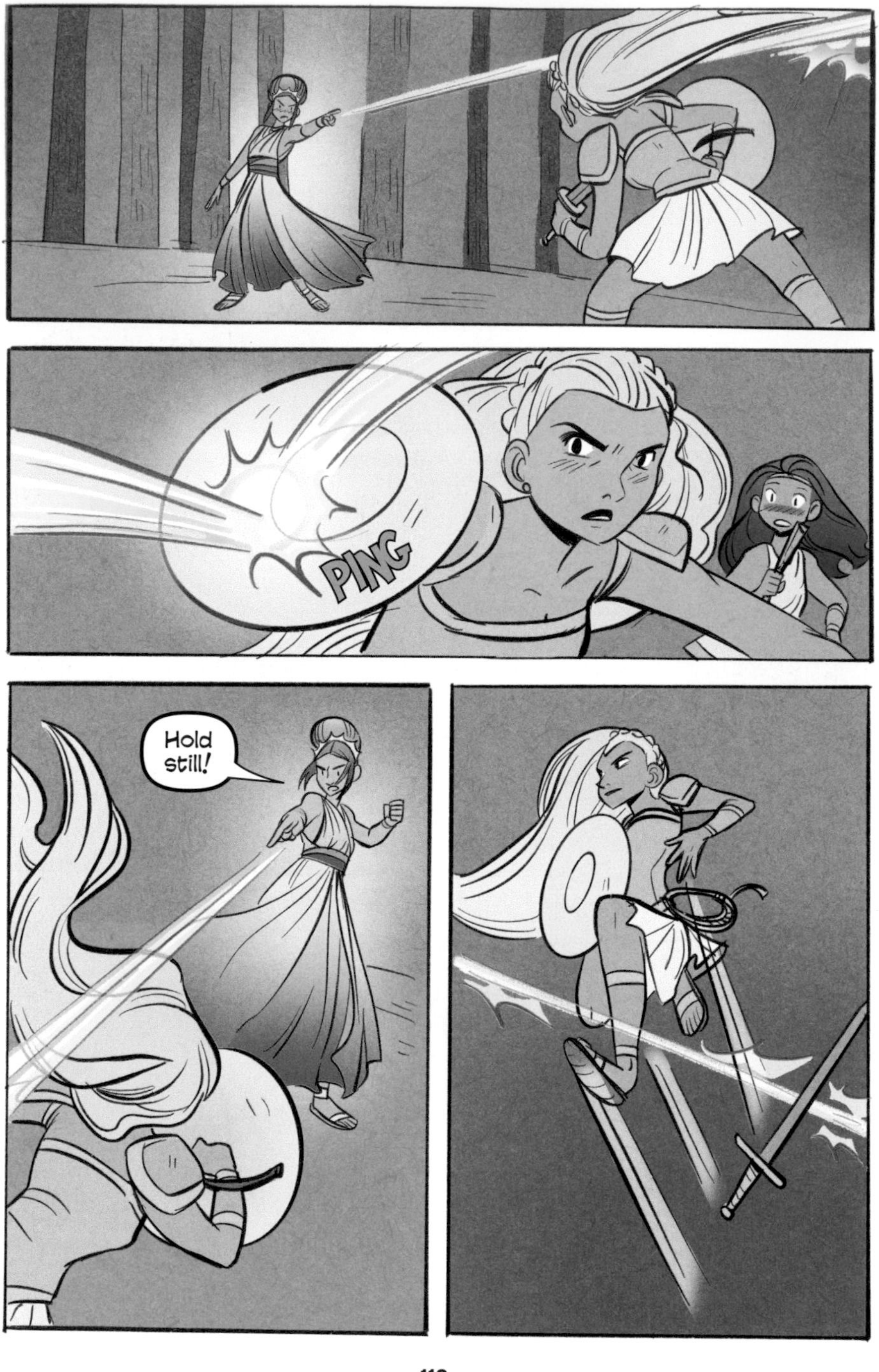
PING
Hold still!

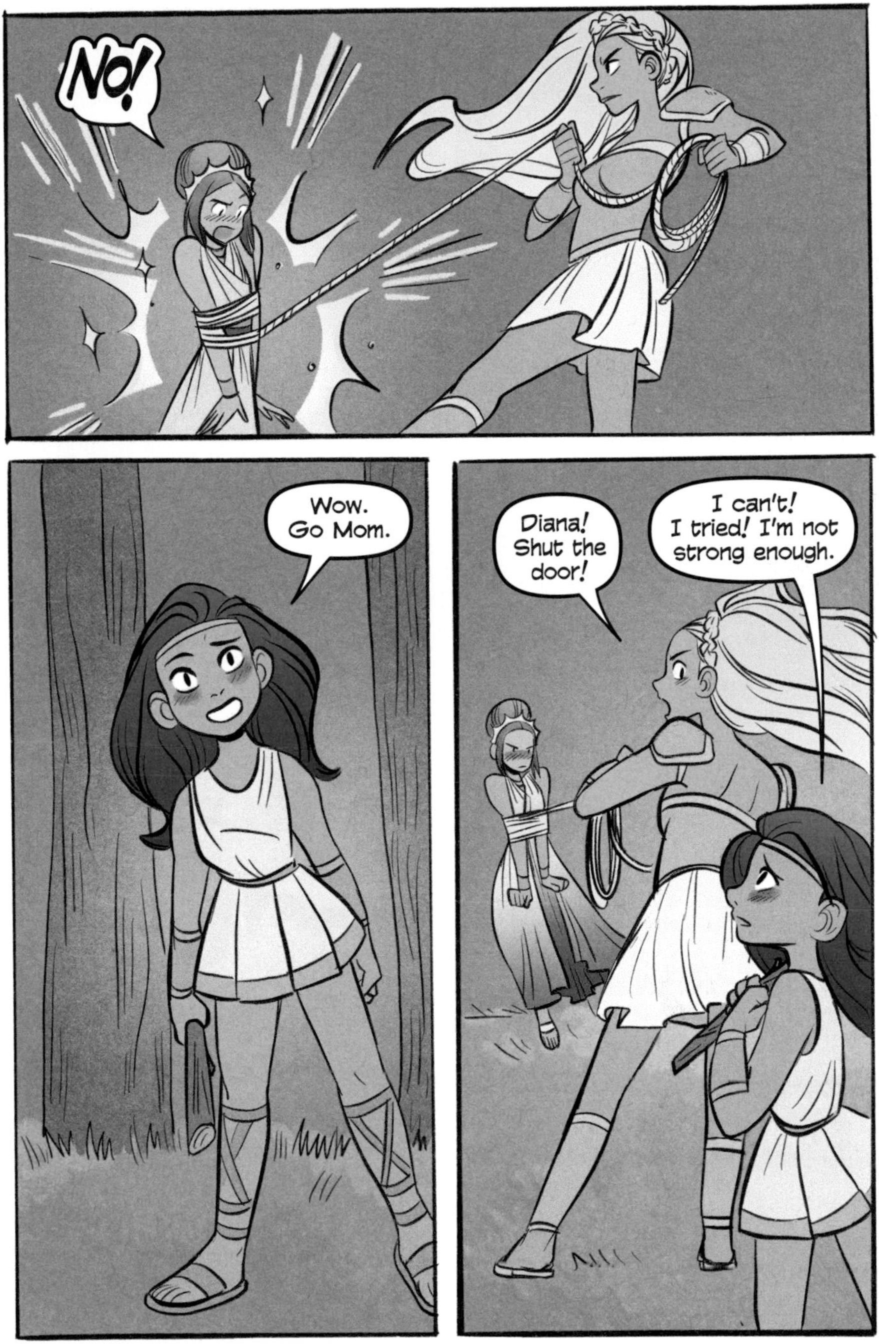
NO!
Wow. Go Mom.
Diana! Shut the door!
I can't! I tried! I'm not strong enough.

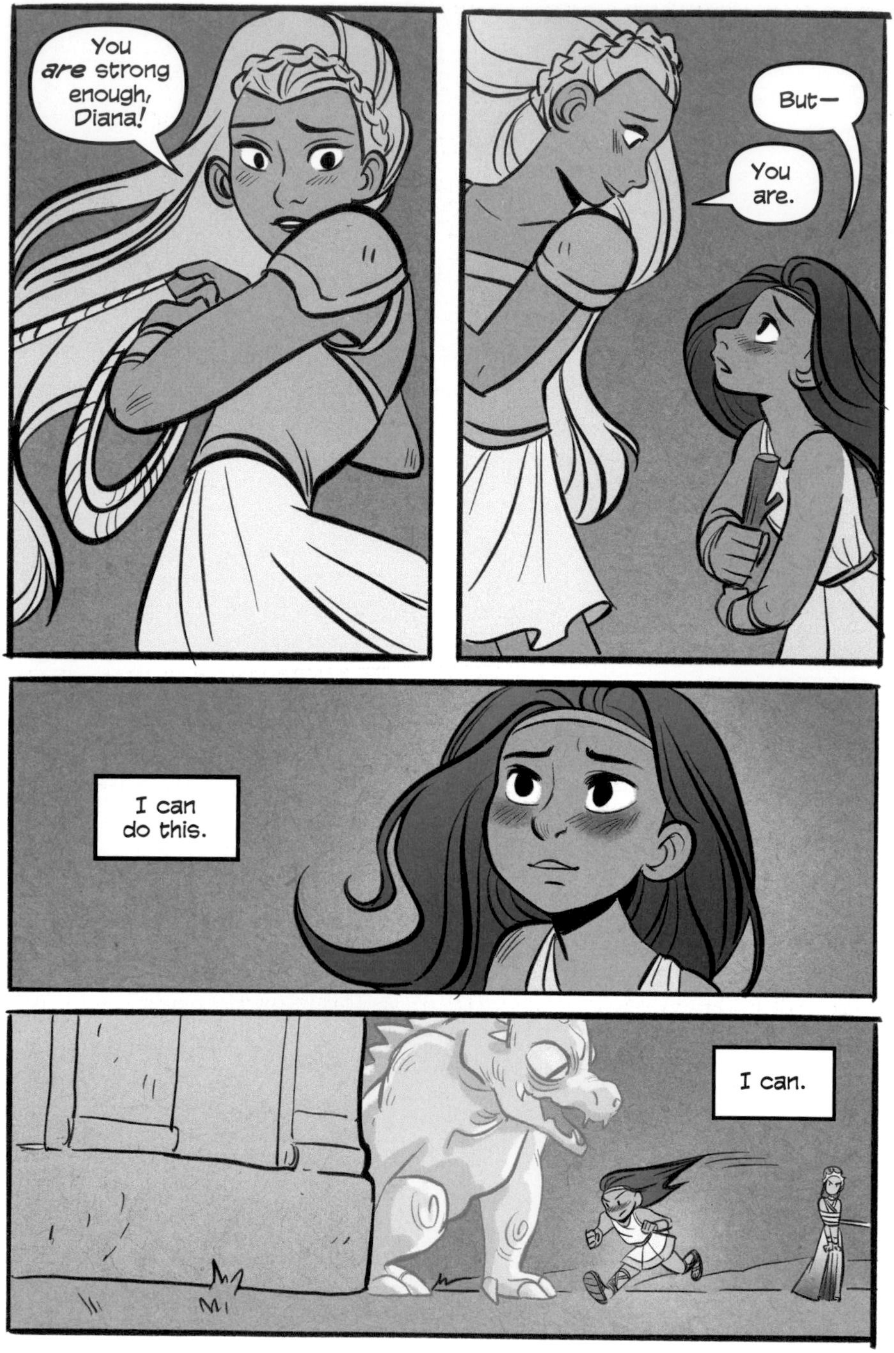
You *are* strong enough, Diana!
But—
You are.
I can do this.
I can.

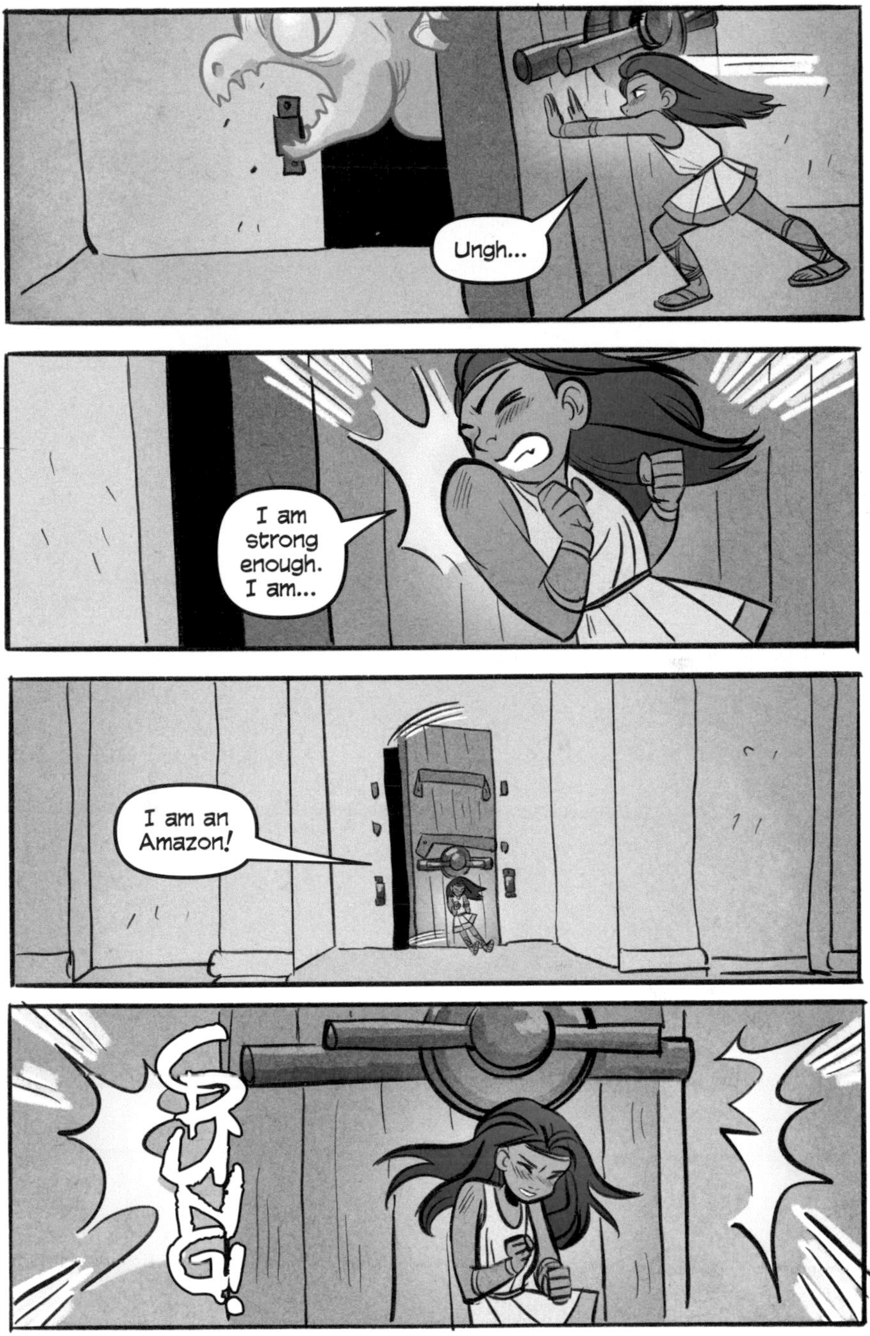
Ungh...
I am strong enough. I am...
I am an Amazon!
CRUNG!

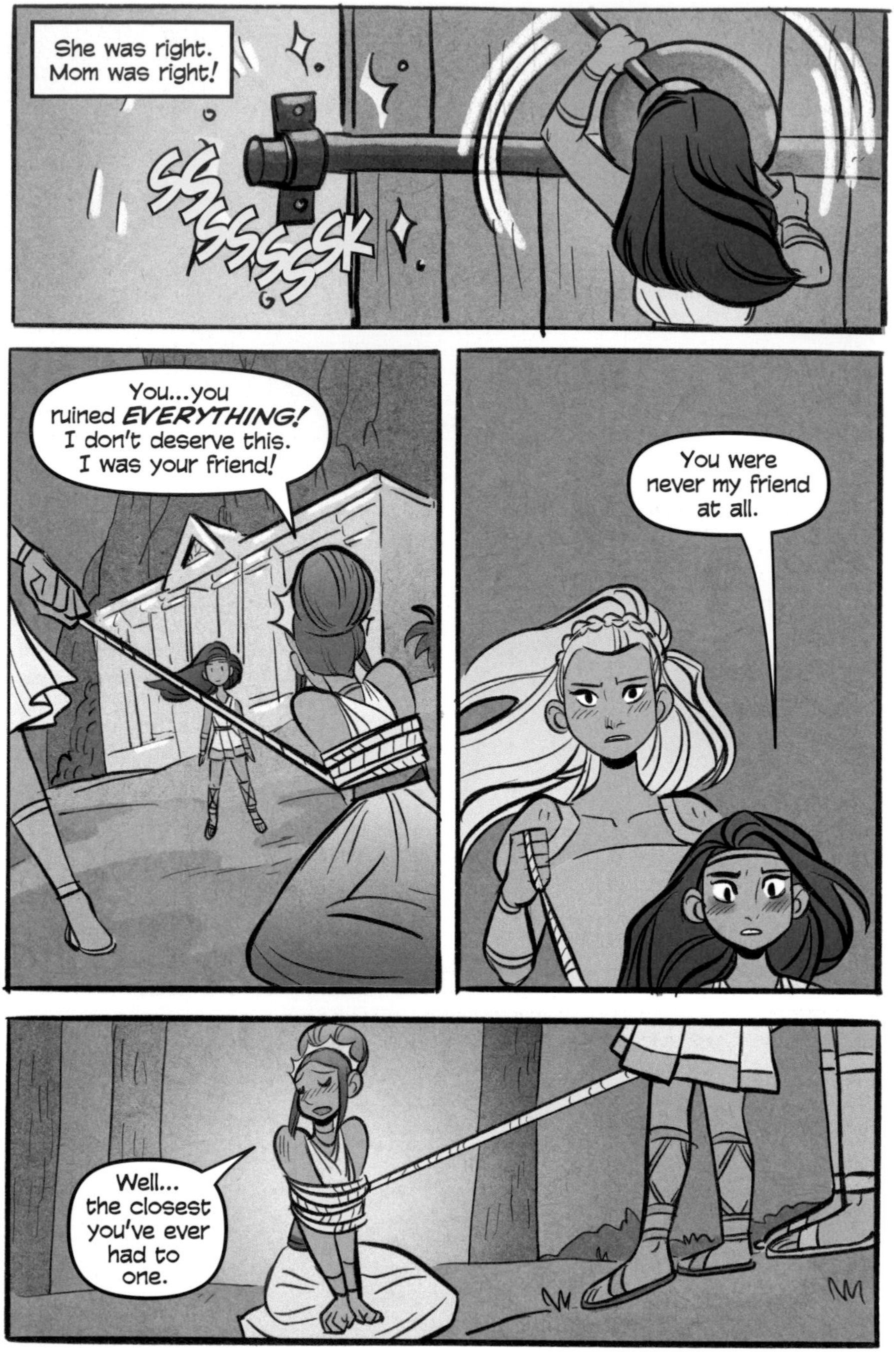
She was right. Mom was right!
SSSSSSSSK
You...you ruined EVERYTHING! I don't deserve this. I was your friend!
You were never my friend at all.
Well... the closest you've ever had to one.

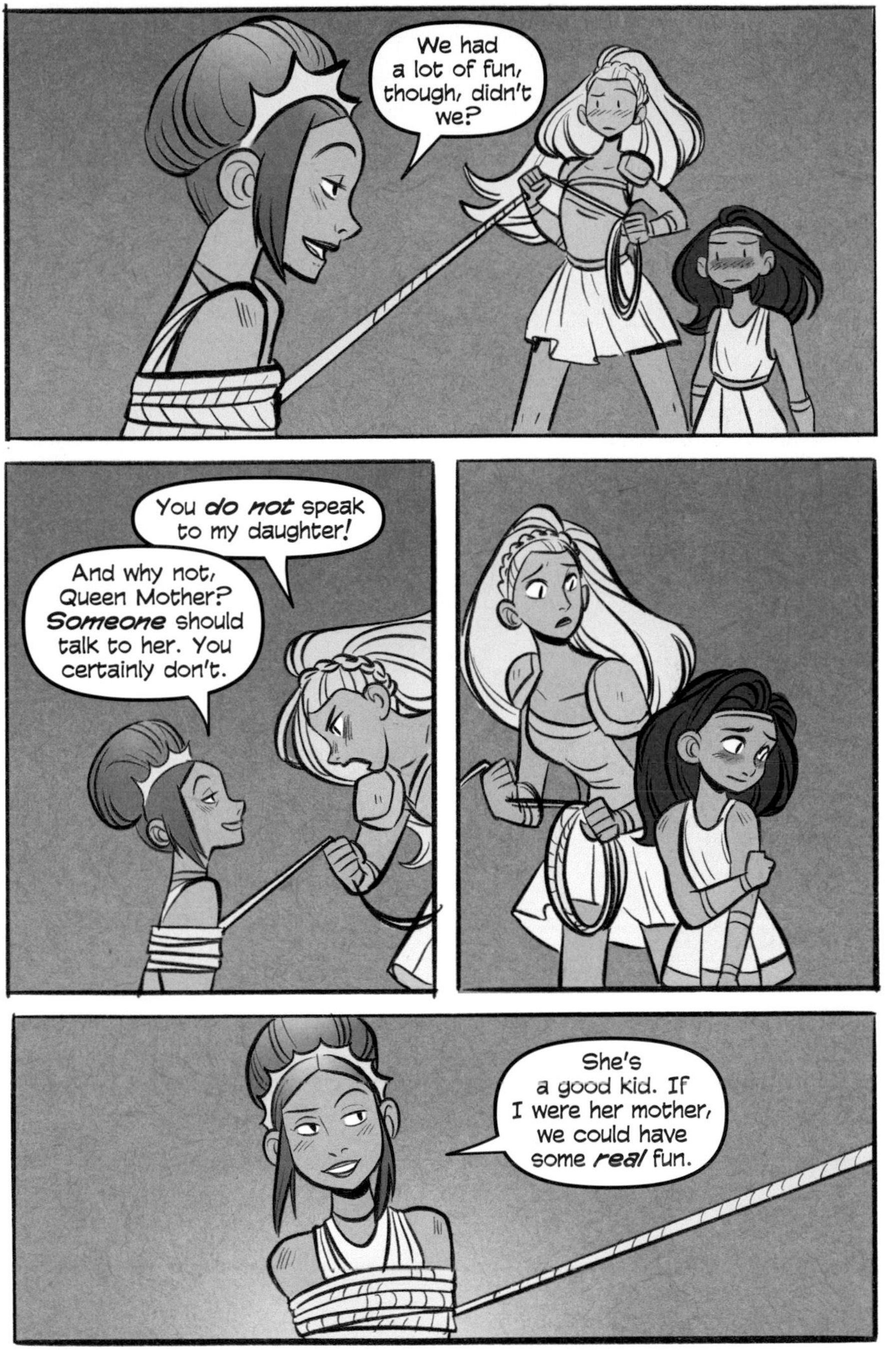
We had a lot of fun, though, didn't we?
You *do not* speak to my daughter!
And why not, Queen Mother? *Someone* should talk to her. You certainly don't.
She's a good kid. If I were her mother, we could have some *real* fun.

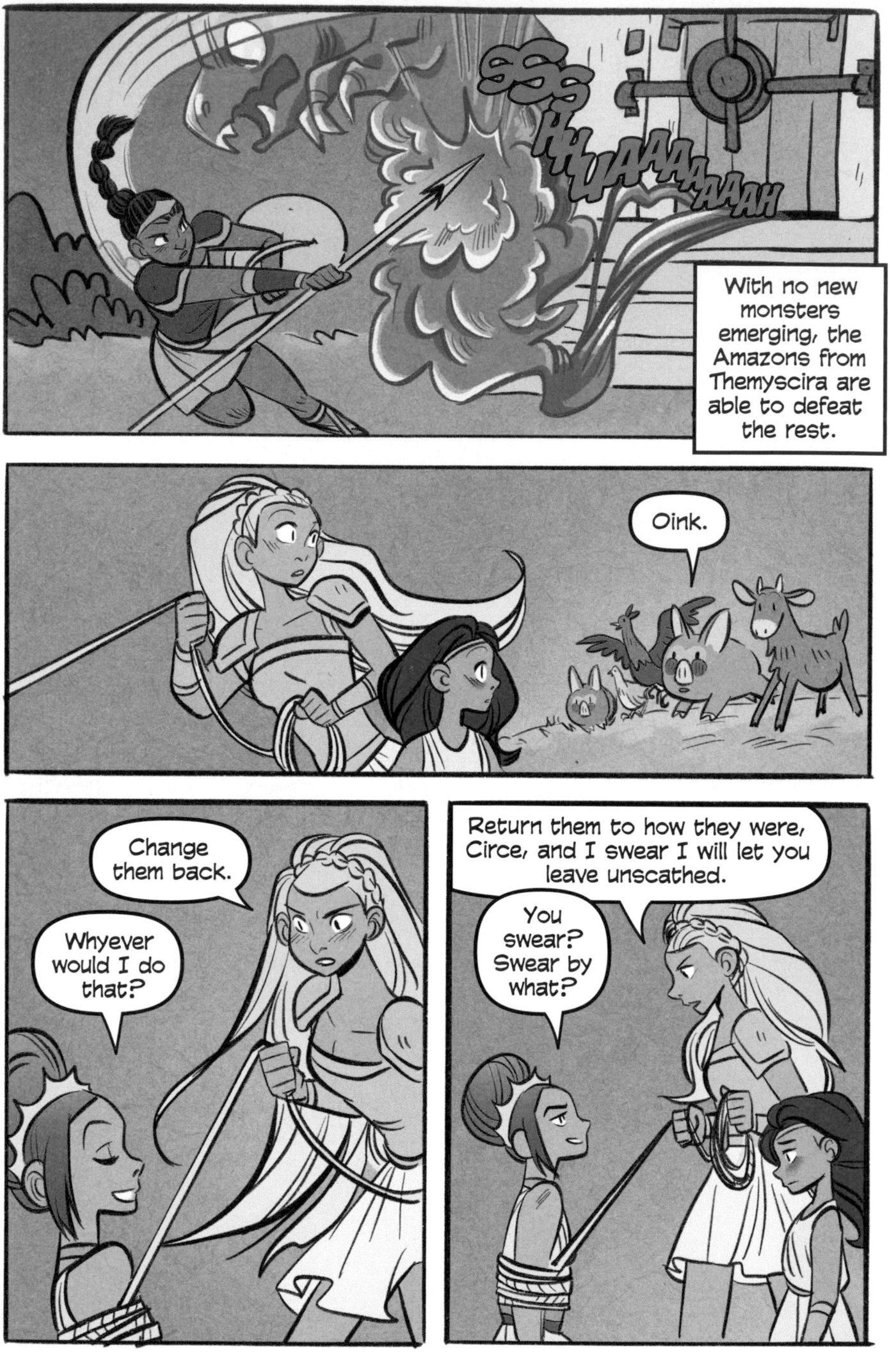
SSSHHUAAAAAAAAH
With no new monsters emerging, the Amazons from Themyscira are able to defeat the rest.
Oink.
Change them back.
Whyever would I do that?
Return them to how they were, Circe, and I swear I will let you leave unscathed.
You swear? Swear by what?

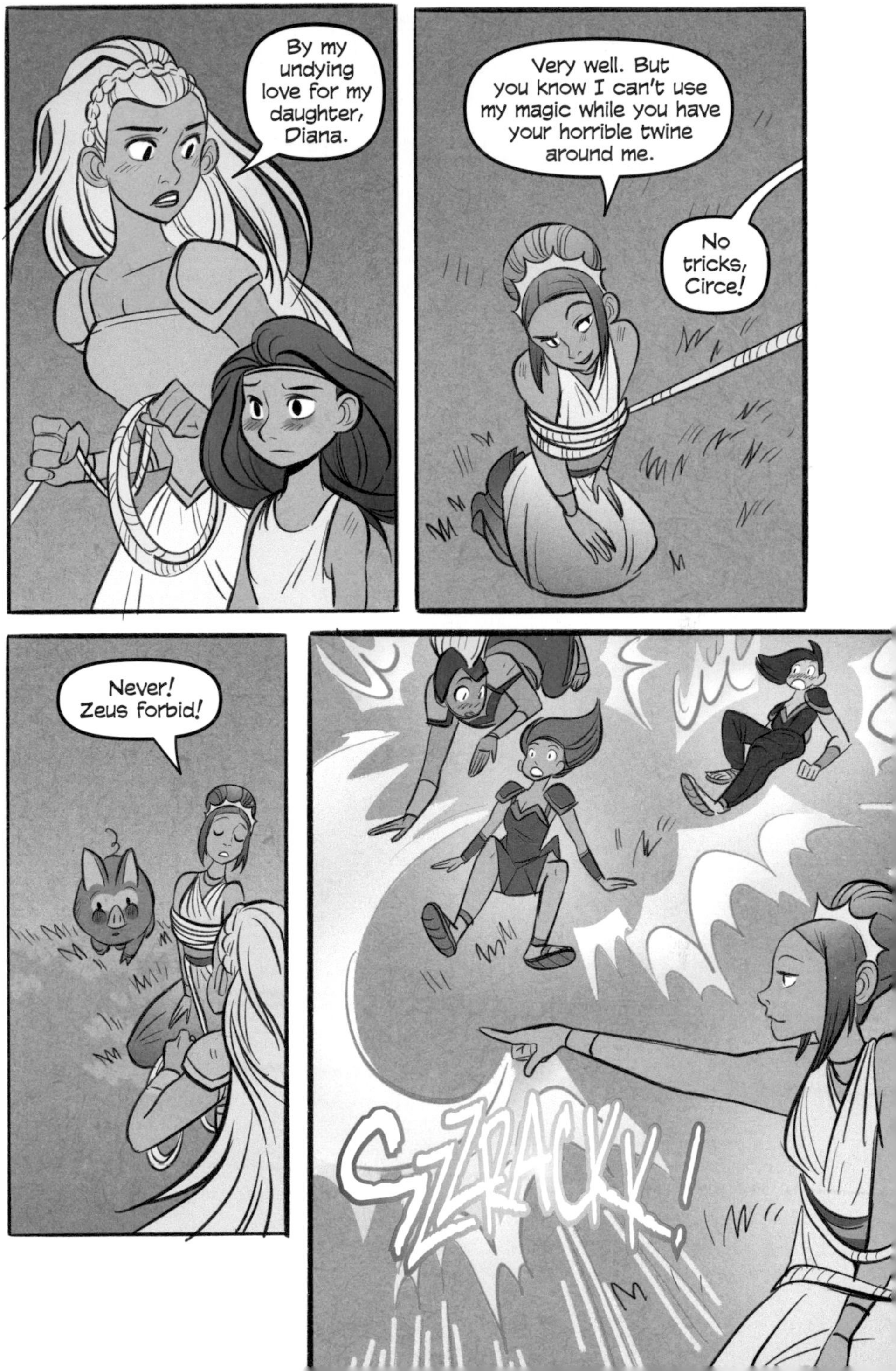
By my undying love for my daughter, Diana.
Very well. But you know I can't use my magic while you have your horrible twine around me.
No tricks, Circe!
Never! Zeus forbid!
SZZRACKK!

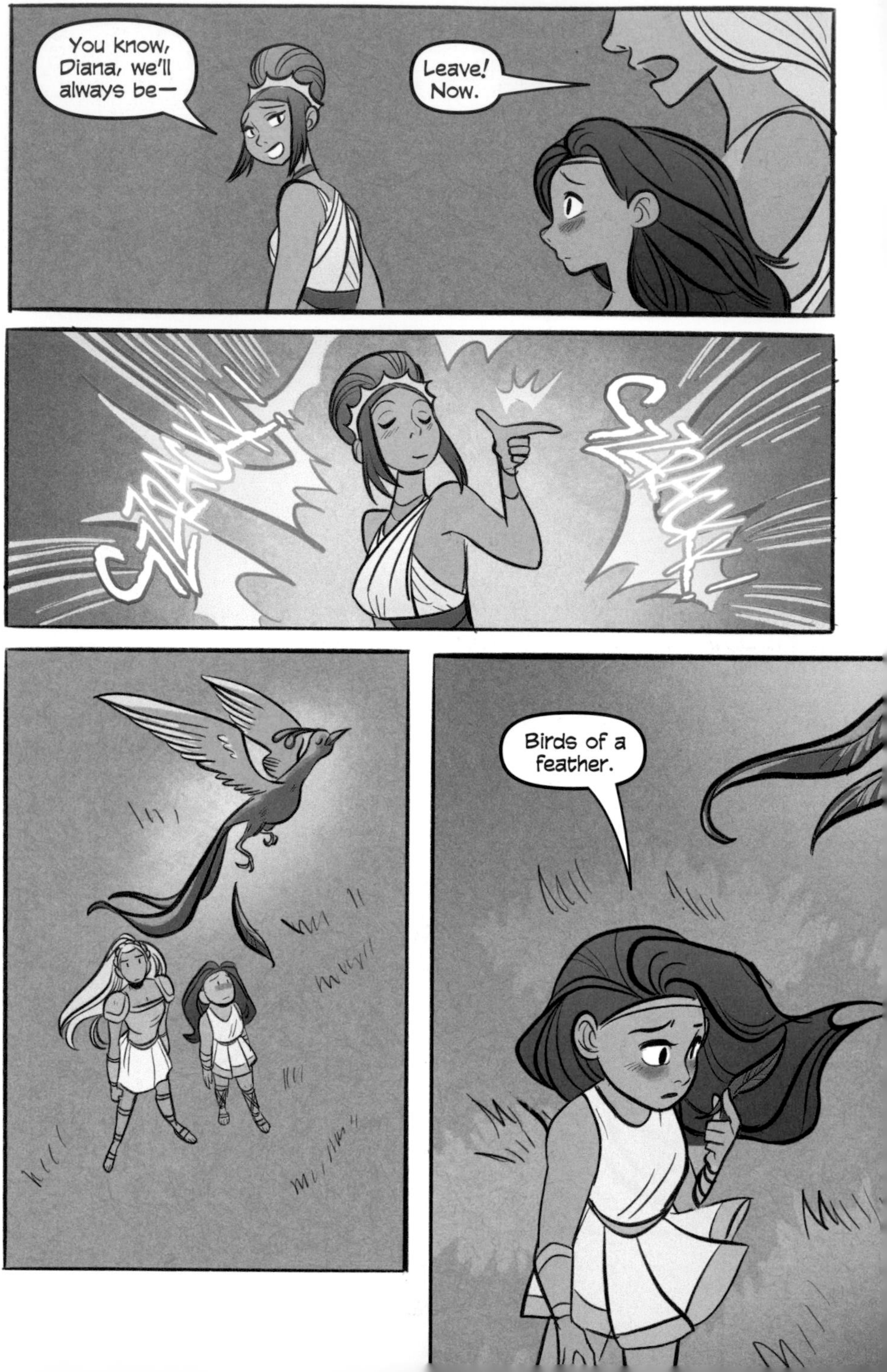
You know, Diana, we'll always be—
Leave! Now.
SZZACK!
SZZACK!
Birds of a feather.

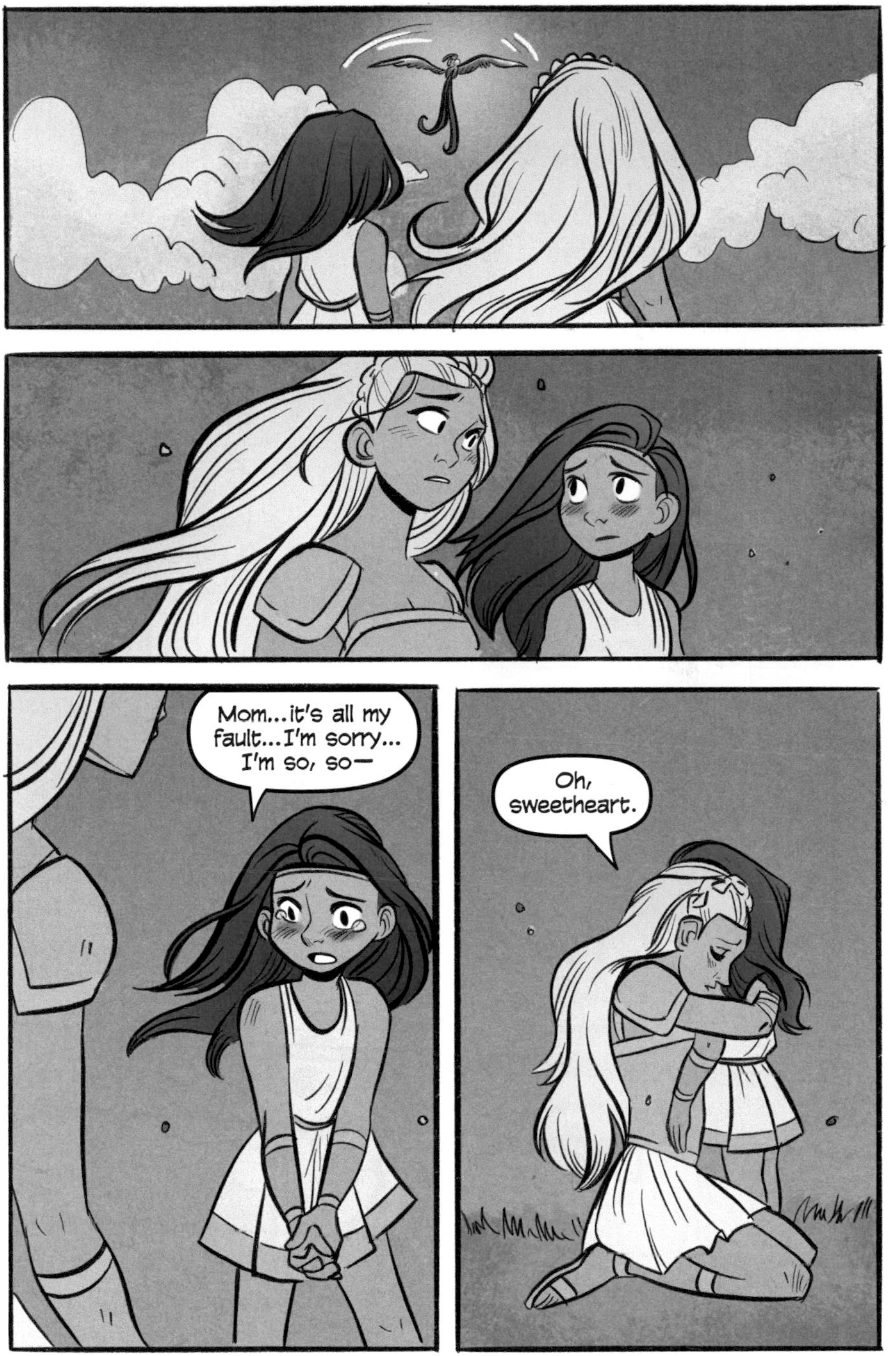
Mom...it's all my fault...I'm sorry... I'm so, so—
Oh, sweetheart.

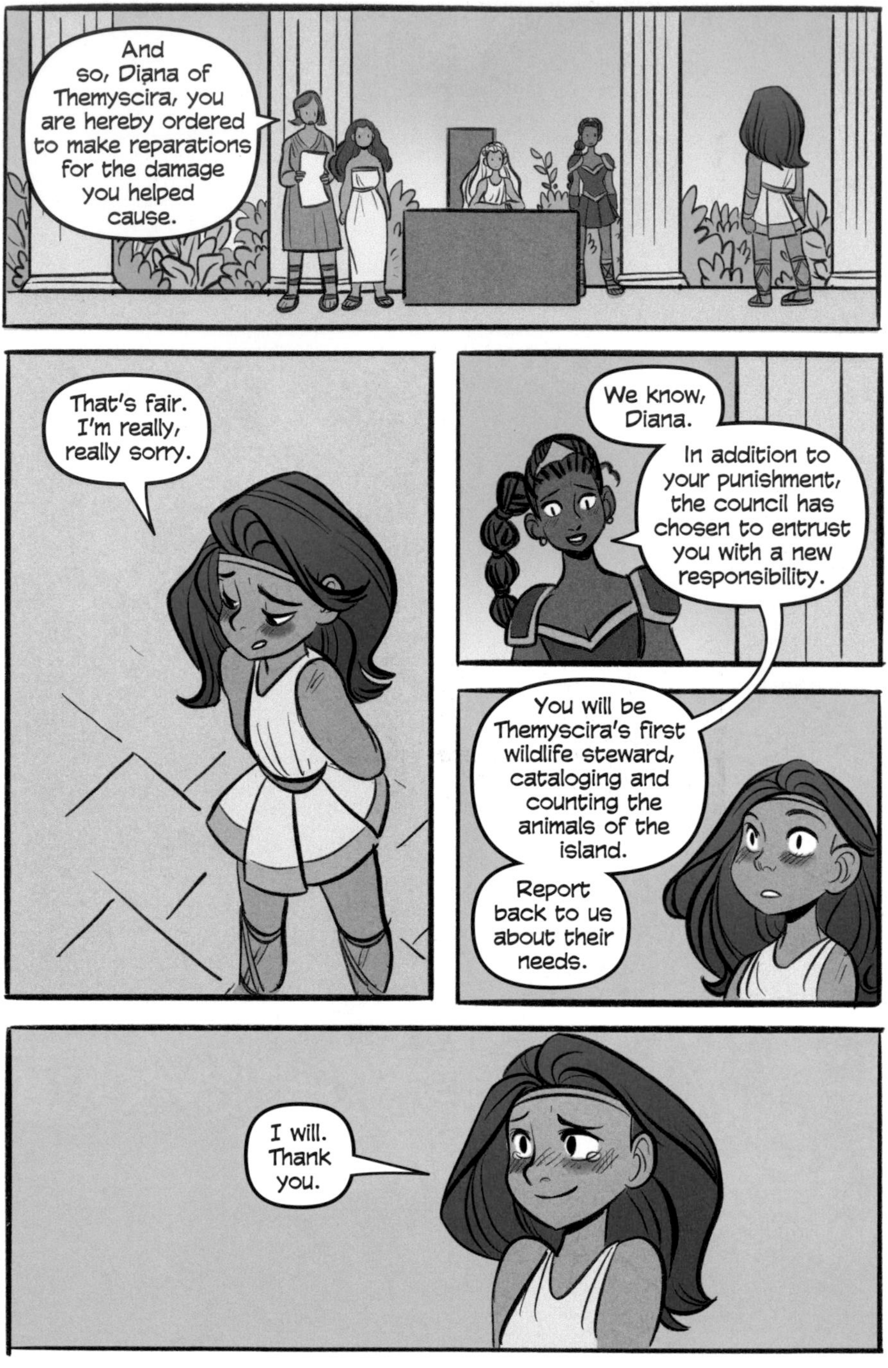

And so, Diana of Themyscira, you are hereby ordered to make reparations for the damage you helped cause.
That's fair. I'm really, really sorry.
We know, Diana.
In addition to your punishment, the council has chosen to entrust you with a new responsibility.
You will be Themyscira's first wildlife steward, cataloging and counting the animals of the island.
Report back to us about their needs.
I will. Thank you.

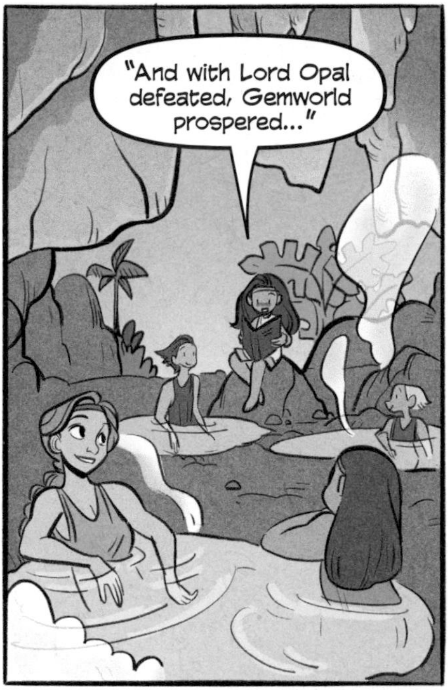
"And with Lord Opal defeated, Gemworld prospered..."
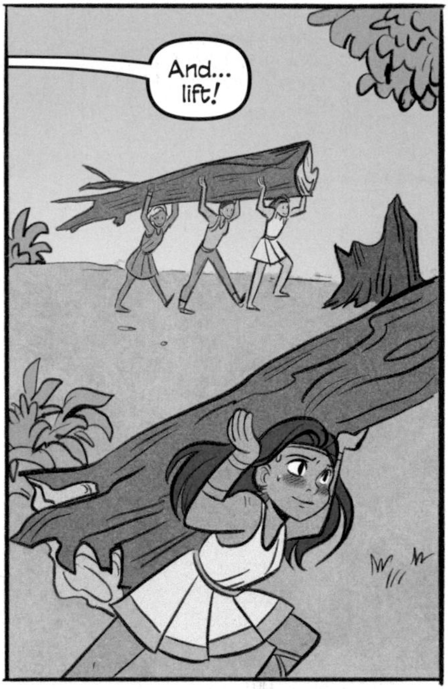
And... lift!
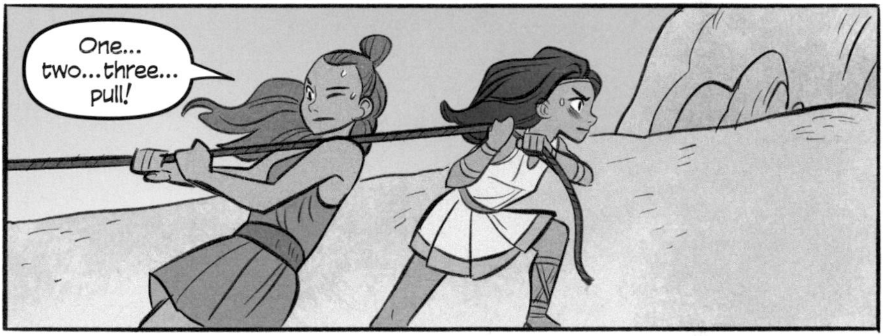
One... two...three... pull!
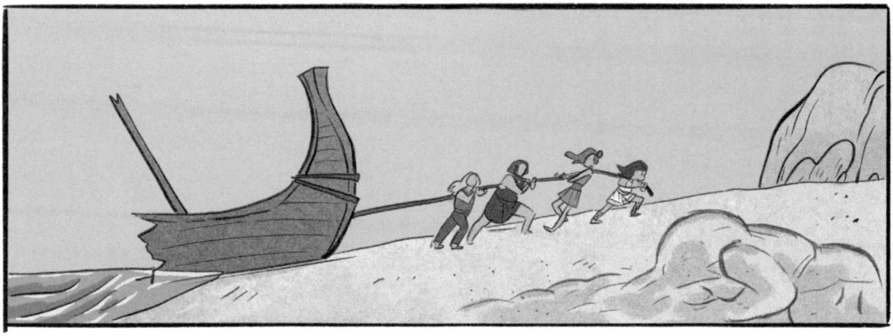

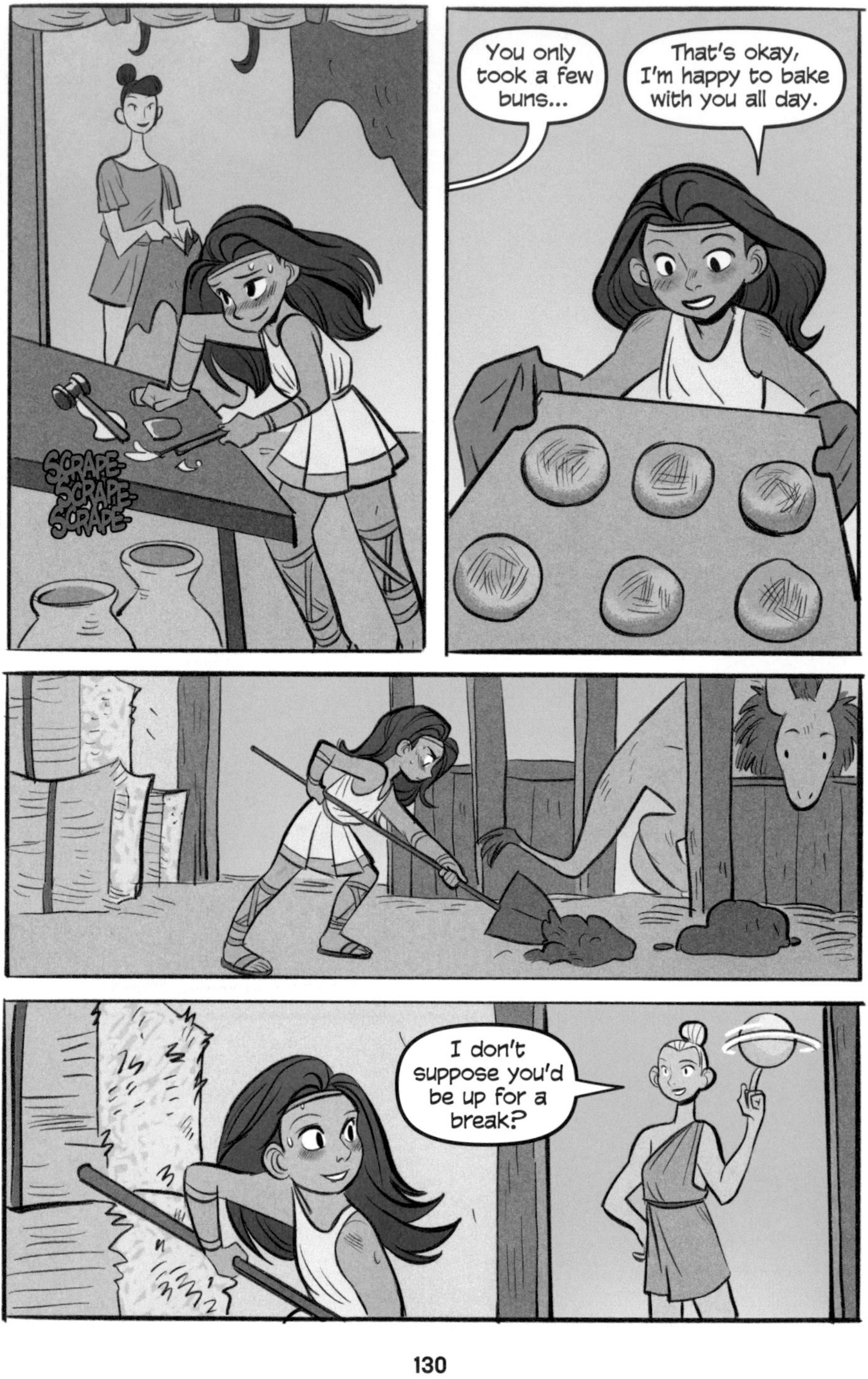
SCRAPE-
SCRAPE-
SCRAPE-
You only took a few buns...
That's okay, I'm happy to bake with you all day.
I don't suppose you'd be up for a break?

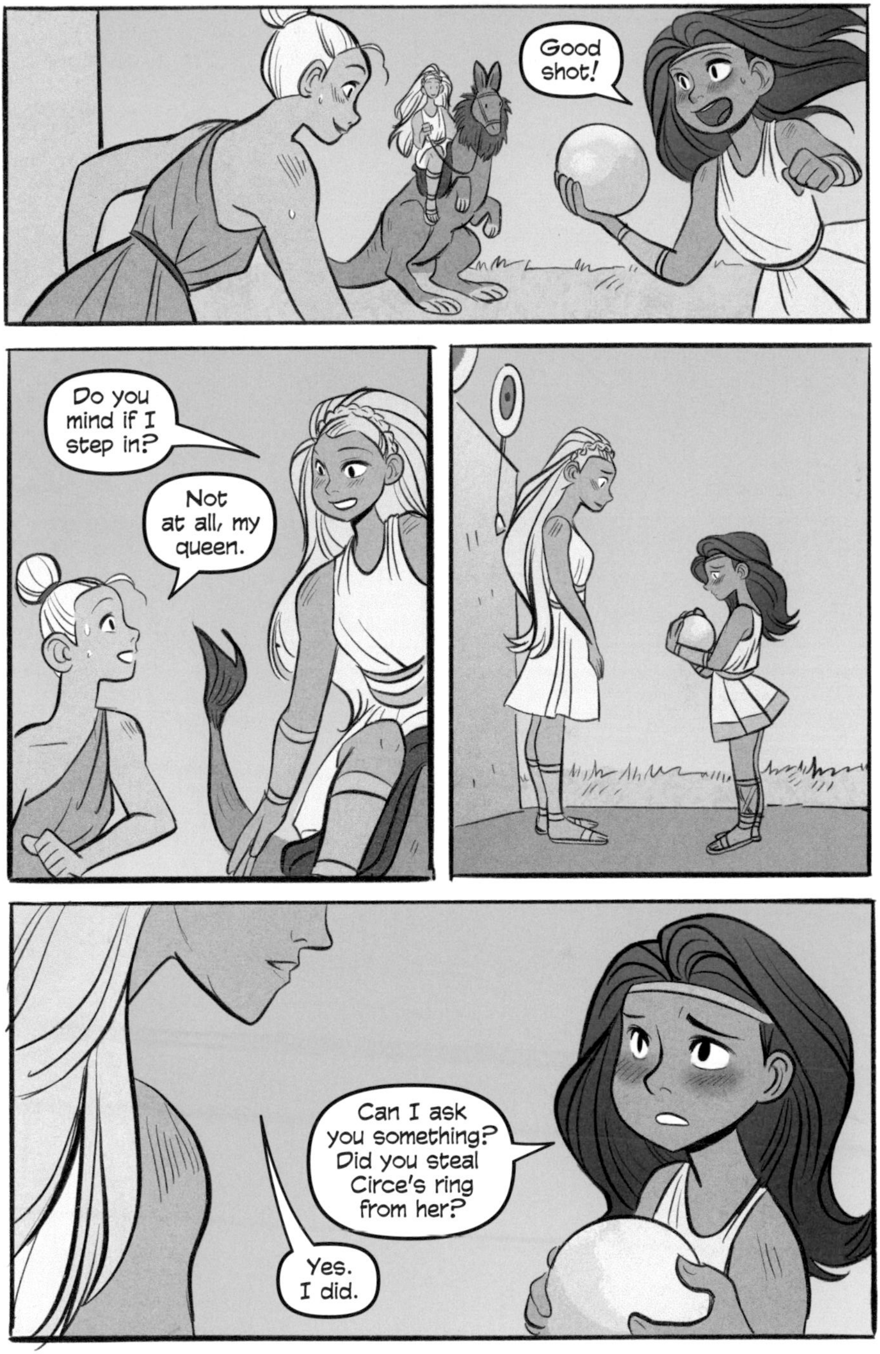
Good shot!
Do you mind if I step in?
Not at all, my queen.
Can I ask you something? Did you steal Circe's ring from her?
Yes. I did.

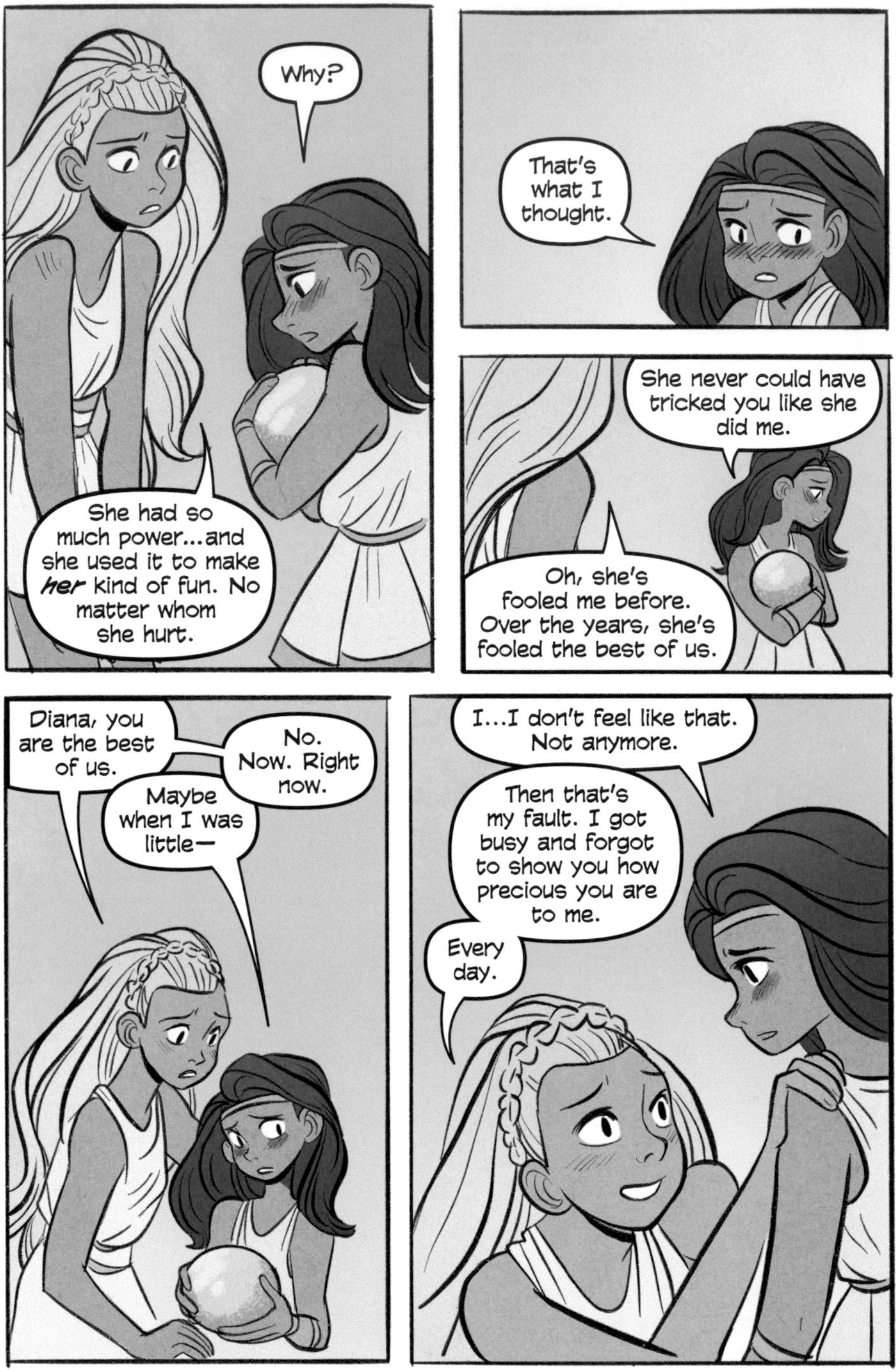
Why?
She had so much power...and she used it to make *her* kind of fun. No matter whom she hurt.
That's what I thought.
She never could have tricked you like she did me.
Oh, she's fooled me before. Over the years, she's fooled the best of us.
Diana, you are the best of us.
Maybe when I was little—
No. Now. Right now.
I...I don't feel like that. Not anymore.
Then that's my fault. I got busy and forgot to show you how precious you are to me.
Every day.

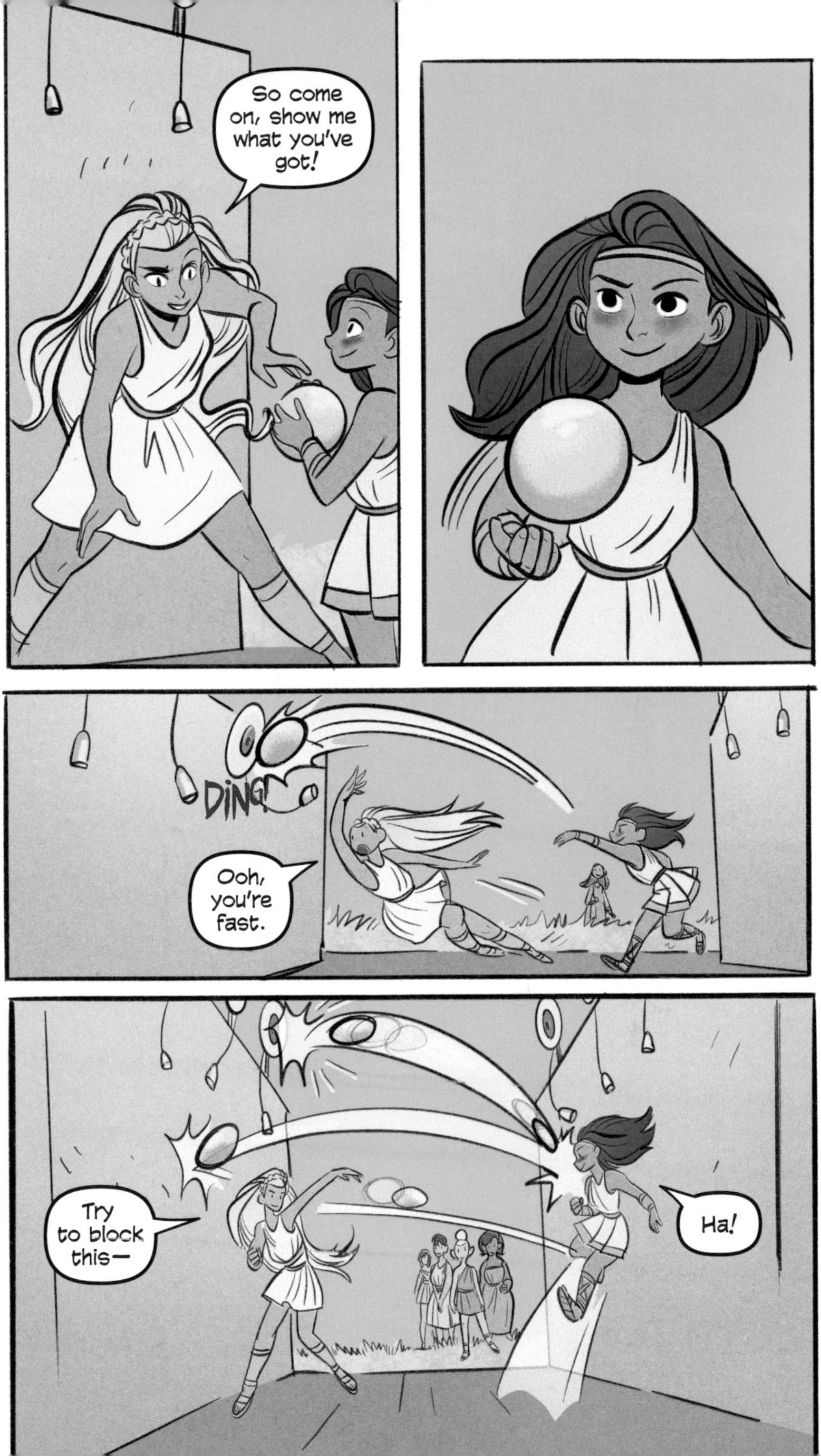
So come on, show me what you've got!
DING!
Ooh, you're fast.
Try to block this—
Ha!

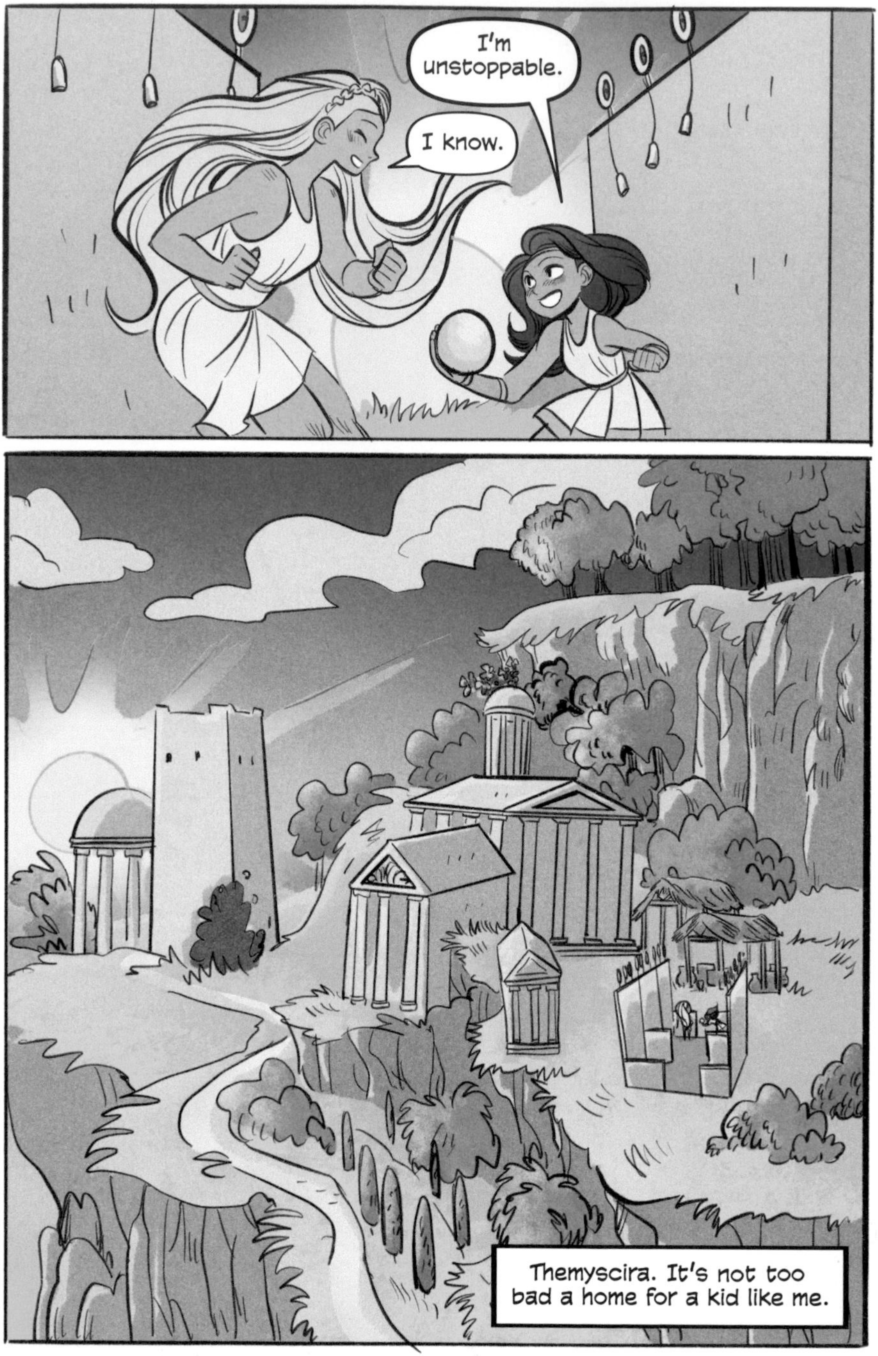
I'm unstoppable.
I know.
Themyscira. It's not too bad a home for a kid like me.

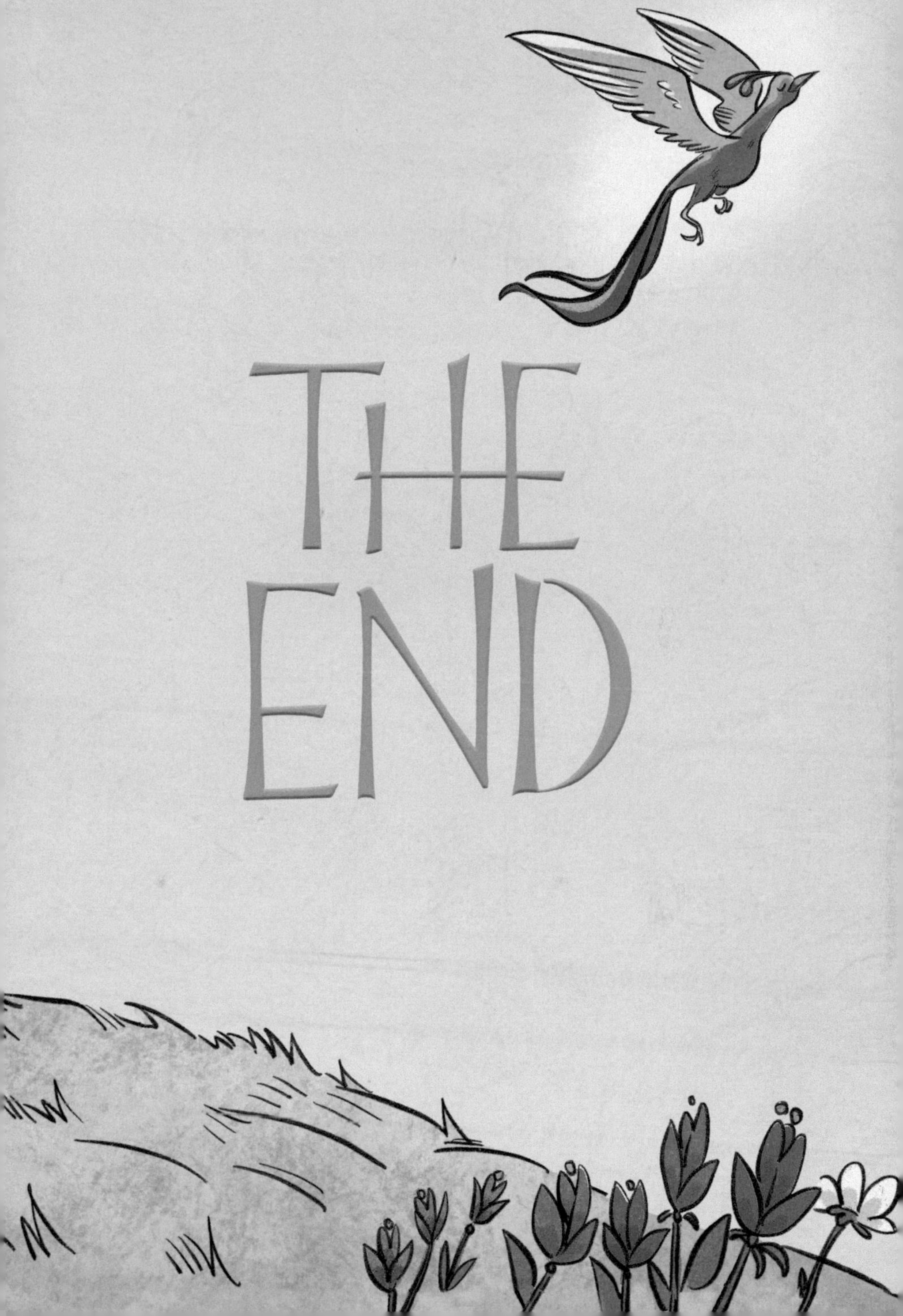
THE END

Shannon and Dean Hale are the husband-and-wife writing team behind Eisner nominee *Rapunzel's Revenge* (illustrated by Nathan Hale), *New York Times* bestselling series *The Princess in Black* (illustrated by LeUyen Pham), and two novels about Marvel's Squirrel Girl. Shannon Hale is also the author of the Newbery Honor-winning novel *Princess Academy*, the *USA Today* bestselling *Ever After High* series, the graphic novel memoir *Real Friends*, and others. Shannon and Dean live in Utah with their four children, who all agree that Wonder Woman is one of the greatest superheroes of all time.

Victoria Ying is an author and artist living in Los Angeles. She started her career in the arts by falling in love with comic books, which eventually turned into a career working in animation. She loves Japanese curry, putting things in her shopping cart online and taking them out again, and hanging out with her dopey dog. Her film credits include *Tangled*, *Wreck-It Ralph*, *Frozen*, *Paperman*, *Big Hero 6*, and *Moana*. She has illustrated several picture books including *Not Quite Black and White*; *Lost and Found, What's That Sound?*; and *Take a Ride By My Side*, and is the writer and illustrator of *Meow! Diana: Princess of the Amazons* is her debut graphic novel.

Lark Pien is an award-winning cartoonist and picture book author. She occasionally performs color work for unique comics that inspire. *Diana: Princess of the Amazons* is her first coloring project with an all-female cast! The naughty, the nice, the brave and capable, she's enjoyed coloring them all.

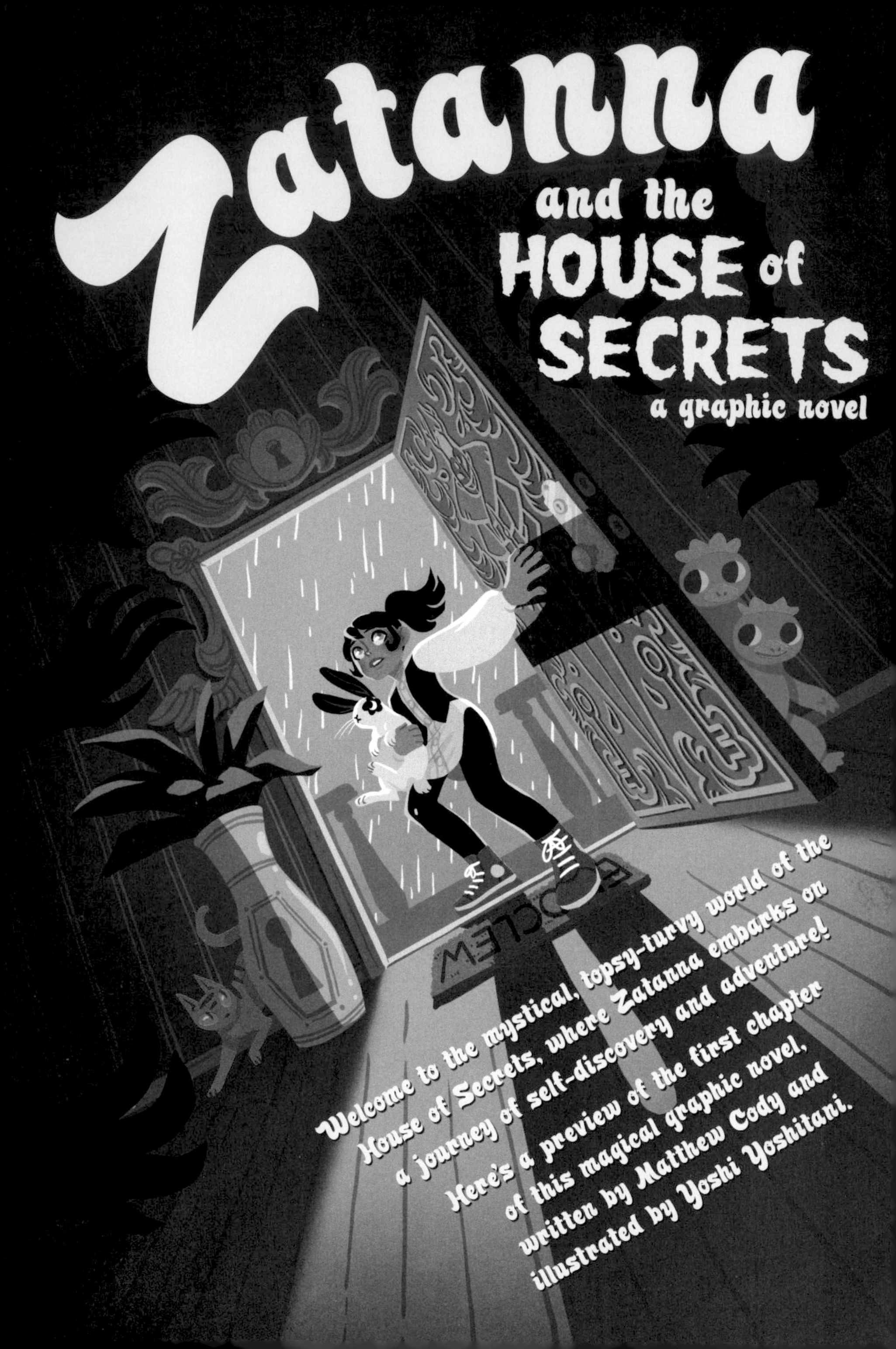
Zatanna
and the
HOUSE of
SECRETS
a graphic novel
Welcome to the mystical, topsy-turvy world of the House of Secrets, where Zatanna embarks on a journey of self-discovery and adventure!
Here's a preview of the first chapter of this magical graphic novel, written by Matthew Cody and illustrated by Yoshi Yoshitani.

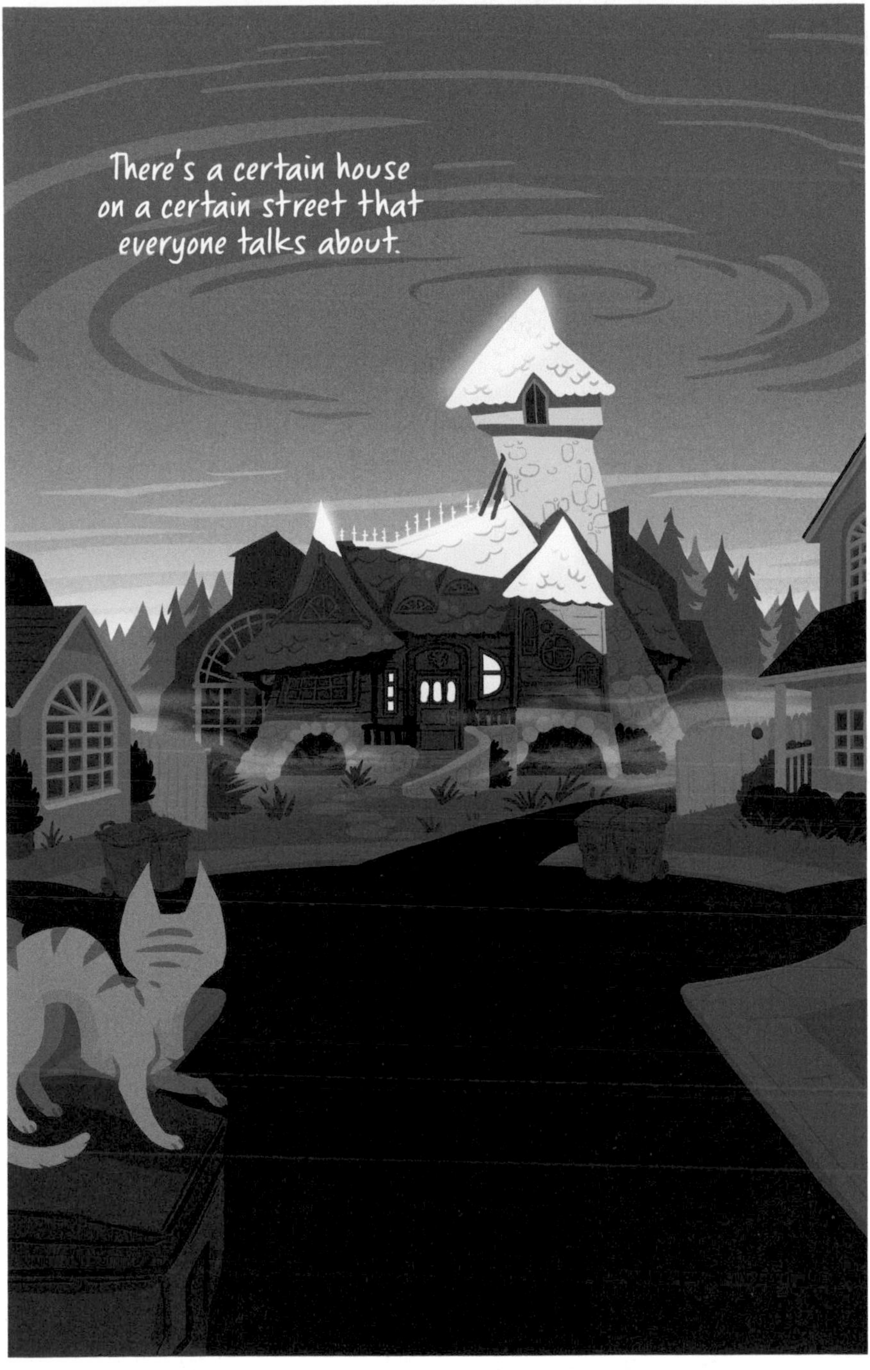
There's a certain house on a certain street that everyone talks about.

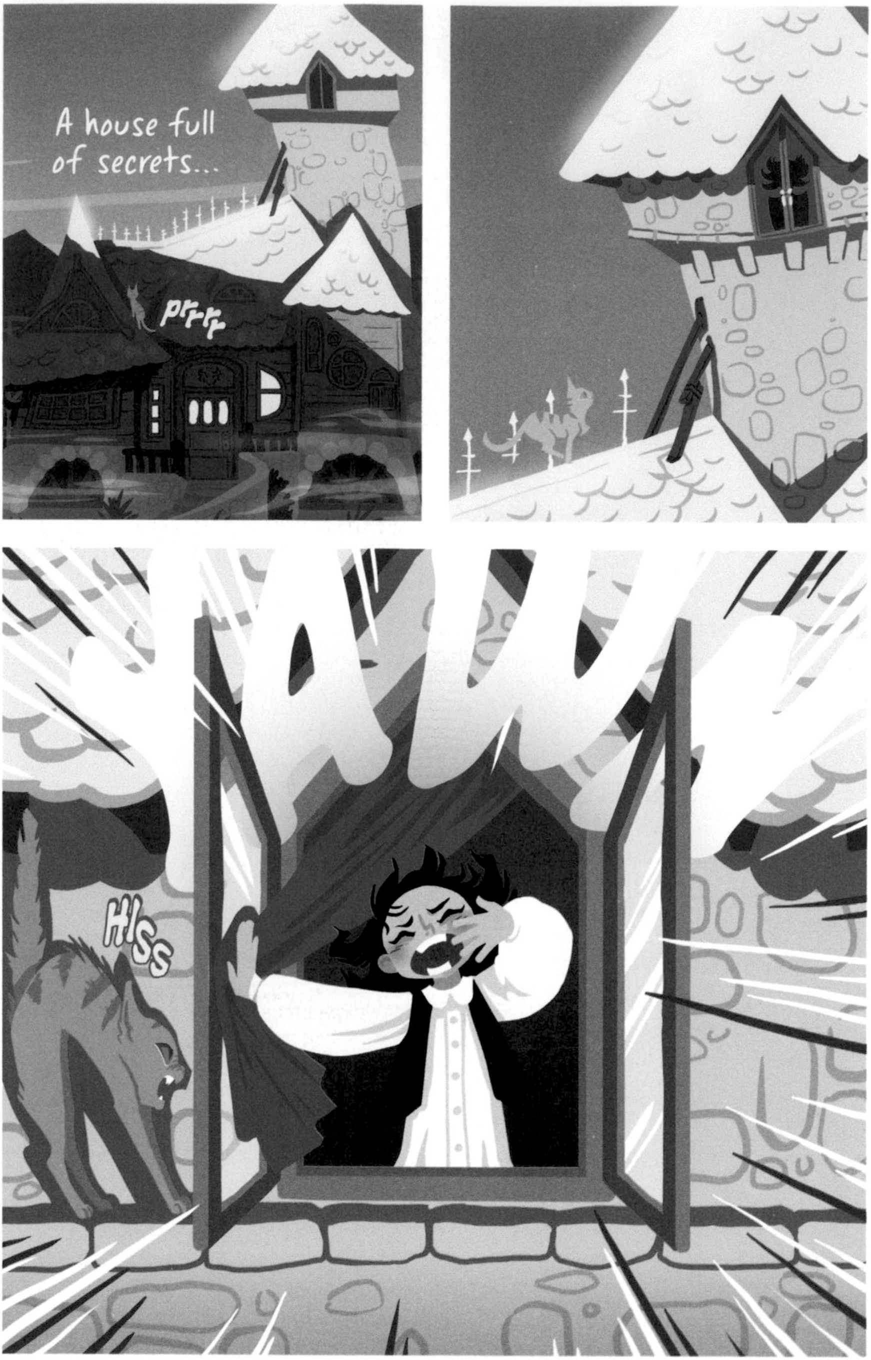
A house full of secrets...
prrrr
HISS

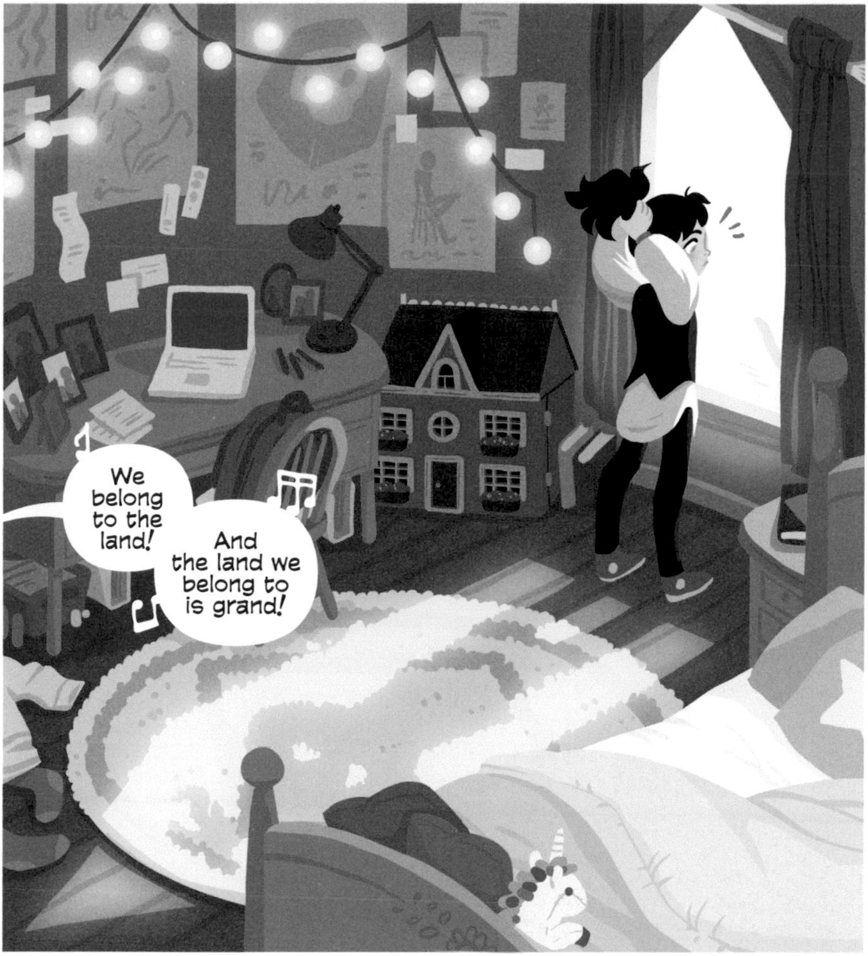
We belong to the land!
And the land we belong to is grand!

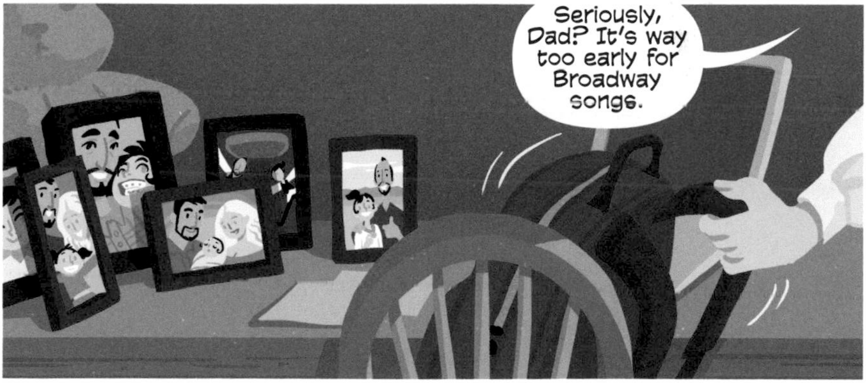
Seriously, Dad? It's way too early for Broadway songs.

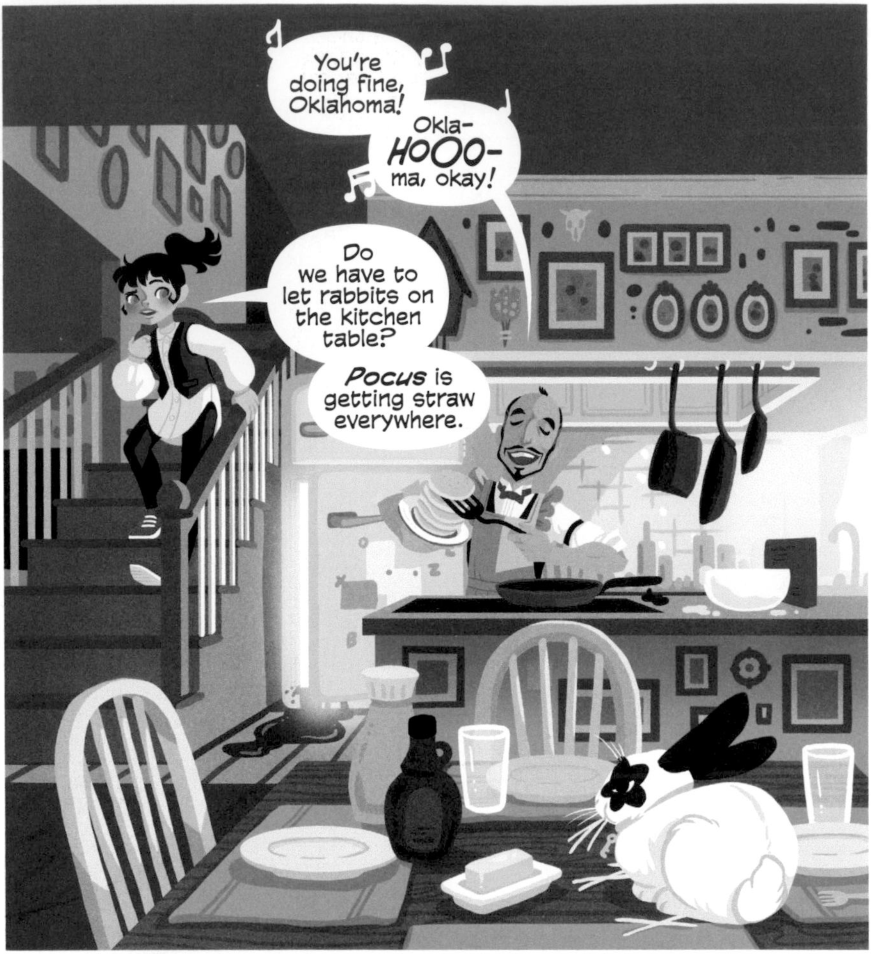
You're doing fine, Oklahoma!
Okla-HOOO-ma, okay!
Do we have to let rabbits on the kitchen table?
Pocus is getting straw everywhere.

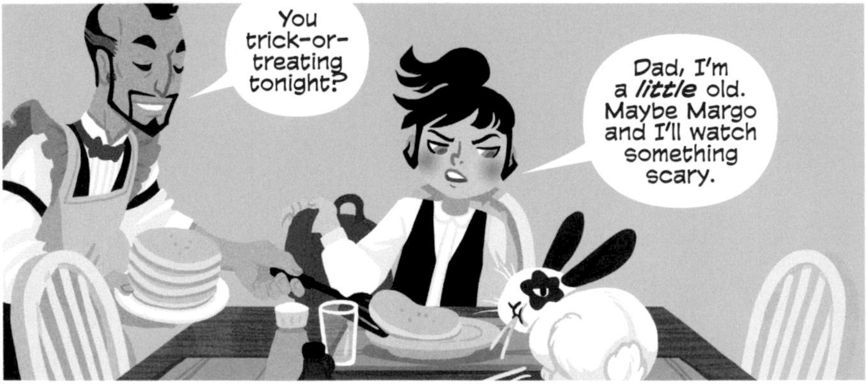
You trick-or-treating tonight?
Dad, I'm a *little* old. Maybe Margo and I'll watch something scary.

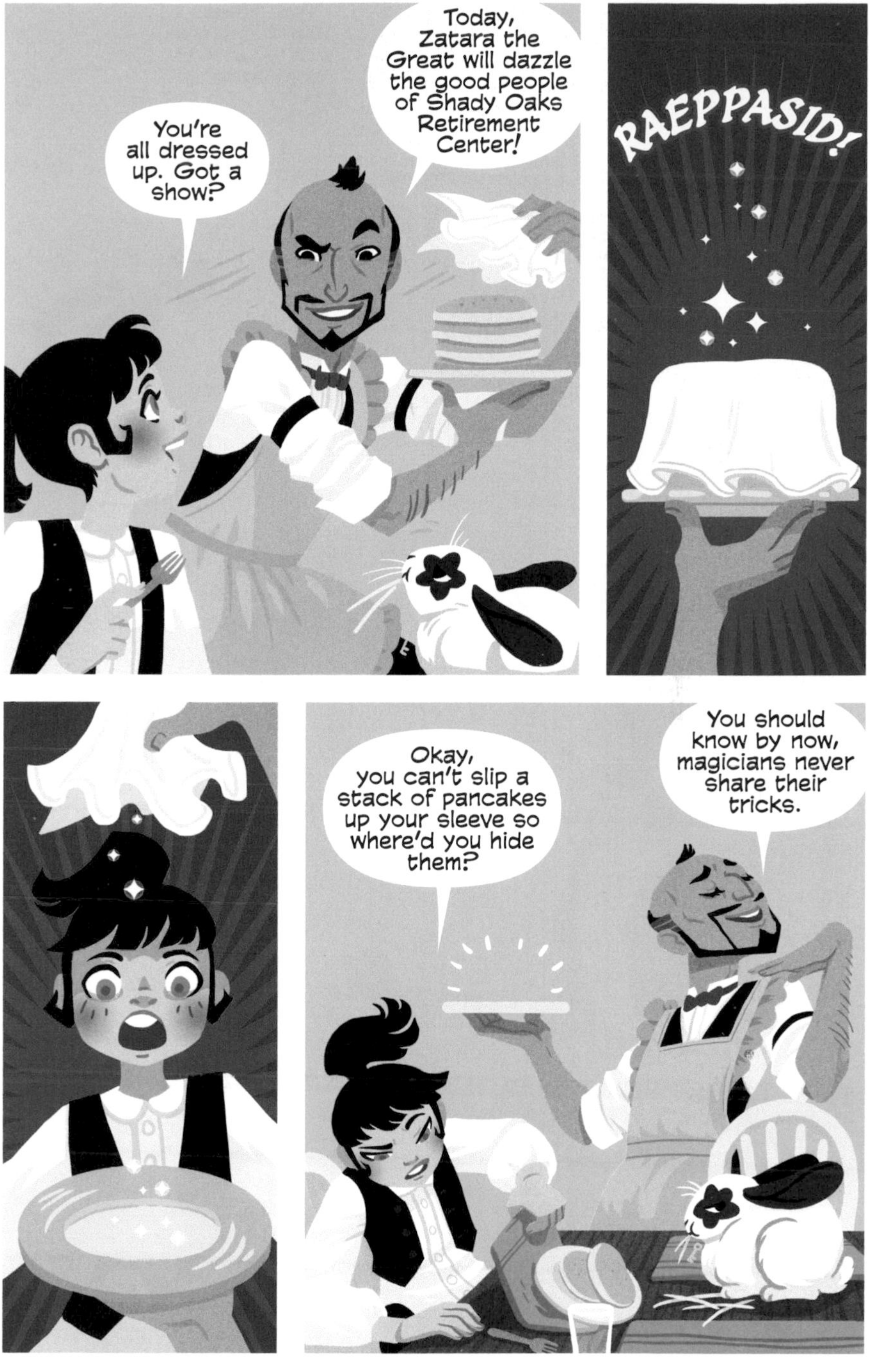

You're all dressed up. Got a show?
Today, Zatara the Great will dazzle the good people of Shady Oaks Retirement Center!
RAEPPASID!
Okay, you can't slip a stack of pancakes up your sleeve so where'd you hide them?
You should know by now, magicians never share their tricks.

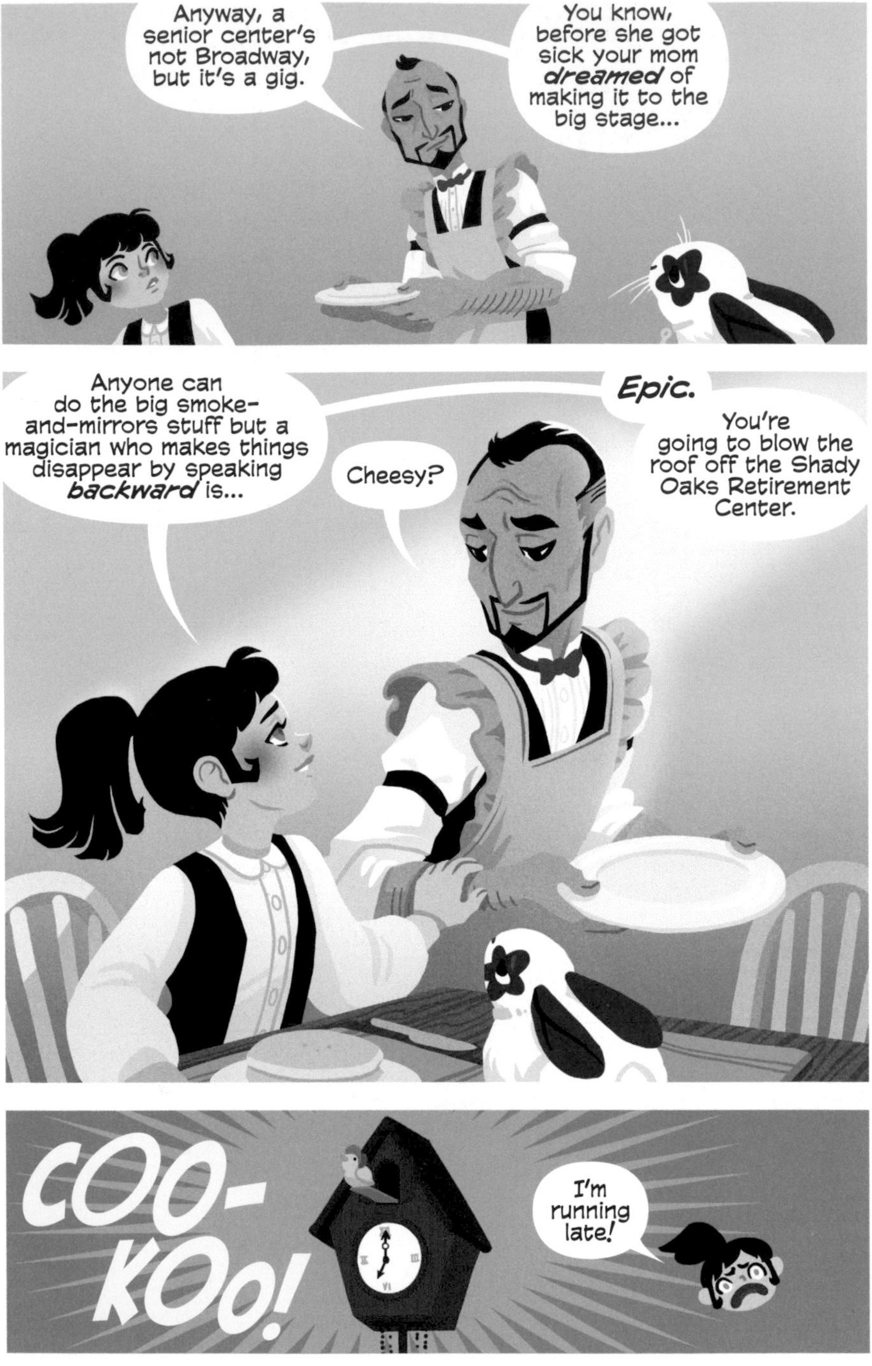
Anyway, a senior center's not Broadway, but it's a gig.
You know, before she got sick your mom *dreamed* of making it to the big stage...
Anyone can do the big smoke-and-mirrors stuff but a magician who makes things disappear by speaking *backward* is...
Cheesy?
Epic.
You're going to blow the roof off the Shady Oaks Retirement Center.
COO-KOO!
I'm running late!

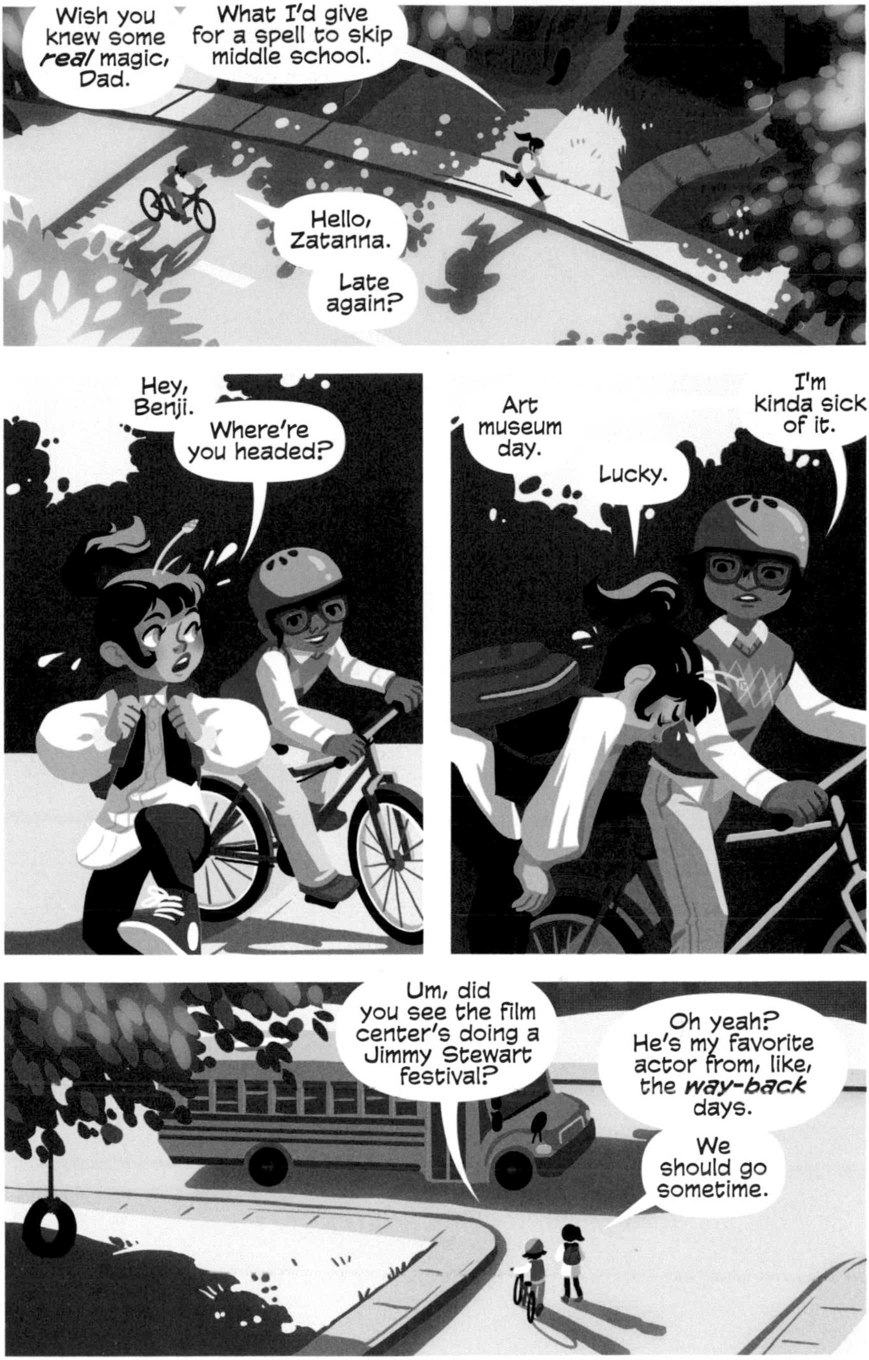
Wish you knew some *real* magic, Dad.
What I'd give for a spell to skip middle school.
Hello, Zatanna.
Late again?
Hey, Benji.
Where're you headed?
Art museum day.
Lucky.
I'm kinda sick of it.
Um, did you see the film center's doing a Jimmy Stewart festival?
Oh yeah? He's my favorite actor from, like, the *way-back* days.
We should go sometime.

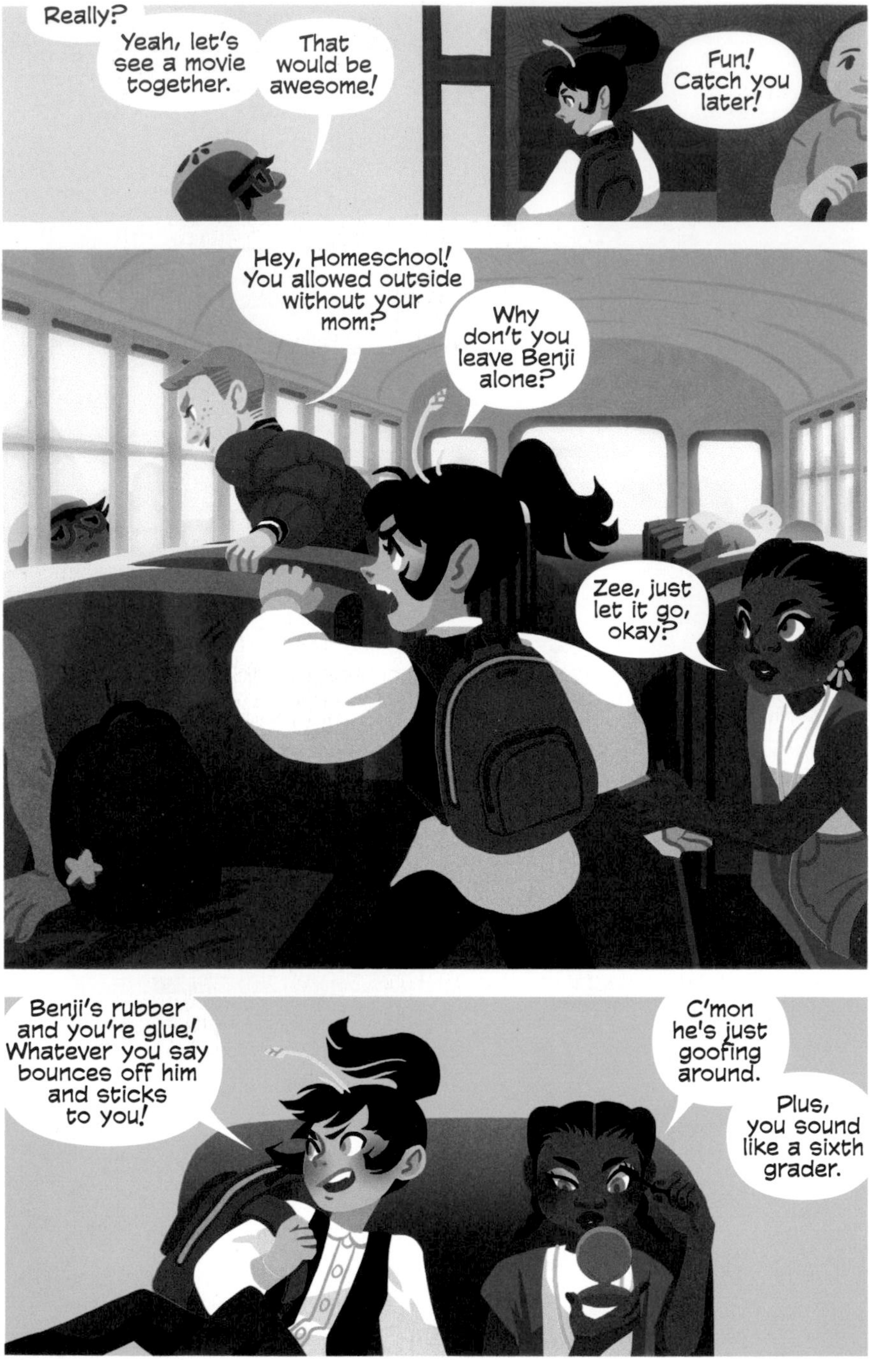
Really?
Yeah, let's see a movie together.
That would be awesome!
Fun! Catch you later!
Hey, Homeschool! You allowed outside without your mom?
Why don't you leave Benji alone?
Zee, just let it go, okay?
Benji's rubber and you're glue! Whatever you say bounces off him and sticks to you!
C'mon he's just goofing around.
Plus, you sound like a sixth grader.

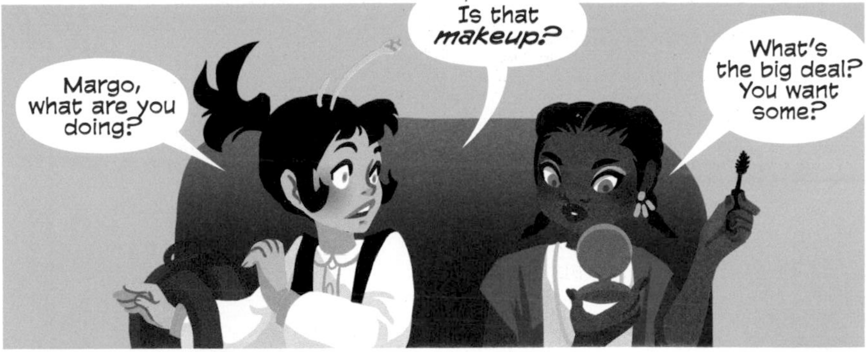
Margo, what are you doing?
Is that *makeup?*
What's the big deal? You want some?

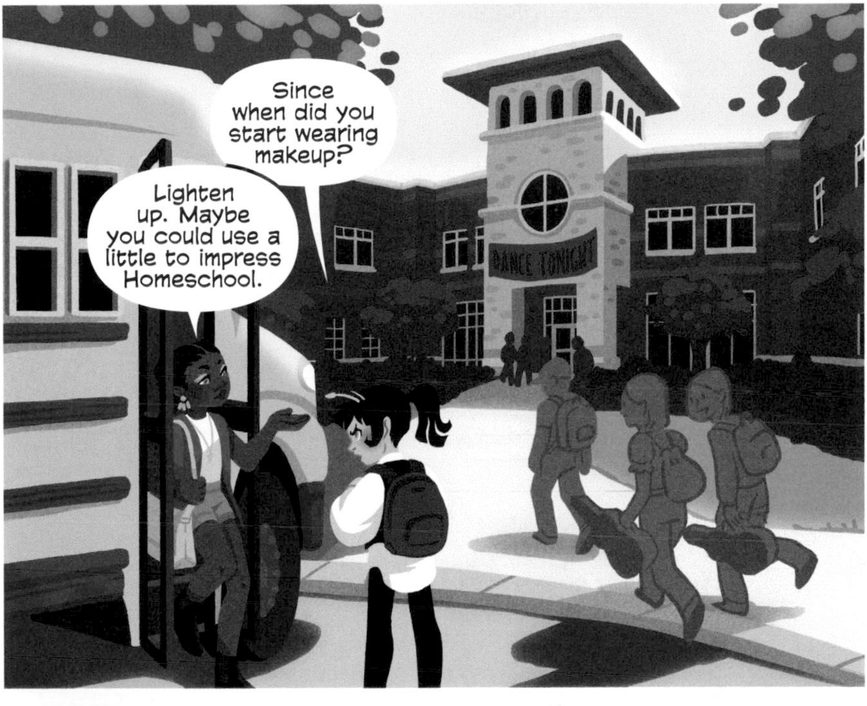
Since when did you start wearing makeup?
Lighten up. Maybe you could use a little to impress Homeschool.
DANCE TONIGHT

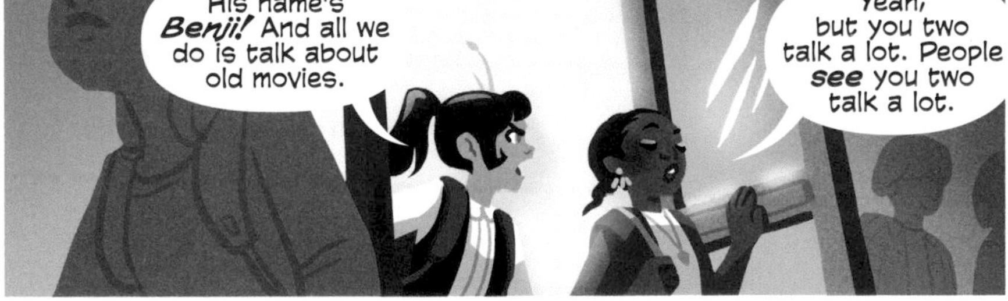
His name's *Benji!* And all we do is talk about old movies.
Yeah, but you two talk a lot. People *see* you two talk a lot.

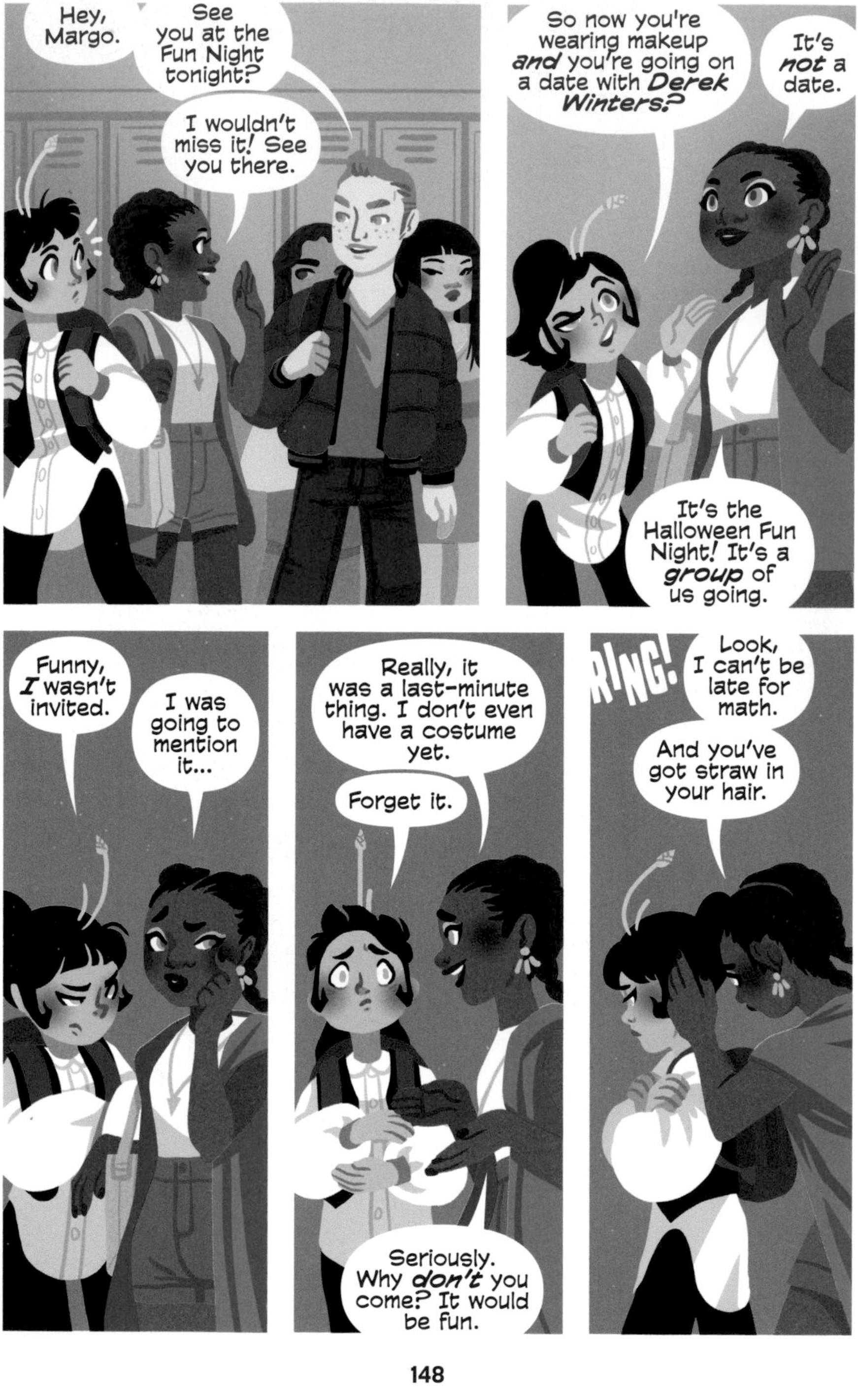
Hey, Margo.
See you at the Fun Night tonight?
I wouldn't miss it! See you there.
So now you're wearing makeup *and* you're going on a date with *Derek Winters?*
It's *not* a date.
It's the Halloween Fun Night! It's a *group* of us going.
Funny, *I* wasn't invited.
I was going to mention it...
Really, it was a last-minute thing. I don't even have a costume yet.
Forget it.
Seriously. Why *don't* you come? It would be fun.
RING!
Look, I can't be late for math.
And you've got straw in your hair.

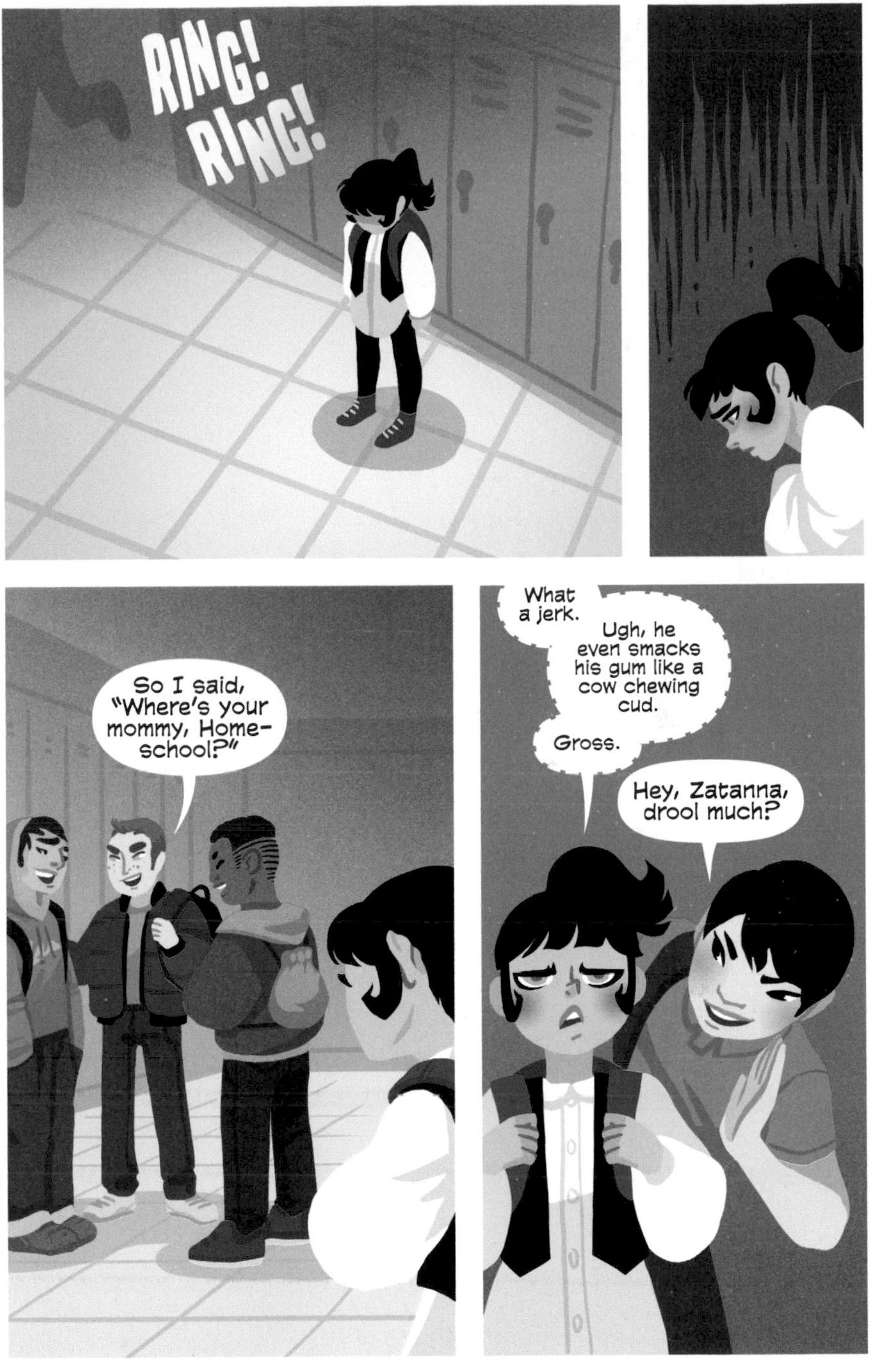
RING! RING!
So I said, "Where's your mommy, Home-school?"
What a jerk.
Ugh, he even smacks his gum like a cow chewing cud.
Gross.
Hey, Zatanna, drool much?

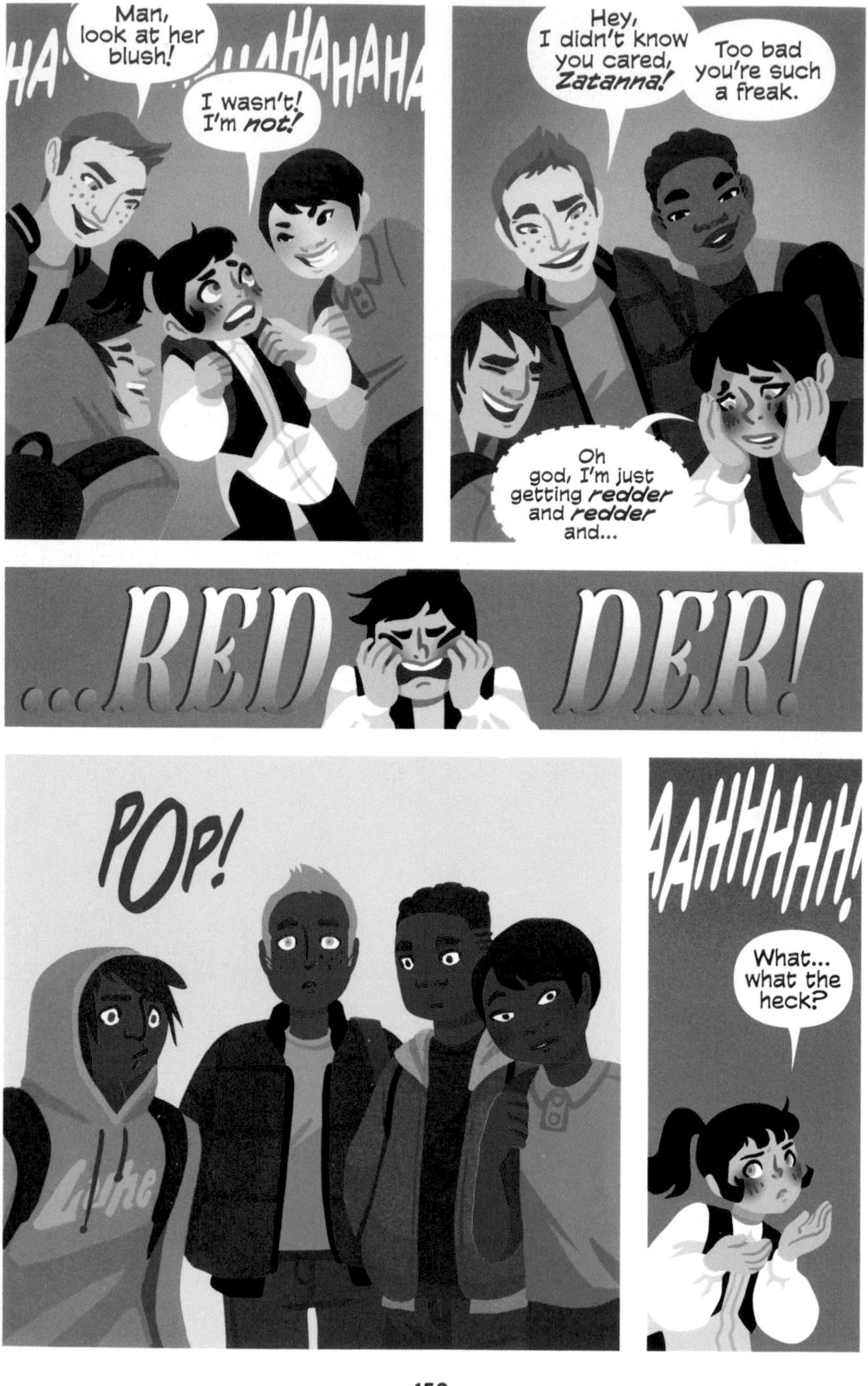

HA
Man, look at her blush!
HAHAHA
I wasn't! I'm *not!*
Hey, I didn't know you cared, ***Zatanna!***
Too bad you're such a freak.
Oh god, I'm just getting ***redder*** and ***redder*** and...
...RED
DER!
POP!
AHHHHHH!
What... what the heck?

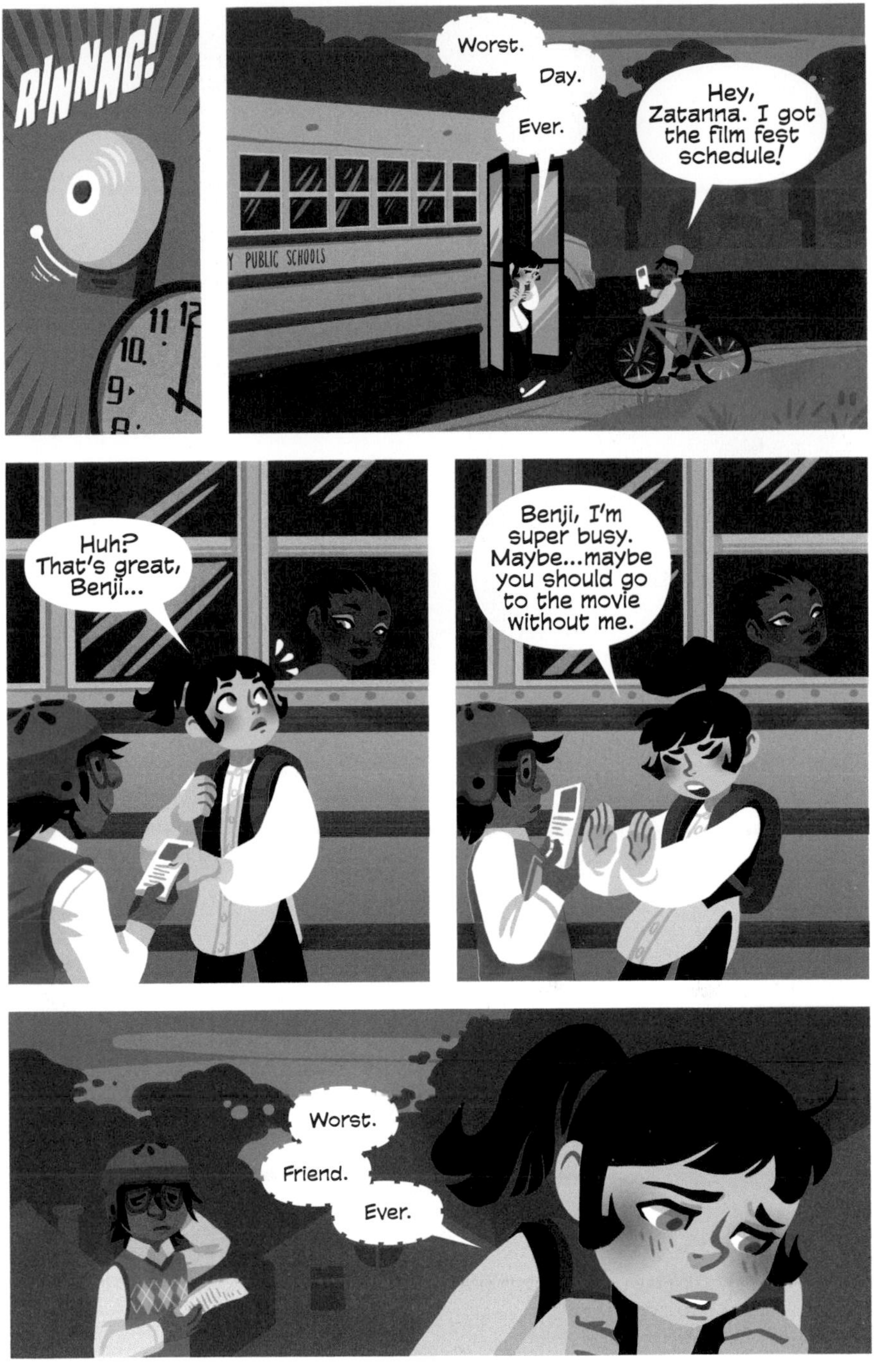
RINNNG!
Worst.
Day.
Ever.
Hey, Zatanna. I got the film fest schedule!
Y PUBLIC SCHOOLS
Huh? That's great, Benji...
Benji, I'm super busy. Maybe...maybe you should go to the movie without me.
Worst.
Friend.
Ever.

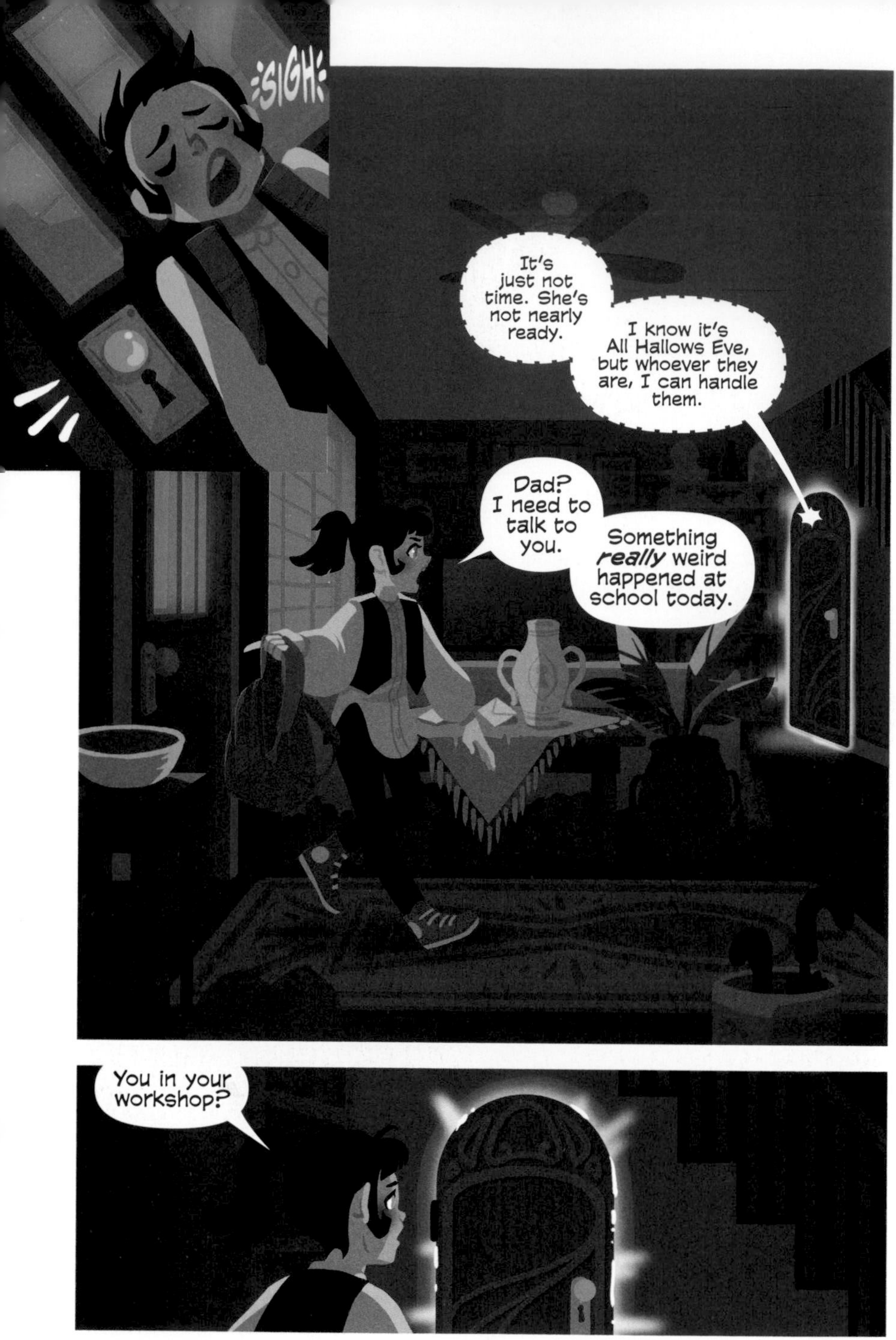
SIGH
It's just not time. She's not nearly ready.
I know it's All Hallows Eve, but whoever they are, I can handle them.
Dad? I need to talk to you.
Something *really* weird happened at school today.
You in your workshop?

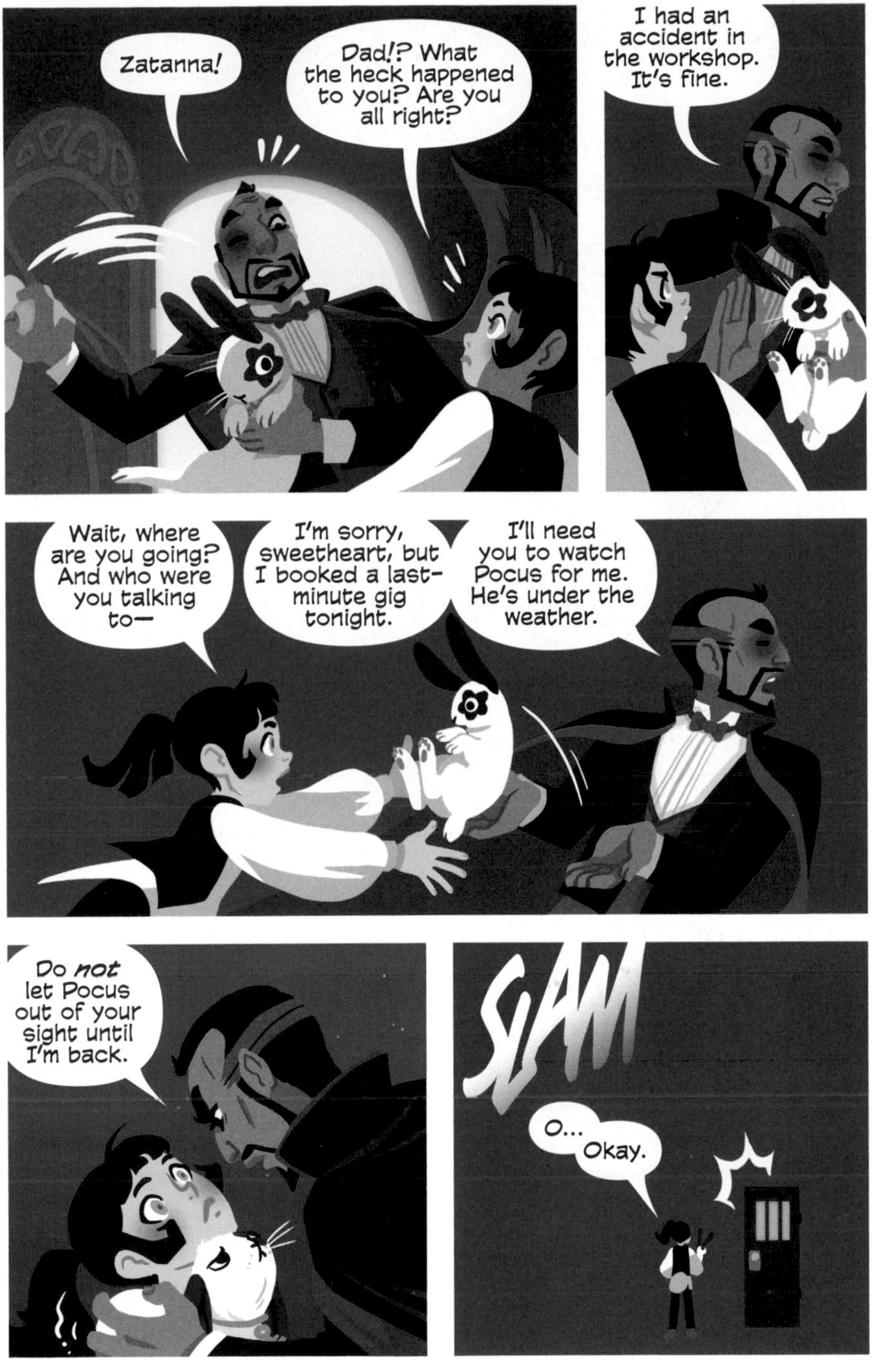
Zatanna!
Dad!? What the heck happened to you? Are you all right?
I had an accident in the workshop. It's fine.
Wait, where are you going? And who were you talking to—
I'm sorry, sweetheart, but I booked a last-minute gig tonight.
I'll need you to watch Pocus for me. He's under the weather.
Do *not* let Pocus out of your sight until I'm back.
SLAM
O... Okay.

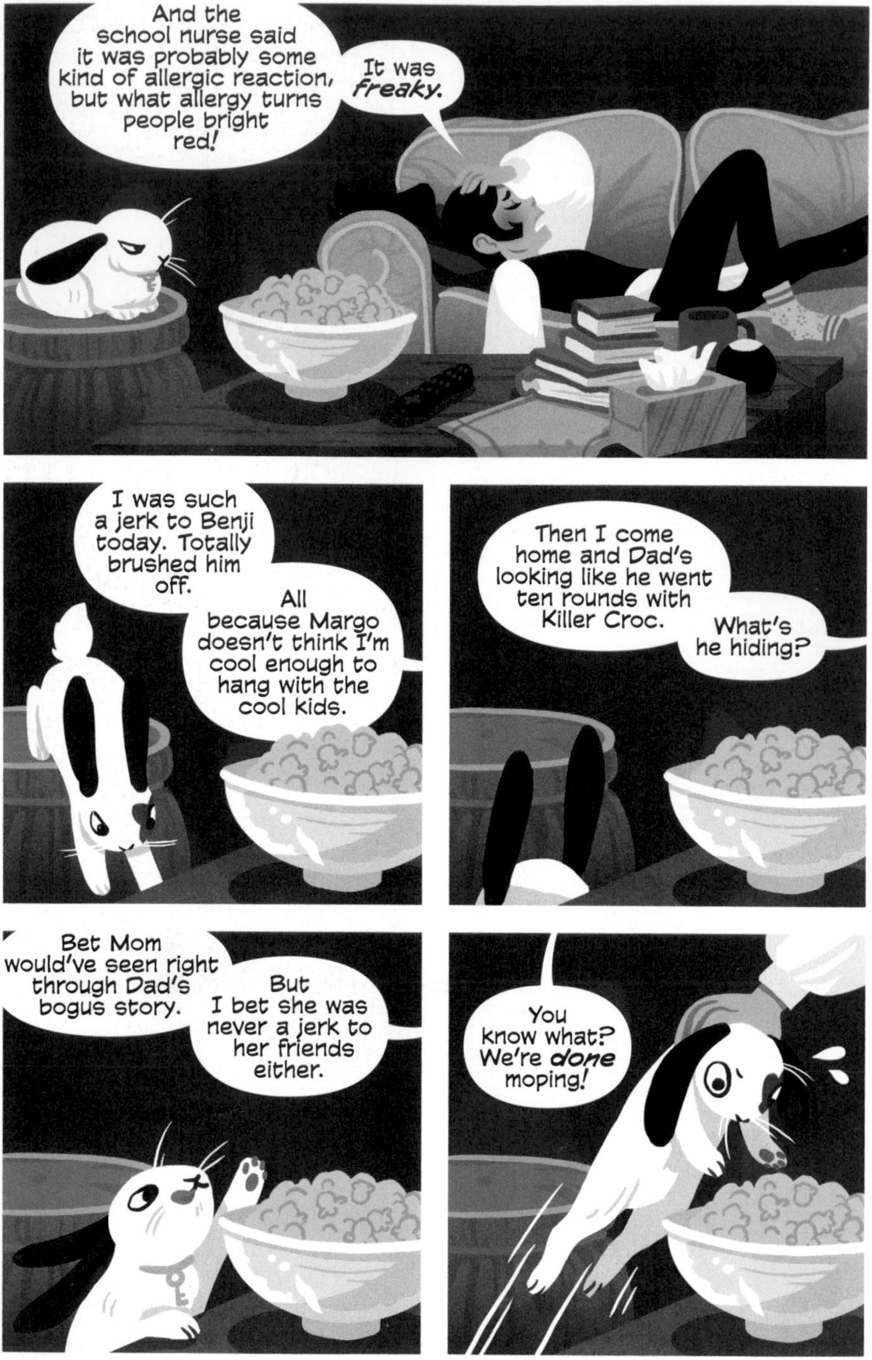
And the school nurse said it was probably some kind of allergic reaction, but what allergy turns people bright red!
It was *freaky.*
I was such a jerk to Benji today. Totally brushed him off.
All because Margo doesn't think I'm cool enough to hang with the cool kids.
Then I come home and Dad's looking like he went ten rounds with Killer Croc.
What's he hiding?
Bet Mom would've seen right through Dad's bogus story.
But I bet she was never a jerk to her friends either.
You know what? We're *done* moping!

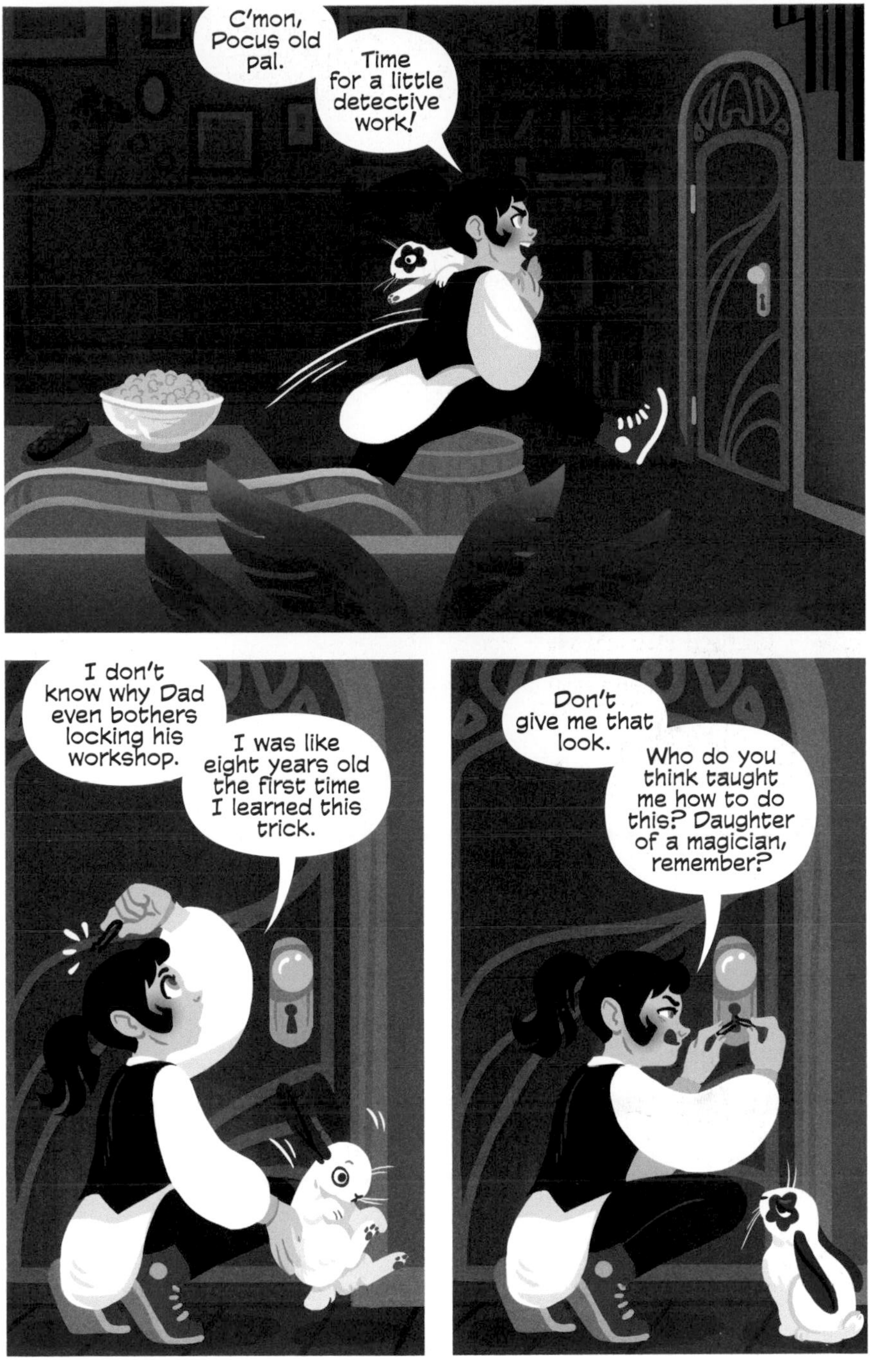
C'mon, Pocus old pal.
Time for a little detective work!
I don't know why Dad even bothers locking his workshop.
I was like eight years old the first time I learned this trick.
Don't give me that look.
Who do you think taught me how to do this? Daughter of a magician, remember?

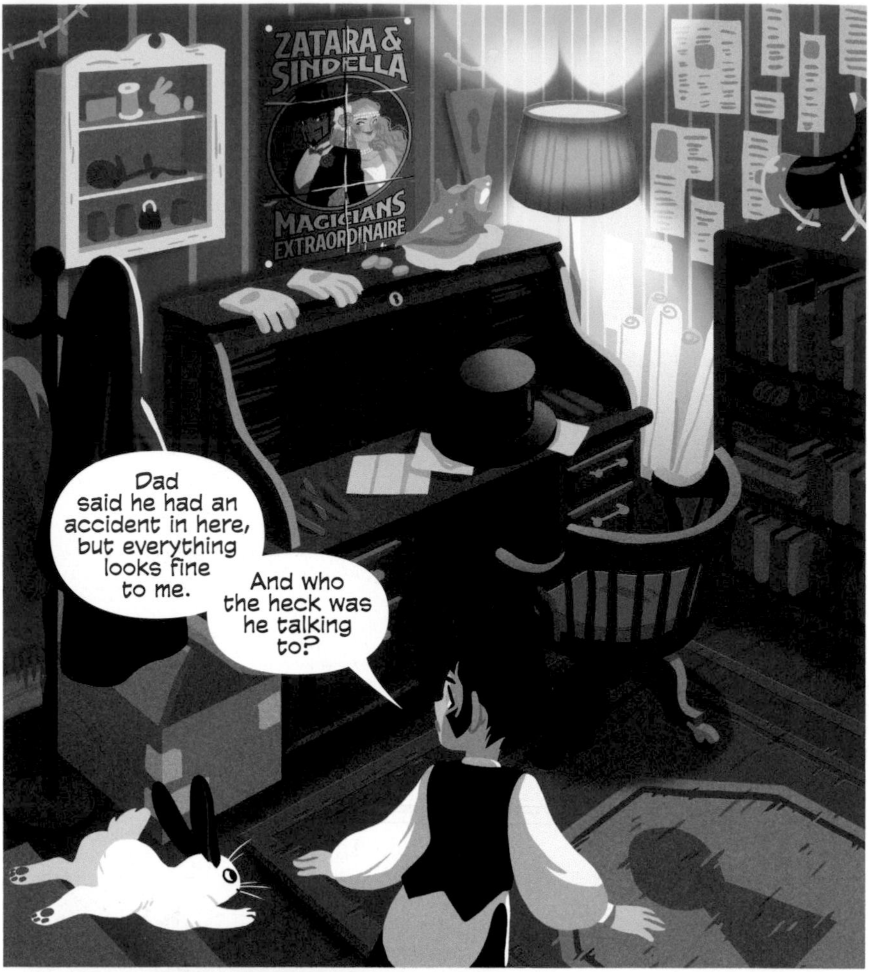
ZATARA & SINDELLA
MAGICIANS EXTRAORDINAIRE
Dad said he had an accident in here, but everything looks fine to me.
And who the heck was he talking to?

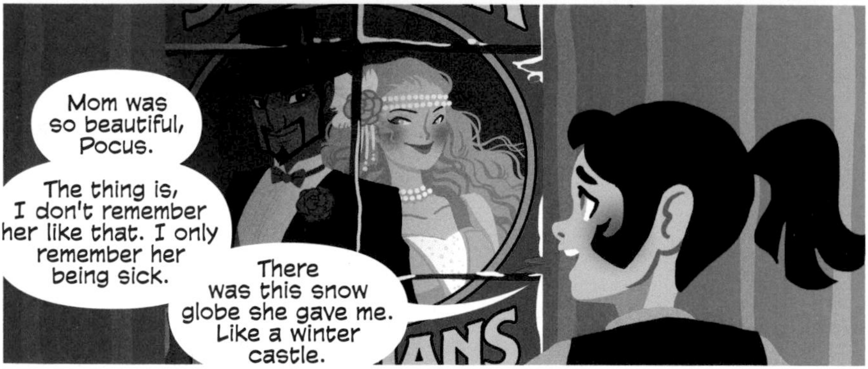
Mom was so beautiful, Pocus.
The thing is, I don't remember her like that. I only remember her being sick.
There was this snow globe she gave me. Like a winter castle.

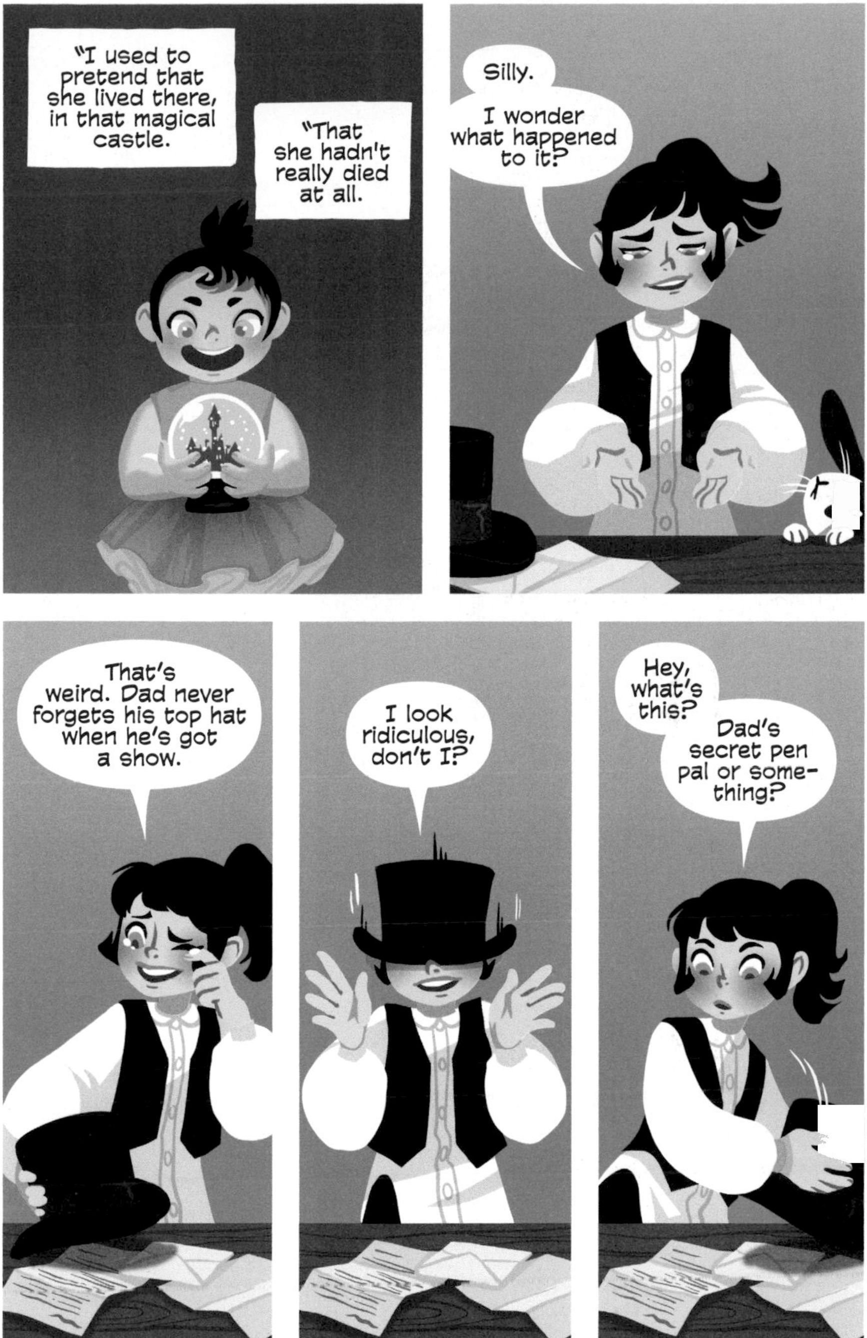
"I used to pretend that she lived there, in that magical castle.
"That she hadn't really died at all.
Silly.
I wonder what happened to it?
That's weird. Dad never forgets his top hat when he's got a show.
I look ridiculous, don't I?
Hey, what's this?
Dad's secret pen pal or something?

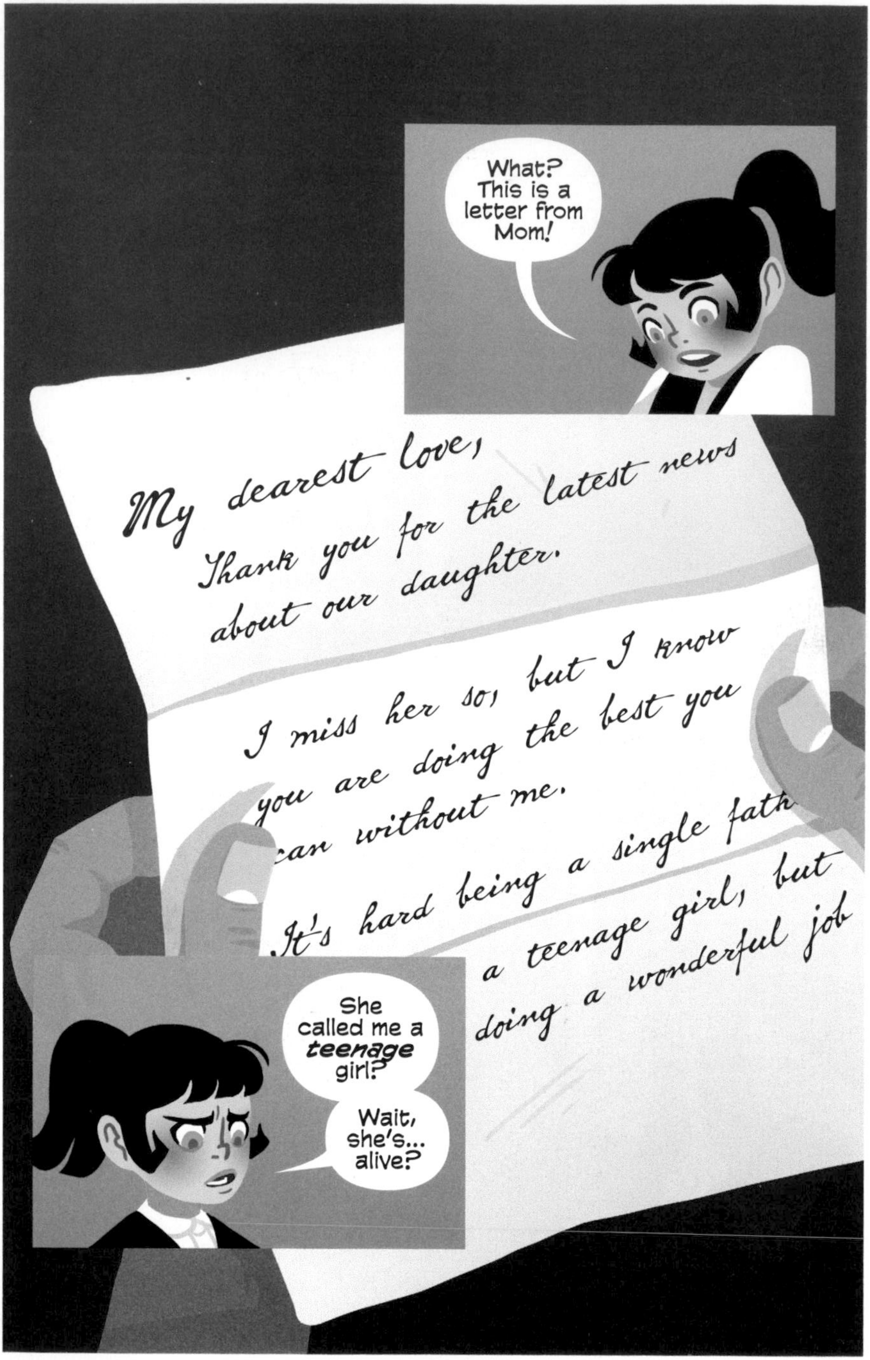
What? This is a letter from Mom!
My dearest love,
Thank you for the latest news about our daughter.
I miss her so, but I know you are doing the best you can without me.
It's hard being a single fath
a teenage girl, but
doing a wonderful job
She called me a *teenage* girl?
Wait, she's... alive?

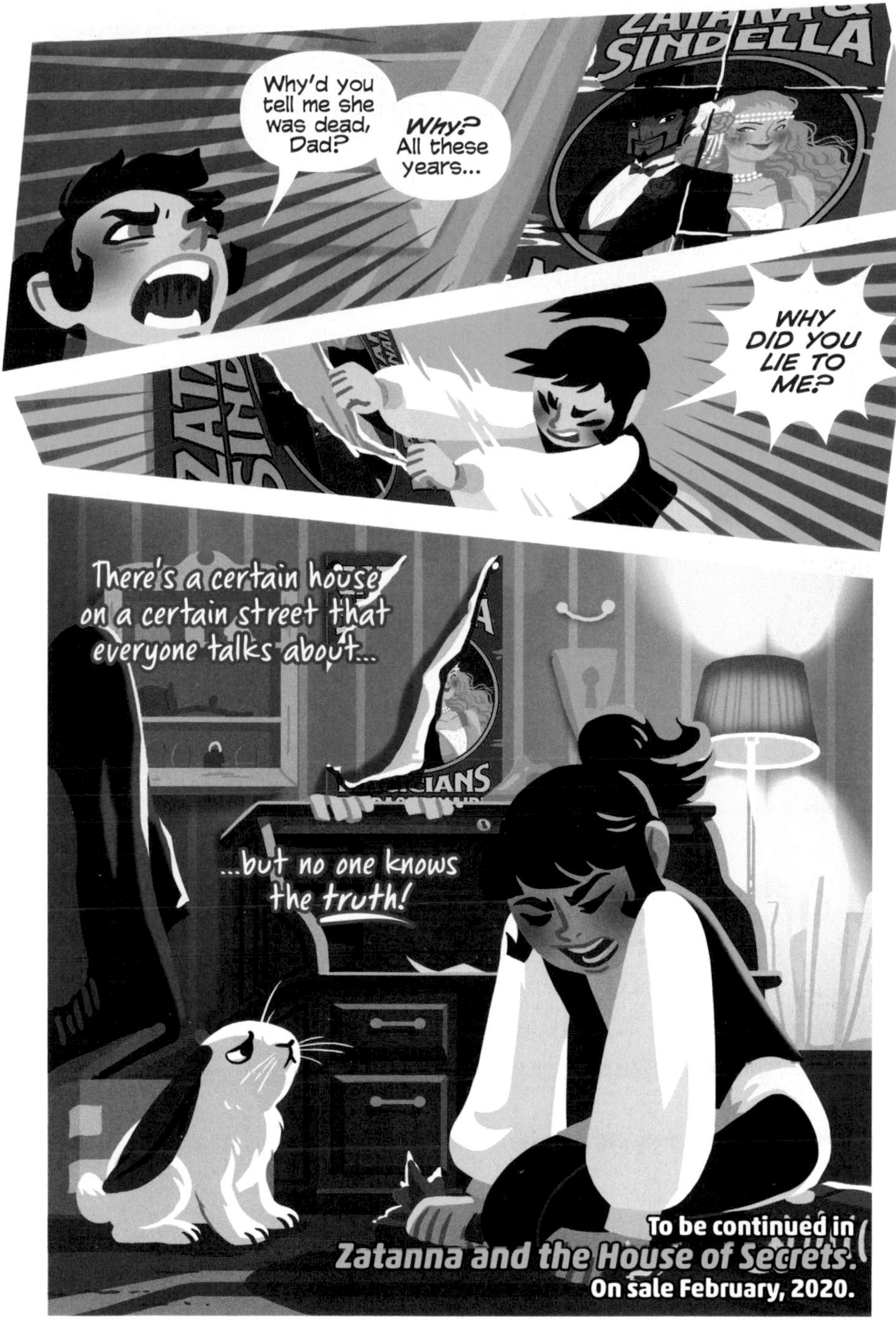
ZATANNA & SINDELLA
Why'd you tell me she was dead, Dad?
Why? All these years...
WHY DID YOU LIE TO ME?
There's a certain house on a certain street that everyone talks about...
MAGICIANS
...but no one knows the *truth!*
To be continued in
Zatanna and the House of Secrets.
On sale February, 2020.

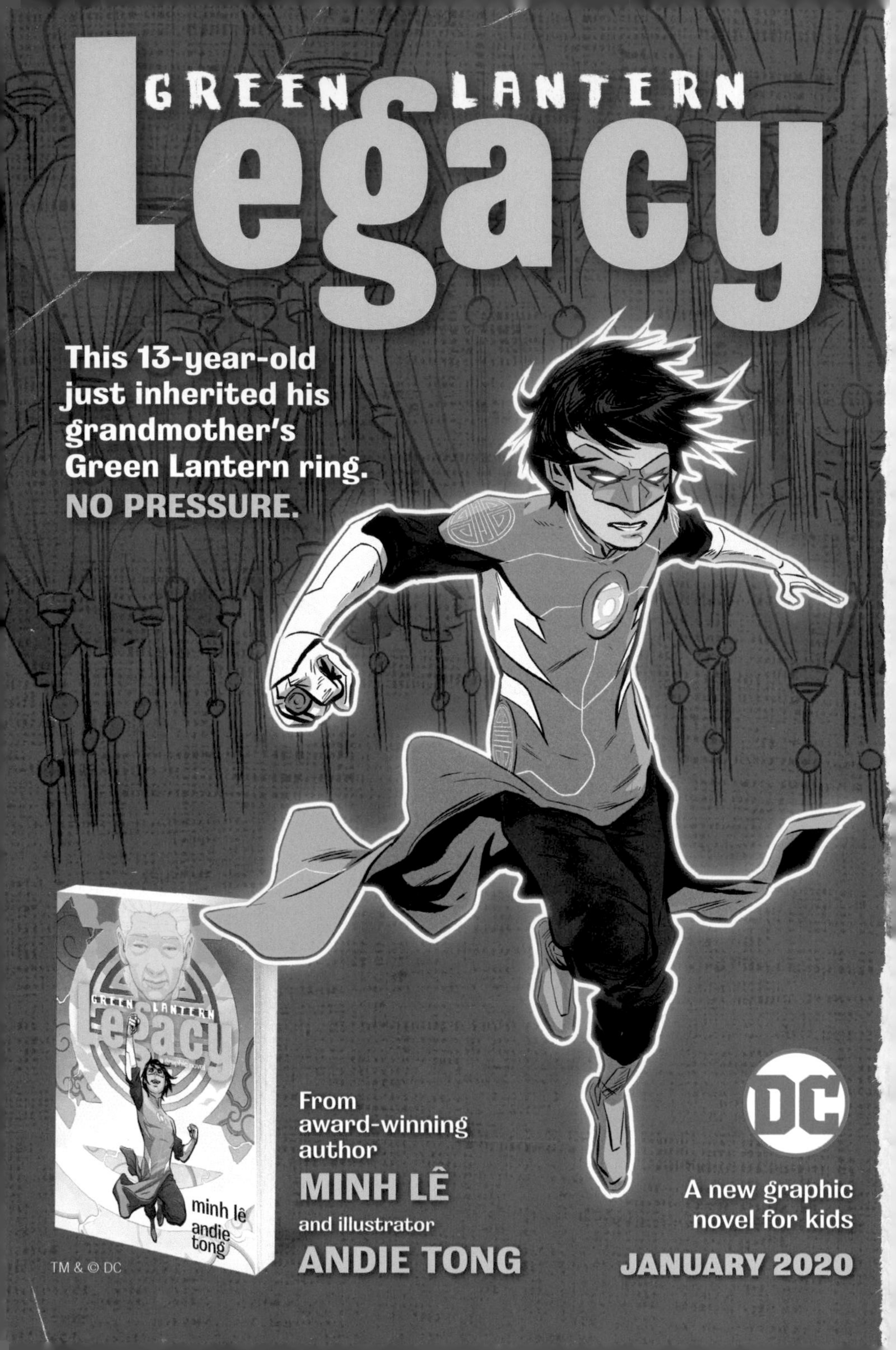
GREEN LANTERN
Legacy
This 13-year-old just inherited his grandmother's Green Lantern ring.
NO PRESSURE.
GREEN LANTERN
Legacy
minh lê
andie tong
From award-winning author
MINH LÊ
and illustrator
ANDIE TONG
A new graphic novel for kids
JANUARY 2020
TM & © DC